D0464334

WINDING RIVER

A Novel
By

Jeff Weir

Grimgribber Books
A Wisconsin Limited Liability Company

Sturgeon Bay, Wisconsin

Grimgribber Books
A Wisconsin Limited Liability Company
P.O. Box 430, Sturgeon Bay, WI 54235

This book is a work of fiction. The characters, names, places, dialogue, and incidents are either products of the author's imagination or, in the case of the names of some cities, are used fictitiously. Any resemblance to actual persons, entities or events is coincidental. All references to laws are references to laws that existed in the State of Wisconsin in 1976, and such references are for fictional purposes and are not intended to be, nor should they be relied upon as, legal advice.

ISBN 0-9726196-0-7

Library of Congress Control Number 2002096066

Design and composition by Impressions Book And Journal Services, Inc., Madison, WI

Printed and bound by Edwards Brothers, Inc., Ann Arbor, MI

First Edition

10 9 8 7 6 5 4 3 2 1

For all of the truly small town lawyers across America, including Jim in Iowa who once told me, "I never made much money practicing law, but I'd like to think I did something important."

"Thus the Barrister dreamed, while the bellowing
        seemed
    To grow every moment more clear:
Till he woke to the knell of a furious bell,
    Which the Bellman rang close at his ear."

—Lewis Carroll, "The Barrister's Dream,"
from *The Hunting Of The Snark*

The Place

1

"Next," a classmate barks as he exits the interview room in the old law school building and smiles at me. I stand, adjust my tie and then enter the room. A slightly built attorney sits at a small table. Late October sunlight streaming through windows dances off the few strands of silver hair on his head and steel rimmed glasses covering part of a face smiling while exuding a sense of stature. He rises and extends his hand:

"Bob Burnett."

"John Hall." I shake his hand.

He points to a chair across the table from him. As I sit, a chill runs through me even though the room, as always, is overheated. Burnett looks me over before his eyes fall on the interview sheet before him. I would describe myself as six feet tall, wide-shouldered but trim, with neatly combed, dark hair and blue eyes, nothing unusual for a man my age. What does he see, though, the crook in my nose and the small scars over one eye, the facial flaws of a former boxer? Or, are those defects shielded by the anxiety and doubt clouding my face?

He mutters as he reads, "twenty-seven, three years in the Army before college, single, work part-time for a Milwaukee law firm. Uh, huh." He sits back in his chair.

According to the clock on the wall behind him, it's almost six p.m. I suspect he's tired of running through his routine all afternoon. I'm tired of interviews, too, tired of saying what I think I should say rather than what I think. And, I'm tired of the appearances. This time of the school year there's always clamor about the impression you must make; what you need to do if you're going to make the firm.

"So you're going to be one of those few January grads, huh?"

"That's right." Rick's name comes to mind, my friend who was a year ahead of me in law school and also a January grad. We were out of step from most of our classmates in another way: we were both Vietnam era vets, although I spent my time in Germany while Rick waded through the rice paddies in Nam. Rick acted as my mentor, passing on his first and second year experiences, along with terrific notes and outlines. On graduation, he opted for a large law office in Chicago.

Maybe it's the weight of the past interviews, the weariness of school and work, the financial struggle, or simply because I'm belatedly reasoning with myself why I signed up for this interview that my attention drifts from the story Burnett tells to thinking about Rick.

If we passed on playing hearts after lunch with two other students, we argued the merits of some case, sometimes one from the morning newspaper. Often the article contained the barest of details, affording our imaginations the opportunity to fill in the blanks. Like a story where a middle-aged man wearing a suit and horned-rimmed glasses stepped into a dorm room, politely asked which of the two students lying on beds was Tony, and after he answered, the man fired three bullets into his chest, dropped a revolver on the floor and asked the other student to call the police.

Cold blooded, premeditated murder? No excuses? Wait, Rick would interject, the dead student was on bail, having been charged with raping the man's only daughter during a vicious attack on her. Her stockbroker father had to have been on planet Mungo, not on earth, when he fired the gun. On graduation, Rick opted for a large law firm in Chicago. Ever since he has been begging me to interview with his firm. I smile at the thought of Rick snickering at me when I tell him I interviewed with a small town lawyer.

Burnett must have noticed my lapse in attention since he hesitates before continuing. He checks the wall clock, then rubs his face before eyeing me closely. "Are you really interested in practicing law in a small town, or are you simply looking for a job?"

The abruptness of the question jolts me. He's getting right to it. Speak up, act like you know what you're doing, Rick would say. So, I do. "It's warm in here."

"Yes, it is. I was going to take off my coat." Burnett stands to shed his suit jacket and waves at me. "Go ahead."

I remove my sport coat and then wait.

Burnett smiles. "That was a clever response. If you don't like the question, answer a question you would like to have been asked." The smile fades. "Don't try that with a judge, though."

"I already did, with a judge who taught a class in school. You're right, it didn't work."

We both laugh.

"It's been a long day, John. You don't mind me calling you John?"

"Not at all."

"I drove down here this morning. I'm not used to these interviews." He rubs his face again. "Here's what I do, what most small town lawyers do: lots of real estate, estate planning and probate, contracts, divorces, small business matters, traffic and minor criminal cases, some collections."

I try to look interested, but the word "mundane" is clutched by my mind. Yet, I recall the two lawyers at the firm where I work after school arguing over the placing of their names on the firm's letterhead. Do I want to spend a legal lifetime moving from forty-second to ninth place on a piece of stationery. What *do* I want?

Burnett continues, and I try to listen while again wondering why I'm in the room. Many of my classmates already have jobs lined up, some with firms they've been working for, some with family ties. Many will head for offices of District Attorneys or corporate legal departments. Some will enter politics or business. The top half dozen have been picked off by the leading Milwaukee firms; the bottom ten are beginning to search for the cheapest walls available to hang their diplomas on. I'm in the vacillating middle: a couple of low grades one semester, and I can smell the sweat from the bottom ten; a couple of aces the next, and I can see the wrinkled brows of the leaders as they anxiously peer over their shoulders. None of those jobs suit me. Still, if I don't want to hire on with my part-time employer, where do I go? I nod approvingly at Burnett who continues:

"What do you hope to accomplish with your law degree, John? If your intentions were to make lots of money or handle high profile cases, you wouldn't be sitting across the table from me. What is it: The elevator stalled between floors? The walk past the conference room, with the fine china in the center of the table, to your assigned cubbyhole? Lack of the required patience to wait for 'trial day'? Or is it the narrow window of the work?"

The curve balls whiz by me. I came prepared to answer questions that aren't being asked. Burnett peppers me with such a mixture of pitches I'm unable to swing the bat. When he lifts his eyes over my head, I realize he knows the answers to his questions; he is cataloguing them for me. Then he lowers his eyes to stare into mine.

"Obviously, you do have a dream, probably like the one I had before I came to the Northwoods forty years ago. We're all dreamers of a sort. At times we're all enamored by the lawyer on the front page of the newspaper or the attorney being interviewed by a TV reporter on the steps of the courthouse. They're pleasant diversions from studying arcane property law or subsection three of subparagraph b of paragraph one of some section of the rules of civil procedure. Most of us would rather stare out the windows of the classroom, if there were any, except, of course, the student who raises his hand and starts a one-on-one dialogue with the professor that saves the rest of us from having to recite during the class."

I laugh. This is a strange interview, and I'm now enjoying every minute of it. "Tell me, why did you go to a small town?"

"I went because I couldn't find the intersection where dreams merge into the road to reality." He reflects before he continues. "I went because I thought it was my only opportunity. I didn't know then it was my best opportunity . . . that happiness, hopes and dreams, misery and sorrow, are not dependent on the population of a place."

He watches me closely, no doubt gauging how his message is being digested by my mind, how well he is maneuvering me to the door he will open for me. It's odd how I feel: strange and yet at ease. One of the things bothering me slips out:

"The Northwoods seems so remote, a place you go to on vacation."

"Yes, people love it so much they spend there the precious moments of their yearly escape from their daily lives, only to return to the existence they profess to hate." He smiles. "You won't have to return."

I smile. I'm beginning to want to confess to the saintly looking man, when I have nothing to confess. Then I let it go; I tell him what I'm after, at least what I think I'm after. "I want to be a part . . . I want to do something important, but I don't want to be one of the big guys anymore. I don't need my name to appear in newspaper headlines or have my face grace the cover of some national news magazine. You know what I mean?"

Burnett's face shows me he was waiting for me to open the gate for him. "Ah, yes, important. What's important? Daily lives in a small town are trivial to outsiders, yet monumental to the inhabitants. A tourist will laugh at the sight of a speeding ticket on the front page of the newspaper. The older woman who received the citation will read the article with horror as she suffers the double indignity of having her lawlessness hung before the community while having her age revealed to those who previously only suspected gray hair lay underneath layers of dye."

As he sees me smile, Burnett removes his glasses and leans back in his chair. The gate is now wide open. The stories are stampeding toward it as they always do from those who have gone before, and I want to hear them even though I know they're part of the seduction.

"After I graduated from law school, I moved to neighboring Big Lakes County and opened my law office over a bank where the president was kind enough to promise to send work my way. I remember the day in the summer when the first client in. I was sitting alone behind my desk, and I heard footsteps on the stairs and up the hall to my door and then the turn of knob until it pulled out and the silence before it was replaced and then the footsteps going back down the hall and down the stairs."

We laugh as he goes on:

"And then there was the sign, the uncooperative sign bearing my name I wedged between protruding bricks underneath the window. When a strong wind blew the sign would sail to the sidewalk and be brought in by irate passersby or be run by cars in the street. I hated scrubbing off the tire marks. How happy, I was when seven months later I was elected District Attorney for Big Lakes County, serving two terms before I was lured to Timber County. At least you won't have to suffer those indignities I so cherish."

While we laugh again, Burnett sits up and puts on his glasses. The smile vanishes as he looks directly as me. "You're a young man with the book of your life before you. Most of the pages are empty. What story will you write on those pages? Will it be the story you want to write or a story others will dictate for you?"

After he lets his message sink into my brain, he leans forward and lowers his voice as he speaks slowly. "Here's the deal: I'll pay you a thousand dollars a month and give you a bedroom over the office. I'll refer clients to you and furnish you other legal work." He smiles broadly. "And, I'll give you all of the advice you can stand. If after a year you decide to stay, we'll discuss a partnership with a plan for you take over the firm when I retire. I'm sixty-seven, and I'm not going to work forever . . . is that fair?"

I'm shocked. He's offering me a job. I came in to look around, not to buy anything. Can I say, "I'm just looking," and then slip around a corner?

The year is 1975. The economy is reeling from the bear market of 1973 and 1974 and high interest rates and inflation. I don't want to head into a section of the business world where a law degree adds nothing more than credentials for the job. I want to be involved in the law. The end of January is three months away. I have to start buying. "Speak up." "Act with authority." Burnett awaits my response.

"It sure is," I say in my most confident voice. We shake hands again. This time I feel Burnett's grip.

Burnett dons his suit coat. "Don't tell the others yet, I want to personally contact them first. Good thing you had the last time slot." He gathers up his papers. "See you at the end of January." As I start to leave, he adds, "Don't forget your snowshoes."

❧ ❧

Elation and panic play ping-pong with my emotions. I hustle out to the parking lot and rummage through the glove compartment of my car for a state map. Only with the aid of the index am I able to locate the village. The book Burnett referred to opens in my mind to a blank page on which I write: *It's a tiny, empty circle surrounded by a forest and countless lakes. A highway runs in and out of it. That's it. For now, I guess I can only imagine the rest.*

A classmate strolls past my car. "Hey, John. How are things going?

"I not sure," I mumble. "I'm going to Winding River."

2

White birch trees stripped of leaves mingle with pines and cedars. Summer cottages, all dark in the winter, circle lakes hidden by snow. I've arrived in the Northwoods of Wisconsin. The sensation I feel is the kind when something special has occurred. Yet, as the late January snow falls heavily with the wind creating random drifts on the road and I see the same pine tree and the same white birch over and over, the beauty of the scenery is overshadowed by a nagging question: Why have I come to such a lonely place? I had alternatives. Is this the end of *The Great Attorney John Hall* of my dreams?

Then a voice sounding like that of a creepy kid reminds me I am not alone.

"You know you shouldn't pick up strangers. You never know what they're gonna do."

The short man with a rough-cut face, wearing a camouflage jacket and an orange hunting cap, slumps in the passenger seat. A strange one. My hope for cheery conversation about the Northwoods when I picked him up north of Green Bay has disappeared along with the asphalt. But how do I audition hitchhikers?

"There was this guy, a tall guy with a handsome face . . . killed a woman who picked him up."

"Is that so?" I shift in my seat and crane my head forward to see more clearly through the windshield over which the wipers have lost control. The trees are now thick and hugging the edges of the road as we enter a national forest. What was the name? Why am I searching for details?

"Yeah, it really happened. I know the guy. He stuck a knife in her."

"That's horrible." Why did I pick up the hitchhiker? I try to ignore him, but he's making me nervous.

"Stuck it in her side while she was driving."

"Sounds pretty gruesome to me."

"Twisted it in, that's what he said. Turned the knife as he stuck her."

I frown as I glance at the man who identified himself as Billy. Another nut? I resolve to quit picking up hitchhikers. Why do I always get the losers? Then my whole body stiffens, and I almost lose control of the car as I see the glistening of the steel blade of the hunting knife Billy is jabbing and twisting in the air.

"Just stuck it right in and twisted it. That's what he said. She slowed down and stopped . . . stared at the knife in her side. Horror was all over her face, he said. He reached across her, opened the door and pushed her out. Then he drove off. I heard the story lots of times. I know it's true."

I begin to sweat in the cool car. Somehow, I must remain calm. "Well I believe it." I grimace as I look at Billy again. "Maybe you should put that knife away."

With a thumb on one side and a forefinger on the other, Billy caresses the knife blade. "It's beautiful, isn't it? You know what I can do with this?"

"I can imagine." I recall two drunken GI's going after each other with similar knives after an argument in a bar. I'm still not sure exactly what happened since I scattered with everyone else who had no stomach for risking his life to quell a fight where there was no victim. I did learn one of the fighters almost died on the way to the hospital. I have to say something, to go along with it.

"It's a beautiful knife, but I'm worried about you getting hurt. The weather is getting worse, and we might run off the road. You really should put it away."

Billy glances at me, hesitates, then slowly slips the knife into a sheath he stuffs into a deep pocket of his jacket. "Did you like the part about the twisting? That's the part I like best."

"I liked it fine, Billy. I really did. Say, why don't you take a nap. Maybe I'll need you to help me drive later."

"You'd let me do that?"

"We'll see what happens."

Nervous, unsure of my next move, for several miles I hear Billy continue with lurid details of the stabbing. Is it all a prelude to him sticking me with the knife? What have I gotten myself into? Difficulty in driving through the falling snow forces me to keep my eyes off the man. What can I do anyway? Slam on the brakes if he pulls the knife out again? Then try to take the knife away from him?

Billy mumbles, "The guy kept her car. It was a big car. I don't know what kind, but it was big and it cost a lot of money . . . and her purse was on the seat . . . and, and it had a lot of money in it, a lot of money."

An orange glow from the first sodium vapor lights of Lenora, the county seat of Timber County, appears as a beacon. As the highway becomes the main street, ruts in the snow from other cars driving over the unplowed road maliciously grab at the tires of my car. Out of the corner of my eye, I see Billy gently patting the pocket with the knife, apparently absorbed in details of his story. I'm no longer listening; instead, concentrating on keeping my car on the road. I know now what I have to do, where I have to go. But, where is it?

Then I sigh as I see it, ahead on the right edge of the street: the courthouse square with a spotlight on the flag flapping in the ill wind. I turn into the driveway leading to the parking lot of the Sheriff's Department. The engine idles while I look at Billy and see the doubt in his eyes.

"I'm going to duck inside and check on the weather conditions. I don't see many cars on the road. Maybe, we'll have to pull in somewhere for the night. Get a motel. Would you like that?"

"Yeah, I'd like it a lot." Billy sits up straight and smiles, the smile quickly fading to a frown. "You're only gonna check on the weather?"

"That's right." I wince; I hate lying, even to an alien to the world of reality. I turn off the ignition and drop the key into my coat pocket.

When I return, the veteran deputy with me walks around to the passenger side of the car and taps on the window with his flashlight. As Billy rolls down the window, the deputy looks at me. "Just what I told you." He again faces the window and speaks in a deep voice. "We've been searching all over for you, Billy. Come on out. It's time to go home."

Billy climbs out of the car, hanging his head.

The deputy sticks out his hand. "I'll take the knife." Billy removes the sheath from his jacket pocket, eyes it longingly, and then hands it to him. "Turn around. You've been through this before. You know I'm going to have to handcuff you for your protection."

After he snaps on the cuffs, the deputy faces me. "We'll see that Billy gets back to the mental heath center. You'll have to come in and give me a statement. They're going to have to keep a tighter lock on him."

I nod affirmatively as I release to the wind a huge sigh. Then, as always, is the next problem: By the time I'm done with the statement, will the snow so blanket the highway I will be unable to drive the last sixteen miles to Winding River? I look at Billy, then at the deputy. "All that, and it was just a story?"

The deputy smiles. "Billy loves that story."

"Who's the tall guy with the handsome face?"

"Oh, that's Billy, too. He plays all the parts. You're lucky he didn't give you the version where he plays the victim." The deputy turns to Billy. "Isn't that right?" Billy keeps his head down and doesn't answer.

Is it true what the deputy told me in his office, that Billy is harmless? What is he thinking now? Does he consider his latest performance a hit?

The deputy grabs the chain on the handcuffs and walks Billy up the snow-covered sidewalk leading to the jail, with me trailing them. Halfway there, the deputy halts and turns around. "By the way, Attorney Hall, welcome to the Northwoods."

❦ ❧

Burnett must have come to the Northwoods in a distant ancestor to my four-door sedan, *Rusty*. In the interview he described her perfectly. *Rusty* is small and afraid of the snowdrifts and her behavior is generally unpredictable. She is too old for the trip, but I have no choice other than to take her. At times, like Burnett had, I hate my car and sense she hates me, too. I admit I expect too much of her, especially considering her life of abuse. I remember when I bought her late one night in a tavern for twenty-five dollars and a six-pack of beer with a promise of a fifth of whiskey to follow. Since I never saw the previous owner again, I drank the whiskey with Rick and another classmate after spring exams and consider my actions justified since the purchase price for the car was too high.

Rusty slips along the highway from Lenora to Winding River, occasionally taking a slide, as though she is a child sliding on ice on a playground. Relief from Billy's departure is losing the battle of my emotions to anxiety from the whiteout.

No more hitchhikers. I recall the clean-cut, young man, wearing a letter jacket, I picked up along a road near an Army base in the South where I was assigned after my two years in Germany. I thought he was a high school kid, that is, until I saw he was wearing handcuffs he was trying to hide from me. I lied that time, too. I said I was going on past the base to town. When I suddenly turned in by the guard shack, I grabbed the soldier, and with the aid of the guard, returned him to custody.

No more hitchhikers. Do I pick them up as a gesture of kindness to my fellow man or for the selfishness of having companionship on a journey? In a way, I admire my classmates who found the cheapest walls and commenced practicing. I want the freedom from the firm; yet, am I unable go it alone? My mind drifts along with the piles of powder on the highway.

Suddenly I feel the big slide, so long and so fast I can do nothing but go along with it. *Rusty* skids off of the highway into the darkness of the night, plunging deeply into a snow filled ditch. As a wall of snow smacks against the windshield, self-preservation comes first: I hope the windshield will keep me from being smothered to death. When survival has passed, anger moves up to tailgate me into useless behavior. "Damn!" I yell as I bang my fist repeatedly on the steering wheel before I sit back.

Tires with good treads would have helped is my first thought; that I couldn't afford them is the second. I stare at the white wall ahead of me. Pretty, with an appearance of purity, isn't it merely a collection of compressed snowflakes that mean no harm? There flashes through my mind a downhill skier I read about who plunged headfirst into a tree well on the backside of a Colorado ski hill, causing the snow to cave in and suffocate him before help could dig him out. I grab the door handle.

I struggle with the driver's door for several minutes before accepting the futility of attempting to open it. First donning a wool cap and a pair of gloves, I climb onto my law books and clothes strewn over the back seat. Lying on my back, I use my feet to push open the rear door enough for me to squeeze out and struggle onto the road again running through the national forest. I estimate I'm no more than two miles from Winding River.

I begin wading through the snow on the road. Since I have no shovel and have not seen a car pass me since leaving Lenora, wading my way out of what I now view as a nightmare where I'm engulfed in a huge white sheet with no ends seems to me the only thing *to* do. Stopping almost as soon as I start, through a swirl of flakes I notice a dim light from a clearing in the woods. As I close the distance to the light, it appears to come from a white, frame house. I continue trudging along the road and then through a yard no longer disclosing the location of its walkway.

My face is grim when the front door opens. A slender woman about my age, with dark hair done in a pageboy and wearing a sweater over a turtleneck, peers out at me. I blurt: "I'm in trouble. My car ran off the road, and I need to call a tow truck."

The young woman looks me over carefully as she speaks. "Are you hurt?"

"No, I'm all right, a little shaken."

"Well, I don't know if you'll be able to get anyone out here tonight. The last report on the television advised everyone to stay off the roads until the snow plows come through, probably late tonight or early in the morning. I can give you a shovel."

"I think it's past that." I realize I have surprised her, maybe even frightened her. I glance back at my path, now being lost for eternity by the wind and new falling snow.

The young woman leans out the door. "You can't stay out there. Come inside."

I hesitate, then brush down my coat and trousers before stepping into the entryway where I remove my coat along with my cap and shoes.

"Don't worry about the snow. We're used to it." She still eyes me closely as I run a hand through my dark hair. She motions me into the living room. "Sit down by the fire and dry your feet."

A black, cast iron stove with the doors opened before a grate stands in the corner to the right of the front windows. I move a chair so I can sit with my feet on the homemade brick hearth. The magic the fire performs by reducing the logs to ashes distracts me for a few moments before I turn to the young woman. She sits in a rocker on the other side of the stove, staring at me. Attractive, but there is something else that immediately draws me to her: large eyes with the dark color matching her hair, friendly eyes both cautious and inquiring.

She breaks the silence. "I'm Ann. I live here with my roommate. I was reading when you knocked on the door."

I look around the room. An open book turned upside down rests on a couch underneath the glow from an end table lamp.

"She's gone to bed. We're teachers in the schools here, and Shelly thought we'd have school tomorrow as usual. The way the snow's drifting and piling up school will start late." She gives me a serious look. "May I ask where you were going?"

"I'm on my way to Winding River to begin practicing law with Attorney Robert Burnett.

Do you know him?"

"I've met him several times. He knows my father." She pauses. "So, will you be living in Winding River?"

"Above Burnett's office." The *deal* runs quickly through my mind, for three months a frequent occurrence. A thousand dollars a month along with a room and referral of clients and legal work is a fair job. But, Rick's firm would have given me a better offer. Still, I didn't want the large firm. I didn't . . .

Ann nods. "Do you want something to drink, like a beer? You look like you could use one?"

"Please, and may I use your telephone to call the Burnetts. They're expecting me?"

"Sure, that is, if you'll first tell me your name?"

We laugh. "I'm sorry. My name is John Hall."

"That's simple enough. Do you have a family coming with you?"

"If you mean, am I married? The answer is no."

Ann smiles as she beckons me to follow her. On the way to the kitchen, she shows me the telephone in the hallway.

❧ ❧

When she returns to the living room with two bottles of beer, I'm leaning over the couch, inspecting the oil painting above it. The scene of a house standing alone in the distance alongside a snow covered road winding through pines into the forefront suggests to me, although I do not know why, that it's her work.

She hands me a bottle. "Were you able to reach the Burnetts?"

"He said the weather was worse in Winding River. He doubts I can get to their home even if my car wasn't in the ditch. I'm to call him if I can't find somewhere else to stay." I pause. "How about motels. Is there one I could walk to?"

Ann meets my eyes. "Well, you obviously can't go anywhere tonight. Sleep on the couch, and I'll get you a pillow and blanket."

"Are you sure?" I speak slowly, forcing the last word upward in a losing effort to lend conviction to my delivery.

"I'm sure."

I return to my chair next to the fireplace as Ann sits the rocker. I glance over my shoulder at the painting. "Your picture reminds me of my trip here. Unfortunately, along the way I . . . " Then it hits me. I shouldn't mention the hitchhiker; how can I do so without going through the whole story. I'm a witness; I'm more than a witness, I'm the victim. Maybe there'll be a hearing, and I'll have to testify. I cannot now tell a story that may differ from my later statement.

"I . . . I assume you painted it?" As soon as I utter the words, I realize Shelly could be the artist. I have to stop reaching conclusions so quickly.

"I teach art. I prefer painting and sketching."

"It's not the kind of scene I witnessed where I grew up."

"Where were you raised?"

"In Milwaukee, on the lower east side. My father died when I was six years old, and my mother raised my younger brother and me in a small apartment. She passed away last spring. It was mostly a tough neighborhood, a place for low income and immigrant families that has slowly been changing through housing projects and younger people renovating houses so they can live closer to the downtown. It was the kind of neighborhood where the hero of the seven- to nine-years-olds was a third grader, living at the opposite end of the block, who not only smoked cigarette butts plucked from the gutters but could flip them further than anyone else. Most of the kids had no dreams."

"And you did?"

"Too many. I'll never live long enough to bring them all to life."

"How does coming to Winding River fit in? Was that a dream?"

"Not at all. In fact, the move may have destroyed my favorite dream."

Ann rises, stokes the fire and returns to the rocker. "What was that?"

"One where I'm the lawyer at the top of the ladder of the top lawyers, the ones who handle the cases with the highest stakes."

She has a puzzled look on her face. "You won't have that kind of practice in Winding River. What brought you here?"

"A lot of things." I think of the wall in my apartment I sat against early in the morning while I waited for the coffee to perk. Once white, the wall is now gray from attacks by pollutants in the city air. I also see the mattress in the center of the barren living room, with a sheet and blanket strangled during a night of tossing and turning. "Mostly, Burnett."

Ann eyes me in a way making me think honesty prevents her from disguising her facial expressions. "So," she drags out the word, "how do you define 'highest stakes'? If you look at it from the point of view of the client, aren't the stakes the highest in every client's case?"

"The big cases go beyond an individual client. They can have ramifications for multiple clients, for millions of people who aren't yet clients."

"I see." She creases her brow as she pauses. "If the city lawyers are arguing all the big cases, where does that leave Sally Smothers in Winding River? Her divorce isn't all that important? She doesn't rate a top-notch lawyer? She gets someone culled from the . . . I'm sorry, that wasn't meant . . . "

"That's okay. You're asking the questions I'm asking myself. I wish I knew the answers. Fortunately, I've found a man who can provide them for me."

She's good at the banter, and I like that. I'm also tired. As my brain finishes sponging up the question, I suspect further statements by me will be weakened by the exposure of my doubts. Anyway, why risk letting it escalate into an argument? I like her. Is it the eyes, the smile, the tone of voice, the mannerisms, the warm presence, the probing of me using logic and intelligence? I've never been able to pinpoint why I like a girl; the reasons are too complicated, too many variables multiplied in too many ways. I simply trust my feelings.

"I think . . . I think you should tell me about Winding River." I see she's disappointed I gave up but quickly recovers.

"It's a small village. Population is about twelve hundred and fifty. Began as a logging town in the late eighteen hundreds when a railroad company set up a land office in the area and sold lots. When the railroad reached here a year later, homes and stores popped up along meandering streets. The area was later re-platted as a village. Timber was harvested from the forests and processed by a local sawmill. Some of the lumber was used here and the rest shipped south on the railroad."

"That's kind of what I imagined this area to be like."

"That's how the village used to be. There's still logging in the forests; nothing like the days when the loggers systematically eliminated all of the virgin timber. If you want to see the hundred-year-old trees, you'll have to drive through one of the Indian reservations, where progress wasn't understood. Most of the people who don't work in the retail businesses here work in the paper mill in Lenora or one of the other small businesses there."

Ann sips from her glass. "It's a small community in every way a community gets to be described as small—small size, small houses left over from the boom days in logging, small stores with small supplies of goods, and some people with small minds."

I smile. I like her sense of humor. "Sounds low key." I try to keep my voice up, but it's fading.

"We're 'north of the tension line,' as they say around here, over halfway to the North Pole from the equator. You'll have your excitement. Some things don't change wherever you live."

We continue talking. Weariness. I yawn. "I saw on a map a river running through the village. Is that where the name of the village comes from?

"Yes. The Winding River flows south, coming into the village on the north end. There it makes a big bend to the east, goes under a bridge on the highway, then makes another big bend and flows south through the village and through many more bends to Lenora, where it's slowed by a dam at the paper mill. Then it continues south until it merges with another river."

"I grew up close to the Milwaukee River. There's always a river around, isn't there?"

Her reply eludes me. I try to listen, but her words are softer and coming from further away. I try unsuccessfully to stifle another yawn.

Ann rises. "Why don't I get you that blanket and pillow." She heads for the stairway to the second floor.

After she disappears, I move to the couch. Isn't that where the blanket and pillow go? I first sit and then lie for a moment on the couch with my head on a throw pillow. Only for a moment. I'll sit up when she comes down the stairs.

3

I wake in the dark in a sweat. Another bizarre dream. A number of college graduates have told me of their dreams about not passing final exams or graduating from school. The recurring theme in mine is not receiving my law school diploma.

Sitting up, I search the room through eyes out of focus. I remember the black stove and the young woman sitting in the rocker and *Rusty* driving into a white wall, and then I remember the young woman some more. I toss the blanket covering me aside. Where did it come from? Then I stumble to the front windows. With no moon, how incredibly dark it is in the country. The snow has disguised true shapes, yet I can view in the darkness snowdrifts lying still throughout the yard and across portions of the highway and the trees standing tall with the quaking all gone.

I find my way back to the couch. Coming to Winding River confounds my wildest dream. Was it a mistake? Part of me frets about the move; the other part eagerly awaits the highway plow so *Rusty* can be released from the snowdrift, and I can get to Burnett's office. What is that saying about law school: *The first year they scare you to death; the second year they work you to death; and the third year they bore you to death*? The boredom has passed. I'm anxious to begin interviewing clients and applying what I've learned in law school to the world beneath the proverbial tower. Still, I attempt to compile a mental list of reasons for coming to the Northwoods. My efforts are sabotaged by thoughts of the young woman. I like her.

As sunlight peeks through the windows, soft footsteps are on the stairs. I stand quickly to check myself. I realize I have not undressed.

"Oh, my gosh. You startled me," gasps a woman about Ann's age, slightly heavier and taller with reddish hair.

"I'm sorry. You must be Shelly."

"How did you know?"

"I'm John Hall. My car, ran off the road last night, and Ann, I mean your roommate, let me sleep on the couch. I guess she didn't tell you."

Shelly eases away from me, toward the kitchen. "I wish she *would* tell me these things."

"You were asleep. Anyway, I'll be going as soon as I get my car out of the ditch."

She brushes her short hair with her hand as she sighs and begins to breathe and speak more slowly. "I guess you wouldn't be here if Ann didn't think it was okay. I'll make a pot of coffee."

We sit at the kitchen table while we wait for the coffee to perk. Well into chatting with her, I realize my questions are mostly about Ann. "Tell me about yourself." She appears pleased by the opportunity.

"Well, I'm the business teacher at the high school. I also coach . . . "

I smile. I nod. I hear broken sentences. My mind wants to think about Ann. I recall the things she said and the way she said them, the tone of her voice, her mannerisms, and I find in it all an embrace of intelligence and grace. Then I return to see the seriousness on Shelly's face as she speaks, and in a lame atonement offer: "Really?"

Ann enters the kitchen and turns on a radio sandwiched between canisters on the counter. "Sorry, Shelly."

It's strange how she says it, less like an apology than a sign of victory.

We laze in the living room, holding cups of coffee and talking round robin. The rumbling and flashing yellow light of a highway plow break through the windowpanes. Ann experiments with diverting the light pattern by moving a hand.

Shelly speaks: "The landlord should be here soon to plow the driveway. He knows we have to get to school." Ann quickly drops her hand.

All Timber County schools will start at ten o'clock today, announces the morning newsman on the radio.

I try to face them both at once. The competition has finally forced through the lingering fog in my head. "I'm going to need a wrecker for the car."

Ann leaps up, while Shelly is still on the rise, and after leafing through the phone directory, hands the book to me to make the call.

When the wrecker arrives, I wade through the snow to the highway, finding no traces of my tracks from the previous evening. After *Rusty* is returned to the road, I thank and pay the quiet, old man. George? I clean the snow off my car with a brush from the trunk, turn on the flashing lights and return to the house carrying a gym bag and clothes on a hanger. Burnett is expecting me at nine o'clock, and I want to be on time.

It's past eight-thirty as I stand, freshly shaven and wearing a sport coat and tie, before the two young women, still sitting in the living room talking and drinking coffee. "I . . ." My impulse is to ask only Ann, but a flash of respect rearranges my words. "I want to buy you both dinner. How about Friday night?"

"Sure," is the word I hear from two directions.

4

The village drapes over the contour of the land along the Winding River like a white sheet thrown over a partially opened reclining chair. The top of the sheet stretches along the crest of a hill on my left, running parallel to the highway. From there, the sheet, dotted with church steeples towering above homes, droops four blocks to the commercial establishments along the highway, the seat of the village. Beyond the businesses on the other side of the road, the white sheet, with more blocks of homes clinging to it, sags over the gentle slope to the edge of the river where it tucks underneath the watercourse. A half-mile from the far side of the river is the national forest.

A front-end loader drops a load of snow from a pile in the center of the street into the back of a village dump truck. Shopkeepers and home-owners shovel their sidewalks and plow their parking lots. They work at a pace and in a manner that keeps their cheeks from ripening past the danger point and their minds from succumbing to the resignation that more snow may fall tomorrow and more the day after that. They know perfection in snow shoveling is a worthless pursuit.

I pass the village hall and attached police station on my left, the volunteer fire department building on my right, and two blocks lined with shops before I begin searching for the left turn onto Spruce Street by the bank Burnett had described to me. The number of persons and cars I pass surprises me; apparently, it's a normal day here.

Coming toward me on the sidewalk is a short man, wearing a cap with dangling earflaps and pulling a coaster wagon with a case of beer in it. Only in Wisconsin, I mumble. I spot the sign for the State Bank of Winding River projecting from the concrete pillared front of the bank.

A pile of snow in the intersection prevents me from turning left so I drive up to the next intersection. As I turn left onto Forest Street, I glimpse an old woman looking at me from a window above a restaurant at the corner. Although I barely see her, the sighting leaves me with an unsettling feeling. Was she watching for me?

After I circle the block to Spruce, I drive up the inclined street that dead-ends at the crest of the hill, in front of Burnett's office. I note how small many of the homes are and that they're almost all two-story, constructed of wood with the windows and porches arranged in the same way. There is no competition among them, as though they had been built not for the tastes of the owners but for some utilitarian purpose. I have never seen an old company town.

I drive straight into the parking lot, past a white sign bordered in black reading *Robert O. Burnett, Attorney At Law*, and park next to four other cars. On the way to the door of the two-story, red brick house, I stop and turn around. The village, colored pure white, is spread before me.

Stepping into the hallway, I sense warmth. To the right is a door to an office, with a stairway past the doorframe. Through the doorway, I see a fire burning in a fireplace and a gray-haired man seated in front of a desk with an open umbrella balanced on it, shading a picnic basket. He spoons scrambled eggs into his mouth from a plate surrounded by bananas and muffins while talking to someone seated opposite him, presumably Burnett.

To my left, is a doorway to a secretary's office. Seated on a couch past the door, opposite the staircase, is a middle-aged man, with thinning hair, wearing glasses and a sweater. He's reading a newspaper, with a dog curled up at his feet. Mahogany floor and trim boards, warmed by off-white plastered walls with pictures of brightly colored scenes of the Northwoods appear intended to lend a dignified appearance to the office.

The yellow Labrador Retriever rises and ambles over to me, wagging its tail with such force it wags its rear end.

"Good morning," grunts the man, briefly looking away from his newspaper.

"Good morning." I smile as I remove my overcoat and hang it on an antlered rack in the corner, then pet the dog.

A trim woman I estimate to be in her fifties, with a pleasant face, rushes into the hallway and grabs my hand. She has the unworried look of one who has mastered the essentials in life. "I'm Margo Lynch, Bob's secretary. Well, you made it."

"In a fashion."

She looks at the man on the bench. "That's Henry Miller, a local realtor." Then glancing down at the dog, "And that's my dog 'Abstract.' She's a successor to 'Deeds' and 'Wills.' She's also overweight because Henry feeds her donuts."

"Very nourishing." Henry appears pained to have to desert his newspaper.

I shake hands with the realtor.

"This is the new associate, huh?"

"Yes he is. And we're happy he's here. If you'll excuse us, Henry." Margo motions to me to step into her office.

"Nice to meet you." As soon as I finish speaking, Henry raises the newspaper back to eye level.

My first thought on entering her office: how does one secretary use two desks? Despite filing cabinets and shelves packed with client files, documents and office supplies, it is somehow a neatly cluttered room.

"Bob is with a client." Margo appears embarrassed and continues in a low voice. "The Dean. He turns every appointment into a picnic, regardless of the weather and despite Bob's protests. Supposedly he comes in for estate planning, but all they ever do is discuss literature. He was a professor and dean of a college in Minnesota." She lowers her voice further. "It will be better for you if he doesn't get to know you."

I laugh. "Literature was not my best subject. I enjoyed the writing part but not the reading. I never seemed to get out of the novels what I was supposed to be getting out of them."

"Well, it's all beyond me." She shakes her head. "While we wait, I'll show you around the office. This, by the way, is the old dining room. Bob keeps promising me he'll buy more file cabinets. I don't like it this way."

I follow her into the kitchen behind her office.

"You'll have full use of the kitchen as well as the other rooms in the building. We're hoping this will be your home for some time."

As she guides me across the hallway to a room behind Burnett's office, I think she is pleasant enough and clearly in charge.

"This is your office, John. And, I hope you don't mind me calling you by your first name?"

"John is fine."

What brings an immediate smile to my face are the two windows, one showing a lot full of pine trees on the side of the house and the other facing the back yard. No cubicle here. The desk, with two client chairs in front of it, faces the door. A bookshelf covers a wall separating the room from Burnett's office. I pick up a triangular shaped, wooden nameplate with the metal plate on one side inscribed, *Attorney John Hall.* "You've thought of everything."

"The telephone man should be here today to put in an extension, and I've ordered a dictating machine for you that should have been here by now. I'm a little upset about that."

"I can wait."

"Do you have your law school diploma with you? I'll get it framed."

"Thanks, I already did that." The diploma dream pops up. "It was the first thing I put in the car."

I follow Margo upstairs to the front bedroom I will be using and then through the other rooms on the second floor. The one above my office is a combination conference room and library. Solidly packed bookshelves cover most of the walls except for two windows lining up with those in my office below. A dark oak table, with six chairs around it, occupies the center of the room.

"I like this." My words surprise me; this is hardly the law office of my dreams. Rick would really be snickering by now. "I take it this was someone's home at one time."

"It belonged to one of the managers of the old saw mill in the early nineteen-hundreds when this was a booming lumber town. Bob got it many years ago at a very reasonable price through an estate. Not one he handled, though." Margo leans toward me. "He wouldn't have thought that to be ethical."

When we return to Margo's office, Henry Miller is gone. Burnett is still with The Dean, so I sit in a chair in front of her desk. Abstract wanders in and plops next to Margo's chair.

For no reason other than idle conversation, I offer: "With all of the snow out there, I find it amazing that everyone is going about their business as usual."

"The snowstorms are part of our life here."

"I even saw a man pulling a kid's coaster wagon with a case of beer in it."

"Huh! That's Eddie Plumber. They call him 'Beeper.' He's the village . . . served a few jail sentences for petty theft and failure to support his family. He got that nickname as a young kid always running around and sneaking up on people and going 'beep beep.' Quit school when he was sixteen, works on and off doing yard work and as a handyman. No one ever expected him to be anything other than an annoyance."

"I take it he's also lost his driver's license."

"Many times, too many times. Then, I'm not sure if he ever got it back to lose."

Margo excuses herself and heads for the bathroom at the rear of the first floor. I stroll around the room, occasionally picking up a file to determine the type of legal work in it. The telephone on her desk rings. After the third ring, I look down the hallway for Margo, and after the fourth ring, I pick up the receiver. "Burnett Law Office."

"I just have a question. Are you an attorney?" It's a young, feminine voice.

"Well, yes, but . . ."

"I'm sure you can easily answer it. It won't take a minute."

My frantic eyes search again for Margo, but she has not returned. "Just a question?"

"Yes. I'll talk as fast as I can. I'm a pretty fast talker anyway. Here's the thing: I'm from Indiana, but I was living in Harris County in Wisconsin for about eight months, and now I've been staying for two weeks with my aunt in Winding River. Maybe you know her, Virginia . . . well that doesn't matter. I'm eighteen, and I got married about six months ago in Harris County. I'd been staying there with my older sister, Kathleen, because I wasn't happy at home, and I met Josè there. He's from Mexico, but he was working on a farm in the county. This is confidential, isn't it? I mean he's not in the states legally; well maybe he is now. Anyway we got married, and I had to have my mother sign because I was seventeen. She didn't really sign, though, because she was in Indiana, and my older sister looks older and like my mother, and she signed as my mother. It's not working. He doesn't like to work, and he keeps getting into trouble. You know, he's nice enough, and he doesn't hurt me or anything like that, but he gets drunk and goes back to Mexico, and he was in jail in Arizona, or maybe New Mexico, and I just don't want to be married to him anymore. So, can I go to court here and get an annulment, or should I get a divorce, that's what Virginia said I should do, because we did have sex and all that, but I don't want to get my sister in trouble, and, anyway, how much is this going to cost because I don't have any money right now?"

A shock wave hits me. This is a dream, another one of those dreams of the impossible law school exam. Find the issues: annulment, void marriage, misrepresentation, fraud, jurisdictional questions, service of process. Arrow like issues cascade on me. It has to be a dream.

"Like I said. It's just a question."

"Ah, I think you should schedule an appointment with . . . "

"Maybe my aunt could give me a few dollars."

"Attorney Burnett may be able to help you, and . . . "

"What's your name?"

"John Hall. I . . . "

"He's really nice to me when he's not drunk, but he's tough. I think he's wanted in Indiana because he beat up my mother's boyfriend when we went to visit her. My mother didn't like him, and he got mad at her and then her boyfriend got into it. My mother didn't come to the wedding. Well, she didn't know about the wedding. You know, maybe they found him, and he's in jail in Indiana. You can check all those states, right? I mean you're an attorney."

"What I'm trying to tell you, Mrs . . . "

"Mindy."

"Mindy, is that . . . "

"If they do put him in jail or prison, will that stop the annulment or divorce? I want to get it over with as soon as possible. But, I want child support. He won't get out of that will he?"

"Child support?"

"I'm pregnant, and I know he's the father. Well, I did have sex with several other guys, but I know he's the father. We can prove that somehow, can't we? I don't want him getting out of child support. Virginia says I should get it. She knows. She was divorced twice. Did I ask you if you know Virginia? Never mind, the thing is . . . "

"You should schedule an appointment to see Attorney Burnett."

"Oh, if you're busy now, I can call back in half an hour."

I put my hand over the mouthpiece of the phone as Margo sits at her desk. "It's Mindy?"

Margo looks alarmed. "Mindy? Good Grief." She thumbs through a rotating telephone card file, parts the tabs, and shoves the file in front of me.

"Ah, here's a telephone number for legal aid in Lenora."

"Will they help me?"

"You said it would be only one question, remember?"

"Oh, yeah. Thanks." Click.

Margo shakes her head and purses her lips. "Don't say anything. She made two appointments to see Bob and didn't keep either one of them."

❦ ❧

The intercom on the telephone buzzes. After answering, Margo ushers me into Burnett's office. It's my first look since October at the man who brought me here. A lanky man with a serious face, though, diverts my attention. He gathers dishes and left over food and places them in a basket on the desk.

Burnett rises and moves quickly to me, extending his head. "John, we're so glad you're here." He turns to the lanky man. "This is The Dean." As I shake hands with the former professor, Burnett adds, "We were discussing his estate plan." He winks at me.

The Dean sizes me up. "Are you a reader?"

"I . . ."

Burnett saves me. "I'm sure he hasn't had time to read anything other than law books."

The Dean gives Burnett a nod along with a pucker of the face. "I'll prepare a reading list for him." He buttons up his coat, then folds the umbrella and tucks it under his arm. "We'll do this again, soon, along with your associate." With his other arm, he lifts the picnic basket and carries it out into the snow.

I see Margo roll her eyes as Burnett moves back to his chair and asks me to sit down. I sit in one of the three chairs in front of the desk that faces the front window. A credenza with files and papers partially obscuring a dictating machine is located behind the desk. The walls are

covered with the history of a man: diplomas, plaques, and framed photographs and letters.

"We've got so much to talk about, John."

Margo starts to leave, stopping to answer the telephone ringing on
Burnett's desk, addressing me as she does so. "I switch it over when I
leave my office. It normally won't ring in your office." She frowns as she
hesitates with the receiver before thrusting it at me. "It's for you."

"For me?"

"Good morning," speaks a patient voice. I'm Attorney Sanford
Smith, the other attorney in the village. I was hoping you had arrived.
I'm looking forward to meeting you. I know how hard it is for a young
lawyer to get started, so I'm referring to you a client with a personal injury case. If it's all right, he'll come in about ten o'clock tomorrow
morning."

"Fine. Thank you very much."

"All right then. Good luck on your practice. Good-by."

I smile. "That was Attorney Smith. He's referring to me a client with
a PI case."

"What?" Margo stands with her hands on her sides.

Burnett shakes his head. "Smith *is* different."

"Different?" snaps Margo. "He's pompous, sneaky . . . "

Burnett puts up his hands, palms forward, and Margo leaves the
room.

"John, you have to understand Margo. A wonderful woman, does
everything around here, been with me for years. But, she knows everybody and everything, and she's not afraid to express her opinions."

"I can see that."

"Smith is everything she said. That's another thing about Margo.
She has that maddening quality to always be right. Say, do you want
some coffee?"

"Please."

Burnett buzzes Margo to bring in two cups. "Anyway, Smith is
about forty, overweight and, admittedly, overbearing. He went to a private college out east and then to a law school out west that no one
around here knew existed. I suspect his grades were marginal. His father
is a third generation owner of the lumberyard and a director and major
shareholder in the bank. He might have been able to buy Smith's way

into school, but not buy the grades." He sighs. "You're going to have to deal with him. Just be careful."

Briskly entering the room with the coffee, Margo proceeds to hand each of us a cup, beams at me and then leaves. She exudes confidence and competency. Maybe she does know everything, everything, that is, she feels is worth knowing.

Burnett glances at a clock on the wall to his left. "We'll go down to Lenora later. We'll drive around the city, have a sandwich, and I'll introduce you to the people in the courthouse. Have you seen your office?"

"Yes sir, I have. I'm very satisfied."

A pained look clouds Burnett's face. "Forget the *sir* stuff. We're not that formal here. You're not here to impress anyone but me, and I don't impress easily, so don't bother to try."

"All right."

Burnett sips from his coffee cup. "Let me stress that we exist here because of our clients. We have to work with them, help them to solve their problems. In a sense, that's what we do. We're problem solvers. First we have to make sure we understand their problems, then figure out how to solve them, and then draft documents or go to court in furtherance of the solutions. Sometimes you're going to find they need a CPA or an investment advisor or a psychiatrist to solve their problems. We can only help them if they have legal problems. We're not qualified beyond the law.

"When you work out the solutions, though, always remember there's a human side of the practice. You don't want to become a technician. I think many lawyers feel their clients are most concerned with results and fees. I'm not sure about that. Results are obviously important, that's why they come to you, and they don't want to pay more than they can afford. In fact, many of them would like your services for free."

I nod my head. "I'm sure of that."

"I believe, though, what's very important to them is to establish a good repoiré with their attorney, their attorney demonstrates to them their files are being worked and keeps them advised on the progress, and, most importantly, there's some understanding, some sympathy for their legal plight."

I sit on the edge of my chair. Burnett has a way of drawing me deeply into a conversation. His communication with me isn't really a conversation since he does most of the talking. Nor, is it a lecture. It's my orientation, and I don't want to miss a word of it.

"Now, John, I have several matters I want you to work on. You're going to begin interviewing clients and going to the courthouse right away. It's the way I got started, the way every lawyer in Timber County got started. I'm sure you'll have lots of questions. Ask. I'm also sure you'll make mistakes, that's part of the learning process, but give it your best shot."

"I will. I appreciate your giving me the opportunity to be here." I pause, thinking I should end it there, but some sense of honesty keeps me talking. "I know I'll make mistakes. I tend to leap at things too quickly. I'll try to keep them at a minimum."

"Good. After we return from the courthouse this afternoon, I want you to finish looking around the building and get moved into your room. Tomorrow afternoon, I'd like you to sit in with me on a new divorce. And, I'd like you to do some research for me on condemnation procedure. I'm the village attorney for Winding River, and the village wants to extend a street, but is having trouble acquiring the land from one of the owners along the proposed route. I need to be prepared to explain the procedures at the next Village Board meeting. Most of eminent domain law is statutory, so look over the statutes carefully, particularly the notice requirements and time lines."

Burnett checks his calendar. "On Thursday morning, I need you to take a court hearing for me at nine-thirty on a default matter. I have a conflict with another case. Margo will put it on your calendar, and I'll go over it with you on Wednesday afternoon. It shouldn't take more than ten to fifteen minutes."

"Okay."

"Let's head down to Lenora." Burnett picks up a briefcase with the leather scuffed and discolored in spots, jams abstracts of title into it, and snaps it shut. "John, I also want you to sit in with me on Wednesday morning when a young woman is coming in on a PI case."

"That's fine. I know there's plenty to learn."

As we put on our coats in the hallway, Burnett continues, "You'll be busy. In law school you study five courses a semester. Here you may work on two-dozen matters in a day, and they may all involve different areas of the law. That's not counting the telephone calls and the walk-ins with different problems."

"I hadn't thought about that, but it's all right with me. I should be taking notes so I can remember everything you're telling me."

Burnett smiles as we walk to his car. "You'll remember. I used to keep most of the facts of my cases in my head. Now, I have to take more notes. Age."

This is the way I want to begin, by plunging in. While the car warms up as we drive down the hill, I shiver. Is it from the cold? Still, the doubt lingers. I'm in a village whose existence I only recently discovered; in an old house with an attorney who no longer craves trial work; the only other attorney in the village may not be a friend; and then there is the dog, following me everywhere, sniffing me for information. Strange. So different from my dreams.

While Burnett points out places on the Main Street, I think of the state map I looked at in the school parking lot. The tiny circle on the map begins to fill in.

5

The Timber County Courthouse is a museum. The two-story, brown-stone building stands in the center of a square block, with the main door facing the highway. Atop the courthouse is a dome with clocks facing in four directions. A newer attachment on the south end houses the sheriff's department and the jail I visited last night.

The jail. As Burnett drives into the parking lot along the north side of the courthouse, I wonder what happened to Billy. Is he now back in the mental health center? What is that old Midwestern saying? *There's only a thin red line between the sane and the insane.* Billy crossed the line; he went across the river.

We ease along the shoveled sidewalk leading from a parking lot to a side door of the courthouse. I point at the walls. "I've noticed that reddish-brown stone on several of the buildings in the village."

"It was quarried on Madeline Island in Lake Superior. Some day, we'll go up to Bayfield and take the ferry across to the island. There's a lot to see in Northern Wisconsin." He turns to look at me. "This isn't the end of the earth up here." He cocks his head. "Then, there are those who claim you can see it from here."

We laugh while we stroll down marbled floor corridors with high ceilings, past museum like doors with aged, black lettering on the windows identifying the offices of the County Treasurer, County Clerk, and Register of Deeds, into the rotunda in the center. We pause to survey the ceiling of the dome that was artfully painted by Civilian Conservation Corps workers during the Depression. If the uses of the building are modern, I reason, the building itself is not. Is it on the list of the National Register of Historic Places? Probably not, there must be hundreds of county courthouses like this one around the country.

"I'll take you around the offices later, John. First, I want to introduce you to the judge. I hope to catch him before he goes on the bench for the afternoon session."

"Sure." Then why doesn't Burnett walk faster so we'll be sure to catch the judge? Burnett's springless steps are measured and confident. They're like his conversations where he's constantly calculating what he's going to say and do, and then speaking and acting with confidence.

We take the stairs to the second floor courtroom. The room is empty except for a court reporter inserting the top of a new tape into his stenographic machine. He appears to be my age, slightly shorter, with very dark hair, handsome, wearing a blue shirt and a tie and carrying a paunch that portrays lack of exercise. He wears the impish face of a prankster.

"Is the judge back from lunch?"

"Yeah, he is, Bob."

"This is my new associate, John Hall. John, this is Angelo Bellini."

"Angie." The court reporter grins as he shakes my hand. "Welcome to the Northwoods."

Burnett puts up his hand. "Excuse us, Angie. I want to catch the judge."

I wave at the court reporter as Burnett leads me into the judge's chambers. Most of the wall space is occupied with bookshelves. A door to the left must lead to the jury room. Behind the judge's metal, county desk is a row of windows with the space between the ones nearest the center containing a framed pencil sketch of him.

"Good afternoon, judge. This is my new associate, John Hall." Burnett gestures toward the judge, taller and stockier than me, with a firmly drawn face. "John, this is Judge Homer Tompkins."

"Ah, yes," The judge rises enough to shake my hand. "Sit down."

I'm more nervous now than I was with Billy. The judge is looking deeply into me.

"Where did you go to school?"

"I went to law school in Milwaukee."

"So did I, about thirty-five years ago. Still formal, have to wear a coat and a tie to class and stand when reciting?"

"Yes. I spent three years in the Army, so I was less fazed by the formal approach than many of my classmates."

The judge shakes his head approvingly. Why is he eyeing me so closely?

"As you know, the idea is that if you are going to be a professional man you should look and act like one."

"I understand." I meant I understand the comment but not the penetrating look and the accent on the word *act.*

Burnett must have caught it, too. He stands up. "Well, judge, we don't want to hold you up. I wanted you to meet John before he appears in court."

"I'm glad you brought him in, Bob." He checks a wall clock. "I don't have anything until one-thirty. In the meantime, do you suppose I could have a few words with Attorney Hall . . . alone."

"Sure, judge. I have to pick up some documents at the Register of Deeds' Office." Burnett turns to me, squinting his eyes. "I'll wait for you outside the courtroom."

I nod as he leaves, closing the door behind him. What's this all about? My anxiety increases.

The judge stands and begins circling the room. "I understand that you slept at my daughter's house last night."

"That was *your* daughter?" I instantly realize it was a mistake to emphasize the adjective of possession. As if I would have done anything differently if she had not been his daughter. Then panic seizes me. Who is the daughter? How could I have not gotten either Ann's or Shelly's last name?

"Now, Attorney Hall, I know about the circumstances. At least, I know about some of the circumstances. She's my youngest daughter, the only one of the three not married. She's . . . well, the point is I'm very particular about my daughters. I'm sure you can understand my concern."

Still staggered by the revelation, I wonder if I should respond, and if I do, what will I say? Which young woman is the judge talking about? The judge has moved around to me. I jump up.

"I know many things are done differently these days. Nevertheless, I urge you to be careful . . . *Attorney* Hall." The judge grips my hand so tightly I recognize it is not a casual shake as he again stares through me.

"And, good luck with your law practice. I'm sure we'll see a lot of each other."

"Thank you, Your Honor. I will be careful." Stupid again. Be careful about what? This is not the way I envisioned my first meeting with the judge. I try to sort it out as I walk back into the courtroom.

"Poof!" Angie shoots me with a partially closed fist, the index finger pointed out and the thumb up.

"You know about this?"

"Hey, this is the Northwoods. We know about all of the foxes and the hounds around here. And, she's a fox."

"Well, I'm not a hound, at least I wasn't last night." I dip my head toward the judge's chamber. "Am I in trouble?"

"Nah, don't worry about it. He's all right after you get to know him. Talk to him about golf. Come over here."

He steers me through a door on the left side of the bench into the jury room. The jury table and some of the chairs have been pushed to the far wall and a putter leans against the near wall, next to the door. Several golf balls rest at various positions on the floor near an over-turned can. We laugh.

People begin drifting into the courtroom. Angie looks out at them. "I live in Winding River. How about we get together for dinner tonight. We'll have a few brews first, at Slider's on the main drag. Sometime after five?"

"I'd like that." I start to leave the courtroom as attorneys file in, then I hurry back to Angie. "By the way which one is the daughter?"

Angie grins as he sits down before his machine and remains silent.

❧ ❧

Burnett sits on a bench outside the courtroom reviewing recorded deeds and mortgages. For the first time, I notice his rumpled sport coat and trousers badly in need of a press. I recall his comment on the way to Lenora that even if I hadn't graduated in the upper third of my class, he would have picked me over the others he had interviewed. He was pleased I hadn't shown up for the interview in a three-piece suit with a Phi Beta Kappa key dangling from the vest. Of course I've never owned a three-piece suit, and the only keys I have are the ones to *Rusty* and my apartment in Milwaukee.

As he leads me down the stairway, he asks, "How did it go with the judge?"

"I'll tell you on the way back to the office."

"All right. I've got an abstract of title to a tract of land being sold in Algona, which is southwest of Winding River. We're representing the seller. I'll show you what we do here."

Abstracts? I forgot about abstracting. Where did I think the dog got her name?

In the Register of Deeds' office, Burnett points out the tract indexes where documents pertaining to title to real estate are recorded. "In metropolitan areas, title to real estate is shown by title insurance policies in about ninety-nine per cent of the real estate transactions. Around here, title to real estate is shown by abstracts in the majority of the transactions. As you know, an abstract is a compilation of the entries in the courthouse pertaining to a tract of real estate, commencing with the United States Government patent down to the present title holder—all of the deeds transferring the property from time to time, all of the mortgages and satisfactions of mortgages affecting the property, tax liens, construction liens, judgments, and other impediments to title."

I try to be attentive. Abstracting?

"Our job when there is a sale of real estate and we represent the seller is to bring the abstract up to date within fifteen days of the date of closing. Then we furnish it to the buyer's attorney who will render a title opinion on it. You get the information from the courthouse, and Margo will type up an extension of the abstract. Not exciting work, but something that has to be done. And, you know, John, it's a great way to learn about real estate."

We move to the Clerk of Court's Office, where, after introductions, Burnett shows me various books concerning liens and judgments. "Remember that as abstracters we simply report what is recorded. It's up to the examiner of the abstract rendering an opinion on it to determine the significance of what's recorded."

My mind wanders, preferring to concentrate on the cute deputy clerk, that is, until I spot the wedding ring. Oh well, maybe there's still a chance with Ann.

In the County Treasurer's Office, we search the tax records for delinquent real estate taxes against the property. In each office we visit everyone eyes me closely. Am I the exhibit "H" they have been waiting for? I sense they're trying to determine if the exhibit is as good as the one they've been promised.

"I know this can be boring work," Burnett acknowledges. "Still, I must stress strongly that we can't miss liens or past due taxes against a tract of land. If we do, we may be on the hook for them."

"Is there a lot of this?" I ask as we walk out of the courthouse.

"Unfortunately, there is, but you'll learn to work it in whenever you're at the courthouse. After a while, it goes quickly. When we're back at the office, I'll go over some abstracts and title opinions with you."

"Okay." It is not okay, though, and Burnett sees it in my face.

"John, I know I'm starting you out with one of the most mundane chores of a small town lawyer. I didn't like it when I started out. Abstracting is not a reason anyone ever gave for going to law school. It's just something we have to do."

❧ ❧

Burnett has both of his hands firmly on the steering wheel as we drive past banks of snow piled high along the sides of the highway leading to Winding River. "So that's Lenora, John, the only city in Timber County."

"Seems like I've heard the name before."

"Maybe you've heard the tale. Lenora was a young woman, sixteen-years-old, as I recall. This was back in the late eighteen hundreds. Story is she took up with a logger, apparently a small, quiet lad. One morning Lenora was found behind the old Koester Hotel with her throat slit. Her young man had disappeared. The murder was never solved, and the young man was never found. It's a sad story that shocked the community, then called Oakview.

"When I was the district attorney in Big Lakes County, out of curiosity, I read up on the case. There was no indication her young man had killed her; rather, it was thought she was killed by a drunken logger whom her boyfriend couldn't fend off. It was assumed the lad ran off out of fear and shame."

"It does sound like a sad story," I acknowledge.

"Well, it's one of those tales of the Northwoods like the Paul Bunyan stories. How much is fact, and how much is fantasy? It's like trying to decipher the stories some of our clients tell us. Anyway, when the community was incorporated, it was named Lenora after her."

"I heard a story something like that, except it happened in one of the old mining towns." I cut off the subject so I can relate the events of the previous evening.

Burnett laughs. "Well, I don't think the judge has a daughter with reddish hair; then, I'm not sure. He lives in Lenora, and over the years I socialized with him mainly at bar association meetings. I've lost track of his daughters."

As we near Winding River, a fully loaded logging truck breezes past us.

"Watch out for them," Burnett warns. "I suppose you've spent a lot of time on the new rules of civil procedure that became effective on January first?"

"We did in school. I had some experience under the old rules at the firm I worked in after school this past year, so I could understand many of the changes."

"You may have to educate me, John. I went to a seminar on the new rules, but I'm so ingrained in the old ones, I know I'll have to be careful."

"I can't imagine that I can help you learn much of anything." Mentoring my mentor?

"I can always learn. If I can teach you anything, it's to learn how much you need to learn."

When we enter the office, I barge into Margo's office, trailed by Abstract.

"Margo, do you know the name of Judge Tompkins' daughter who lives in Winding River?"

She does not look up nor cease typing. "Ann."

"Are you sure?" I immediately regret asking the question.

The typewriter becomes quiet as she gazes at me. "Yes."

"Thanks, Margo."

I bound upstairs to my room. When Margo showed me the room earlier, I noticed it contains the basic furniture: double bed, nightstand, dresser, and spindle back chair. As I stand at the front window over-looking the village, I realize I missed the view. This is a better view than I had in the morning when I lingered in the parking lot. The location of the river is as Ann described it; what she failed to relate is the way the river sweeps through the village. Even though covered with snow, the banks to the water outline the river. The scene evokes for me a powerful feeling. I sense an intertwining between the river and everything around it. The river is a linchpin for a connection I fail to understand.

The national forest lies beyond the river, the pines and cedars wrapped in snow, stretching east and north and south as far as I can see. A small object in the distant white appears to be a ranger tower. I'll have to buy a pair of binoculars.

I sit on the bed. Far removed, I consider, from my two-bedroom apartment in Milwaukee. There the views show an alley running along the side of the building and dilapidated houses across the street from the front. My mother would have liked this place. She always wanted to escape from the city. Now that she is gone and my brother married, I'm alone, in a place I never expected to be in. My eyes run over the furniture again, then up and down the barren walls and bare wood floor. The quietness and simplicity of the room soothes me.

6

Twenty minutes after five. The sun is down. My possessions have been hauled from my car into the bedroom except for my framed diploma, a law dictionary, several of my text books and my outlines from law school, all of which I left in my office. I clean up in the bathroom at the back end of the upstairs hall. Then I head for Slider's.

Located on Main Street, two blocks north of Spruce, my guide to the bar is the reddish glow from the neon sign on the front of the log building reading *Slider's Northwoods Tap*. A long, mahogany bar with a brass foot rail and a matching, ornately carved back bar with mirrors, stretches along the left wall. A mounted, young black bear on a shelf, flanked by deer heads, covers the opposite wall partitioning the dining room. Twenty some persons are in the bar, most of them on barstools, with four at a table playing sheepshead, while a jukebox sends soft music through a trace of smoke.

"You sure know how to cut 'em, Milt!" yells one of the men at the table, as he slams down a card in the Wisconsin version of the old Bavarian game.

"You win. You buy a round," gloats one of the other men.

Angie sits alone at the bar, joking with the bartender. "Counselor! We're holding court. This is Dale Anderson, the owner."

I reach across the bar to shake hands with a short, slightly built man in his thirties with a thin face. His crew cut defies the prevailing long hairstyles. His eyes tell me b.s. is allowed, that it's part of the place, but he'll know it when he hears it.

Angie looks at me. "They call him 'Slider' from his baseball days . . . reportedly the best shortstop and base stealer ever to come out of Winding River. Played at the U in Superior. He's famous."

Slider laughs. "We don't have any famous people from Winding River. We don't have any famous anything. That's the beauty of the place."

"Catch him one on me." Angie opens his wallet and throws a ten-dollar bill on the bar.

"Beer is fine."

Slider moves down the taps and draws off a large mug of Wisconsin brewed beer.

Angie grins at me. "Well, counselor, did you find out the name of the daughter?"

I pause before hoisting my mug. "Is that the topic of discussion?"

Slider smiles. "Gossip is a Northwoods virus. It's particularly contagious when the doors are shut against the winter."

"It began spreading the moment old George pulled your car out of the ditch," adds Angie.

Quiet George? "If I buy the next round, will you wise guys solve a dilemma for me: stay away from Ann and see Shelly to make the judge happy, or stay away from both of them?"

"Ooh," Angie and Slider chime. "We'll have to think about that."

I face Angie. "Where are you from?"

"He's a Yooper," Slider answers for him.

"The Upper Peninsula of Michigan. I left after high school to go to court reporter school in Milwaukee. After many of the iron ore mines in the U.P. closed down in the sixties, there weren't the opportunities there anymore. At the time I finished my training, Tompkins' court reporter retired. I guess no one with experience wanted to move up here. Hard to understand that, isn't it Slider?"

"Can't imagine that." Slider polishes the outside of a glass with a bar towel.

"How is it that you live here rather than in Lenora?"

"I found a nice cottage on the other side of the river. When the ice is off, I can come home, pop open a can of beer and drop a line off the end of the pier. And when the ice is on, Slider will take me on his snowmobile to his shanty on Oval Lake so we can ice fish."

"Drink beer and play cards in the shanty," Slider corrects.

I drain the mug. "I suppose if I get invited I get to use the ice auger to drill the holes in the ice and keep the fire going in the stove?"

Thumbs up, index fingers out, Angie shoots Slider. "I told you he was a smart guy."

I like both of them. I suspect Angie is going to be trouble, but I can't help but like him. He reminds me of guys I knew in the Army and in college who got me in the middle of embarrassing or costly situations and then evaporated, but somehow the guys were always fun.

"I'll get the next round," I tell Slider, handing him my empty mug.

My watch reads nine-fifteen when I drive into the office parking lot. The dinner I ate at seven o'clock at Slider's was a brat and some fries, along with an appetizer of fried, breaded cheese curds. "Perfect," I tell myself, the food I've been living on for years.

I tuck my hands into the pockets of my jacket as I stand in the lot and let my eyes roam the village below. Inside the houses I know stories are being enacted: some buoyed by laughter and happiness, some cloaked in lust and deceit, and some perpetrated by violence and cruelty. I wonder how many of those stories will be told to me some day and what I will do after I've heard them. I recall Burnett's remark, "You never know what the next call is going to be about or what strange matter the next client will bring in." What about the clients themselves? What will they be like? And, am I ready for them?

Inside the dark hallway, I fumble for the light switch. I feel relief when the light comes on, and I leave it on all night.

The Clients

7

The alarm clock on the nightstand buzzes. Six o'clock in the morning. I rise for my first day of practice. Yesterday didn't count since all I did was listen to others. As I pull on jeans and a sweatshirt, I peer out the window. Many houses have lights on and a few cars are struggling in the streets. More snow fell during the night, and the moving cars have been cleared of the flakes except on their tops, which look like powder puffs. In my haste to get downstairs, I stub my toe on the nightstand. My curse echoes off the bare walls and floor. After ten years of barracks, dorm rooms, and seedy apartments without carpets, I find strange comfort in the sound.

On the way to the kitchen, I realize I should have gone to the grocery store. A note from Margo on the table reads: *Cereal in the cupboard . . . Milk and orange juice in the refrigerator . . . Will bring fresh donuts and make coffee.* I find a stale donut and munch on it as I set up the coffee maker, the extent of my culinary arts. While the coffee brews, I stumble across the hallway into my office.

My law school diploma hangs on the wall behind the desk, next to the window, and a clock now hangs over the doorframe. An appointment book at the top of the desk lays open to Tuesday, January 27, 1976, the left side of the book for appointments, the right side for keeping track of time. Margo must have come in during the evening. On the left page she has written:

10:00 - *New PI Case*
12:00 - *Lunch w/Bob*
 2:30 - *Meet w/Bob on New Divorce*

I flip the page to Wednesday.

9:00 - *Ginger Buckman PI*
1:00 - *Meet w/Bob re Schultz v Herdina*

I flip to Thursday.

9:00 - *Schultz v. Herdina DJ Hearing*

The next page is empty. This is the beginning. Am I ready to take on clients and dispense advice? Whether I made the right choice in coming, I *have* come and now that I'm here, I have to do what the diploma implies I am capable of doing. The moment I first walked into the barracks at the reception station in basic training in the Army flashes through my mind. A young recruit who knows it all since he arrived the day ahead of me lies on an upper bunk, wearing a khaki T-shirt and fatigue pants. His head is propped on an elbow and dog tags dangle from his neck. The recruit yells, "Go back home! It's not worth it!" I cannot go home now any more than I could have then.

I return to the kitchen, pour a cup of the fresh coffee and carry it upstairs to the library to begin researching eminent domain law. The bookshelves contain a complete set of Wisconsin cases, many of the oldest volumes with tattered or missing covers; a set of annotated statutes with cases referring to the statutes; legal encyclopedias; a set of federal cases; and various treatises and sets pertaining to specific areas of the law.

Whenever I stand before shelves of books in a law library, I am awed by the magnitude of the law. The law reaches with its octopus-like tentacles into virtually every aspect of human life. Society cannot exist without rules of conduct created by the law. In college, I read philosophical essays about questions without answers. In legal forums, rightly or wrongly, the keepers of the court are forced to provide answers to the questions before them. The litigants did not seek answers to eternal, unanswerable questions. They sought answers only to those countless questions that provide a path to weave through the fabric of life without knowing why. The answers crafted by the courts are bound in the books before me. I feel humble in their presence.

I kneel before a set of books on municipal law and browse the index until I locate a section titled *Eminent Domain*. This time a year before I wondered what use I would ever make of a course on municipal law I was then beginning. Now I remember my professor discussing condemnation in this type of situation, by a city for a road extension. Burnett is right; most of municipal law is statutory, few court cases interpreting the law compared to an area like personal injury law. There is less reading to do; then, there is less guidance when the statutes are ambiguous.

I further recall my professor commenting that even in times of old English law, every man had free use and enjoyment of his property, subject to the right of the government to appropriate the land for public use, upon the government paying compensation to the owner. A simple enough concept, I think. As I skim through the text, what is not so simple are the lengthy sections and subsections packed with requirements of notice, time lines, and specific forms of action. I finish the coffee and dig in; I've never waffled on working.

In the midst of the research, I pause to glance at the bookshelves. Will my name appear among the names of the lawyers handling appellate cases printed in future volumes of the books before me? Wouldn't that be the closest brush I'll ever have with immortality?

At seven fifteen, I eat a bowl of cereal and take a shower. When I bounce downstairs with a dress shirt and tie on, I hear Margo typing. Abstract naps at the feet of Henry Miller who sits on the couch with a doughnut in his mouth, looking himself like a retriever, while he reads the newspaper. Miller doesn't look up as I step into Margo's office and sit down.

"Thanks for hanging my diploma and setting up the appointment book."

Margo lifts her unpainted fingernails from the typewriter keys and takes a drink from her coffee cup. "Well, I hope you use that book. I mean to keep track of your time. God knows I have to beat Bob into doing it."

"Actually, we haven't discussed billing."

Margo grimaces. "Our hourly rate is thirty-five dollars an hour, except we take most personal injury cases and collection cases on a percentage of the recovery. You write down your time, and I'll post it to the books and bill it monthly."

"All right."

"You can think whatever you want about the practice of law, but if you don't see it as a business, you'll never make much money at it. Don't pay attention to Bob when he tells you how when he first began practicing law here getting a new client was harder then walking up the hill to the office in an ice storm; so he had to be careful about what he charged clients." Margo looks wistfully past me. "I've never understood whether sympathy for the depressed of the Depression locked up Bob's attitude on billing, or he simply doesn't care about money." A smile returns to her face. "Anyway, good morning."

"Good morning." I inch closer to Margo and lower my voice. "Is Henry here every day?"

"Every day. That's another part of the business. He brings us all of his real estate work, and we furnish him the morning newspaper and fresh donuts and coffee. After a while, you won't notice him any more."

Chuckling, I leave Margo's office by the hallway door so I can walk past Miller on the way back to my office. I hear a grunt when I say hello but receive no further recognition from a face that never appears from behind the newspaper. Abstract's eyes follow me, her body staying close to the source of morning doughnuts.

As I sit at my desk, I eye the dictating machine that arrived late in the afternoon on Monday. It's similar to the one I used at the law firm. I pick up the appointment book and on the right hand page at seven a.m., write in: *Village of Winding River, Research condemnation procedures—1.10 hours.* Not keeping my book on municipal law was a mistake. I did, though, keep my torts book, and I remove it from the bookshelf and begin leafing through the pages, even though I have no idea what the *New PI Case* at ten o'clock concerns. I decide to review some of Burnett's open and closed PI files to determine the kind of notes he takes on initial client interviews.

⌘ ⌘

Margo buzzes me on the telephone intercom my appointment has arrived. I lead into my office a small, bushy-haired man in his late thirties, wearing a mustache, with shifty eyes and his right arm in a sling.

The man sits on the edge of his chair, eyeballing the office as he speaks. "You're the new lawyer, huh?"

"That's right. I've just graduated from law school. If you want someone with more experience, I could set up an appointment with Attorney Burnett."

"You gotta license to practice, don't you?"

"Yes, I do." I should get it framed to match my diploma. "I believe Wisconsin is one of two states in the United States that has a 'diploma privilege,' meaning that if you graduate from one of the law schools in the state and meet certain other requirements, you get admitted to the bar automatically." I point over my shoulder. "There's my diploma on the wall behind me."

The man shifts in his chair as his nervous eyes again flit around the office. "I got this injury, see." He lifts his right arm slightly.

"I see." I pick up a pen and a legal pad from my desk and sit back in my chair. "Tell me how it happened."

"I was comin' from the grocery store. You know where that is?"

"The one on the main street?"

"Yeah, that's the one. There's this big parkin' lot on two sides of it, and I was goin' across it when I fell and hurt my right arm. Can't even write."

"You just fell?"

"No. I slipped on some ice. Went right down."

"When did this happen?"

"On Tuesday, January thirteenth about ten in the morning." He shifts in his chair again. "Bud's gotta be nedgilent, and I want you to handle this for me."

I ignore the corruption of the word negligent. "Who's Bud?"

"Bud Wills. Him and his wife own the store."

"Is the arm broken?"

"Almost. It's real sore, and Doc Smeatshum says it's gonna take a bunch of treatments, and I could have perm . . . perma . . . real damage."

"Who is Doc Smeatshum?" I try to write it all down.

"He's the choirpractor in Lenora."

I hesitate. "You mean chiropractor?"

"That's right. He's my doctor."

"Did he take x-rays?"

"Yeah, and he said I got a real mean bruise . . . and maybe some damage to nerves in the arm."

"He put a sling on it?"

"Nah, I had one."

"You've been injured before?"

"Oh yeah, lots of . . . I mean, ah, I been in other accidents." He sits up in his chair.

I look at him for a moment. "Did you notify the store owner of the fall?"

"Right away, and I had him call the police, and they made a report."

My eyes drop to my list of prepared questions. "Did you miss any time from work?"

"Oh, yeah. I'm keepin' track."

"What's your occupation?"

"I'm self-employed."

"What kind of work do you do?"

"All kinds of stuff."

"Well, where do you work?"

"At my house."

"Doing?"

"All kinds of stuff."

Rats. I wish I had phrased the last three questions differently. I'll get the answers later. "As you can understand, I'll have to look into this matter."

"Sure, that's what I want you to do. Get a copy of the accident report and get a medical report from Doc Smeatshum. Send a letter to Bud and Clara that you represent me, and send a copy to their *insurance* company. Here's the name and address." With his left hand he slides a slip of paper across my desk.

I glance at the paper. "We handle these kind of cases on what we call a contingency fee basis, that is . . . "

"I know, a quarter if you settle it before trial, a third if there's trial. I mean, ah, that's what I heard."

Who is this guy? I fill in the blanks on a contingency fee agreement and on an authorization for obtaining medical information, forms

Margo gave to me. As soon as I slide the forms across the desk, his left hand goes right to the places to sign and inks his name.

He slips my ballpoint pen into his pocket as he stands. "I want you to get on this right away."

"I'll do that. I'll be in touch with you as soon as I get the reports and review the matter." I escort the man to the front door and then walk into Margo's office.

She shakes her head. "After I saw him, I was going to tell you. Then, I thought you have to find out some things for yourself."

"What do you mean?"

"That's 'Suits.' He used to come in here until even Bob couldn't stand him anymore. He unloaded him on Smith. I told you about Smith."

"Suits?"

"I don't know how to describe him." She looks at me but not in a seeing way. "He was arrested one summer when he was a teenager for selling flowers he pilfered from the cemetery to tourists. Talk to Bob." She looks away and immerses herself in papers on her desk.

I start to speak, then shrug my shoulders and walk across the hallway to Burnett's office and knock on the doorframe.

Burnett turns his chair toward the door. "Good morning, John. I was going to look in on you, but I had to go to Lenora first thing this morning, and when I got back you had a client with you."

"Margo called him Suits."

Burnett leans back in his chair and takes off his glasses. "Oh no, it was Suits? Tell me about it."

I sit down and relate the interview to Burnett.

"You know, he may have looked over the lot until he found some ice and then fell down, but we don't know that. Look at the police report and Smeatshum's report. When you read Smeatshum's report, though, take into consideration he's a plaintiff's doctor, very supportive of his patients. In any event, I suspect his injuries are minor."

"I think you're right." The interview spools through my mind. "I had him sign a fee agreement and medical authorizations, but I forgot to tell him not to talk to anyone else about the case."

A smile creeps into Burnett's face. "You don't have to worry about that. I hate to say it, John, but he knows more about the ins and outs of a PI case than you do."

"I'm sure he does." I slump in my chair. "I shouldn't have been so quick to jump into it. I was thinking that it was my first client, and, in a way, I brought the client into the office. Some client."

"Don't worry about it. Let's see what turns up. He might make have a cause action for the fall, and if it's not legit, we'll tell him we're not going to handle it anymore. In the meantime, have Margo locate the Baxter divorce file. It's a closed file. You can review it before my two-thirty appointment to see how the divorce process works."

I ask Margo to find the Baxter file and to send the requests for the reports on Suits. Then I spend the rest of the morning examining abstracts of title and rendering title opinions. I also try to reconstruct the manner in which I arrived at Winding River, altering facts to comply with logic. When that fails to work, I console myself with the indisputable facts that I have windows in my office and when I look out those windows, I don't see a freeway interchange.

8

I can tell Burnett feels sorry for Brenda Krueger as soon as he sees her. It's partly her appearance, the unkempt hair and sweater askew on her shoulders attesting her mind is on more urgent matters. Mostly, it's the way Brenda sits, with one hand clasped over the other, and avoids Burnett's eyes as she speaks in between sobs. She carries the weight of a disastrous marriage on her small body.

"I was seventeen when I got pregnant the first time, during my senior year. We got married about a year later. I'd known him since grade school, and I knew he was a troublemaker. At first, though, he was always real good to me."

"Did he hit you before you got married?" A bruise on her face and her demeanor must tell Burnett he can eliminate the preliminary questions.

The words come slowly, "Before. He was always jealous of any guy who talked to me too much, and he blamed me for things I didn't do. When our second son was born, all he could talk about was the expense. Then he got fired from his job. He started drinking a lot, and if I said or did anything he didn't like, he would go crazy, throw things around . . . hit me."

Burnett gives her some tissue. With each answer, I become more agitated.

"I know I should probably divorce him." Brenda pauses while she dries her eyes. "But, I wasn't raised that way. I mean, in my family we always tried to work things out. Bill won't talk about his problems. He thinks they'll go away if he ignores them."

55

"Did you ever call the police?"

"Several times. And then Bill would say he was sorry and be real nice to me for a while, and I would drop the charges. He *is* good with the boys, but I'm afraid they'll grow up to be like him. He said his father beat his mother, and she took it and I should too."

"Well you shouldn't," I interject, instantly sorry I've spoken.

Burnett catches my eyes, signaling me to calm down. Then he continues:

"I know it's difficult for you to talk about this, Brenda. Understand, though, if you're going to commence divorce proceedings, you have to have grounds for it. There's talk about Wisconsin adopting 'no fault divorce.' Right now, you need grounds. In your case, likely it's cruel and inhuman treatment. Did your family and friends know about the beatings?"

"I tried to keep them secret, but he beat me real badly once, and I had to go to the hospital. That was the first time I talked to the police. The hospital must have a record. I finally told my mother everything. She's the one pushing me to get a divorce."

Burnett looks at me, then back at Brenda. "Well, it's up to you. It sounds like your situation isn't going to get any better, especially if he won't participate in counseling or even discuss it. And, I hesitate to say this, but he could seriously injure you. Then there are the boys. How old are they?"

"Nine and six."

"You're right. They should not be a party to that. Who takes care of them when you're at work?"

"They're in school. I get home before the school bus gets there. I work the first shift at Northern Stamping in Lenora."

Burnett looks at me again. "John, why don't you explain the divorce procedure?"

How much detail should I give her? I wish I had rehearsed this with Burnett. I paraphrase my notes. "We'll file a summons and complaint at the courthouse in Lenora. The complaint will state that you meet the residency requirements, state the grounds, and the types of relief you want, that is, custody of the boys, child support for them, alimony for you, division of your property. We'll also file a request for a temporary hearing before the family court commissioner for Timber County, which will probably be scheduled within a week of the filing. At the temporary hearing, the commissioner will set forth rules for you and your husband to live by until the final hearing before the judge: who is going to live in the house, who pays what bills, visitation rights for your husband, assuming you get custody of the boys . . . "

"You mean," she interrupts as she looks up, "I might not get custody?"

Burnett breaks in. "Brenda, will your husband object to you having temporary custody?"

"I don't know. I don't know what he'll do, but I doubt he'll agree to anything. I think he'll go crazy and go after me."

Burnett speaks again. I'm relieved he's taking over. "We'll get the commissioner to issue a restraining order for Bill to stay away from you after the temporary hearing. When we file the papers, because of recent abuse, we should be able to get the judge to sign a restraining order requiring Bill to stay away from you before the temporary hearing. If you feel it's necessary, we can argue that any visitation with the boys be away from the home. Even if the judge doesn't order it, you can have someone at your house when he comes to visit them."

On a nod from Burnett, I run a pen through my notes until I find a place to continue: "Copies of the papers we file will be served on Bill by a deputy sheriff."

Brenda raises her eyes for a moment. She looks like she had been slapped in the face. "Papers? I hadn't thought about the papers. He has to get papers doesn't he? I'm really afraid of what he'll do when he gets them." Her head sags as she says softly, "Papers."

"I understand your concern." Burnett nods as he ponders his next remarks.

Burnett knows the risks. I recall our conversation at lunch yesterday about clients who were assaulted, beaten, seriously injured after their spouses were served with papers. A few times the victims had been the husbands. He remembered the woman who was polite with the deputy serving papers on her, and as soon as the deputy left the house, she hit her husband over the head with a rolling pin, knocking him unconscious.

"Brenda," Burnett switches to a fatherly voice, "we'll do everything we can to help you and to protect you. Unfortunately, there's only so much we can do."

"Can't I get some kind of simple divorce?"

"There is no such thing as a simple divorce. Everyone would like their divorce to be simple; that's rarely the way things turn out."

"Well, what will all this cost me?"

It sounds to me as if the question was posed for a reason other than an answer.

"We usually charge . . . " Burnett shoots a guilty look at Margo's office. "We can work out the fees. Understand, though, if there's a battle over custody of the boys, our fees will be quite a bit more."

"I don't know. Won't things be worse than ever? Won't it make the fighting worse?"

Brenda no longer wants answers; she's stalling. She apparently sees both paths of the fork in the decision between starting and not starting a divorce leading to dead ends.

"Hopefully, it won't. We can't, though, offer any assurances because we simply can't predict the outcome. All we can do is try to help you achieve a better life than you have now."

As she again stares at the carpet, Brenda still grasps her right hand with her left, as though afraid if she lets go of it, the right hand will be gone.

Burnett glances at me then looks at Brenda. "If it's all right with you, I'll have my associate, John, take you into his office to obtain more detailed information. Keep thinking about what you want to do. We want you to feel that you've made the right decision."

She is even smaller now, with a wretched face as she speaks in a voice barely audible, "It's all right."

Burnett turns to me. "John, have Margo give you the divorce intake form I use and a financial statement form she will have to fill out for the court commissioner. If you have any questions, buzz me."

I guide Brenda to my office before I obtain the forms Burnett mentioned. She sits across from my desk with her head hung slightly but her eyes raised. I'm trying to figure out how to begin when she speaks:

"I wasn't pretty; I wasn't smart; and I wasn't good at sports. You know, how important those things are in high school. I guess I turned to the wrong things. I made some bad decisions." She lifts her head as she sighs. "Can you do as Attorney Burnett said, can you help me to have a better life?"

I have difficulty responding. I feel as though I'm about to capsize into the river along with my boat as it rocks in an unexpected wake of responsibility. She continues to stare at me. Her eyes confirm for me that she has suffered for the past nine years far more than I can understand. Law school has prepared me for many things; it has not prepared me to answer her question. I finally respond in the strongest voice I can muster. "I can try, Brenda."

I peek at the clock Margo installed above my office door: 6:05. Brenda has gone home, along with everyone else. A copy of the summons and complaint and other initial papers from the Baxter divorce file are strewn on my desk, and I have altered them to create a rough draft of the pleadings for Brenda's divorce. The opening part of the summons reads:

State of Wisconsin	County Court Family Court Branch	Timber County

Brenda C. Krueger
321 Birch Street
Winding River, Wisconsin,

Plaintiff

V   Summons

Case Number No._____

William E. Krueger
321 Birch Street
Winding River, Wisconsin,

Defendant

I stare at the papers. Should I keep for myself a copy of the first pleadings I have drafted as an attorney? What for? I was never a collector. Life always moved too fast for me to have time to collect the past. I write a note to Margo to have the pleadings typed by late afternoon tomorrow so Brenda can sign them when she stops in after work.

My mind drifts to Brenda. Although I have been in my share of fights over the years, I have never understood how a man can hit a woman, especially one as small and timid as Brenda Krueger. If Burnett had not given me the chance to handle the divorce, I would have asked him for it. At the same time, I'm being strangled by feelings of inadequacy to handle the task. Law books are full of stories of conflicts and how to resolve them from a legal standpoint. Where, though, in those thick books of legalese is it described how we lawyers should deal with the emotional aspects of our cases? Burnett says I have to adopt a professional posture, not let myself get too emotionally involved in my cases. How, though, do I maintain that posture after spending a couple of hours with a Brenda Krueger?

I need a beer. Realizing I haven't thought about dinner and have not gone to the grocery, I decide to drive down to Slider's. Then as I recall Angie said he wouldn't be around this evening, the phone rings. "Burnett Law Office."

"Hi. This is Shelly, from . . . "

"Yes, Shelly, it hasn't been that long ago."

"I guess not. You invited us to dinner on Friday, and, well, Ann can't come. So, it will be me."

"I see. That's fine. Is she okay?"

"Oh, yes. It's . . . "

"I don't need an explanation. I'll pick you up around six at your place, and you can let me know where you'd like to go."

"I'm looking forward to it. I'll see you then."

Ann is the one I want. Still, I invited both of them. As I hang up the phone, I wonder whether the judge had a part in Ann's decision. Will she slip out of my life as easily as she slipped in?

I drive down to Wills Grocery and buy a TV dinner. Bud Wills comes over to the checkout counter and introduces himself. Wills seems like a nice guy, the kind of person who would keep his parking lot as clean and safe as possible. I decide not to mention Suits.

After I heat the TV dinner in the kitchen, I realize there is no TV in the building. So, I eat the dinner in my room, listening to my stereo while I toss scraps to Abstract whom Margo left for the night. Maybe she thinks I'll hang around the office if I have company.

The back door is barely open when I discover the temperature has taken a precipitous drop. Abstract tries to nuzzle her way out the door so I drag her back into the hallway while I grab a parka and zip it up over my jeans and sweatshirt. Still shivering, I try not to breathe too deeply the frigid air while Abstract takes her time finding the right spot. Though she has been good company, there are the practical aspects, I decide. What is the yipping I hear in the deep woods beyond the end of the backyard? Coyotes? Margo told me to keep Abstract on her leash, which I undoubtedly would not have done without her caution. What do I know about dogs? Now I'm glad I did. Though, isn't Abstract a distant cousin to the coyotes?

I let her inspect the first floor while I flop down on the couch in the hallway, my head on a cushion. Light from the lamp on the end table floods my face. I reach up and turn the house into darkness, and then let my mind wander back through the day. My excitement has dissipated through the release of nervous energy. Tired. Still, I finished my first day as a practicing lawyer, a day far different from any of those in my dreams. I began to answer questions from ordinary people rather than from professors, texts and exams. How deceptively easy the questions were stated; how hard the answers were for me.

Tomorrow . . . tomorrow . . .

9

Banging. Banging from somewhere. Now barking. Barking much closer to me. I look for the clock on the nightstand next to my bed, but somehow I'm on the couch in the hallway. The pounding resumes. Is that a diesel engine running in the parking lot? Abstract barks at the front door. I have to stop falling asleep on couches.

As soon as I open the door (why isn't it locked?), Suits lets himself in. He wears a wool cap and a heavy coat with an empty sleeve. He claps his gloves together.

"Did you send those letters sent out?"

What the hell? I'm not ready for this; I need coffee. I rub my eyes. "They went out yesterday afternoon."

"Good. See, I want you to get on this. It's important."

"I am. I'm working on it. What time is it?"

"I'm goin' back to the doctor. This really hurts." Suits unbuttons his coat to reveal the arm in a sling. "This is serious. I'm in real pain."

"We're looking into this, as I told you we would."

"Good. You know I may need surgery. Smeatshum is very worried." Suits eyes me closely. "I'll be back later. We have to keep on this. You know I can make you some money." He pauses like he's gauging the effect on me, and then hurries out, leaving the door ajar.

It takes a strong push to shut the door against the intruding wind. What have I gotten himself into with the bushy-haired man? Abstract sits on her haunches, gazing up at me. I pet her before stumbling into the kitchen to brew a pot of coffee.

When Burnett sticks his head in the doorframe of my office, I'm leaning back in my chair dictating information to be typed in on forms for a real estate closing.

"Good morning, John. What did Brenda decide?"

"I gave a draft of the papers to Margo." I set the speaker of the dictating machine on my desk. "How did she happen to come in here?"

"Her mother referred her to me." Burnett steps into the office and sits in one of the client chairs. "I did some estate planning for her and her husband a few years ago."

"Is that how most of the work comes in, from referrals from other clients?"

"A lot of it. Some of it comes from referrals from other attorneys, the telephone book, the sign in front. Most divorces come in on referrals. Divorce is such a personal experience most people don't look up a lawyer in a telephone book. I suppose her mother felt comfortable with me. After all, they did share their financial matters with me, and as you know, financial matters are usually considered sacred."

"I'm concerned for her."

"And you should be. Except for death, there is nothing that affects an individual and the individual's family like a divorce. Rarely is a divorce concluded easily, except where the parties are young, with no children and little income or property. Even in those cases I doubt that it's done painlessly. It depends largely on the attitude of the parties toward each other. A man as seemingly uncaring and violent as Bill Krueger, who won't attempt to discover the sources of his problems, poses a real threat to Brenda."

I *am* worried. "Will I have trouble getting a restraining order?"

"No. Based on the affidavit by Brenda, the judge will grant one until the temporary hearing." Burnett rises and begins pacing the room. "As I said, you should be concerned. But, don't ever let a client make a divorce your divorce."

"What do you mean?"

"Don't get so drawn into the divorce that you lose your perspective. To properly advise your client, you must stand outside of a situation so you can look at it objectively. Some clients either don't understand that, or don't want to understand it. They think you're not interested in their case."

I nod as I let him go on:

"And, John, be aware that a divorce client will sometimes attempt to shift her anger, resentment, hurt and frustration to her attorney. Even though the attorney gets the divorce she wanted and gets her a good settlement, she may still be unhappy, and somehow that unhappiness will be the attorney's fault."

"That doesn't sound like Brenda Krueger."

"No it doesn't. She's the flip side—timid, beaten down, despairing, convinced that it's all her fault."

"I'm sure divorce cases are all different."

"They are, and another thing, divorce cases are usually unpredictable. There's some wrinkle, some bizarre turn of events, some thing perhaps you should have seen coming but you don't. And then there is always your opponent, trying to get an edge, trying to get something from your client to impress his client. Even after you've handled a number of divorce cases, something will astonish you. Let me tell you a story."

Burnett sits down again. "A number of years ago I represented a young woman in a divorce, and she bugged the hell out of me to get a final hearing before Christmas."

"She wanted it before Christmas?"

"Oh, I've had several clients over the years who wanted their divorce finalized before the holidays, even though from a tax standpoint it was often a poor move. I guess they didn't want to spoil a time that had always been pleasant for them. Anyway, I got a final hearing date for December twenty-second. I had her testify. Then, since her husband didn't have an attorney, the judge questioned him. While he was testifying, he began crying. Then she started crying. The judge pronounced them divorced, and as the husband got off the stand, she rose from her seat next to me and moved around to the front of the table. They were headed to embrace each other when she stopped in front of me and through clenched teeth said, 'You son of a bitch. You divorced me.'"

❧ ❧

Ginger Buckman is what I expected. When I took the tape of my memo to Burnett on the Village condemnation into Margo to type, I asked her about the PI client coming in at nine. "Tough," she described the young woman, then modified the word to "different." Different from the rest of the family, whom Margo described as fairly normal—the father an accountant with offices in Winding River and Algona; the mother the manager of the family business; and the two older sisters, both honor students.

Margo claimed Ginger sought unique ways to skirt conformity. At nineteen years of age she had managed to compile a minor juvenile record and a long list of school infractions and absences. Skimming only that part of high school that interested her, she graduated near the bottom of her class. Since then she has worked at various jobs, most recently as a waitress at the River's Edge Supper Club. Daily, she travels to Lenora to visit her boyfriend who is serving a six-month sentence in the county jail as part of a bargained plea for selling drugs. At least, Margo sighed, she no longer dyes her hair bright red or green.

"It happened about ten thirty in the evening last October," explains Ginger. Her speech is flat and her face expressionless. Wearing a motorcycle jacket over a heavy sweater, she sits across from Burnett's desk. A pair of crutches lay next to her chair.

I positioned my chair next to the desk so that I also face her. She is a suspect brunette, the hair cut short and probably dyed to cover up true blonde hair that might, along with her pretty face, cause more heads to turn her way. About five feet six inches, she is trim, a condition I guess is due less to conditioning than a lack of interest in eating.

"Do you remember the exact date?"

"The sixteenth . . . a Thursday."

"Go on."

"I was going south on Main Street on my motorcycle, and they were driving . . . west on Forest Street. They went through the stop sign, turned right, swerved into my lane and then back into their lane and kept going. I had no choice; I had to swerve to my right to get out of the way. I over corrected and tried to turn back to my left. Then I lost control of my bike and hit the street. The bike came down on top of me and skidded to the curb."

"And you were still underneath the bike?"

"Until the bike hit the curb. Then it bounced off of me onto the sidewalk and went across it and smashed into the wall below the window of Jorgenson's Bakery."

"And you say their car never touched your bike?" As he speaks, Burnett stares at a diagram of the accident on a copy of the police report.

"That's right. That's the point; I had to get out of their way as quickly as possible."

Burnett continues to stare at the police report. "And, you couldn't recover to your former position in your lane?"

"I had to swerve so quickly, I couldn't control the bike." She scowls. "I wish I could have. I wouldn't be suffering like I am."

"How far did their car go into your lane?"

"I don't know, it happened so fast, it's hard to say . . . pretty far. I think I was about in the middle of my lane."

"Where were you coming from?"

"North of the village . . . visiting a friend, a girlfriend. I was on my way home."

"Had you been drinking, that is, drinking alcohol beverages?"

"No." Ginger drags out the word.

"Take any medication?"

"Noo . . . well, I am a diabetic. Nothing else." She moves slightly and winces. "Look this isn't my fault."

Burnett sits back. "I'm not suggesting it is, Ginger. I want to know exactly what happened. This is an unusual case. Both of the sixteen-year-olds you claim were in the car are unwavering in their statements they did not run the stop sign, never caused you to swerve, or saw your bike, that they weren't even in the area that evening. And, there is no physical evidence, nor are there any witnesses, to the contrary."

"That's because they're lying. They're scared. I'm sure Jeremy figures he'll lose his license if he tells the truth. He's kind of a punk anyway. Tommy is his best friend, and he's a punk, too. Tommy set fire to the Lutheran Church when he was twelve."

Burnett nods. "I remember the incident. They may act differently in a deposition or in court when they're put under oath. Still, if the police couldn't break them down, they may stick to their story."

"They're lying. The little creeps."

I sense Ginger is disgusted to have to answer the questions, as though they are a waste of time. They have been asked before and somehow Burnett should know the answers. If Brenda Krueger is a sympathetic individual, Ginger is someone I want to chastise and send to bed.

Now, though, she is an adult, and all anyone can do or say is that she's "tough," or more politely, "different" and then ignore her.

Burnett turns over a page on his legal pad. "Well, Ginger, let's talk about your medical situation."

"I broke my left leg, below the knee. I've got pins in it. Broke my left elbow. Scrapes and bruises all over my left side. My left knee and hip also still bother me. The doctor said they weren't broken, just badly bruised. Except for the leg and the elbow, he thinks everything else should be cleared up now. I don't think he believes me about the pain I'm still having."

"Any head injuries?"

"No. I had my helmet on."

"Did you go to the hospital in Lenora?"

"Yes . . . in an ambulance. I can still hear the siren."

Burnett continues to explore her injuries and other damages and after she agrees to hire us to represent her, has her sign the same contingent fee agreement and medical releases I used with Suits. After he observes Ginger limp out the front door, aided by her mother who came to pick her up, Burnett addresses me. "What do you think?"

I ease over to the fireplace to seek warmth from the fire Margo started earlier in the morning. My back faces the fire as I stand with my arms folded against my chest and speak. "Obviously, this is no Suits case. I believe her story, and she has real injuries. Problems, though."

"Yes." Burnett removes his glasses and begins wiping them with a tissue. "What do you see as the issues?"

"Obviously liability, although someone must have seen or heard the accident. It wasn't that late."

"The police didn't come up with any witnesses." Burnett puts his glasses on and picks up the accident report. "It happened on a Wednesday evening. During the week, most people around here go to bed by ten o'clock. The first shift in the mill at Lenora starts at seven."

"The taverns must have been open, customers coming and going."

"They probably were, but the last thing we need is a drunk for a witness."

"Well," I argue, "we have her testimony. She won't make a likeable witness. I'm having trouble liking her, but her story is believable. Why else would she spill her bike like that? According to the police report, the road conditions were good. There's no evidence she was speeding."

"Distracted. Fell asleep. What about the fact that she's a diabetic? What if, for some reason, she failed to take her insulin shot, got low blood sugar, lost her senses?"

I shrug and wave my hands. "I didn't think about those possibilities. Aren't they defenses the other side is going to have to prove?"

"Sure they are. I want you to think this through. Are there other issues?"

I ponder the question. "Causation would hinge on the doctor's report saying her injuries were caused by the accident, and we'll have to show the accident was caused by the sixteen-year-olds."

"All right."

"It's not clear to me at this point the extent of her present injuries, and what kind of medical treatment she'll need in the future."

Burnett purses his lips and nods. "The medical reports from the doctor and the hospital will answer much of that. In addition to the arm and the leg, it sounds like she has some 'soft tissue' injuries. If the doctor says she has reached the maximum point of healing for those injuries, from an objective viewpoint, how much of her problems are subjective, and how long will they go on? How do you prove subjective complaints other than by the victim? And, you've seen what kind of witness she's likely to be."

"Yes."

"Now don't misunderstand me. She may well have pain in areas other than the arm or leg, even an enormous amount of pain. She may indeed be suffering as she claims, but how do you convince a jury the pain is there by her testimony alone, that it's there because she says it's there? Especially, if her doctor won't back her up."

I sit down again. How did I expect this was going to be easier than anything else lately? Maybe examining abstracts is more exciting than dull headaches and cramped feet. Entries in the abstracts are less slippery facts, though I know they may exist as a result of fraud. "Should I go on?"

"Sure."

"Okay, then there's the question of damages."

"Questions as to what damages? You can tally the medical bills and prove lost wages. Her insurance company has paid for the damages to her bike."

"Pain and suffering. I suppose, though, since that's another subjective item . . . difficult to put a price tag on it."

Burnett bobs his head. "That's where experience comes in. Dealing with these kinds of cases over the years, dealing with the insurance companies and adjusters, and trying PI cases to juries, you get a feeling for what a particular injury is worth. What about permanency?"

I sit back. Permanency? While I mull a response, Burnett answers it for me.

"In addition to everything, else, if the doctor says she has a permanent injury, she is entitled to compensation for it. In this case, if she has pins in her leg, there will no doubt be continuing problems, and an elbow injury is nasty. This is an area where her doctors rule, except as the other side can contradict them with their own doctors. And, of course, it depends on how much the jury believes her complaints."

"I understand."

"Anything else?"

I think for a moment. "There's one thing I'm curious about. If we prove liability and damages and receive a favorable verdict, how will we collect from a couple of kids if there's only the minimal liability insurance coverage on the car?"

Burnett cants his head as he raises his eyebrows. "According to the police report, the car Ginger described is owned by Jeremy Wilson's parents. We'll assume for now Jeremy was driving it with their permission. Knowing them, I'm sure they carry adequate liability insurance to cover Ginger's damages. Even if they don't, since Jeremy is under eighteen, under Wisconsin law, we can join in the lawsuit the parent who sponsored him as a driver to recover from the sponsor any 'overage' above the insurance limits."

"I see." Actually, I see, and I don't see. Where are we now? After three years of intensive reading in law school, then discussing the facts and issues, I'm used to the professor asking questions and the pupil fumbling wildly for answers. Where, though, has the Socratic trail led us? "So what do we do now?"

Leaning back in his chair and looking at the front windows, Burnett hesitates before speaking. "Normally, I refer PI cases to Matt Willock in Ridgecrest. He specializes in PI cases. I do it on a referral basis, continuing to act as local counsel, and we work out a percentage split of the fees. I haven't had enough experience in trying these cases."

I'm stunned. Impressed with Burnett's trial experience in other matters, it never occurred to me he would not try a personal injury case. My surprise is reflected in Burnett's face as he speaks:

"You know, it 's difficult to be both a good corporate attorney and a good trial attorney. Sometimes, I wonder whether the British have it right with the solicitor and barrister system."

With the reckless move of a novice, I attempt a leap far wider than any jump I've ever made. "I want to handle this case. If we can't settle it, I'll try it."

Burnett frowns. "I appreciate your eagerness, John, but we have to think about our client. In our profession, enthusiasm and effort usually don't equate with experience. I say *usually* since occasionally beginning lawyers, with the aid of a constant of ignorance or arrogance, manage to make an equation. I expect that won't happen here. She deserves the best representation she can get. In this case, she's going to need an experienced attorney."

"Give me a shot at it, Bob. I've got the time. At least we can investigate it further, do the groundwork. We can always bring in Attorney Willock if we need him."

The pensive look. I sense the energy of his mind as Burnett sits in thought, staring at the front windows for some time before facing me.

"All right, do some investigation, understand, though, we'll probably refer it." He shakes his head. "I hope I won't regret this."

🐟 10 🐟

When I hear clacking from Margo's high heels on the hardwood floor outside my office, I glance at the clock above the door. Almost noon? Since I returned to my office after my long discussion with Burnett, I made changes to the Krueger divorce papers and gave them to Margo for retyping, handled several telephone calls, worked on two real estate matters, talked to Suits who appeared in my doorway without notice, examined several abstracts and dictated title opinions, reviewed Burnett's notes on Ginger Buckman's case and had Margo send out the requests for doctor and hospital reports. Maybe I'm being overly eager on Ginger's case, without the knowledge and experience to back up my promises. Burnett must have had something in mind, though, or he wouldn't have let me proceed with the investigation.

Margo beams as she steps into my office. "I baked a tuna casserole and some cookies. Let's have lunch."

"Great." I jump up and trail her and the smell of tuna to the kitchen. "Where's Bob?"

"He went to the courthouse. I expected him back by now."

I pour myself a glass of milk and sit at the table as Margo takes the casserole out of the oven and sets in on a hot pad in front of me. "Smells good. You know, I was surprised when Bob told me he didn't try PI cases."

Margo hands me a plate and silverware. "He feels personal injury cases, unless they're minor, are a specialty. Besides, he always has more work than he can handle, so he refers some matters to other attorneys."

"Why didn't he take on an associate?"

"He did, a couple of times. Either they were unhappy or their spouses were unhappy, so they left." She dishes out the casserole. "Look at the temperature this morning. Fortunately, it has risen, but it's still below zero. Not everyone wants to spend their winters this way." She pauses to taste her work, by the smile on her face apparently pleased with the results of her test. "I know one of them didn't like the variety of work—constantly picking up something new, something different, something beyond his knowledge—and working with the constant interruptions."

I listen as I devour her casserole. "This is very good."

"Thank you. I like to cook." She has a wistful look. "Since my children have grown up, Red and I eat out more, or have simple meals." Margo puts down her fork. "I want you to know that Bob is a very good trial attorney. He served two terms as the District Attorney for Big Lakes County before he came here."

"Why did he come here then? Isn't the D.A. job a rung on the ladder to a county judgeship?"

"Sometimes. Bob was never interested in becoming a judge. Too confining he claims. He likes the idea of owning his own business." She wrinkles her brow. "Even if he doesn't always run it like a business."

I hide my grin as I bring the plate of cookies from the counter to the table, along with another glass of milk. "Tell me about your family."

"Well, Red . . . his name is Jim, is a foreman at the mill in Lenora. He has always been active in the community—was the Village President for some years, a past president of the Lions Club, presently is a deacon in our church. Our two girls are married. One lives in Madison, the other in Minnesota, and . . . "

I see a look in her face I've not seen before. In spite of her strong-mindedness, not being afraid to interject herself when she feels it necessary, she is almost always smiling, seemingly happy. "I didn't mean to pry . . . "

She catches herself. "That's okay. We also had a son. We lost him in Vietnam in nineteen sixty-seven. He was twenty years old. His name was James, too."

"I'm sorry. I guess I was fortunate I was sent to Germany when I was in the Army, although, at the time I felt like I missed out on the action."

"It was something he wanted to do. The girls weren't interested in law, but Jimmy had talked about it. So we had hoped he would go to college and then maybe law school. Since Bob and Vera's son and daughter pursued other careers, Bob also hoped that Jimmy might some day wind up here. It wasn't meant to be, was it?"

"I guess not."

"A Marine Corps recruiter, in dress blues, came to our house with a telegram advising us that Jimmy had been killed in combat. He told us that it happened during an operation in a northern province in South Vietnam. He was sympathetic, but he didn't offer details. I don't think he knew anything else. He couldn't answer the one question any parent wants to know in that situation."

"What's that?"

"Whether he suffered."

"I'm sure he didn't." I wish I had some basis for the remark, some way to assure her.

We finish eating and then clean up the kitchen mostly in silence. I put my arm lightly around Margo's shoulders before I return to my office.

❧ ❧

Burnett pokes his head into my office on his way to the kitchen. "Sorry I missed lunch. That's how it goes, though. There's always something throwing you off schedule."

I wave Burnett into my office, then have him close the door. "I had lunch with Margo, which was fine. She's a good cook. Unfortunately, I inadvertently led her into discussing her son."

Burnett leans against the closed door. "Red took it harder than she did; it was a real blow to both of them. It was a tough time around here then. I tried to give her some time off, but she worked harder than ever. Margo's life has always been neat and orderly and to that point, under her control. Everything has its place, and there is a reason for its existence. She couldn't reconcile Jimmy's death with her world."

"I didn't know."

"Of course, you didn't. Don't worry about it." Burnett folds his arms. "You know, John, Margo likes you. You're the first associate I've had here she's approved." He frowns. "Just don't mess with how the office is run."

"I know that."

"I'm going to catch a bite to eat in the kitchen. Why don't we go over the Schultz collection during the lunch? It's a simple motion hearing."

After Burnett finishes, I again review my notes and Burnett's notes, along with the police report, on Ginger's accident. Then I drive to the police station. The Chief handled the accident. He relates what he knows, adding nothing to what Ginger furnished. I determine the Chief checked the neighborhood and his sources without locating any witnesses. I also ask him about Suits' fall. The Chief had not handled the complaint but furnishes me a copy of the report.

As I drive back to the office, I make a mental note to stop in Slider's after work to determine whether he knows anything about Ginger's accident. An accident like hers had to have been a "happy hour" topic.

Back at the office, I again examine abstracts. A ringing phone gives me a needed break.

"Mr. Hall," a feminine voice speaks, "my name is Sharon Vande Hei. I'm a teacher at the high school. If you can fit it into your schedule, would you be willing to speak to my senior class when we have 'Career Day.'"

"Would you mind calling me back in five years?"

She laughs. "I realize you've only recently graduated from law school, but I'm sure you can speak about your job for half an hour or so."

I roll my eyes. Then I think: *job*? Is that what it is? I carry a leather-covered toolbox, containing a legal pad and pleadings in it, and I have a head full of methods of findings answers to questions. I listen to people I don't know who ask questions for which I must find answers. Then I search for the answers, or the lack of them, and pass the search results on to the questioners. That's it. Mostly indoors work with no heavy lifting but lots of anxiety, uncertainty and mental fatigue and no guarantee of when, or if, the next questioner will come. Advertised that way, who would apply for the job?

"Mr. Hall?"

"Sure I'll come. When do you want me there?"

"I'll call you back when the date for Career Day has been set. Thank you Attorney Hall."

"You can call me John."

"All right, John. Bye."

Abstract wanders into the room. I gaze into her deep brown eyes. "Two choices who spread my name around the school system, and they're both female teachers."

~ ~

Brenda stops at the office in the darkness of the late winter afternoon to sign the papers for her divorce. She sits underneath the intense illumination from the florescent lights above my desk. She still has difficulty facing me. After she finishes reading the papers, she sets them on the desk and looks past me. "I'm not sure I can do this."

"As Bob said, it's up to you. Based on what you've told us and on what we've been able to learn about you're situation, we believe this is the action you need to take. Unfortunately, again as Burnett said, we can't be sure how smoothly the divorce will proceed." I pause, hoping Brenda will speak, but she remains silent, gazing at the window behind me. "I've already told you this will be my first divorce case, so I'll be learning along with you. Of course, Bob will back me up."

"I don't know. I'm afraid."

"Afraid of Bill?"

"Afraid of everything . . . Bill, having to take care of the boys by myself . . . being alone." Tears are creeping down her small, pale cheeks.

I take a box of tissues from my desk and hand it to Brenda. "You know, even though we start the action, that doesn't mean you can't change your mind and have us dismiss it. I hope you won't do that, though."

She doesn't respond. She continues to look away from me. What's going through her mind? What else should I say to her? "I know this is a hard thing for you to do, probably the hardest decision you've ever made. Yet, it's a decision you have to make. You can't let yourself continue to be mistreated. You have to protect yourself, as well as your boys. Perhaps you need more counseling before . . ."

She interrupts without facing me. "My counselor wanted me to see a lawyer."

"Well."

Brenda sits in silence. I wait. Finally, she wipes her face before she looks at me with her watery blue eyes for what seems to me a long time. It's a look of detachment. She gingerly slides the legal documents to the edge of the desk, hesitates for a moment while she again peers into my eyes, then signs the papers and quickly leaves my office.

"Call me after he's been served the papers," I yell after her.

I walk slowly down the hallway to Burnett's office and duck my head in the doorframe. "Brenda signed the papers."

"I saw her leave." Burnett motions for me to sit down.

"Bob, are we doing the right thing?"

Logs are crackling and spitting as they disappear in the fireplace while wind rattles the storm windows. Burnett starts to reply but a sudden howl of wind causes us to stare at the windows. He speaks to the wind:

"Except for the snowmobilers, the ice fishermen and the cross-country skiers, the winters here are not much appreciated. You can't fight the elements, though, because the weather is an unpredictable opponent. So you either make peace with that part of the calendar or suffer months of misery."

When we look away from the windows, Burnett replies: "Remember that she came to us. She solicited our advice on the divorce process. Our clients want us to explain to them the law concerning their situation and then give them a recommendation on the course of action they should follow. It's up to the client whether to accept our recommendation. When the advice sought relates to divorce, you have to be very careful. Brenda had to make the decision herself, which she did. Now we'll see how it turns out."

"Did you ever wish you had a crystal ball?"

Burnett laughs. "Of course, that's the dream of all lawyers. Since we don't, you'll have to try to predict the outcome without one. The more you learn about the facts and the law pertaining to your case—absent a client who is not telling you the whole story, a dishonest witness, or a prejudiced trier of fact—the better your prediction should be."

As I rise to leave, Burnett adds, "And, you'll have to make adjustments to your predictions as you go along to account for the surprises. They'll come with the suddenness of a howl of the wind in the winter."

11

The clank of a cell door slamming shut echoes throughout the Sheriff's Department. I stand patiently in the lobby facing a counter with no one behind it. Through a small window in a door to my left, a burly jailer is visible as he walks past jail cells toward me, swinging a large metal ring of keys. He unlocks the door and steps into the lobby.

The deputy sheriff glances at the counter before turning to me. "I guess Florence left for a minute. Can I help you?"

I set my briefcase on the counter and extend my hand as I speak. "My name is John Hall. I'm a new attorney in Winding River."

The deputy shakes my hand. "Bob called this morning and said you'd be in with some papers to be served."

"They're right here." I open my briefcase and take out three copies of the summons, complaint, and other documents and hand them to the deputy. "I filed the originals with the Clerk of Court. These are authenticated copies, one to be served on the defendant, one for your return to the Court and one for return to our office."

"I'll let Florence know." The jailer lays the copies on the counter. "Bob told me to be sure the deputy serving the papers keeps an eye on the defendant."

"There's a history of domestic abuse by him. She's afraid he won't liked being served."

"They seldom do." The deputy cocks his head. "Most of the time there isn't a problem, that is, as long as we're there."

Nodding, I thank the deputy and start to leave. Then I turn back. "By the way, what happened to Billy, the hitchhiker I dropped off here on Sunday evening?"

"Oh, yeah, I heard you brought him in. He's back in the mental health center. He's got a problem, but he's never hurt anyone." The deputy screws up his face. "Then, you never know."

I exit the jail onto the shoveled walkway leading to the courthouse. For Brenda's sake I hope there won't be an altercation when Bill gets served. I'm nervous, but not about Brenda's situation; it's the *Schultz Case.*

Burnett prepped me on the procedures for the default hearing, and I have them written down. I sat through a mock trial in law school as part of a defense team, and several times in between classes, I sat in the back of courtrooms at the Milwaukee County Courthouse to observe the proceedings. This is different; this is for real; this is me doing it alone. My stomach begins to gurgle.

As I walk down the marbled floor toward the courtroom, I try to quiet the squeaking of my wet shoes. A husky man, wearing a work jacket, work shirt and cap, all dark blue with *Schultz Plumbing & Heating* on them, squats over a wooden bench outside the courtroom door.

"I'm John Hall. I assume you're Carl?"

"Right." Carl grabs my hand.

I sit on the bench, setting my briefcase next to me. "As I'm sure Bob explained to you, this is a so-called 'Default Judgment Hearing,' default meaning the twenty day period listed in the summons to answer the complaint expired and Mr. Herdina failed to submit an answer or contact Burnett or you about it."

"That's right," Schultz wheezed. "I got nothin'."

"Bob then filed an affidavit to that effect along with a motion for judgment based on the pleadings. The reason you're here is in case the judge wants some testimony from you to show the amount due to you for your work on Herdina's home."

"I got my file."

"May I see it?"

Schultz hands over a manila folder with bent corners and smudge marks, one of them being a perfect fingerprint. I thumb through the papers, pausing briefly to examine some of the papers. Handing the file back, I rise and stretch my shoulders. "Unless you have questions, let's go in."

Schultz shakes his head and follows me into the back of the courtroom. We move into the second row of benches. After shedding my lined trench coat on the back of the seats, I smooth out my sport coat and tie. Ahead of the rows of seats are two counsel tables – set side by side, about four feet apart, each with three chairs—facing the judge's bench on a raised platform twenty feet away. The jury box is to the left of the tables. To the right of the bench on the platform is the Clerk of Court's seat, occupied by a deputy clerk shuffling papers. I met her when I filed the Krueger divorce papers earlier, and she smiles at me. On the left of the bench is the witness box with Angie's seat below it.

The judge has not come on the bench. Along the wall to my right are a dozen framed photographs of older men. Angie stares out a window overlooking the highway at the end of the snow-covered lawn. He turns to see me looking at the pictures. "All prior county judges, a history of Timber County." He gives me a thumbs-up sign. "Just remember what I told you, and you'll be all right."

"Got it." I remember what Angie said the night before at Slider's: At the beginning of a hearing or trial always address the court by saying the five most important words in the courtroom.

Angie points to the counsel tables. "Sit up here with your client. You're next."

"Does it matter which one?"

Angie sits down before his machine. "Usually, the plaintiff sits at the table to the left facing the bench, the defendant to the right."

My stomach is growling. I fiddle with my file and a legal pad before me on the table, trying not to respond to the wild calls from my abdomen. There's no bailiff in the courtroom, so when the imposing Judge Tompkins walks in, clad in a black robe, the deputy clerk cries, "All rise!" The judge motions to everyone to sit down.

Before the judge can speak, the courtroom door bursts open and an attorney and his client rush in. The attorney is wearing a three-piece suit, the trousers bulging at the waist, and his thick, black hair is slicked back on the sides. The client sits at the defendant's table while the attorney, who remains standing, addresses Tompkins: "Sorry, Your Honor. I hope we're not late."

"You're not late." Tompkins looks irritated. "I don't know why you're here, though, Mr. Smith."

"Well, you see, Your Honor . . ."

Tompkins puts his right hand up, shutting up Smith who sits down. "Let's call the case first, and we'll put this on the record, whatever it is."

The deputy clerk hands Tompkins the court file. He checks the title on it. "All right, this is *Schultz Plumbing and Heating versus Joseph Herdina,* Timber County Court Case Number 2831."

My stomachache has yielded priority to shock.

Tompkins turns to me. "Please state the appearances."

"Ah, Attorney John Hall of . . . the Burnett Law Office here for the plaintiff . . . and, ah, the plaintiff, the owner, Carl Schultz, is here."

"Attorney Sanford Smith of Winding River appearing for the defendant, Joseph Herdina who appears in person."

I notice how Smith emphasizes the "ford" so that his name rolls out with the elegance of three words. I suddenly feel dizzy. Smith and Herdina are not supposed to be here; they are not part of the script Burnett gave me. Is Smith going to present a defense now? I'm not prepared for a trial. I want to shout at the judge: *Burnett said this would only take ten minutes!*

Tompkins leafs through the file. As he sets it on the bench, he again addresses me. "Proceed."

Running rapidly through my mind is the scene in my Real Property Law class where my strict professor begins a discussion of *The Rule In Shelley's Case.* "But by virtue of the Rule, the state of the title is: life estate in B, and . . . ? Mr. Hall. What else?" I jump up and begin babbling. I tended bar the night before and am clueless. "So," the professor scowls, "You've been reading *Alice In Wonderland* again instead of your assignment." Then the snickering and stifled laughs begin as they always begin by those who are not standing up.

"Mr. Hall."

Snapping back, I begin: "May it please the court."

"Wait a minute." The judge frowns as he lowers his head to peer over his bifocals. "Mr. Hall, while we try to abide by the required formalities of the courtroom, we're not that formal here. Just tell me why you're here."

"Yes, Your Honor." I shoot a disgusted look at Angie, who has his head down, then look at my notes on a legal pad, running a finger down the lines. "This is a Default Judgment Hearing. As shown by the affidavit of Attorney Robert O. Burnett of Winding River, attached to the motion for judgment, neither Mr. Herdina or anyone else, answered the complaint or contacted our office regarding the matter within the answer period. The complaint asks for the sum of one thousand sixteen hundred and fifty-three dollars for plumbing and heating work performed by the plaintiff on Mr. Herdina's house." I can hardly get the words out, but now that I'm into the hearing, my stomach has calmed down.

The judge turns to Smith.

Smith stands up. "You see, Your Honor, Mr. Herdina contacted our office. He misunderstood the summons as to the time limit and thought he could . . ."

The judge glares at Smith. "Did he also misunderstand the Notice of Motion for this hearing that I see was served on him?"

Smith smiles. "Your Honor there has obviously been a number of misunderstandings here, and for the court to be fair with my client, I think . . ."

"Are you suggesting the Court doesn't know how to be fair?" Tompkins face is flushed.

"Of course not, Your Honor. I just want you to understand this is one of those cases where things got confused and in fairness to everyone involved . . ."

Tompkins removes his glasses again and continues to glare at Smith." You haven't filed any affidavits. Do you have a proposed answer? Do you have a defense?"

"Again, Your Honor, due to the continued confusion in this matter, we would like an additional ten days to answer the complaint. We expect to set forth numerous defenses, including a substantial counterclaim against Mr. Schultz."

"*Mister* Smith."

Smith bends down to whisper to his client and again faces the judge. "Of course, Your Honor, under the circumstances, we wish to be reasonable. Could I have a minute with Attorney Hall?"

"You're wasting . . . All right."

Smith eases over to my table as I stand up to talk to him. "Look, there's no reason to turn this into a lengthy case, probably a jury trial. I'm sure your client doesn't want that. Neither does my client. The way to handle this is to put the hearing off for thirty days, and if we haven't settled it by then, you can take your judgment."

Out of the corner of my left eye I see Angie almost imperceptibly shaking his head negatively. What does that mean? "I think the only confusion is what you're creating. I came here to get a judgment against your client."

With a rigid face, Smith studies me for a moment. "You're new here, and you've got a lot to learn." He pauses. "But, I want to help you. I'll make this as simple as possible. Take your judgment today, but agree on the record that you won't have the judge sign the judgment or docket it for thirty days. That way it won't affect Mr. Herdina's credit rating, you'll still have the judgment, and he'll get the extra time to pay your client, with interest of course."

Great. This is a victory as I see it. I get the judgment today; we won't have to return to court; and if Herdina doesn't pay the amount due in thirty days, I can have the judge sign the judgment, docket it with the Clerk of Court, and proceed with collection efforts. That's the way it first runs through my mind. The afterthought is what action will Smith take in the next thirty days? File some pleadings to set aside the agreement?

I look at the judge. "Your Honor, would it possible for me to have a short recess to talk to my client?"

"Is it necessary?" Tompkins immediately dismisses his question. "If that's what you want, keep it short."

"Yes, Your Honor." I whisk Schultz out of the courtroom as Smith, looking irritated, leads Herdina back to the jury room.

I see the bewildered look on Schultz's face but gently push him down on the bench outside the door. Then I race down the hallway to the Clerk of Court's office and call the office. Margo tells me Burnett has a client. When I insist on speaking to him, she puts me through. I quickly explain the situation.

"Absolutely not." I can tell Burnett is irked but not at me. "Don't make any deals with Smith. I've heard some rumors Herdina is trying to sell his house. He probably doesn't want the judgment docketed because then it would be a lien against the house and would have to be dealt with at closing on the sale. If you do it Smith's way, they can close the sale in two weeks, and Herdina is free of the judgment lien. We'll be chasing him forever, or not at all. Schultz is not going to want to spend a lot of money starting a lawsuit in some other state."

"I'm sorry. I didn't think of that. You're right."

"Hang tough, John. If we have to try the matter, we will. Call me as soon as it's over."

"Thank you." I hang up and race back into the courtroom with Schultz huffing behind me. Tompkins is still sitting on the bench, chatting with the deputy clerk while Smith and his client sit quietly. I sit at my table. "I'm sorry for the delay, Your Honor. We wish to proceed with the motion for judgment. It's our position the defendant has not shown any reason for you not to grant the motion."

For the first time since I came into the room, the judge is smiling. "I'm glad you finally got around to that, Mr. Hall." He turns to Smith. "Anything else, Mr. Smith?"

"Judge, perhaps you would consider postponing . . . "

"Based on what?"

"Well . . . "

Tompkins intensifies his glare.

"Nothing further."

"Finally, we're getting to the conclusion of something that should have taken about ten minutes." He looks down at the file. "I find the defendant is in default. Based upon the affidavit of Attorney Burnett and the documents attached thereto and all of the other pleadings filed in this matter and upon Attorney Burnett's motion, judgment is hereby granted in favor of the plaintiff and against the defendant in the sum of sixteen hundred and fifty-three dollars, plus court costs. . . . Mr. Hall, anything further?"

I rise. "Since this was scheduled as a default hearing, Attorney Burnett prepared a proposed judgment." I hold up the document.

"Bring it up here." As I move forward, the judge stops me. "First, give a copy to Attorney Smith."

What else do I not know? I fumble through the papers on my table, find a copy and hand it to Smith. Then I stumble after I whack my knee against a front leg of the counsel table.

"Mr. Smith?"

Smith scans the proposed judgment before answering, "Nothing."

"Then I'll sign it," Tompkins scrawls his name. "Court is adjourned."

The judge disappears into his chambers as Smith and Herdina start to leave their table. I rise and reach for Smith's hand. Smith starts to ignore it, then lightly shakes it.

A smirk emerges on my face. "Thanks for referring Suits to me."

Smith begins to utter a comment, instead abruptly leaving the room with Herdina trailing him.

"What exactly happened here?" asks Schultz. "When do I get the money?"

❦ ❧

On the way to the Clerk of Courts Office after I call Burnett, I wonder how much of the collection process Burnett has explained to Schultz. Apparently, Schultz either doesn't understand the lawsuit or, most likely, doesn't care. All he wants is to get paid for his work. How to accomplish that chore is why he hired an attorney.

When I walk into the Clerk of court's Office, the deputy clerk who sat in on the hearing strolls to the counter. I hand her a check Margo prepared for the docket fee. "Would you please docket this judgment for me."

"Sure." She smiles at me. "You know you did all right."

"Nice of you to say that." I haven't had time to think about my performance but am sure I don't want to see a film of the proceeding. Angie zinged me, then redeemed himself with the headshake. Or, was he talking to himself? He probably didn't know what Smith was pulling, but knew that it was Smith. I bumbled and mumbled my way through the hearing. Still, I got the judgment. How many of my classmates were in court alone in their first week after graduation?

In an effort to put the hearing behind me, I hurry along the corridor toward the main door of the courthouse. I stop to read a plaque on the wall near the entrance. The plaque contains the names of county residents killed during American conflicts. The inscription *James B. Lynch, Vietnam, 1967,* appears on a metal plate near the end of the list. I step up to the black directory with white letters inside the entrance, then take the stairs to the Veterans Affairs Office.

"Do you have any information on the veterans listed on the plaque downstairs," I ask the older, bald man who is stuffed into an opened collared shirt.

"I don't have their files if that's what you mean? I handle benefits and help veterans with other service connected matters."

"I understand. I was curious if you know anything about the James B. Lynch who died in Vietnam in nineteen sixty-seven."

"Yeah, I knew Jimmy, knew him before he went in." He rummages through some papers in a drawer before pulling out a sheet of paper. He reads off Jimmy's unit and some minor details regarding his death. "That's as much as I know."

"Thanks." I smile and leave. I decide not to introduce myself. It might get around that I'm checking up on Margo's son. Wouldn't she wonder why?

❧ 12 ❧

I duck into Margo's office. She's smiling again. Without aiming, without any intention of hitting it (how did I know it existed?), I struck her point of vulnerability. I'm happy she has cheered up, but not surprised. She impressed me the first day in the office as the sort of person who doesn't dwell on negatives, the kind who either turns a negative into positive or buries it. On the other hand, how can anyone ever completely bury the loss of a child?

She picks up her coffee cup. "How did it go?"

"Well, let me put it this way: I'm glad the hearing is over. I learned something, though."

"What's that?"

"To expect the unexpected."

Margo smiles in a knowing way but moves on. "I scheduled an appointment for you for one o'clock with the Sunstroms . . . about wills." I nod approval. "In the meantime, Bob said you should get started on some income tax returns." She hands me two files. "These are short ones. Our clients are anxious to get their refunds."

"I'll get them done today . . . perhaps with a little assistance from you."

I sit down in my office. I feel better, a lot better. It's not that the stomachache, the anxiety, the doubt about going into court alone, are all gone; I prevented Smith from suckering me into a deal I didn't have to make. I know the business world, the legal world included, turns on deals. Any deal, though, is a contract where each party gets something of value from the other. What would I have gotten from Smith other than making him go away? I haven't shied away from fights for a long time, and I'm not going to start now. At the same time, I recognize Smith is my senior, someone to whom I should show respect. Still, Smith hasn't shown me any respect. Didn't he try to take advantage of me?

My eyes drift to the two files I set on the desk. Income tax returns?

⁓ ✦

Paul and Jean Sunstrom sit on the edge of the couch in the hallway, apparently eager to be "Next." I guess they are each in their mid-thirties. When they stand, I decide they could be cutouts from a poster for wholesome milk. Margo warned me they are very religious.

Paul pumps my hand. "Thank you for seeing us on such short notice." Then he steps aside as Jean shakes my hand and thanks me.

As they sit in front of my desk, I sense they're embarrassed. They look at each other in a seemingly courteous effort to allow the other one to talk. Paul finally speaks:

"I guess it's about time we had some simple wills made. We've put them off far too long."

"Actually," Jean adds, "we've put them off until the last minute. We're flying to Florida on Saturday morning for a vacation without the kids."

"I'm sure we can get something whipped up by tomorrow afternoon." They look relieved as I gather background information on them. Interrupting my thought process is the question whether I have promised them something I can't deliver. I should have checked with Margo first.

Paul speaks again: "We don't know a lot about estate planning. I'm a sales rep for a manufacturing company in Lenora. We've never had a lot of money or property . . . donate a lot to the church . . . never thought a will was necessary. Then a few weeks ago we attended a dinner and seminar on estate planning held by the bank. What caught our attention was a discussion about providing for your kids in case, well, you know. We have an eight-year-old daughter and a six-year-old son."

"Exactly the purpose of a will. What are your intentions?"

Jean's turn: "We want to leave everything to our daughter and son, equally. At the seminar they talked about setting up a trust for them in case something happens to us."

"That is something you need." I begin to describe trusts, trying to edit my comments as I go along to eliminate too much technical data. I tick off the questions: When can the children first have access to the money? For what purposes—education, medical expenses, living expenses? To what age do you wish to provide for them?

After we work it out, Paul asks Jean, "Do you have the paper where we wrote the names of the guardians?"

She rummages through her purse and hands the sheet to me. "Our first choice is Paul's brother and his wife; second are my sister and her husband."

"You've come prepared. Understand, though, naming them in the will does not bind the court. Normally, a judge will accede to the wishes of the testators, absent some circumstances such as the proposed guardians being in jail or otherwise unfit at the time."

I finish answering their questions, and then I remember the catastrophe question. "We need to determine what you want to do if something happens to all of you at once." I see the shock in their faces. "It's something extremely remote, I know. It's my responsibility, though, to try to cover everything. If all of you, the children included, are in a common disaster, sorting out what will happen with your estate could be very tricky . . . figuring out which one of you died first . . . even if by a matter of seconds."

Jean stumbles over her words, "Right now we're only worried about the two of us. Our kids aren't going with us."

"I understand. If you're going to prepare wills, though, you need to cover all of the contingencies. I know we could redo them when you get back, but what if you're busy and don't have the time . . . " The more I attempt to explain the provision, the more I agitate them. What do I do now? I have taken their hands and led them down this path. Are they going to tell their friends I'm a zebra hunter; that most people when they hear hoof beats at the window, look for horses, but this guy looks for zebras?

On the way to the front door, I'm unable to stop myself from going back to it. "I didn't mean to upset you. The common disaster provision was simply something we needed to discuss."

They nod and force smiles as they shake my hand. They are very religious, very forgiving. "Will I consider attending services at their church?" they both ask me. They no doubt wonder why I didn't spend more time on the trust and the guardians. I decide to have Burnett run his routine by me.

Margo is standing in the doorway to her office when I close the front door. "They're a very nice young couple. If you'll give me your notes and a list of the provisions you want, I'll type a draft of the wills."

"You heard?"

"Some of it."

She follows me to my office door where I hand her the notes from my desk. "If you're not too busy? I notice you worked until six last night."

"Some things need to be done right away. I'll call the Sunstroms and schedule an appointment for tomorrow afternoon for them to come in and sign the wills. Bob and I learned the hard way about putting off the preparation. We've had clients die before their wills were signed. Luckily, Bob was able to work around those situations."

As Margo returns to her office, Burnett hurries down the hallway. "Good job on Schultz. Now we'll see if Smith will call because there *is* a pending sale on the house."

I follow Burnett into the kitchen to get coffee. "I'm surprised Smith didn't have something more than a bluff."

He laughs. "I think he's run out of excuses: the Clerk of Court's Office must have misplaced the answer, he was intentionally led astray by the plaintiff or the plaintiff's attorney, whatever might possibly constitute excusable neglect in not filing a timely answer. The judge has heard them all."

Burnett pours cups of coffee for us as we stand at the coffee maker on the counter next to the sink. "Listen, John, I would like you to sit in with me on a real estate closing tomorrow at nine o'clock at the bank."

"Sure." I fetch a bottle of cream from the refrigerator.

"We're representing the buyers. Henry Miller is the realtor. The sellers' attorney, though, will handle the closing. Henry always gets one of the attorneys or the bank loan officer to close it." Burnett shakes his head. "He even gets his wife to do the closing statement."

"You know, Bob, Margo was right. I haven't noticed Henry the past couple of days."

As I cross the hallway to my office, I hear Burnett chuckling. First clearing an area on my cluttered desk, I wade through the two tax returns, reading the instruction booklets as I proceed. Who goes to law school to prepare tax returns? When I finish the second return, I wonder whether the mundane will become routine.

❦ ❧

When Margo tells me Brenda Krueger is on the phone, I glance at the clock as I pick up the receiver: 5:15. "Did Bill get served?"

Her tremulous voice causes me to press the receiver hard against my ear. "A deputy served those papers on him and told him some things. Bill stared and stared at the papers. His face got really red. I could tell he could hardly control himself, but the deputy was watching him pretty closely and told him not to make problems."

"What happened then?" I grab a legal pad and write down the date and Brenda's name.

"Well, Bill got some clothes and other stuff, tossed them into the cab of his pickup and sped out of the driveway. He wouldn't talk to me, but told the deputy he was going to his parents' place. They live in the north end of the village."

I'm relieved. "What about you and the boys?"

"I'll call my mom and dad after I get off the phone with you. They're going to come over to help me pack clothes and the kids' toys. We're going to their house."

My body tenses as I consider her response. Burnett advised me Brenda should stay in the house during the divorce, especially until the Temporary Hearing; otherwise, Bill will have the argument she doesn't need the house because she has somewhere else to go.

"I don't know if that's a good idea, Brenda. Why don't you stay in the house and have your mother or both of your parents stay with you for awhile."

"No. They don't like it here. They're as afraid as I am he'll come back. I have to get away until he cools down."

"You think he'll move back in?"

"No. He'll stay with his parents. He wouldn't know how to make meals and take care of himself. What we're worried about is Bill coming back and starting something."

"Listen, Brenda, be sure to call me if there are any problems. Call me any time."

"Thank you, *Mister* Hall. I will."

"And, Brenda, the temporary hearing before the court commissioner is set for Tuesday afternoon at four o'clock at the courthouse in Lenora. I assumed the time would be all right with you since you get off work in Lenora at three o'clock."

"That's okay. I'll stay in Lenora after work until the hearing."

"Good. I'll meet you in the main lobby of the courthouse about three-thirty so we can go over your finances again. Tomorrow, drop off the financial statement I gave you so Margo can type it."

While we are talking, Margo waives good-by to me as she leaves the office with Abstract trotting behind her. Burnett has already left. I hang up the phone and sit back to mull the Kruegers' situation. I suspect the divorce is not going to be this easy.

I move around the corner from my office to the door underneath the staircase to the second floor and switch on the basement lights. Since Margo gave me the tour of the place, I've been curious what's below the first floor.

A few spider webs notwithstanding, it's cleaner than I expected. Against a back corner, the rough stone walls box out what I figure is some kind of room, perhaps a cistern. I recall a similar enclosure in the basement of an old house owned by an aunt and uncle. To the right of the cistern is a short stairway to the outside covered by slanted, double doors, and to the far right, the pressure tank and overhead water pipes feeding the building. On the other side of the stairway is an oil furnace and beyond it an abandoned coal bin, apparently once fed through a now sealed window. The rest of the basement is empty and dry, but cool, warmed only through heat escaping from the heat ducts to the upstairs.

It will do, I assure myself as I continue to assess possibilities. The gyms I trained and boxed in when I was younger weren't much warmer. Besides, I'm not going to box again. When I quit, I vowed never to go back. This will be exercise—wielding a few weights, pounding a punching bag, rapping a rhythm on a speed bag. I can spend some evenings creating the semblance of a gym. Burnett won't care. Maybe I can get Angie and Slider to help me . . . well maybe Slider.

I inspect my hands. They're soft now. I'm not as hard as I used to be. Moving around with my back to a bare bulb, the light casts a shadow on the wall. I move into a boxing stance. Then I smile and go back upstairs to my office.

Through information, I locate a telephone number for a classmate I haven't seen since high school, the name coming to me in the basement. I call Tim Waters.

"Tim, you're out west of Milwaukee now?"

"That's right. I'm running a small construction company out here I started a few years ago. How about you?"

"I'm up in the sticks . . . Winding River . . . practicing law."

"I always knew you'd do something like become a lawyer. And, here I am, working my butt off trying to keep my company going."

I laugh loudly. "Company? Who owns a company? I don't own any-thing but a beat up car and some used law books." Waters laughs. "Seri-ously, Tim, you went into the Marine Corps right out of high school, didn't you?"

"Yeah, I did. When you went into the Army."

"Right. Were you *in country* in sixty-seven?"

"Yeah."

"I know the Corps is a lot smaller than the Army, still not that small, but did you ever hear of a marine named Jim Lynch from Winding River, killed in a northern province of South Vietnam in sixty-seven during some operation there?" I relate the information I received from the Veteran's Service Officer on the outfit.

After a long pause, Waters responds: "No, I don't recall his name. I'd need more info. Sounds like it was a search and destroy operation. There were a lot of them . . . a lot of marines killed. My company lost twenty-four men in one afternoon, not to mention seventy-three wounded."

"Tim, if you can find out anything about him, mainly how he died, would you let me know? It will mean a lot to a woman I know."

"I'm not big in the veterans' organizations, but I keep in touch with several guys I was in with, and they know other guys. Maybe I can find out something."

"I'll owe you big time. Just because I'm up in the Northwoods doesn't mean I can't help you. I'm licensed to practice throughout the state. So, if you need help, call me."

"Deal, John. I'll try to find something on Lynch. And good luck in . . . what's the name of the town you're in, Wild River? I never heard of it. How did you find the place?"

"It found me."

~ 13 ~

Burnett guides me toward the front door of the State Bank of Winding River. The classic small town bank, he tells me. Large pillars and tall, narrow windows in front lend the impression of a larger bank than it is inside. A teller counter along the left wall faces a stone fireplace graced with a somber portrait of the bank founder hanging over the mantle. In the back of the room, a paddle fan clicks slow revolutions, forcing hot air down from the high ceiling onto desks crammed in front of a safe with its door wide open.

Mark Petersen, a forty-some year old, tall, broad-shouldered man with a weathered face that suggests to me he is a banker inside the body of an outdoorsman, leads us to a conference room on the second floor. Our clients, the buyers, Jerry and Judy Larsen, are waiting for the closing at a long, oval table with a highly polished surface. After witnessing the Larsens' enthusiastic greeting of me, Burnett whispers to me: "I want you to become involved in their legal matters, particularly a business they're starting."

I nod agreement. Burnett has apologized to me for pushing me into so many different areas of the law so quickly. At the same time, he flatters me, alleging my eagerness and competence, considering my lack of practical experience, give him high expectations for me. It prompts him to give me the chance to show I can handle the practice. He reveres his deceased mentor, Charles Eggleston, for treating him the same way. I appreciate his faith in me that I can make the next jump; yet, I feel stress as he keeps raising the bar.

Petersen furnishes coffee to us and refills the Larsens' cups before addressing them. "Well, let's go through the loan closing." He picks up the first paper from a stack of prepared documents.

"I always start with the note, the promissory note, since all of the other documents tie in with this one. This is the piece of paper stating we're loaning you the money to purchase the old warehouse near the train station along with additional money to remodel it and to purchase equipment." He looks around the table and smiles. "And, that you'll pay the money back to us. Those are the basics of the loan."

The Larsens have a stack of copies of the same documents in front of them. Jerry holds up his copy of the note. "If that's all there is to it, how come we've got all of these documents with small print crammed on them?" He laughs at his remarks.

The banker returns his laugh. "I wish there weren't, then I wouldn't have to go through all of them with you."

I think of Burnett's comment on the way to the bank that Petersen would rather be out on the ice today, in his fish shanty with pop-ups set for the lines in the water through the hole in the ice, and that his wife, who is president of the Winding River Women's Club, would be happy he was out there if he wasn't going to be at the bank.

"The mortgage," Petersen points out after the note has been signed, "provides security for the loan. It provides the bank with a lien on the real estate, which includes the building, you are purchasing. Later, we'll review documents granting the bank a lien on the personal property, that is, the machinery and equipment you are buying. The mortgage will be recorded with the Register of Deeds."

With me looking over his shoulder, Burnett is following Petersen's comments. Jumping ahead of the banker, Burnett scans the forms that are familiar to him, then slides the stack of documents in front of me. His attention has drifted elsewhere. Is he thinking about the Larsens? He told me Jerry grew up in Winding River. His father, who worked in the mill at Lenora, and his mother had been clients. He suspected Jerry would return to the village eventually, as did many of the village's young people who left for college or technical school, or the military, or just drifted from their roots for a number of years. There is Burnett insisted, something about the Northwoods—the rivers and the lakes, the friendly people, the calmness masking the sense of purpose of most of the residents—that draws them back. He's sure more of them would return if there were employment opportunities compatible with their education and vocational skills.

When the loan transaction is completed, Petersen leaves the room to have copies of the signed documents made for the Larsens and to invite Henry Miller, along with the sellers and their attorney, up to the conference room to close the real estate transaction. Burnett follows him out, on the way to the bathroom.

"What type of business are you starting?" I ask the Larsens as we wait.

"A small manufacturing operation," Jerry answers. "We've got several things planned, the big one securing an agreement with one of the gun manufacturers to make firing pins, something I've got a line on. I don't want to put everything into one product, though."

"That's interesting. I didn't realize something like firing pins was contracted out. I assumed the whole firearm was made by the gun people."

"I know that's a common misunderstanding of manufacturers. Many companies with multiple part products contract out some or all of the parts and then do the assembly. It's cheaper that way." He pauses to sip coffee. "We're going to need you guys to form a corporation for us. Can we get in next week?"

"Sure. We'll set up an appointment."

Miller strolls in with the sellers and their attorney, followed by Burnett and Petersen. Burnett sports a wry smile. During the drive down the slope to the bank, Burnett laughed as he alleged Henry has the perfect business for himself. Marrying into a family with money, Miller does not have to hustle like most realtors. All he has to do is wait until prospects spy his office on Main Street and walk in, find out what they want, and then get somebody else to do whatever is needed. If there are ever any obstacles, Henry will lapse into a nap. He received an affiliate award from his national franchiser for outstanding real estate sales in 1975.

The seller's attorney from Algona, Dick Minor, a short man with early signs of balding but a partially compensating dark moustache, walks everyone through the papers. Minor is exceptionally well organized. After passing out a closing checklist, Minor goes through it item by item, from insuring that all of the contingencies in the offer to purchase have been met, through reviewing the title insurance, the warranty deed and the closing statement, to making sure the keys are turned over after the money has changed hands. Henry sits with the silence of an innocent bystander and appears to miss his newspaper.

"And that's it." Minor ends it on an up note.

Appearing to snap out of a trance, Miller rises and grasps Jerry Larsen's hand and then his wife's hand. "I want to be the first to congratulate you on your splendid purchase." Miller shakes the rest of the hands around the room, gives everyone a Miller Realty ballpoint pen, and then disappears with his commission check stuffed into his shirt pocket.

Burnett's wry smile returns. As we leave the bank, he whispers to me: "Miller always took photographs for the *Winding River Record* of the sellers passing the keys to the buyers. Apparently Henry has abandoned the practice as being too much trouble. It's going to create holes in the front pages of future editions of the paper."

Minor catches up with us on the street and speaks to me: "I think there's a bar association meeting next week in Lenora. Hope you can make it."

"I intend to bring him." Burnett waves goodbye to Minor.

I watch Minor walk around the corner to his car. "Seems like a nice guy."

"He is a nice guy. More importantly, he's someone you can work with, someone you can trust. John, if you need help on something, and I'm not around, he's someone you can rely on."

❧ ☙

As soon as I sit down in my office, Margo buzzes me to pick up the telephone.

"Good morning, Mr. Hall. Attorney Sanford Smith here. How are you this morning? Beginning to get the hang of the practice?"

I hesitate. "I'm doing okay."

"You did a good job for your client yesterday. Now, it looks like my client is going to be selling his home. So, we'll be paying off the judgment next Thursday at closing. Send me over a copy of your proposed Satisfaction of Judgment, and we'll swap the original for the sixteen hundred and fifty-three dollars at the closing."

I hesitate again. "That amount plus the interest on it and the court costs. Remember you told me if we held off on the judgment, you would pay the interest."

"Attorney Hall, my client is barely getting enough money from the sale proceeds to cover the mortgages and other liens on the property, let alone the closing costs. Surely you're not going to hold up Mr. Herdina for a few days of interest and some minor filing fees."

"My client is entitled to every cent. Why should he take less?"

"Attorney Hall, we're not planning to appeal the judge's decision, but I'm sure you understand we could do so given the egregious manner in which the judge handled the hearing. It makes sense for us to dispose of this unfortunate matter as simply as possible. Surely you're not serious about interest and costs."

I grit my teeth. As if he's serious about appealing. I'm being pushed around again. I can take a lot of things, but I can't take being pushed around. "Pay the whole amount, or I won't furnish the satisfaction."

I hear a click on the phone. "The prick hung up on me," I say to myself as I slam the receiver onto the phone.

Burnett, walking past the doorway, backs up when he hears my words. "Who was that?"

"Who else? Sanford Smith." I speak through clenched teeth. "He's a big prick. I don't know how else to describe him."

Burnett sits down. "Well, that is a good description of him. He is big and . . . What did he want?" He listens carefully to my reply before continuing. "You have to learn how to work with him. You're going to constantly run into him on your cases. You're going to run into him in the village, at the courthouse, at the grocery store. You have to . . . "

"I know that." I cut him off. "I know I should handle Smith better, but he pisses me off."

"That's the way he is, and he isn't going to change. Remember, John, there will be times when you'll want concessions on a case from him—excusing of interest so that you can get something for your client, an extension of time to answer a complaint, agreement on postponing a hearing or a trial because you have a conflict. You can't try every case. Your clients would not want you to. You're going to need to settle cases with Smith, perhaps making compromises you're not happy with, if, of course, Smith is also unhappy with the compromises he has to make."

I sigh. "I know. I'll learn to work with him. In this situation, though, I don't think I should give up anything, especially after the way he jacked me around in court."

"Then don't. But, be civil with him. Use a little finesse." Burnett grimaces. "Don't be a hard ass."

I look at Burnett before laughing. "You're right. I'm not usually like this. He gets to me." I begin to grit my teeth again. "He's such a pompous, condescending prick. He's . . . "

Burnett shakes his head as he leaves the room.

14

Following Burnett's recommendation, I decide to eat lunch at Wally & Laverne's Restaurant on the corner of Main and Forest Streets. When I pass through the door, I feel as though I've entered a time portal. I'm a kid again. The black and white, checkered tile floor and the metal stools with padded red tops lining the counter, together with the sizzling, greasy looking grill and a juke box, flashes signs of the 50's.

Burnett claims the restaurant is the best place in the village to get a quick meal. The soup and sandwich special is good, the service is as slow as I've experienced. No one among the locals, waitresses and cooks exhibits any movements described by the word "fast." Like the rest of the people in the village, they exhibit a sense of purpose and a sense they know how to achieve it. They're simply cranked down several notches.

A fat salesman sitting next to me is red in the face from waiting for his check. "Christ, this place is slow." He checks his watch and eyes the other customers on the stools before he faces me. "Don't any of these people work?"

"Well, I don't . . . "

"What do you do?"

"I'm an attorney. Actually, I just started . . . "

He gives me a pathetic look. "An attorney? Christ, what does an attorney do in a place like this?

"What an attorney does in any other small town, I guess. Real estate . . . "

After checking the menu board above the grill, he dumps several bills on the counter. Easing off the stool, he faces me again. "Must not be a lot of real estate work in this town if you're eating in this place." He shakes his head and moves out the door.

An older man in bib overalls on the other side of me shrugs. "We get some like him in here all the time. What in the hell is he in a hurry to sell?" He yells at the blond, overweight waitress, wearing lots of lipstick, behind the bar. "More coffee, honey."

The pleasant feeling lingering with me after lunch disappears as I walk into the office and see Suits sitting on the couch with a stack of files on his lap.

He rushes up to me, holding out the files. "I brought all these over to you. You'll be handlin' everythin', now."

As I remove my coat and hang it on the antlered rack, my first wish is that I had a one o'clock appointment. My second wish is that Suits would go away, mad or not. Since neither of the wishes will be granted, with tentative fingers I accept the files thrust into my hands. "Come into my office."

I drop the files on my desk as Suits sneaks into a chair. Even his mannerisms are beginning to stir fear in me, fear I will make some colossal blunder to add to the one in taking him on as a client.

Suits rises from his chair enough to pick up the top file and fling it toward me. I catch in a reflexive action. "This one's my divorce. You gotta get up to speed on it right away. Lots of stuff goin' on."

"Where did these files come from?"

"Attorney Smith. Handed 'em all over to me. Didn't even argue about it. Even made out the transfer forms or whatever you call 'em."

"I'm sure he did. Look, we're still investigating your personal injury case. We don't . . . "

"That's okay. We got plenty of time on that one. Statute of Limi . . . We've got three years to file a suit."

"I know that." I'm peeved as I leaf through the divorce file. "You've got a hearing next Wednesday before the judge on criminal charges?"

Suits straightens up in his chair. "Ah, there's nothin' there. I shouldn't have to go to court for that."

I examine the copy of the criminal complaint in the file. "It says here your wife was given the right at the temporary hearing to reside in your home." I read on. "And, that you were arrested for breaking in, breaking down the kitchen door."

"No, no. I went there to get some tools I needed to fix my car, and when I was knockin' on the door, I tripped over a planter and fell through the door. It was an accident, hurt my shoulder." His left hand rubs the top of the sling on his right shoulder. "I told her I'd fix the door."

"Come on. If that's true, why didn't you go back outside to wait until she got you the tools?"

"She didn't know where I kept 'em."

I shake my head. "And that's why when the police came you were hiding in a closet?"

"Yeah. That's where I thought the tools were."

"You were sitting down underneath a pile of dirty linens."

"It was hard to see in there . . . dark, real dark."

"And that's your defense?"

"Yeah. And, it had been rainin', and the back porch was real slick."

"What?" I check my calendar. "This happened last Sunday afternoon. It didn't rain then. In fact, it was snowing all day. I know that for sure."

Suits stares at the ceiling, folding his arms. "You're right, snow." He leans forward and excitedly points at me. "It was wet snow, real slippery. And that's why I didn't see the planter, 'cause it was covered with snow."

I imagine Tompkins listening to the defense. Will he pad the fine for lying? "I don't know. I'm getting awfully busy." I pick up the files and start to extend them across the desk.

Suits jumps up and backs outside my reach. "Look 'em all over good. And, she's not gettin' the grill. I bought it, and I want it." He stands in the doorway. "I'll ride down to the courthouse with you."

"Wait . . ." Suits twists around the doorframe into the hallway. By the time I reach the entryway, he has disappeared, leaving the door ajar.

Margo buzzes me to pick up the phone. "John Hall."

"This is Carl Schultz. You know anything more about getting the money?"

"I talked to Herdina's attorney this morning. It appears they're going to close the sale of his house next Thursday."

"That Smith is somethin', huh?"

"More than something, he's a . . . " Burnett's admonition interrupts me. "He's different."

"Okay. You let me know, huh?"

"I'll do that." After I hang up, I swivel my chair to face the side window. The rays of the morning sun have gradually been shielded by a grayish-white sky now hanging over the village like a gigantic blanket from which small flakes drift harmlessly to the snow cover and lose their identities. I hope the snowfall will not begin in earnest before morning. It's Friday afternoon, and I'm looking forward to my date with Shelly tonight, even if she is my second choice.

Turning back to my desk, I ponder my choices of unenviable work: the files Suits has left, several abstracts to be examined, or a new stack of income tax returns. Margo allows me to select "none of the above" when she informs me over the telephone intercom the Sunstroms have come in to execute their wills. I'm relieved; I ask her to escort them into my office and to bring the wills with her.

The Sunstroms are pleasant, yet I sense they're still unsure of me. I have them read over the wills carefully as Margo watches them and waits to witness their signatures. I stifle my temptation to revisit the common disaster provision, and they don't bring it up. When we finish, I walk them to the front door amid repeated thanks from them for completing the wills in time for their trip. Ann is right, I decide, most of the residents of the village are likeable people.

I peek my head into Burnett's office. "Nice folks, the Sunstroms."

Burnett looks up from his desk. "It's always pleasant when the good people come in. Unfortunately, in our business we see a disproportionate number who are dishonest, immoral, uncaring . . . thoughtless, vengeful, unreasonable, and whose attitudes and conduct are otherwise twisted by their lack of character and common sense. Some are merely stupid. They're all called clients, though, and they may all need representation."

"Where do you draw the line in representation?"

"Well, certainly where they are proposing action or conduct that is, or could be considered, illegal, immoral or unconscionable. The real problem arises when they're not likeable individuals. You'll find many of those in criminal defense work, but some in your civil practice. You don't have to like them to represent them. At some point, though, you have to ask yourself whether you want to represent an individual who's difficult to communicate with, makes unreasonable demands upon you, or perhaps is not telling you the whole story, the balance of which will surprise you in court."

"It's on a case by case basis?"

"That's right. You can't, though, shy away from your obligations as a lawyer. You're going to get some public defender work, and whether you like the individual has nothing to do with your duty to your client to provide the best representation you can." Burnett smiles. "Margo wishes I would get rid of several of our clients. On the other hand, as soon as I point out they help pay the light bills, she clams up."

🞇 🞇

She buttons her overcoat as she lets me in through the front door. "I'm ready to go."

I stand inside the door, perplexed but suddenly happy. "I don't understand."

"Do you need to?" Ann asks.

"Usually I do. Right now I don't."

"Let's say I have a very understanding roommate."

"Good enough for me." I take her arm and lead her out to my car. "Where do you want to go for dinner?"

"How about the River's Edge? Have you been there yet?"

"No I haven't, but the place sounds familiar."

Ann directs me down Main Street to Forest, where we turn toward the river. I again spot the older woman in the window above Wally & Laverne's restaurant at the corner. We drive over a narrow bridge to the other side of the river where we turn left onto River Road and immediately turn left again in to a crowded parking lot next to the supper club. The newer log constructed building contrasts with Slider's weathered log tavern. Parking far from the front door, we hurry through the cold wind into the building.

The place is packed and noisy. It's "B Night" in northern Wisconsin: battered perch, broasted potatoes, and beer or brandy drinks. We check in with the hostess before elbowing our way to the bar and ordering drinks. Ann finds a vacant barstool, sitting on it with her back to the bar as I stand in front of her. I speak first:

"Thanks for coming. Why didn't you tell me your father was the judge?"

"It didn't come up in the conversation. Would it have made a difference?"

I pause. "It might have."

"Was he rough on you?"

"He left no doubt in my mind he expects his unmarried daughter be seen in the company of a gentleman."

"Are you a gentleman?"

"Usually. Would it have made a difference?"

"It might have."

I laugh. "I assume you know your father's court reporter, Angie Bellini? Doesn't he live around here?"

"Yes, I do. I certainly do. He lives down the road a couple of blocks."

"What does that mean? Did you go out with him?"

"A couple of times."

I pick up a drink from the bar and hand it to her. "What happened to the follow up?"

"I didn't like his story. It was all middle. Every day is the same. There's no progression." She strokes her glass. "I think the end and the middle are going to turn out to be the same."

"Do you like people's stories?"

"I love them. When I was a young girl, I used to ride my bike down to the courthouse and sit in the last row of seats in my father's courtroom to watch and listen, especially during the summers when I could go in on Monday morning during his intake on criminal and traffic cases. My father didn't like me going down there and mixing with the defendants charged with crimes and drunk driving, but I went anyway. Sometimes I couldn't get enough facts from the proceedings to make a story out of it, or maybe the facts weren't presented like a story. My father would scold the District Attorney for not presenting a case with a beginning, a middle and an end so he could follow it. The D.A. would scramble it up."

We laugh.

"What's my story?"

"I don't know yet. I haven't heard or seen enough."

I laugh. "You know when Angie said you were a fox, I thought he meant foxy, like in good looking, which you are, but you're also sly, aren't you?"

"Am I?"

I laugh again. "I think I'm going to like this."

The hostess hustles up to us and points out our table. We carry our drinks to a table by a window overlooking the river, the water iced in place and swept with snow. As we sit, I nod at the older couple at the next table. The bearded man is wearing a fur cap and a plaid, wool shirt with red suspenders over it, and the woman across from him has her head covered by a dark, wool tam topped with a white pompom in the center. I look at the log walls and roof trusses and decide the older couple belongs in the Northwoods.

The table is small, and I feel very close to Ann. I debate whether I should ask her to go to Milwaukee with me tomorrow to pick up the rest of my clothes and other belongings. I'm not anxious to return alone to an apartment where I spent most of my life.

The waitress bounds over to us. Ann greets her and introduces me. I'm discovering everyone knows everyone else in Winding River. After the waitress takes our order, I watch her move away, wondering how Ginger Buckman could possibly fit in this place.

"Getting to know the girls around here?"

I break my stare. "I was thinking about a client I realized worked here. You know that's all I can say. I don't know much of her story, but I wish I did."

"So you like stories, too?"

"It's part of my job. Every client has a story. I'm now one of the attorneys you watched in court trying to tell a story."

"Can I come and watch you?"

"At this point, you would quickly lose interest."

The waitress returns with a basket of rolls and two salads.

"You're very intense about what you do, aren't you?" Ann asks as she inspects her salad.

"That's true."

"You're having a hard time relaxing now because you're thinking about her case?"

"That's true, too. I may have taken on more than I can handle. It wouldn't be the first time."

"Can't you put it aside for awhile?"

"I guess not."

I observe Ann take a roll while we talk, break it in half, then break the halves into quarters, and then break the pieces further, buttering a piece that suits her before eating it slowly. "You're different."

"You think so?"

"You like to take things apart, analyze them."

"That's true."

"How is it then that you're an art teacher? Aren't you fighting your left brain?"

"Umm, maybe. I like art that depicts reality, real life drawings. I like to draw. When I sat in my father's courtroom and the stories were boring, I sketched anything in the room."

"I like the sketch behind your father's desk."

"How did . . . you're smart, aren't you?"

"Am I?"

Ann laughs. "I think I'm going to like your story."

❧ 15 ❧

A telephone rings. Where is the sound coming from? There's no telephone in the park. I hold hands with Ann as we stroll past park benches. Burnett stands on a box in front of one, explaining a trust document to an older couple sitting on the bench, while Margo wraps, with the precision of a machine, contracts at a vendor's cart. Should I stop around the curve and kiss Ann? I think I kissed her before, but aren't sure. I glance over my shoulder to see if the dog is still tailing us.

When my eyes open, the park disappears, and I read 12:24 a.m. on the alarm clock perched on a stack of magazines on the nightstand. Then I understand there *is* a telephone ringing. It's too loud to be coming from downstairs. I remember the extension Margo had the lineman install in the library.

"Hello. This is John Hall." I breathe hard from the run to the library. I also shiver in my underwear. At first, I hear only sobbing.

"He broke everything . . . everything."

"Brenda? What are you talking about?"

"Bill. He went to the house last night while I was at my parents home with the kids and broke everything . . . broke all the dishes, the lamps, picture frames . . . ripped apart cushions and pillows and sheets . . . sawed up the furniture. There's nothing left." She begins sobbing again. "What will I do, Mister Hall?"

Burnett is right, some bizarre thing. What do I say? "Is Bill there now?"

"No. The police arrested him. They said they were going to hold him in the cell at the police station until they talked to the District Attorney."

"Where are you?"

"At my parents' home. We went to the house after a neighbor called my mother and said she'd called the police when the noise woke her up. When we got there, Bill was in handcuffs. He'd ripped out the phone cords and smashed the phones, so we had to come back here to call you."

"Just a minute, Brenda." I run back to my bedroom, don a robe, and race back to the phone. "Sorry. I can't fathom this. It's incredible. Did the police talk to you?"

"They asked me about the divorce, so I showed them the papers saying I had the right to live in the house until the hearing."

"What about Bill. Did he say anything, offer any explanation?"

"He said it's his property, too, and there's nothing in the papers that says he can't break everything if he wants to."

"Well, he can't." I try to mentally read the family court commissioner's order. "Among other things, the court order prohibits him from disposing of any of your property without the permission of the court. He certainly disposed of it."

"What should I do, Mister Hall? What if they let him go?"

"I'll call the police. I hope they hold him overnight at least. Depending on what they charge him with, since it's Saturday, he could be held for court until Monday morning. I'll let you know."

"We're going back to the house with some boxes to see if there's anything we can save. There's no phone there."

I don't want to go to the house; well, I want to see it but not go there. How do I do that? I told Ann I would pick her up at seven-thirty to go to Milwaukee with me for the day. Going to Brenda's house, though, is the right thing to do. "I'll meet you at the house. Do you or your parents have a camera?"

"Bill and I have a small camera, but I don't know what happened to it. My parents have a thirty-five millimeter."

"Good. Get one of them to photograph everything before you do anything else."

"Okay, Mister Hall."

"And, Brenda. I'm sorry. I wish I knew something else to say."

"Don't worry about it, Mister Hall. It wasn't your fault." She sobs again. "I'm glad I started the divorce. Thank you." She hangs up.

I pull the robe up around my neck and slump in a chair at the conference table. If I hadn't persuaded her to commence the divorce, she would still have her property. Temporary possession of their home is now a moot issue. When Brenda and Bill divide up their property, Brenda's proportionate share of the destroyed property can be subtracted from Bill's share of other property; good in theory, worthless in reality. Since they rent the house and each has an older car with no equity in it, what other property is left to divide?

❧ ❧

Five minutes after seven a.m. An empty police car with the engine running and the exhaust blowing a cloud of smoke is parked in front of the village hall and police station. I pull *Rusty* into the parking lot. I'm tired. By the time I finished surveying the damage to the Krueger home, consoled Brenda, and returned to bed it was almost three o'clock. Sleep evaded me for an hour after that as I continually rethought my advice and actions.

A young, Scandinavian looking officer emerges from the station. I briskly walk over to him and say, " I called earlier in the morning but no one was there so I left a message." My hot breath is creating steam in the air as I speak.

The officer invites me to sit in his squad car. "I got the message. I'd just come on duty. The chief and the other part-time officer arrested him. We're going to hold him, probably over the weekend. I haven't gotten in touch with the D.A. yet."

"What are the charges?"

"This is one of those domestic relations situations we usually don't like to get involved in. No one was assaulted or injured. He destroyed a lot of property, but at this point whose property is it? Basically, it's a civil matter. There was, though, the neighbor's complaint about the noise. So, probably the only charge would have been some breach of the peace citation."

I'm dejected. If he's released, will he go after Brenda next? "That sounds like a misdemeanor at best, probably an ordinance violation. You can let him go on a signature bond, can't . . . Wait a minute, what do you mean the only charge *would have been*?"

The officer smiles. "He fought the arrest. So, we'll have him charged with resisting arrest, a felony. He'll have to go before a judge or a court commissioner for bail on that charge."

"All right!" I shake hands with the officer and ease out of the police car. "Call me or Bob Burnett if you need anything from us."

Suits files riffle through my mind like cards being shuffled in a deck. I climb back into the police car. "As long as I'm here . . . " I ask the officer if he knows Suits, whom I reluctantly refer to as a client, and whether he has knowledge of an automobile accident in September where Suits' car was rear-ended.

"Oh, yeah. I investigated that one. The lady who ran into him said he slammed on the brakes for no reason. He claimed a deer ran in front of his car, so he had to stop. There were skid marks but no indications he hit a deer. The lady was alone. No witnesses. I don't know." He shrugs. "It was like all of his accidents, who can say exactly what happened?"

"All of his accidents?" I shake my head as I again exit the car. "Thanks."

The officer leans across the front seat to speak as I begin to close the door. "I will tell you this: the car was a junker, and an insurance adjuster investigating the accident told me your client purchased it two days before the accident. See you."

≈ ≈

After I pick up Ann and drive onto the highway, I relate as much as I can of the early morning events without betraying client confidentiality. She looks concerned as she asks me whether I need to stay in Winding River. I allay her fears when I tell her Burnett agreed to cover for me if Brenda needed help before I returned.

I screw up my face. "When I told Bob my first thought on hearing what happened was that I wanted to find Bill and beat the crap out of him, Bob told me he was pleased I had heeded his admonitions on self-control and not getting too personally involved in a case." We laugh.

"At least you understand your problems."

"Some of them." I study the light snow cover on the road. Is *Rusty* up to the drive? "I feel sorry for Brenda. I hope she'll be better off in the long run."

"Better Bill beats up their property than Brenda."

"I like that. You're right, as usual."

Ann smiles at me. "You know you shouldn't tell a woman she's right all of the time. You're waiving your right to further argument. No good lawyer ever does that."

I turn to her. "Why is it that I'm getting to really like you?"

"I object! That's my question."

"There you go again. You're trying to keep me off balance, aren't you?"

"Am I?"

I reach my hand over to squeeze her hand. Last night was sizing and verbal fencing. Now she'll want to know more about me; she's the kind of woman who seeks answers. She has me in captivity and will begin to probe me. I'm too tired for the drill.

"I'll tell you what," Ann suggests, "since we have to drive for over four hours each way, this is a good time for you to start your story at the beginning."

"I don't remember the beginning."

"Start when you can remember."

"You know, I'm tired. You want to drive to, say, Green Bay while I take a nap?"

"No. I'll drive after you tell me some more of your story. And, don't leave out the details."

"What if I can't remember more than a half an hours' worth?"

"Then I'll have to pry it out of you. I learned a lot sitting in my father's courtroom."

I give her a quick glance. "I hope I don't ever have you as an adverse witness. You're tough." I rub my hand over my face to get the blood flowing. "Look, you don't want to hear about what toys I played with or how many times I got drunk in the *gasthauses* in Germany. What are you after?"

"I want to know why the first thought in your mind after hearing about Bill Krueger's escapade was to beat him up? Is that the way you handle things like that?"

"Not in a long time."

"What do you mean?"

I glance at her again. "You're trying to open me up too soon. I'm not ready."

"Well then, tell me what kind of toys you played with and how many times you got drunk in the *gasthauses* in Germany."

I laugh. I knew from the start she wasn't going to be easy, one of the traits that attracted me to her. "Here's the deal (I am beginning to understand the usefulness of the phrase): I'll drive to Lenora, then you drive to Green Bay while I take a nap, and then I'll drive to Milwaukee. While we're there I'll answer your question."

"Hmm. I would be giving up a lot. How do I know that you won't brush me off with some vague or silly answer?"

"If you don't like my answer, then you get to kiss me as much as you want."

Ann laughs. "That's clever. I accept your offer."

❧ ☙

The three-story apartment building comes into view as I drive down the narrow east side street. How different the facade looks from that of Burnett's office. They're both old, brick buildings. Although Burnett's office is older, the red brick is clean and relatively undisturbed from its initial state, while the cream brick of the apartment building has been darkened by years of coal soot and gasoline fumes. The Winding River building has not yet suffered progress.

As we climb the stairs to the top floor apartments, I reminisce about tenants, past and present. The two flights to the third floor are long and steep. I now understand why the climb to the second floor of the office seems so easy. An older woman comes out of a second floor apartment as we pass. She stops to greet us. I introduce Ann, and after we chat, give the woman a hug goodbye.

Going up the flight to the third floor, I explain the woman's husband was a librarian who bought books at annual library sales to the point where most of the walls in their two-bedroom apartment were lined with bookshelves. She invited my brother and me to peruse the books and take them home. And her husband, before he died, brought home children's books when they had no children. The couple owned an intellectual island in the middle of a polluted and neglected lake.

Ann helps me carry my remaining property down to the car. As I take a last look around the apartment, she moves to each window to check the view. "I could do some interesting sketches from here. They would be drastically different from the views I've sketched before. Sadder views."

I ease over to her. "They would be big city views. There are many stories behind the shingled roofed, deteriorated wood houses you see from these windows."

Ann faces me. "You don't think there are as many stories in the view from your bedroom above the office?

"I don't think the stories are as important."

"Important to whom? The details of Brenda Krueger's divorce will never be published the way the details of the divorce of a famous actress would. Outside of her family, few people will ever know much about it, but isn't Brenda's divorce a more important story to her than all of the others in the world?"

I turn away from her to look out the window, although I know I won't find a reply among the dingy rooftops across the street.

"You're been brainwashed by the larger size falsehood," Ann continues.

Her question seizes my dilemma in going to the Northwoods as though she were squeezing my throat. I'm unable to voice an answer. My mind allows me to escape the answer by shifting to comprehension of the significance of the empty room. Memories of my parents, of lying on the worn carpet reading the books I selected from the downstairs neighbors' library, of holidays and of bleak times all rush into my mind. Leaving the place behind ends a long period of my life. Still, I no longer have a reason to be here.

I take a second last look around the room, hoping to etch it in my memory. Then I turn to Ann. "Let's get out of here."

The couple that manage the building are not home so I slip the keys underneath their door. I usher Ann to my car parked below the window where we were standing. While the car warms up, my eyes run up and down the street and then fix on a dirty white, clapboard house. Countless times over the years I stared down at the house, always wondering if Toby and his sister and their mother were all right. I knew that most of the time they were not, yet I did not know what to do about it.

Ann tugs at my coat sleeve. "Is something the matter?"

I shift the fan to a lower setting before replying. "I'm going to give you my answer why I wanted to find Bill Krueger. I didn't want to talk about it. You were right; I was going to make up some excuse or lame story to meet my part of the deal. Seeing the house across the street again, I've changed my mind. I guess we don't know each other very well, yet I can't think of anyone else I would want to talk to about it."

Ann gently touches my arm. "You don't have to if you don't want to. I can see this is going to be something more than I expected."

"When I was in grade school I walked about eight blocks to school. There were always fights. I didn't grow a lot until I was in high school, so I got picked on more than others. At first, I would take a beating and go home. It wasn't in my nature to fight. After a while, I got tired of being beaten and fought back, usually not very well but sometimes enough to keep my attacker from bothering me again.

"My mother didn't like it but knew she couldn't do anything about it. This was a tough neighborhood, and she knew I had to learn to handle myself. So she persuaded me to join a local youth club to take up boxing. She didn't want me to get that involved, just enough to learn to protect myself. Maybe she hoped it would help me to take care of my brother." I pause. My latest frailty seems to be confessions, first to Burnett and now Ann.

"You really don't have to go on."

"I eventually got involved in amateur boxing tournaments. Different than the professional fights you see on TV—three rounds, no draws, smaller ring. I started as a lightweight and when I quit I was a middleweight. I won my share of bouts but lost some key ones. Contrary to what she hoped, I really got into the boxing. It was the only sport I did get into in high school." I turn off the fan.

"What I'm leading up to is . . . Toby Williams, the kid across the street. Seven years younger than myself, he looked up to me. Once I pulled another kid off of him. After that he kind of followed me around like a puppy. He was a hyper kid whose life was bent out of shape by his father who was a drunk and a rotten man who beat his wife and his kids. Several times I looked down from that window in the apartment and saw a police car in front of their house. Sometimes the police arrested him, and once he was gone for some months, probably in jail. It went on.

"Then one night when I was a senior in high school, Toby came running up the stairs to our apartment and begged me to go with him to his house because his old man was giving his mother a terrible beating. I went. Since then I've never been sure I should have gone. I lost control. I beat his father until I almost killed him, even Toby had to get me to stop. His sister was hysterical, his mother injured but not much worse than other times. I told his father if he ever did anything to his wife or the kids again, I would come back and end it for him. Then I took Toby and his sister and mother home for the night.

"It wasn't my intention to hurt him; I just wanted him to stop beating the poor woman. It wasn't right and no one was stopping it."

Ann sits quietly and waits for me to go on. What does she think? I should have waited for a time when we knew each other better, but the story spills from lips I'm unable to seal:

"It was wrong what I did. I know that now, but at the time I created for myself justification. I should have called the police. As I understood it later, he sat around the house getting drunk and late in the evening he wandered several blocks onto a main street and got run over and killed by a bus. I tried to help them, and my mother went over and tried to help, but Toby's mother became very belligerent. I don't think she blamed me. She just didn't want it to end that way.

"A couple of months later, Toby and his sister and mother moved away, I think to Indiana. And that was it. The police came around investigating. They knew Toby's mother occasionally struck back with household objects. Anyway, he was so mangled by the bus it just went away. I quit boxing and promised my mother and myself I would never fight again. After awhile I realized I had liked the idea of boxing more than the boxing itself."

"That's a heck of a story." Ann touches my arm again. "And you've never told that story to anyone else?"

"My mother and brother knew, and the Williamses."

"I suppose you blame yourself for his death, maybe one of the reasons you went into the Army as soon as you graduated from high school."

I think for a moment. "I went into the Army to ease the burden on my mother. I sent her part of my paycheck every month." I pause again. "I'm sure it figured in, though."

"I wonder how my father would have judged you? I sat through an assault trial, and as I remember, he said the law is that you can use only such force as is necessary to overcome the force used against you, something like that."

"That's right. That's why I was wrong. I went too far. I wanted him to stop it before he killed her."

"What if you hadn't stopped him? What if he had killed her? And you knew you could have stopped it?"

"I could have stopped it and left."

"Umm . . . and then he starts up after you're gone and beats her to death."

"I've thought about that many times. The point is, I have to conduct myself within the law, and I didn't do it. I should have called the police and let them handle it."

"Sounds like there wasn't much time." Ann sees the downcast look on my face. "You didn't make him get drunk and stagger up to the street where he got run over. I'm wondering whether he walked in front of the bus on purpose. How do you know that he didn't know he was a rotten man?"

"I think you could give me an eloquent defense, and your father would be proud of you and agree that I didn't cause his death, and then he would find me guilty of aggravated assault. I got away with one. That was over ten years ago, and the statute of limitations has run. I've gotten my punishment because I have to think about it. I think . . . ah, hell, let's go over to Farwell Avenue. There's a bar where I know the owners, and we can have a few drinks and catch a late lunch."

"That won't change anything."

"It might change my attitude."

"I'm trying to put this thing together." Ann speaks slowly. "When Brenda Krueger laid her problems on you, it started coming back, didn't it, the beatings, the destruction, the torment, and you wanted to end it again?"

"I only thought about going after Bill. I wouldn't have done it. It's different now."

"Then why do you still have this hostility in you? You can't let it go. You can't keep yourself from getting in the middle of it like Burnett warned you."

"You're right. He's right. Burnett said we're supposed to help our clients solve their problems. What do I do? I talk Brenda into filing for the divorce so she can get away from the beatings and raise her sons in a better life, and look what happens. Now she's got nothing—no husband, no property, forcing her parents to take her in as well as the children, probably having to help support them."

Ann shakes her head. "Come on now. You're over analyzing everything. You can't make everything come out right to the last detail. It doesn't work like that. My father always said that you give the best advice you can give, then you live with it, regardless of how it turns out. He said you can drive yourself crazy always looking over your shoulder, second guessing yourself." She moves closer to me and puts her arm around my neck. "Let's go over to the bar on Farwell Avenue and have a drink. I've heard enough stories for now."

I feel drained of everything in me. "I can't believe I told you all that."

Ann leans in front of me. "Just because I liked your story, does that mean I can't kiss you?"

16

"How did your weekend go?" Margo asks as I amble into her office for my first human contact of the day. Even when we speak soon after her arrival each morning, Margo appears as though she has been working for hours, performing the details created by herself for a job I suspect came with the hastiest draft of requirements.

"You must not have talked to Bob."

"No. He isn't in yet."

She swivels her chair toward me as she sips from her coffee cup. I briefly mention the trip to Milwaukee and dinner at the Burnetts' home on Sunday afternoon where I took Ann at their insistence. Then I relate Brenda's woes. Margo listens carefully; she is a listener first. The lines developing in her brow and around her mouth convince me she cares before she condemns.

When I finish she asks: "Does she plan to move back into the house? If so, I can try to get the Homemaker's Club to help her."

The question is a good one for her to ask, a hard one for me to answer. Should Brenda risk the move? "I talked to her briefly last night. She wasn't sure what she wants to do. Her parents will let her stay with them. So, I'm debating whether to ask the court commissioner at the temporary hearing on Tuesday for permission to terminate her lease. If no one is going to live there, I think she should try to cut off the rent as soon as possible."

"That makes sense. Does he have an attorney?"

"Brenda said he isn't going to hire one, claims he doesn't need one."

"Which means, of course, you will have to deal with him directly. That should be interesting. Better be careful."

I nod. "I'll worry about that later. Right now, I'm concerned about Brenda. She understands the source of her problems: him. She's struggling with the obvious solution."

Margo digests my remarks before she replies. "She'll get on with it. It may take some time, but she'll get on with it. That's the Midwestern way."

She picks up one of my time sheets. "You're doing a good job keeping track of your time. One thing you may find helpful: at the end of the day add up the time. If it doesn't generally agree with the hours in the day you've worked, go over your time sheet to see what you've missed. Of course, I've repeatedly suggested that to Bob, and he smiles and thanks me and ignores it."

I give her a quizzical look. "You really want to help Brenda, don't you? You'll do anything to help a client. At the same time you're so concerned about our billings, about . . ."

"One is charity, the other business. We engage in both here, unfortunately, too much of the former. Someone has to be the business manager of this operation."

"I have nothing against making money. In fact, there was a time when I planned to make as much money as fast as I could. The plan was part of my dream." I see vapor trails of the dream drifting on the horizon of my mind.

Margo still appears uncertain of me, nevertheless assuring me, "You're going to do fine." She reaches for some typed notes, then holds them up to me. "I have to get this press release to the *Record* before it's old news about your coming here. What are your hobbies, your other interests?"

"I don't have any hobbies, never had time for them. Since I was young, it was school and work, except for the Army when it was work and sometimes school."

"You must be interested in something besides practicing law."

Except for Ann, I'm determined to keep the boxing buried in the archives of forgettable history. The story line on the gym in the basement will be that it's for exercise. "Let's see: I'm doing estate planning for my car. I'm checking bankruptcy law regarding my debts from law school. I like to drink beer, probably do more of that with Angie and Slider. Oh, and most of all, I like Ann Tompkins. How's that?"

"I'm not amused. You're not helpful. I want a sincere list by tomorrow morning." She leans toward me for emphasis. "I mean that."

I laugh as I walk toward my office. "Add to those items my recent discovery of some personal failures. I'm a confessor, and I'm not very good at driving in snowstorms."

For the next forty minutes I wade through documents in Suits' divorce and criminal files, closely examining the criminal complaint. Finally dropping the files, I dial the District Attorney's number in Lenora. While I wait for the ring, I cradle the receiver between my chin and shoulder so I can grab a legal pad and a pen.

"This is Brian Wellcamp."

"Brian, this is John Hall. I'm the new attorney in Winding River practicing with Bob Burnett."

"I heard you were in my office last Monday afternoon. I was over at the Sheriff's Department. Sorry I missed you. Plan to be at the bar meeting tonight?

"I plan to be. Listen, Brian, I'm representing. . . . " As I struggle to get it out, I hear Brian laughing.

"Sorry, but that's funny. He makes his way through the attorneys." Brian laughs again. "I hate to admit this, but Suits is so . . . I almost like him. He has such imagination you sometimes lose your focus."

"That's why I'm getting sucked in." I pick up the copy of his criminal complaint and scan it as I continue. "There's a hearing before the judge on Wednesday on the fiasco at his wife's residence . . . "

"Right, fell through the door and wound up hiding in a closet. That's vintage Suits."

"Would you consider some type of ordinance violation rather than a misdemeanor disorderly conduct? I assume you're not serious about the breaking and entering."

"It's Monday morning, and I'm in a good mood. The thing is he has to stop going over to his wife's place. They have no children. He has no reason to go over there. If you can work out something with her attorney in the divorce case, then get the judge to approve a creative order for him to stay away from Norma, with some teeth in it if he violates it, I'll drop the charges. Also, he must pay for a new door and the cost to install it."

"Great. I'll get on it right away and get back to you. See you tonight."

All right. I make a fist with my right hand and punch it forward. Then, looking at the fist, I quickly open it. When I reviewed Suits' divorce file, I discovered Norma's attorney is Dick Minor. I dial his number in Algona. Minor is even more cooperative than I hoped. I'm beginning to understand why Burnett respects him; Minor is willing to look for solutions.

I scribble notes as I speak. "So the deal, as I understand it, is Suits cannot come to Norma's home for any reason without permission from your client, through you, or permission from the court."

"Correct. But, I want it emphasized in the order that he's prohibited from hanging around the area and from following her or intercepting her as she leaves the area. And, he has to pay for the door up front. I don't want to chase him for payment."

"Fair enough." I'm pleased. This is much better than trying to deal with Sanford Smith. It's a simple solution, without trickery, to a thorny problem. My distaste for Smith continues to grow.

After pouring another cup of coffee in the kitchen, I call Suits who argues with me about the details before agreeing to the settlement. I ask him to bring in another two hundred dollars to add to his retainer; then I call back to Minor and Wellcamp. The D.A. says he'll tell the judge the hearing is probably off. Before he has it cancelled, though, he wants to see the order and know Minor has approved it. I agree to get it done.

As soon as I hang up, I begin dictating the order. Halfway through, the phone rings again. "This is Jerry Larsen. You may recall we discussed setting up a corporation, or whatever, for our new business. We'd like to get an appointment to see you?"

"How about Wednesday at ten o'clock?"

"That's fine. We want to show you the building to give you some idea what we plan to do with it. So, allow time for a tour of the premises."

"Okay, Jerry. I appreciate your calling me."

I resume working on the order. I'm beginning to feel like an attorney, shifting back and forth between matters. Though, how should a novice small town attorney feel? I need to prod Burnett for more stories of his beginning days in practice. In spite of anguish over Brenda's situation, I'm also enjoying myself. Barely putting a coat on one client and ushering him out the door as another one enters and sheds a coat on the entryway rack, keeps me interested, eager to greet the next walk-in.

❧ ☙

"You Attorney Hall?" A short, middle-aged man with a large head and a strange eye set, wearing a deep blue parka with the hood up and his hands in the pockets, stands in the doorframe.

Where did he come from? Margo must have stepped out of her office or she would have warned me. I jump up and move to him. "I am. Come in and sit down." I try to shake a hand but both of the man's hands remain in the pockets of his parka.

"Benny." He pulls a traffic citation out of a pocket and hands it to me as we sit down. "I got this ticket."

I begin reading the ticket.

"The butcher sent me."

"Who?"

"The butcher. You know, Bear Path."

"Bear Path?" I lay the ticket on my desk.

"Yeah, you know. The butcher said you was in his place on Sunday night . . . week ago."

"You mean that little tavern sandwiched in between some mobile homes and an abandoned store about sixty miles south of here? You're talking about the guy who sold me some gas for my car because the gauge was on empty?" Maybe that's where I should have ditched Billy. But, then I didn't know about the knife.

"Yep. He used to run the store there, him and his wife. He was the butcher. Now he runs the tavern." He smiles proudly. "He sent me."

I eye the man for a moment and then pick up the ticket. "Looks like you were speeding on the highway outside the village limits of Winding River."

"That ain't right. They don't get you for that."

"Why is that? According to the citation, you were going seven miles an hour over the speed limit." I inspect the ticket closely, noting a state trooper issued it. "One of the village policemen or a county deputy sheriff might not issue a citation at that speed. The state police may be tougher."

"But, see that ain't right."

"It's speeding, Benny. I can't do much for you. If you'd been going, say, another five miles over, I could try to get the citation reduced to save you points. Get it reduced to a three-point rather than a six-point violation. You were going seven over, so that's a three-point violation. I can't do better than that."

"No, it was only two over. I shouldn't get no ticket for two over."

I re-examine the citation. "Benny, you were clocked going sixty-two in a fifty-five zone. That's seven over, not two."

"No. Don't you understand? They give you the first five."

Trying to stifle a laugh, I explain it again but see Benny isn't buying it.

"The butcher says you don't get a ticket if you're going less than five over."

"But, . . ."

Benny stands up. "I'm gonna get the butcher to explain it to you."

"Okay." I hand the ticket back and watch Benny stuff it, along with his hands, in his parka and slowly move out the door.

Shaking my head, I grab another cup of coffee from the kitchen and duck into Margo's office to find out if she knows the man.

Margo looks up from her typewriter. "Where's he from?"

"Bear Path."

"No, I don't know him. That's a strange area, though. There's a lot of inbreeding down there." She resumes typing, after a few moments looking up to see me staring at her. "I know, but it's true."

"I'm sure it is."

I head back to my office, pausing to turn around in Margo's doorway. "As soon as I finish drafting an order on Suits' criminal case, I'm going to see Earl Schmidt. Bob said Earl has trouble driving so I should go out to his farm."

♌ ♍

Following the route Burnett explained to me, I drive two miles south of the village and then head west on a town road, over the same ridge that runs under the office. The car is warm from the bright sun burning through the windshield. I admire the strange formations on the trees created by wind blown snow. I'm still north of the pine tree line that sets apart the dairy farms to the south. As I drive further west from the national forest toward Algona, the woods part in places, leaving open fields. Then coming over the crest of a hill I see Earl's farm.

At the far end of forty acres of open land is an aged, two-story, white frame house with siding boards missing, showing the underlying black insulation. Off the far side of the house is a hip roof barn, the roof bare of shingles in places and the sides weathered gray. Attached to the barn is a concrete silo partially covered by leafless vines. An abandoned stone smokehouse, with a large tree projecting from the middle of the roofless building, sits behind the house, near a leaning garage. Torn apart automobiles and trucks, along with a rusted assortment of outdated farm equipment, rise above the snow. I'm no farmer and can't imagine what lies in the fields beneath the snow, but I know the farm died a long time ago.

Smoke drifts from a metal chimney pipe extending above the garage. As I pull up to the front of the building, a small, wiry looking old man with a weathered face, wearing double flannel shirts and a leather cap with earflaps, comes out the door. Burnett told me Earl is ninety-one years old. "Good morning," I say as I climb out of *Rusty*, carrying a legal pad in one hand. With the other, I shake a thin hand with a surprisingly strong grip.

The old man leans toward me, as if he has not heard me, then straightens up and raises a finger. He fiddles with a hearing aid. "I forgot. I had it turned down. There was a guy come by this morning wanting to hunt rabbits, and I told him to take off and turned it down when he kept after me. Hell, I feed the rabbits." He chuckles. "Come into the shop."

The single, large room is surrounded by workbenches with tools hanging above them and shelves crammed with large parts and jars full of screws, nuts and bolts, nails and other small parts. A table saw, band saw, drill machine, welding tanks and equipment, and disassembled motors and machines occupy much of the rest of the area. In the center of the room is a large wood-burning stove.

While I inspect a boiler connected to the stove, Earl walks over to the boiler, and taps a foot on the floor. "It heats the floor. The stove heats the water, and it's circulated through pipes under the floor." He smiles. "I built it."

"Burnett said your nickname is 'Tinker.'"

"Ah." He waves his right arm. "I like to putz around." He worms his way to a shelf where he shuffles through parts and pulls out a large clock from which he brushes dust with his shirtsleeve. "This clock used to hang in the bank in Winding River. They got that big fireplace . . . "

"I've seen it."

"Well, I rigged up a deal to catch the downdraft in the chimney so that it wound the clock. They used it for a long time." He shrugs. "Things change."

Earl replaces the clock before working his way back to the stove. He motions for me to sit in one of two chairs at a table with a checkerboard on it, beyond blistering distance of the stove. "Old Ed, from down the road, comes in a few days a week to play. No one ever wins. We always wind up doing something else before we finish."

"How old is Old Ed?"

"Hum, I think Ed's in his eighties now." Earl catches my smile and laughs. He reaches for a coffee pot on the back of the stove. "You want a cup?"

"No thanks. I've had enough this morning. How can I help you?"

Earl pours himself coffee. "I need to do some *es*state planning."

"Do you have a will?"

"No. Never had one made. Myrtle and I were always going to get ones made; we never did. Anyway, everything we owned was in both our names. Attorney Burnett took care of transferring her share to me when she died six years ago. He told me to see him about a will." He waves his hands. "It never got done."

"Do you have assets other than the farm?"

"My pickup and a few dollars in a savings account; they tell me at the bank when there's no more in it. I don't use checks; pay cash for everything. And, I got social security. That's about it. I never made much money in my life, never cared to. The main thing was I liked being my own boss, and doing what I wanted to do. Myrtle and I farmed, had dairy cows, for a long time. As a farmer you get to do a little of everything—plant and harvest crops, take care of the livestock, breed cows, be a vet, a mechanic, a bookkeeper—a lot of hard work, but you don't punch a time clock. Oh, I did that once in a while. When we really needed money, I worked in the mill at Lenora. Mostly, I made it here."

I lean back in my chair, crossing my legs and placing the legal pad on my thigh. "Sounds like you don't have a complicated estate. Tell me about your heirs? I understand that you don't have any children, and I assume your parents are deceased. Any brothers or sisters?"

"None. I'm the last one in my family." He sets his coffee cup on the checkerboard table. "What I've been thinking about is giving my farm to the government to add to forest lands, something like that."

"I know there are several conservation groups interested in acquiring farmland."

Earl further wrinkles an already wrinkled face. "I've read about some of those organizations. I'd rather give it right to the government. I'd like to see most of this place returned to the woods."

"I can help you look into the matter. You'd have to consider the tax ramifications. To treat the gift as a charitable donation, you'd have to give it to an organization qualified by the IRS as a tax deductible, charitable organization. You would . . . "

Earl laughs as he puts up his hands to stop me. "I don't need tax deductions. I don't pay any income taxes."

"I was thinking about reducing estate taxes."

He removes his cap and shakes it out. "Here's the other thing. I don't know if I'll have anything to leave."

"Why's that?"

"I owe the bank in Winding River about twenty-seven hundred dollars, and I've got no way to pay it." From his shirt pocket, Earl pulls out a folded sheet of paper, unfolds it and hands it to me.

A letter from Sanford A. Smith, Attorney at Law, to Earl P. Schmidt, dated January 2, 1976. Smith advises Earl he represents the bank, and unless Earl pays the bank the money owed within thirty days, Smith is going to commence an action in county court to foreclose the farm.

"I've got until February third. No way can I come up with the money. Myrtle was sick quite awhile with cancer. We had insurance, but it didn't cover everything. We used up all our savings with her illness and the funeral." He shrugs his shoulders and sticks out his hands, "So, that's it. It's okay, though, I had a good wife, and I got to do what I wanted to do in life. If there's going to be nothing left, then that's the way it'll be."

Earl's plight is obvious. I seek solutions. "You've got more land than you need to live on. Why don't you sell some acres to pay off the mortgage?"

He perks up. "Exactly what I thought, been trying to do it for years. But, nobody wants to buy any land from me. I've had it listed with several realtors, and they showed it to lots of folks. Then they don't want to buy it. I guess they don't like the view. All that stuff you see out there, though, that's all I got, and it all means something to me. I never know when I'm going to need a part or a piece of something. I lived through the Depression when you learned never to throw anything away."

"What about selling some of your vehicles or farm machinery? Maybe have an auction."

"Ah, it's all junk to them. They won't pay anything for it."

"How about some type of refinancing?"

"Nah, not with my record. The bank won't do it, and I don't blame them. I borrowed the money, and I should pay it back." He shrugs his shoulders and sticks out his hands again. "So, that's it."

I rise and ease around the room, touching things as I walk. Earl sits and watches me. "I'll have to think about your situation."

"That's fine, I'm not going anywhere, at least I hope I'm not. You never know."

"Do you have copies of your loan papers? I'd like to review them."

"In the house." Earl slowly gets to his feet, massaging his lower back as he rises.

We enter through the back door, which Earl can only partially open due to piles of newspapers stacked against the wall behind it. The kitchen table and counter are clean, but the rest of the room is as cluttered as the shop. The walls of the dining room and living room are hidden behind huge stacks of old magazines and newspapers and cardboard boxes.

Earl points to the piles with pride. "If I need to look up something, I've got it all here." He pulls a magazine out of a stack and hands it to me.

The date is April 1938. What can Earl possibly want from the magazine? I wonder if anyone from the bank has inspected the premises in the last twenty years. By the time the bank pays to have all of the junk and other personal property removed from the premises and then the buildings and silo torn down and removed, does the property have a negative value?

Earl digs the loan papers out of a drawer in a hutch in the dining room. "I think that's all I got, except for some other letters from the bank. They're in the shop."

Back in the shop, Earl hands the letters to me. I take another look around the room. On a shelf near where I'm standing is a metal contraption with grooved slides welded together to form what looks like a tangled, miniature roller coaster. "What's this?"

"It's a marble rack. I built it years ago for a neighbor kid. Somehow I got it back." He moves over to me. Rummaging through items on the shelf behind me, Earl pulls out a dusty cloth bag. After he blows the dust off the bag, he opens the drawstrings and removes a marble and places it on the top slide. It rolls slowly down the slide, then up another slide, down again and continues a roller coaster ride until it shoots onto the floor. "How do like it?"

"Great, Earl." I pick up the marble and hand it to him. I *am* intrigued with the gadget.

Earl removes the rack from the shelf and hands it to me, along with the bag of marbles. "Take it with you. Have some fun with it." He laughs. "You'll be the only lawyer around with one."

"Thanks, but you ought . . ."

"Nah, take it. Maybe you can find some kid who would like it."

17

I plop in a chair in front of Burnett's desk, speaking as soon as he raises his eyes to mine. "Earl could have driven to the office."

"Yes, he could have, though with difficulty."

"You wanted me to see his place."

Burnett leans back in his chair and removes his glasses. "Yes."

"Your clients are very important to you."

"Yes, they are, and now you have the time to get to know them."

"How does that square with not getting too involved in your client's case so you don't lose perspective?"

"If you know things about your client, have an understanding of who your client is, it will help in your representation." Burnett opens a lower desk drawer, and puts a foot on it as he leans back again. "On the other hand, John, you still must have the ability to pull back from it all, to become detached, as if you were an outside observer. When you do, all those things you've learned about your client will aid you in your appraisal of the situation. You may be able to view a small woods rather than a clump of trees."

I shake my head. "I thought about Earl's situation on the way back to the office. I don't know what we can do for him." I hand Burnett the letter from Smith.

Burnett reads it and hands it back. "After the Summons and Complaint are filed, we should file a Notice of Appearance for Earl. Assuming Smith proceeds correctly, and you should review the pleadings carefully before making that assumption, there's probably no defense, so no Answer is necessary."

"I can file some kind of Answer to stall it, rather than let Smith get a quick default judgment."

"No, you should not file anything that may even appear to be a frivolous Answer. In any event, since the property is a farm over twenty acres, any Sheriff's sale won't be for over a year. Hopefully, in that time, you can come up with a solution."

I nod again. "I'll talk to Smith. Maybe I can get him to hold off for awhile."

"Good luck."

"Yeah, you're right. What about fees? Is this going to be a pro bono case?"

"To some extent. Bill him, and he'll pay." Burnett's eyes dart to Margo's office and back. He lowers his voice. "But, go easy on the billing."

In my office, I check the mail on my desk. I chuckle as I read a goofy card from my brother and then stand it endwise on the corner of my desk. A letter from an adjuster with Grocers Mutual Insurance Company acknowledges receipt of my letter of representation of Suits and asks me to contact her regarding the fall at Wills Grocery.

From near the bottom of a stack of files on my desk, I pull out the *Schultz v. Herdina* file and begin dictating from a formbook a Satisfaction of Judgment. Then I dictate a letter to Sanford Smith with a payout figure I calculated with interest through Thursday. I tell Smith I'll exchange the Satisfaction for receipt of the funds. There's no sense in calling him to attempt to get a delay on the foreclosure of Earl's farm. Smith will want to trade off any concession he would give Earl for something off the Schultz judgment. I think I owe it to Schultz to get him every cent. How can I trade Schultz's money for a delay of Earl's foreclosure?

I take the dictation into Margo.

She looks up from her typing. "We have cake for lunch."

"You baked a cake?"

"No. Mrs. Sunstroms' mother brought it in this morning. She said her daughter baked it Friday afternoon. They appreciated your last minute help."

"That's nice."

"You should send them a thank-you card." Margo opens a drawer in her desk, rifles through cards, pulls out one and hands it to me. "Sign it . . . legibly."

After lunch with Margo, I stare at a stack of abstracts, a separate stack of income tax returns, and a miscellaneous stack of files. Ignoring all of them, I began reading Earl's loan papers. Soon I yell, "yes!" I make a few notes and toss the papers aside. Then I drive to Lenora and as preparation for Brenda Krueger's temporary hearing, sit in the back of the courtroom while the Family Court Commissioner presides over a hearing.

On the drive back to the office I stop at the police station and discover that Bill Krueger had been before a judge in the morning and was released on bail. I probe for more information on Ginger Buckman's accident, but discover nothing further from the police. At the office, I call Slider and ask him if he's found out anything. He hasn't, but he'll ask around.

I scoot my chair to the window behind my desk. In the fading sunlight, I see a buck and two does wending their way through the snow-covered pines in the vacant lot between the office and a home down the street. I watch them until they are spooked by a barking dog and flee, their tails up, showing the white fur underneath.

❧ ❧

Burnett and I enter the old, four-story hotel through the side door leading into the bar. The upstairs rooms are now apartments. A dozen plus lawyers, all wearing sport coats and ties, except for a woman in a dress, are seated or standing at the bar talking, most of them waving their hands as they speak. Burnett leads the way, introducing me to the attorneys. On the way to Lenora, Burnett explained there are about twenty-five lawyers in the two county bar association, including the two district attorneys, county corporation counsels, a few retired attorneys who practiced elsewhere and the vice-president of one of the banks in Lenora. It's obvious the attorneys are enjoying themselves.

"Good to see you again." Dick Minor extends his hand to me as Burnett drifts off. "Let me buy you a drink." He motions the bartender over and introduces me.

"Beer is fine." From my inside coat pocket, I pull three folded sheets of paper and hand them to Minor. "Draft of the order we discussed, along with two copies of a stipulation signed by Suits. I assume you'll get your client's signature. If you can give me a call tomorrow morning, maybe we can get this wrapped up. I gave a copy to the D.A."

Minor nods as he stuffs the folded sheets into the inside pocket of his sport coat. He takes a bottle of beer from the bartender, hands it to me, and then raises his bottle and clanks it against mine. "Good luck here."

"Thanks." I take a swig on the bottle. "Tell me about Algona. I assume you're not the only lawyer there."

"It's smaller than Winding River. There're two of us in practice there, a semi-retired attorney and me."

"How did you wind up there?"

"I was born there. I never wanted to live anywhere else. When I graduated from law school, I tried to get in with the other lawyer, but he wanted to remain alone. So I joined the ranks of the sole practitioners."

"It had to be tough starting out on your own."

"You're right. What kept me going was the other attorney being very helpful. There was enough work to go around, so he never perceived me as a threat." He grins. "You know the old saying, 'If there's one attorney in town, he'll starve to death. If there're two, they'll both earn a decent living.'"

I laugh. "That could apply to Winding River." I search through the attorneys at the bar. "Smith isn't here."

"He knows no one likes him. Anyway, since he's smarter and more competent than the rest of us and has repeatedly informed us of those facts, what would be his purpose in coming here?"

"Why couldn't he be in Algona?"

"Because we wouldn't let him." Minor laughs. "Actually, he's good for business. He's not nearly as smart as he thinks. Tell me, why did you decide to come up here?"

"I've been trying to answer that question. This isn't what I expected to be doing."

"What did you expect?"

"That I would be a big city lawyer, handling high profile cases and making lots of bucks."

"You'll never be that here. There aren't any big cities in these counties. Once in a great while there's a sensational murder case, but some city lawyer usually winds up with the defense. And, no attorney here makes a lot of bucks."

"I don't have a good answer. I worked in a large firm during my last year in school, and it didn't appeal to me. Perhaps I should have opted for a smaller firm in Milwaukee or Chicago."

"Why did you go to law school?"

"Basically, I wanted to get ahead. There were other reasons. My senior year in college a law student roomed in the house I lived in. Interested in politics, he thought a law school education would help him with the legislative process." I try to recall an image of the gregarious student. "He had an aura of importance about him. The enthusiasm he exhibited in preparing for his classes, the excitement in his voice when he discussed politics and the law and what he believed in was contagious. I thought, and I still think, he'll do something important someday. Anyway, he motivated me to think beyond college, to do something other than get a diploma and hit the streets looking for a job."

Minor has a far off look on his face. "I guess most of us here got motivated by someone or something; otherwise, we wouldn't be here."

"I don't know, Dick, I'm not a legal scholar and never will be. I'm also not a crusader. I just like helping people and want to do something important. I want to make the kind of impact on people's lives that other people made on mine." Someday will I spool back the reels of my life to this fork in the road? I signal the bartender to bring us another round.

"You don't think you can do that here?"

"A lady friend of mine has me thinking about that. She would ask, 'What is it you consider important?' "

The bartender sets a bottle of beer before each of us.

"Thanks for the beer, John. I noticed at the closing on Friday that you seemed to be enjoying yourself."

"I am. It's . . . I feel like I'm being left out."

"Left out of what?"

"The big game? I'm not sure anymore."

Minor catches the look of doubt on my face as the lawyers begin moving into the dining room. He pats me on the back. "Well, John, you won't be left out here. This is the only place in the world where you can attend a meeting of the Timber and Big Lakes Counties Bar Association." He pauses. "We may not have impressive credentials, but we can make a lot of noise."

The Practice

18

There she is with her head down again. Brenda Krueger sits on a wooden bench in the rotunda of the courthouse, holding her hands together and staring at the intricate design in the marble floor. I wonder if she sees anything. The scene reminds me of a case discussed in law school where a lawyer asked a witness whether the witness had looked through the keyhole in a door after hearing commotion inside, and the witness said, "Yes," and the lawyer went on, failing to ask if the witness had *seen* anything.

"Hello, Brenda." I sit next to her. There are those people who I always want to help, often without knowing why. In her case, the why is easy. "Are you okay?"

"I'm all right. Sometimes, I'm down. Other times I'm glad I'm going ahead with the divorce. I couldn't take it anymore."

"Look at me." Brenda lifts her head as it turns. "This isn't your fault. This isn't the way you wanted your marriage to turn out. I know you did everything you could to prevent this from happening."

"I tried. After the first year we were married, I knew we were going to have problems. They kept getting worse, and Bill wouldn't do anything to change." She starts to cry.

I reach in my coat pocket to extract a small package of tissue. "I thought I better bring some."

Brenda wipes her eyes. "Thank you, Mister Hall. You've very kind."

"You know, Brenda, you can call me John."

"Thank you, Mister Hall."

Opening my briefcase on my knees, I take out her file and remove a four-page form. "I had Margo type up the Financial Disclosure Statement form you dropped off at the office. I need to have you sign it." I close the briefcase so she can write on the top and hand her a pen.

She signs the form and the copies. "We've got a lot of debts, don't we?"

"You do, though I suppose your situation is not that unusual." I take the pen and the forms back. I start to give her a copy of the documents but decide to wait until we get into the hearing room. She has other things on her mind.

"Most of the debts piled up when Bill was laid off or got fired. He was fired twice, once for showing up drunk and once for swearing and attacking his foreman."

"Whatever temporary order the Family Court Commissioner makes, there probably won't be enough money for both of you. Although, if your lease is terminated, and you each live with parents, you won't have rent and then . . . "

"I doubt that will be true. Bill's parents will probably charge him rent. They're that kind." She wipes her eyes again. "I'm thinking about moving back into the house. My parents and a friend will help me fix it up. My parents don't have much either, and I can't expect them to take care of me and the boys."

"What do you want to do? I need to know what to argue to the court commissioner."

Brenda looks at me. "What do you think I should do?"

"I think . . . " I stall as I try to separate friendly advice from legal advice. "As I stated, from a monetary standpoint, and that's important in your situation, you would be better off living at your parents' home. On the other hand, I understand there are other considerations. How about your lease? Do you have a written lease, or is it a month-to-month tenancy?"

"We have a written lease. We renewed it last August."

"There may be a problem if your landlord doesn't want to let you out of the lease."

Brenda perks up, a serious look on her face. "Oh, I don't think so. After what Bill did, I'm sure our landlord would love to get rid of us."

"I'm sure you're right. Well, unless you change your mind, I'm going to take the position for you that you're going to move back into the house once it's cleaned up."

"And get some furniture. He even sawed up the bed frames and cut the springs."

"He must have been very tired when he got done."

"Oh, he's very strong, especially when he's half-drunk."

I start to snicker, thinking she has a sense of humor despite her problems, but stop when I see her eyes wide open underneath a wrinkled brow. "Let's go upstairs."

As we step into a conference room near the courtroom, I switch on the light. The room is almost sterile: a conference table with six chairs, a smaller table in the corner with a telephone on it, and a wall clock. That's it.

"We'll sit on this side." I gesture to my right as I set my briefcase on the table. Then I fold my coat in half and drop it on a chair.

Brenda hangs her coat on the back of a chair next to mine and looks around the room. "This is the, what do you call him, commissioner's courtroom?"

"It is today. The judge is using the courtroom. Anyway, this is an informal hearing."

Lester Erickson, a bantamweight man in his forties, light hair and a small chin, wearing glasses and a checkered sport coat with and tie, enters the room. After I introduce the family court commissioner to Brenda, he sits at the end of the table by the door and meticulously spreads the contents of his briefcase. He checks the clock showing 4:05 p.m.

His voice is high pitched as he says to Brenda, "Is your husband going to be here?"

"I don't know," Brenda answers in a lower voice.

"Mr. Hall, have you been contacted by an attorney representing . . ."

Bill Krueger storms into the room, slams the door shut, and slouches in a chair across from Brenda. Stocky, with a stubby beard, he wears a green and brown cap and a worn jacket over a hooded sweatshirt. He fits the image of his present occupation of a construction worker laid off for the winter and drawing unemployment while he hunts, according to his own schedule of seasons, whatever in the Northwoods comes into his path. I understand how Bill demolished his home, and with the scowl on his face, recognize he is capable of demolishing the room and everyone in it.

Erickson fidgets with his papers, avoiding eye contact with Bill, as he addresses him. "Are you represented by an attorney?"

"Don't need one."

"All right. Do you have a financial statement?"

"Don't need one."

Erickson fiddles with his papers again.

Observing the continuing scowl on Bill's face, I feel my hands curling into fists. The man appears to be ready to explode. I attempt to disperse the acrimonious air. "Here's our statement." I hand the original to Erickson and slide a copy across the table to Bill, who ignores it.

Erickson scans the statement and addresses Bill. "Have you looked over your wife's statement?"

"Don't need to."

"Well, Mr. Krueger, if you're not going to furnish any financial information, I'll have to proceed based on the information furnished by your wife." He pauses for a response, but there is none.

I glance at Brenda before speaking to Erickson. She's staring at her lap. "Mrs. Krueger wants to continue to reside in the house." I relate Bill's arrest for the Friday night rampage. Then stress Brenda will attempt to remake a home there in spite of the destruction of their household goods.

"Any objections, Mr. Krueger?"

Bill smirks and glares at Brenda.

"All right." Erickson begins filling in a Temporary Order form with carbon copies. He checks off a box indicating that Bill is to vacate the home immediately. "Mr. Krueger, is there anything you need to remove from the home?" Hearing no response, he makes another check on the form.

Erickson looks at me. "How about custody of the children?"

"Brenda wants temporary custody of the children, and any visitation rights will have to be at set times and away from the home. There's a history of physical abuse of my client by Mr. Krueger."

Bill straightens up and faces Brenda. "Well, you little shit head. Are you telling everybody about us now?"

Brenda jerks her head up. "Yes I am. I should have told about you long ago. And, and, I'm not a shit head, you are."

"So, Mr. Krueger, you have no objection to the custody arrangement?" Erickson waits before he makes another check on his form. "Next we need to address the issue of child support. Reviewing the financial statement prepared by Mrs. Krueger . . ."

Bill leans across the table. "Money, I gave you all my money."

"You gave me what you didn't drink up."

Rising, Bill takes out his wallet and flings the bills in it at Brenda. "Here's your money. It's all you're going to get, you worthless piece of crap."

Clearing his throat, Erickson breaks in. "We need some civility here. We need . . . "

Brenda jumps up and throws the money back at Bill. "I don't want your money. I want back the nine years I wasted on you."

"Oh, yeah. You want it again, don't you? You want me to straighten you out." Bill starts around the far end of the table.

Erickson leaps up and retreats to the door.

I spring out of my chair and pass Brenda as Bill comes around the far end of the table toward me. I'm activated not by any conscious thought process but by instinctive reactions developed on the streets of my youth. I stop and put up open hands. "Calm down, Mr. Krueger."

"Up yours, asshole." Bill swings at me. I block the shot with my left forearm and with my right hand, immediately grab the lower part of Bill's blocked arm and twist it up into a hammerlock. Using my left hand to clutch the back of Bill's jacket, I push him against the wall and look for Erickson. He has crept into the corner and is dialing the phone.

Brenda tries to get around me to get at Bill. Blocking her way, I feel my hold weakening as the muscled Bill wiggles and bends over. Damn, he's strong.

"I'm through with you." Brenda tries to get a leg around me to kick Bill. "I'm not taking it any more."

I want Erickson's help, but he's now backing into the hallway. As I lose the hammerlock, I wrestle Bill to the floor. A deputy sheriff races in and pushes Brenda aside. While I use my body to pin Bill to the carpet, the deputy gets a cuff on Bill's right arm, then edges me off and cuffs the other arm. With my help, the deputy straightens Bill up and drags him into the hallway as another deputy arrives.

"You're all a bunch of shit-asses," Bill yells as the deputies drag him away. "I'll get you Brenda. I'll get you some way. I'll do . . . " His voice fades out.

I try to calm myself as I shuffle back into the room. It has been awhile; I need to get in shape. Boy, is he strong. I wouldn't have made it as a wrestler.

Brenda is sobbing and shaking. "I don't know what happened to me. Am I in trouble?"

"No, you're not. What happened is you've begun to lift a huge weight off your back." I help her to sit in her chair.

Re-entering the room, Erickson has the appearance of an accident victim in shock. He stares at his form, as though seeking sanctuary in the structure of the intersecting lines on the paper. I watch him with disgust before I dismiss my feelings toward the slight attorney. After all, Bill is out of Erickson's weight class.

The three of us sit in silence until I address the court commissioner: "So, what do we do now? Proceed without him?"

He glances at me and then at his form. "We've already reached agreement on who will reside in the home and on custody." He picks up Brenda's financial statement. "I'll finish the order as far as child support and alimony based on the sworn information furnished." Erickson looks at me again, his face flat. "Do you think it will make any difference what I order?"

I shake my head sideways. Brenda has retreated into herself. She stares at the carpet, holding her right hand with her left.

掕 掓

"Hey, Slider," I call out as I enter the taproom. Despite the afternoon wrestling bout, I'm excited, excited for Brenda. She made an unexpected, but needed, turn in her life. If only for a few moments, she released some of the anger pent up in her over the past nine years. I hope she won't turn back.

I move down the bar to Angie. "And here we have the infamous court reporter of Timber County."

"Be careful how you choose your words, Hall. Remember, words are my business."

"Not that you do anything with words other than take them down." I wink at Slider who sets a stein of beer before me. I turn back to Angie. "What was going on in the courtroom at four o'clock?"

"Probate hearing. Unbelievable. You should have been there."

"I had a temporary hearing on a divorce. Talk about trouble."

"Yeah, well *this* was something to see and hear."

I feel deflated as I hear Angie go on. I know, though, I can't discuss my cases with these guys, even if the conversation is limited to events they will soon hear about. Burnett has warned me about shooting my mouth off, especially in a tavern. Besides ethics and confidentiality considerations, in a village where the residents all know each other, the idea of their attorney blabbing about their case in a tavern will not set well. Worse, Burnett claims, is to get drunk and embarrass yourself in public. From the first day, he has preached the professional person's code of conduct.

Angie continues. "It's all public record now. And, of course, you guys would never let it be known that the finest court reporter in the Northwoods can't keep his mouth shut."

Slider leans an elbow on the bar. "Of course. Now tell us about it."

"This old guy has four children. His wife is dead. He owned a nice piece of lake property with the family home on it. He knew that they all wanted it. So, what did he do? He made a will himself leaving the property to the child who is the highest bidder."

"What?" Slider frowns. "Why didn't he give each one a one-fourth share?"

"That's seems logical." Angie drinks from his stein. "According to one of the children, he wanted to create as much money for the estate as possible, but wanted to make sure at least one of his children got the place. So, he didn't want the property sold outright and then the sales proceeds divided up among them."

Slider is shaking his head. "That's nuts, absolutely nuts. I mean, yeah, three of them will get more money if they bid the price up, but the buyer gets stuck with the tab and . . ."

Angie cuts him off. "But, the buyer gets part of the extra money he's paying as part of his one fourth share of the proceeds, and he gets the property which is what they all want. Of course, if they keep bidding, eventually the buyer is going to have a hellava tab."

"Great for family reunions," I add.

Slider is still skeptical. "What kind of lawyer would write that will?"

"It wasn't a lawyer. Like I said, he wrote it himself."

"Is that any good?" Slider looks at me.

"A holographic will, that is, a will written by the testator, may be admissible in Wisconsin, provided that certain conditions are met, like the testator being competent to make it, having it properly witnessed . . . "

Angie points a finger at me. "Exactly what the judge said, and he met all of the conditions. Still, what a crazy thing to do, huh? Then, the guy didn't make any provision for disposition of his personal property. After the sale of the house, proceeds from the sale of everything else were left to the children in equal shares. The problem is, the kids had all been promised certain items. Now they find out that if they can't agree, everything gets sold, and they divide up the sale proceeds. And, they couldn't agree. They were all bickering, yelling at each other." Angie sips from his beer stein. "It's true what they say about estates; some are worse than any divorce."

"What a mess," Slider mumbles.

Angie grins. "On the other hand, the decedent beat some attorney out of a hundred bucks for drafting a simple will."

Slider shakes his head. "Jesus, Angie, you're a cynic."

"Yeah, and I don't get paid for being one like the lawyers do. Isn't that right, John?"

"I've had enough law for one day."

While Angie and Slider go on, I wonder if I could ever be a judge and sit in court all day listening to the lies, the quarreling and the petty complaints of many of the litigants, let alone deal with the devious, pompous and grandstanding attorneys. I know I would lack the "judicial temperament" that supposedly allows judges to hear and see it all while maintaining their normal blood pressure readings and suppressing their urges to strangle litigants and lawyers.

Angie motions to Slider to fill our steins. "When we finish these, let's go across the road and see Mary."

"Mary?"

"She's a bartender at Alma's. You'll love her."

"I think I should go home, wherever that is."

"Ah, come one. We'll have some fun."

❧ ❦

Angie carries something in a small paper bag. Now what? We cross the highway and stroll into the smoky and dimly lit tavern with a sparse but rowdy crowd. Behind the bar with a hand on one of the taps is a young, dark haired woman, wearing a tight sweater. She's so top heavy I'm surprised she doesn't topple forward. We take barstools near the far end of the bar as the bartender follows us and the rest of the eyes at the bar follow her.

"Beer, Angie?"

Angie coughs and clears his throat. "I'm not feeling well."

"What's the matter with you?"

"I don't know. Give us two beers, one for my friend, John."

"You have a nice looking friend. I hope he has better manners than you do."

Angie strains a sick laugh. "As if this is the House of Manners."

When she moves up the bar to draw the beer, Angie leans toward me. "They call her 'Mattress Mary.'"

I laugh. "I'm not surprised."

Under the counter, Angie hands me the bag. "Now look, when I nudge you with my elbow, take the can out of the bag and empty it on the bar. Be careful, because I've got the lid off."

"What?"

"Shush. Do it the way I told you."

Mary sets the glasses of beer before us. Angie coughs again and then starts gagging.

"You don't look very good." Mary is frowning as she picks up Angie's twenty-dollar bill from the bar.

"Maybe a little beer will clear my throat."

She looks at me and then moves to the cash register to make change, standing with her back to us. Angie elbows me. He starts gagging again and then lets out a blat as I spread the contents of the can on the bar.

Mary turns around and sees the mess on the bar, grabs her mouth and runs for the ladies room. The other customers stop talking and look toward the end of the bar. Grinning, Angie grabs the empty vegetable soup can from me and holds it up. The other customers hesitate and then roar.

I can't help laughing, at the same time worrying about Mary. "You rotten guy, Bellini."

Angie goes around the end of the bar and picks up a rag. He rapidly cleans the bar, dumps the rag and the mess in a trashcan, and then moves back to his barstool before Mary appears, shuffling across the room.

"What?" Mary goes behind the bar. "Where's . . ."

Angie sets the can on the bar. "I love vegetable soup, don't you, John?"

"Absolutely."

Mary stares at us, her face reddening as she pursues her lips. She begins frantically searching the bar and then the back bar.

"Uh, oh," Angie whispers to me as he scoops up his money except for a ten dollar bill. "She's going to throw something. Put a ten spot on the bar and get out of here."

The other customers are still laughing as we run out of the bar and go back across the highway toward Slider's.

"Damn it, Bellini. You did it to me again. That was a dirty trick."

"Funny, though, huh?"

"Sort of, but not for Mary. Look, I don't need the trouble. I'm trying to get accepted here."

Angie halts on the sidewalk in front of Slider's, grabbing my arm as he wrinkles his face. "Trouble? What are you talking about? She'll throw up any time for twenty bucks."

19

Creaks from my steps on the floorboards in the hallway ruin my attempt to sneak into my office to start the day.

"Where's my list?" Margo yells at me.

I back up and slink into her office. "Look, I don't know what to say. Can't you make up something for the *Record*?"

Margo ceases typing and faces me. "No. And while you're here, I got a call this morning from Mrs. Jensen. She lives above Wally & Laverne's." Margo narrows her eyes as only she can. "She was awakened last night by two young men singing and carrying on in the street. She didn't know one of them, but thought the other one was *that court reporter*. She thought I should know about the matter."

I feign concern. My headache makes it easy for me to keep from smiling. "I've heard Bellini drinks a little. He seems like a nice guy, probably got carried away."

"And you have no idea as to the identity of the other young man?"

"Who is this Mrs. Jensen? Is she an older woman? I think I saw her on the morning I arrived here and again on Friday evening."

Margo appears as though she has let slip a secret. "She's an invalid, taken care of by her daughter and son-in-law." Margo hesitates, now appearing as if she is uncertain whether to spill the rest of it. "She runs the switchboard for the village gossip line."

"And you're on the line?"

"No. She knows I won't give her any information, so I'm not on the line. She calls me when she feels I need to know something. She's also the Chief's downtown informant."

"Really. I wonder if she knows anything about Ginger Buckman's accident?"

"I already checked on it. She had gone to bed. The line opens early in the morning." Margo comes back to it. "You didn't answer my question."

"I'll work on the list this morning. It's going to be a short list. I'm not very complicated."

"I'm finding that not to be true." Margo narrows her eyes again. "Watch yourself, young man. This is a small village."

"Okay, mom." As I turn to walk back to my office, I see Margo try to hide the smile on her face. It's Angie's fault. He's the one who keeps telling me I should lighten up, though perhaps not that much. What has Burnett told me? "When you're alive people think of you for your work; after you're gone, they remember you for your conduct." Margo's right. I'll have to watch it . . . to watch Angie.

Sorting out the files on my desk, I pull out my notes on the review of Earl Schmidt's loan documents. Should I call Smith and point out the problem? Is that the right thing to do? I doubt Smith would do the same for me. Still, I have to talk to him. Ultimately, something has to be worked out or Earl will lose his farm. He owes the money; no one disputes the fact. *Call Smith re Earl* I scratch on a small pad. Since it's bound to spoil my day, I decide to place the call later on.

What to do about Ginger Buckman? The doctor's report hasn't arrived. Burnett warned me doctors don't reply quickly. Paperwork, especially dealing with lawyers, is one of the least pleasant parts of their profession. Anyway, until we can prove liability by something other than the unsubstantiated testimony of a questionable plaintiff, do we have a case? She definitely lost control of her motorcycle and suffered injuries, but why did she lose control? Is she telling the truth? Are the murky waters of her involvement with the drug-pushing boyfriend washing over the accident? I toss her file on top of Earl's file.

On Tuesday morning, Minor and Wellcamp told me they were satisfied with the order I prepared. Minor is going to have the judge in Suits' divorce case sign it, and Wellcamp is dismissing the criminal charges, reiterating he will not do so again. I slip the file on the bottom of the stack of Suits' files. I review Suits' other files, deciding nothing needs immediate attention. There's no point in calling the adjuster for Grocers Mutual until I get the medical report from Dr. Smeatshum.

I return to Margo's office, carrying a legal pad. "I forgot to mention that Brenda Krueger is going to move back into her house. So, if you can do anything for her . . ."

"I'll bring it up to the Homemakers."

"Thanks."

Walking quietly across the hallway to Burnett's office, I notice Henry Miller and Abstract appear deep into their own worlds, which I imagine are equally uncomplicated.

When I knock on the doorframe Burnett looks up from the *State Bar Bulletin* he's reading. "Come in."

"I might as well tell you now, because you're going to hear about it when you go to the courthouse." I sit down and summarize the wrestling match at Brenda's temporary hearing.

Burnett begins to laugh and cuts me off. "Margo told me all about it when I came in."

"What? She didn't say . . ."

"That's Margo."

"Bob, I didn't come here to fight."

"Sure you did. That's part of a small town lawyer's job. Of course, we use gentleman's rules."

"Bill Krueger is no gentleman."

"You should have known he wasn't from your conversations with Brenda. You're going to have some of those situations, especially when the other parties don't have attorneys to caution them on their behavior at the hearings."

"I was told when I came here I would have some excitement. Ann was right."

"Be careful you don't get hurt. You haven't seen the last of the weird characters."

Shifting in my chair, I put my right ankle on my left thigh to create a temporary desk and place the legal pad on it. "The Larsens are coming in at ten o'clock to discuss setting up a corporation for their new business. What are your thoughts on the type of business entity they need?"

Burnett leans back in his chair and removes his glasses. With a pensive look clouding his normal cheerful face, he begins with his familiar, "Well, John." It's exactly what I want to hear. When I return to my office, the first three pages of the legal pad are filled with notes. It's a primer that could be titled, *Considerations In Forming An Entity For A Small Business.*

❧ ❧

"My name is Ed Witt," the caller identifies himself. "I'm calling from Chicago. My wife and I are purchasing a tract of land in Timber County near Winding River. I was referred to you by the realtor handling the matter, Henry Miller."

"Yes, I know Mr. Miller." He *is* good for business. "How can I help you?"

"Mr. Miller said he would drop off at your office a copy of the offer to purchase and a spec sheet on the property. He said the sellers are furnishing an abstract, I believe he called it, and that I should get you to examine it for me."

"Sure, I can do that. Are you financing the purchase through a bank? If you are, I'll also need to do an opinion for the bank."

"No, we're paying cash. It's a vacant lot. We like the area and want to build a home there some day."

I scribble notes on a legal pad. "Has the offer to purchase been signed, or will Henry be dropping off a draft?"

"It's signed. It's scheduled to close in about thirty days. Is there a problem?"

"I'm wondering if you asked the seller to furnish you a survey?"

"No, we didn't. It's a vacant tract of lands in the woods. Mr. Miller said he would show us the corners, although that's going to be somewhat difficult because of the snow."

"You should get a survey. There could be encroachments, that is, overlaps of your boundary lines by neighboring properties. There may be old fences that through adverse possession could constitute the boundary lines rather than the legal description. There could also be unrecorded easements, like a road or a hiking trail, that allow continued use through what's called an 'easement by prescription.'"

After a pause, Witt speaks, "We didn't think about those things."

"Did you discuss with Henry whether the land will *perk*, that is, pass a soil percolation test? In other words, will the land support a conventional septic system?"

"We're not going to be building anything on it for some time."

"When you do build on it, you'll have to have approval for some type of sanitary waste disposal system. You want to know if a percolation test will show that you can have a standard septic system, rather than a mound system or, worse, a holding tank which needs to be pumped regularly. What about zoning? Is the land zoned, and if so, is it zoned for residential use? Can you even build on it?"

Witt pauses again. "I don't know about those things. I'm a buyer for a retail clothing company. We saw the *For Sale* sign, looked at the lot with Mr. Miller, fell in love with it, and signed an offer. Now you've got me worried." He sounds downcast.

I curse myself. I should have waited until I reviewed the offer and the spec sheet. Maybe my questions are answered. What am I doing chastising a new client like a teacher scolding an unprepared child? I have overdone the "sounding knowledgeable" routine. I should have practiced on Abstract what Burnett has been teaching me.

"I didn't mean to upset you, Mr. Witt. I imagine that you and your wife are excited about acquiring some land here. It is beautiful country. I'm sure you'll love it here. A couple of days ago I was watching some deer through my office window thinking it was such a beautiful setting, the serenity of . . . "

"Do you think we should try to cancel the offer and start over?"

"You can't do . . . No, I'll see that everything gets checked out. I . . . "

"I suppose you think we were a little impulsive."

Me? "Not at all. I'll look over everything carefully, and then we can discuss it further. In the meantime, *don't worry about it.*"

Nice job, I congratulate myself as I hang up. Scare the hell out of a new client, then attempt to back peddle by acting like a representative of the Timber County Chamber of Commerce, and finish with the four words Burnett told me clients fear the most. Now my headache is worse.

⁂

The Larsens come in smiling broadly, Jerry swooping his right hand in for a shake, followed by Judy's enthusiastic grip.

"Like your place." Jerry looks around the entrance hall. "Burnett's my parents' attorney, but I don't recall being here before."

"Nicely decorated." Judy adds. She admires the painting above the couch.

"I'm sure the credit belongs to Margo." I direct them into my office while Margo brings them coffee. I wonder why they bother to drink it; they don't need the caffeine.

At the bank I focused on the loan documents and the procedures and failed to inspect the Larsens. Jerry is slightly taller than myself with light hair; Judy is also tall, with blond hair. Both are in their early thirties, with athletic trimness, and move with an air of urgency. Burnett told me Jerry grew up in Winding River while Judy was raised in southwestern Wisconsin. They met in college. I remember they are both "talkers" and fast talkers; so fast I have difficulty in keeping up with my notes.

After I counsel them from Burnett's primer, Jerry nods slowly. "I'm impressed."

"I'm learning."

Judy takes notes as I speak, and it becomes clear to me she will be the administrative end of the business while Jerry handles operations. Both have the personalities to handle sales.

Judy is also asking the questions. "Since our primary concern is liability, should we form a corporation?"

"As I discussed, there are advantages and disadvantages to all of the types of business entities: sole proprietorship, partnership, corporation, joint venture. Since your business will be involved with manufacturing, in view of the increasing number of product liability lawsuits, you need to attempt to shield yourselves from personal liability. In other words, you should try to restrict any liability to a corporation so that in the event of a judgment against your business, the judgment holder is forced to satisfy the judgment from the assets of the corporation rather than from your personal assets."

Judy appears uncertain. "The business will have product liability insurance."

"Only up to a certain amount. If a judgment is entered against you for more than the amount of the insurance, you'll need protection against the overage. Wouldn't you rather have that judgment against the corporation than yourselves?"

Both nod affirmatively. I glance at Burnett's primer. "Even though you form a corporation, though, you will still have to hold yourselves out as a corporation; that is, always show the corporate name on letter-heads, billings, and purchase orders and sign documents as a corporate officer on behalf of the corporation. So creditors, for example, won't be able to argue they thought they were dealing with you personally. So the creditors won't, as they say, be able to 'pierce the corporate veil.'"

Judy is still taking notes. "I understand."

"After the Articles of Incorporation have been approved by the Secretary of State, and we obtain a corporate record book for your business with the stock certificates, you'll hold an initial stockholder's meeting. Before the meeting, I'll send you a memo concerning matters to be covered."

Jerry raises a finger. "Where does our accountant fit in?"

"Who's your accountant?"

"Gilbert Buckman. He has an office in Winding River."

"I think he has a daughter named Ginger."

Jerry looks at Judy who shrugs. "I've been away for a number of years."

"Well, talk to him before we file for the corporation. He can advise you on the tax consequences of using a corporation versus the other entities. There's a difference in tax rates. Also, you will have to decide whether you want to elect to be treated for tax purposes as a 'C corporation' or a 'Sub S corporation.' With the latter, losses could flow through to your personal income, reducing taxes. That's an election you'll have to make with the IRS, and there are time limits on making it."

Jerry nods again. "What about the name? Is that something we need to know now?"

"I was getting to that." I stick closely to the primer. "I'd like to know the name before I file papers with the Secretary of State's Office. Recognize you won't be able to use a name that's already in use, or close to a name in use. Normally that's not a problem if the name is specific. Do you have a name in mind?"

Jerry checks with Judy before he speaks: "J & J Manufacturing Company, Inc."

"Hum. That name may be in use, or something so close to it that the State won't allow it. Though, we can check the name before we file the papers."

"Okay," Judy speaks up, "How about J & J Larsen Manufact . . . "

"That may be okay. Still, there are a lot of Larsens in Wisconsin."

Jerry interrupts. "Why not Winding River Manufacturing Co., Inc.?"

Judy gives approval as I nod my assent.

"All right then." Jerry jumps up. "Let's go down to the river and look over the site of the future largest manufacturing company in Winding River."

Judy rises and laughs. "He knows there aren't any manufacturing companies in Winding River. We'll be the largest one the day the doors open."

As they don their coats in the front hall, Jerry faces me. "By the way, we're planning to go downhill skiing in the UP on Saturday with our two kids. Why don't you come along? We'll drive up early in the morning. The lifts stop running at four o'clock. We'll catch dinner on the way back."

"Interesting that you brought that up. Ann, that is, Ann Tompkins . . . Jerry, do you know her?"

"Her father is the county judge, isn't he?"

"That's right. Ann suggested we go skiing."

"Perfect." Judy tugs at my coat sleeve. "Bring her along."

"Okay, I will." I halt as we approach the Larsens' car in the parking lot. "The only thing is, I've never been skiing."

"Not a problem." Jerry smiles at me, the smile quickly disappearing. "You do have health insurance, don't you?"

✿ ✿

"You need to work on those income tax returns," Margo reminds me I pass her office after lunch with the Larsens at Wally & Laverne's.

"I know. I'll work on them this afternoon."

After I sit down at my desk, I stare at the pile of tax folders. I try to recall anything Burnett mentioned to me about abstracting and income tax returns during the October interview. The way I heard Burnett describe the position, the job carried with it promises of glory. I conjure an absurd image of myself running alongside other lawyers across a battlefield, with abstracts in one hand and income tax returns in the other hand: *The Charge of the Small Town Practitioners.*

I push the pile further back in the corner of my desk and call Dick Minor. "Thanks again for helping me on Suits."

"I'd like to think he'll stay away from Norma. Knowing Suits, I doubt it."

"Unfortunately, you're probably right. Say, I heard you have a jury trial coming up next week. Mind if I sit in the back of the courtroom to watch some of it?"

"Not at all, if it goes. It's a small PI case, and there's a slim chance it will get settled."

"How many days?"

"Probably a day and a half, possibly two days. Tompkins moves things along, so the jury selection usually proceeds quickly. I'll have my secretary send you a copy of the pleadings and the Pretrial Statement so you'll have some idea of the facts and the issues."

"Thanks. I know I've got a lot to learn, and Burnett doesn't have any jury trials coming up."

"In return, John, you can help me and the other attorneys. We're always looking for an attorney to act as a guardian ad litem for minors that are the subject of a custody dispute in a divorce case. Many attorneys don't want to bother with GAL appointments, especially in child custody cases. Tell Tompkins you'd like to receive such appointments, and he'll be happy and so will most of the attorneys. Burnett can fill you in on your role in representing the interests of the children."

"I'll do that."

I hang up, sigh, and tackle the tax returns. After wading through the first return, I take Earl's marble rack off of the shelf and run a few marbles through it. Then I debate whether calling Sanford Smith will be worse than doing another return. I decide it will be, but call him anyway.

"The closing will be at the bank."

When I hear the patient delivery of Smith's words, I grit my teeth. "I'll give the signed Satisfaction for the Schultz judgment to Mark Petersen this afternoon." Burnett warned me against sending it to Smith with a note to hold it in trust until the amount due on the judgment is paid. Either deliver it to Petersen or bring it to the closing and exchange it for a bank check for the balance due, he suggested to me.

"All right."

Smith sounds irritated. It's probably the wrong time to talk about Earl, yet I have to do so eventually. "Have you got a minute to talk about Earl Schmidt?" No reply. "I'm representing him, and he showed me your letter about his delinquent loan." I again pause for a reply; there is none. "He seems like a nice old man. I want to help him."

"Tell him to pay the balance due on his loan."

"He'd like to. He knows he owes the money. But, he doesn't have the funds to pay the balance. He could make payments. Isn't there some payment schedule we can arrange that will satisfy the bank and eliminate the necessity of a foreclosure?"

"Like forgiving of delinquent interest? Or stopping accrual of new interest?"

"That could be part of it."

Smith utters a snide laugh and then begins a diatribe. "Well, Attorney Hall, isn't this the simple request I made of you a few days ago? Of course it's different now, because *you* want something . . ."

"I expected your response. But, I can't trade off the interests of one client for another."

"No one asked you to. You were asked only to give my client a small break . . ."

"He didn't need a break, though, did he? I mean if he did, since he didn't get it, how is he closing now?"

"I'm trying to be patient with you, Attorney Hall. You've got a lot to learn about dealing with other attorneys. You . . ."

"You mean attorneys like you?"

"In answer to your question, Attorney Hall, I don't have time to talk about it. Good day."

"Wait! You're going to have problems with . . . " I hear the click. Damn it, he hung up on me again. I hate that guy.

I need some fresh air, even cold air. I stomp out in the snow most of my irritation on the way down to the bank to give the Satisfaction to Mark Petersen. I remind myself about making an effort to establish a working relationship with Smith. Who, though, got things between us started the wrong way? What the hell was I supposed to have done, let him get whatever he wanted?

The irritation resurfaces when I return to the office and discover the tax return pile has not magically disappeared. I ignore the returns and begin drafting a contract for one of Burnett's clients. When Margo yells "good night" as she leaves with Abstract, I drop the speaker of my dictating machine, and echo her parting remark. Then I bound up the stairs to my bedroom, change into sweat clothes and bounce down to the basement.

With a used punching bag hanging from one floor joist and my old, black leather speed-bag hanging from a framework I rigged to two other joists, the front part of the basement has begun to resemble a gym. I pick up a pair of gloves, pull them on and approach the speed-bag. Maybe, I can persuade Ann to paint a face on it. I know whose face it will be.

First I built a rhythm—the front of my left fist punches the bag on an angle to the right, then as the bag comes back, the side of the fist hits the bag, causing the bag to move in the opposite direction, then my right fist punches the bag on an angle to the left followed by the side of the fist, again reversing the bag's direction. I increase the speed. I'm rusty, out of sync, so I keep starting over. In spite of the cool basement, sweat appears on my clothes. I switch to a hand over hand routine, picking up as much speed as I can. It feels good. Tension dissolves in my body.

Suddenly, I stop and stare at the swinging bag. Who would believe anyone could be tense in Winding River?

~~ 20 ~~

Thursday morning. Through the front window in my bedroom I gaze at the snow still covering the village and the forest beyond. The clouds on the horizon are thick and a dull gray. Everything looks cold and unfriendly. The scene augurs an ugly day.

After I eat breakfast and begin working at my desk, the mood inside the office also becomes glum. For the first time, Henry Miller steps into my office, carrying a packet of papers. "Hum," he mumbles. Under arched eyebrows, his eyes sweep the room before he eases himself into one of the client chairs.

I'm surprised. This is the first time I've observed in Henry's face a sign of concern; this also the first time I've observed in Henry's face a sign of anything. The slow voice in which he speaks makes me think he's pacing himself.

"I got a call yesterday, two calls in fact, from Ed Witt. He was deeply distressed."

"I know. I was going to talk to you about the situation this morning."

Miller tosses the packet of papers on my desk. "Here's the offer, the spec sheet, and the abstract. Everything you needed. It would have been helpful, if you had looked at these, and talked to me first, before you riled him."

"I know." It wasn't enough I had to backpedal from Witt yesterday, now I have to mollify Henry. "I didn't mean to upset him. Like Bob, I appreciate your referrals."

"Witt's principle concern was that the offer doesn't call for a survey. I see no need for one. The lot was staked out, along with an identical one next to it. Both are located within the boundaries of a larger parcel

160

owned by the seller. When the other lot was sold, the seller's title was clear." Henry leans forward and drums his forefinger on the desk as he raises his voice. "I know that property well. There are no roads or easements across it. It abuts a town road, so there's access to the lot. The seller will warrant the description. What's the problem?"

"I don't know there is one. I felt I should point out some of the things he needed to be aware of."

"Umm. Well, let's work together in the future. We don't need unhappy clients, do we?"

"No, we don't."

"Don't overwork these matters. All he needs is the abstract examined."

"As an attorney, though, I have an obligation . . . "

Miller's face resumes its normal blank expression as he rises and disappears into the hallway. When I walk to the bathroom ten minutes later, Henry is working the crossword puzzle in the newspaper and wiping powder from a doughnut off his mouth, while Abstract keeps both of her eyes on him.

I read the spec sheet and the offer and most of his questions *are* answered. The spec sheet indicates the property is not subject to zoning since it is located in a township that has not adopted the Timber County Zoning Ordinance. Perk tests have been done, and at least part of the property will support a conventional septic system. As shown by the abstract, title to the land rests in the sellers, with no liens against it. The metes and bounds descriptions for the parcel and its adjoining twin have been prepared by a surveyor; and the parcel lies within the property previously deeded to the seller. Still, if it were my property, I would want the survey.

I call Witt and backpedal some more. Burnett says all attorneys at times become tap dancers. What do I do here, a soft shoe? Witt is defensive, but thanks me. Did Henry tell Burnett? Probably not. There would be too much exertion involved.

The pile of income tax returns has been pushed closer to the center of the desk. Margo? I push the pile back and finish drafting the contract for Burnett's client, a lease for a commercial building in Lenora. I haven't drafted a commercial lease before, and despite referring to leases Burnett has drawn and to form books, I'm unsure of some of the provisions, leaving me dissatisfied with the draft. As I prepare to discuss it with Burnett, Margo buzzes to alert me Mark Petersen is on his way into my office.

"Here's your check." Petersen hands me the payment for the Schultz judgment.

I lay it on my desk. "Thanks for bringing it up here. Carl will be happy."

"I needed the walk."

"Have a chair."

Petersen pulls a chair back so that when he sits his long legs do not bump against the desk. "How's it going? You look a little distressed."

"I had a matter yesterday I didn't handle well. I think I've got it squared away. I'm finding currents in the river can be more treacherous than I thought."

Petersen smiles. "We all get those days. Been out ice fishing yet?"

"No. I want to, though. Angie Bellini, the court reporter, and Dale Anderson said they're going to take me out."

"I don't know about Bellini. Slider and I are going out on Sunday, if you want to come along."

"Great. I'm going skiing on Saturday for the first time. If I survive, I'd like to go."

"Okay, we'll expect you. By the way, I'd like to refer some business to you if that's all right with you."

"That's fine. I would appreciate the work." Maybe the weather is changing. Glancing sideways out the rear window the glum is still there. "Doesn't Sanford Smith do the bank's work?"

Petersen screws up his face. "Sort of. There's not much I can do about the bank's work. Still, there are always customers and new people moving into the village asking us for referrals to an attorney." He appears to reconsider his comments. "Maybe I *can* slip you a few things for the bank."

"Thanks. You know, almost everyone I've come in contact with in the village has been very nice to me, a few little eccentric. Smith, well . . ."

Petersen stops me as he stands up. "No need to explain."

   ❧ ✍

"A young man is waiting to see you." Margo leans across my desk and whispers, "I don't like the looks of him."

Lifted by Petersen's visit, I whistle softly as I stroll into the hallway. As soon as I see the man, I quit whistling. Of medium size, built like Bill

Krueger, the man is wearing a wool coat and wool cap, each dotted with holes. The cap is pulled down over his forehead so little of his face shows between the cap and the top of a heavy, dark beard. He ignores my hand and doesn't offer his name.

After we sit in my office, I wait to get the attention of the man as he examines the room. The butcher from Bear Path sent me another? When he turns to me, I try the introductions again: "I'm sorry, I didn't get your name, Mister . . ."

"Everything we talk about stays here, right?"

"There is a legal privilege in Wisconsin between an attorney and his client as to their conversations."

"You don't tell anybody about what we talk about?"

"That's what the privilege is about."

"You know about criminal matters?"

I hesitate. "Yes. I took several courses in criminal law in law school, and I worked as a student aide with the Public Defender's Office for awhile."

The man stares at me through the vision block between his cap and beard for what seems to me a long time, although it is perhaps only for seconds. I return the stare, and find I am peering into empty eyes. Since we sat down, the expression in the man's face hasn't changed.

"Can you help me if I want to turn myself in?"

"You mean you committed a crime?" The man nods, almost imperceptibly. "What did you do?"

"I killed a man in Detroit. I shot him in the back of the head five times, twice when he was standing and three times when he was on the floor. . . . I ran out of bullets."

I freeze. First of all, I should have phrased the question differently, not what did he do but what is he accused of doing. I know better. Obtaining a confession from a client in a criminal matter limits my options, such as allowing the defendant to take the witness stand where he may deny the crime, thus committing another crime: perjury. Besides, now I'm also apprehensive. This guy is no Billy. I recover enough to speak, although I have no sense how long it took me to do it. Seconds, minutes, moments are now equal marks on the ruler of time.

"You want me to talk to the police or the district attorney?"

"I want a deal. The guy owed me. He had it coming."

"I could make some calls and see what I can do."

"I killed before. That was different. I did my time. You understand?"

"I can understand . . ."

"I don't want to go back to Jackson. I'll take any place but Jackson."

Obviously a prison, but where? "When did this happen?" I pick up a pen and poise it over a legal pad. I'm now desperate to be admitted to an asylum of details.

The man with the empty eyes watches me. "You ever do this before?"

"No." I'm reluctant to give the answer, but the truth is that I've never done anything remotely like it. Anyway, I know he knows it.

The man eyes me again before moving to the wall behind my desk. He studies my diploma. As he returns to his chair, I fail to see any emotion in the narrow opening of his face. His barely audible voice asks:

"You got out of school two weeks ago?"

"That's correct; however . . ."

"I made a mistake."

The man shoves a hand into his coat pocket. I slowly adjust myself in my chair, as if seeking a more comfortable position. I'm trying to follow the hand. Where did this guy come from?

"You're the wrong guy for the job."

The room is not warm yet I am perspiring. "Like I said, I could make some calls. Mister . . ."

"This was a bad mistake." His hand moves deeper into his pocket.

"There are things we can do."

The man checks my office again. "Who else is here?" His hand is moving still deeper into his pocket.

I squirm in my chair. Is he reaching for a gun? "Just the secretary; she's in another room where she can't hear anything." Only partially true, and Burnett is in his office. What if I somehow divert his attention so I can use the speaker of the intercom? No, that may set him off? I'll raise my voice. Maybe Margo will sense something is wrong. And, do what? Maybe I should grab him. Grab him? He came to me for help. When will I begin violating the privilege? How can there be a privilege if he's going to shoot me? My imagination has run amuck, that's it.

The man begins to slowly remove his hand from the coat pocket. "I don't like this."

"Why don't I look into this for you." I'm talking faster. "I don't need a lot of details now."

The hand keeps coming out of the pocket.

"I shouldn't have told you anything."

The hand is almost out. As it emerges, I jerk backwards.

The hand is holding a pack of cigarettes. The man removes a cigarette from the pack and plunges his hand back into the pocket for a pack of matches. My chest sinks. I try but cannot speak.

The man stands up and lights the cigarette, dropping the match on the floor. "I won't be back."

Since I still cannot speak, I watch silently as he leaves the room. Scrambling to the doorframe, I see him walk slowly to the front door. As he passes Burnett's office, he looks in, then stops and turns back to look at me. He leaves the door ajar as he goes out.

I bolt to the window in Burnett's office and watch the man go down the driveway, cross the street and continue toward Main Street. He doesn't look back.

Burnett looks at me. "Who was that?

"Some guy with empty eyes who shot a man in the back of the head five times." I collapse in a chair.

Margo rushes in. "Are you all right, John?"

"I thought he was going to shoot me."

"Shoot you?" Margo's face turns pale.

Burnett leans forward in his chair and speaks in a serious voice. "We'd better talk about this."

"You're right. I need to know more about confidentiality. I need to know more about a lot of things."

☙ ❧

Slider turns to check the clock on the wall behind him before speaking to me. "Little early for lunch, isn't it?"

"I'm not here for lunch. Give me a shot and a big beer."

"You're not smiling." Slider reaches for a bottle of whiskey, pours a shot, and then moves down to the taps to draw off a sixteen-ounce glass. "So what happened, you get fired?"

I toss down the shot and take a swig from the glass. "Confidentiality."

"Can't say, huh? How come they don't have a requirement like that for bartenders? I hear all kinds of stuff I shouldn't spread around."

I take another long draw on the glass. "Let me ask you something. If you wanted to murder a man, and you decided to shoot him in the back of the head, how many bullets would it take?"

Slider eyes me closely while he calculates his answer. "One, maybe two. Depends on where the bullet goes in."

"Think five would be enough?"

"If they were large caliber hollow points, and you used five, there wouldn't be much left of the front of the skull." He sips from a coffee cup. "What are you up to, anyway? This isn't like you?"

"I'm not up to anything. Some days are worse than others, that's all."

"Usually that doesn't cause you to have a shot and beer at eleven fifteen."

"Give me another shot. I'm done for the day."

Slider fills up my shot glass, then pours some whiskey in his coffee cup. "Okay, pal, here's to you." He raises his cup.

I salute him with the shot glass, quickly downing the whiskey and sending beer after it. "Burnett's right, you can't help him escape, nor can you help him remain at large, and if you know he's about to commit a crime, the privilege doesn't apply."

"You know I've got my hands full with Angie. I don't need another one."

I manage an abbreviated laugh. "It's been a strange day. It started with those dark clouds. Then it was down hill, then up and then down, sort of like being a marble rolling through a rack. You know what I mean?"

"I don't think I do. In my job, though, you don't have to understand much. It's more nodding and timely filling glasses."

I empty the beer glass and hand it to Slider. "Another one, then fry me a couple of burgers."

"You got it." Slider eases down the bar and yells at his wife through the pass-over into the kitchen before filling the glass. "By the way, I've been meaning to tell you. Alma said Beeper was in her place the other night. She thinks he knows something about your client's accident."

I perk up. "Ginger Buckman, the accident with the motorcycle?"

"That's the one." He sets the glass on the bar in front of me.

"I would have guessed Beeper drank at home. I see him toting home cases of beer."

"He goes to Alma's in the evening once in a while. I won't let him in here any more."

I let the glass of beer sit. "Why's that?"

"The last time he was in here he was drunk, and he fell and hit his head on a table on the way to the floor."

"Liability, huh?"

"No, I got insurance. I called the police station, and they got an ambulance to pick him up and take him to the hospital. The ambulance guys, though, were really pissed."

"Isn't that their job?"

"Beeper had lice, and they got all over the ambulance. I heard those guys had a hell'ava time cleaning it up."

I miss the last sentence, but smile when Slider laughs. "You think he knows something, huh?"

"Talk to Alma."

"Good idea." I hand the full glass of beer back to Slider. "Do something with this." As I step off the barstool, I add: "I'll be back for the burgers in half an hour. And have plenty of hot coffee. I'm going back to work."

All the way to the door I feel Slider's questioning eyes burning my back.

❧ ✲

As I drive toward the south end of village, I'm curious how much Beeper knows about the accident. I plan how to deal with him. Alma confessed Beeper was drunker than usual when he was babbling about the accident. What did "drunker than usual" mean? Wasn't he either drunk or not drunk? Then I think about drunk driving. There *are* levels of intoxication.

Still overcast and cold as I pull up to a dirty yellow, one-story house a block west, but still close, to the river. A car whose stripped body indicates it's used only for parts is parked alongside the house. Visible in the backyard is a swing-set, showing rust where snow fails to cling to it. Next to the front door is a faded red coaster wagon.

The woman who answers the door reminds me of those barmaids in the beer halls in Germany who could carry three steins of beer in each hand. I step back from the door as she steps into the doorframe, with a deep frown on her face.

"What do you want?"

"Is Mr. Plumber home?" I try to show an earnest face and project a professional posture, even though she obviously sees me as a door-to-door salesman.

"If he is, what do you want him for?"

"My name is John Hall. I'm an attorney. I believe he has information relative to a case I'm working on."

"He's busy." She moves back and starts to close the door.

"I'll only take a minute of his . . ."

The door is suddenly thrust open as she is pushed aside by a much smaller, beer-bellied man who without his cap with earflaps is bald. Shoeless with creases on his cheek, it appears he has been napping on the couch. "Get inside so I can close the door."

I enter the house, carrying my briefcase. My first sense of the living room is the smell of zoo animals.

"What's this about?"

"I understand you have information about a case I'm working on, an automobile accident on Main Street last October."

"Oh yeah, that. Sit down." He points at a stuffed chair with a protruding spring. "I gotta get a beer."

I remove my coat and drop it next to the chair, avoiding the spring as I sit down. While Beeper is in the kitchen, I scan the living room: a small room in a small house with well-worn furniture and an absence of anything that can be read. It's the kind of room I won't remember except for the smell in it. The huge woman glowers at me while she strains the wood chair she is draped over.

Beeper guzzles a bottle of beer as he returns. "So whataya wanna know?"

I place my briefcase on my knees while I remove a legal pad, then close the case and put the pad on top. "Did you see the accident?"

"I saw it."

"Tell me what you saw?" I take a ballpoint pen from my shirt pocket.

"That young girl, she was goin' down the street on a motorcycle . . . "

"Going south, toward Lenora?"

"Right. She was comin' up on Forest. Them two boys were comin' on Forest toward Main." He stops to drink from the beer bottle, slightly over shooting his mouth and wiping the excess on the front of his shirt-sleeve. "They never stopped. They just kept comin'. Went right past the stop sign onto Main, into her lane. Then they got back in their lane and kept goin'. They were both laughin.'"

"You could see them? Wasn't it dark then?"

"Street light by the intersection. I seen 'em."

"Did you know who they were?"

"I've seen 'em before. I don't know their names. Not the one drivin', the other one, he was the kid who burnt down the church."

"Burnt part of it," corrects his wife

"Stay out of this," Beeper yells. The woman scowls as she sits back in her chair.

"So what did the young woman on the motorcycle do?"

"What could she do?"

Exactly, I say to myself.

"She got out of the way . . . crashed the bike up on the sidewalk. She was in the street by the curb."

"Did you know her?"

"She used to work at the checkout counter at Wills. I heard she was workin' at the River's Edge then."

"What time did it happen?"

"I don't know, maybe ten." Beeper finishes off the bottle and chases after another one.

I smile again at the woman who turns away. Beeper is a third of the way through the bottle when he returns.

"I have to ask you this . . . " I pause to allow Beeper to belch. "Were you drunk then?"

The woman laughs loudly with Beeper joining her.

"Hell, I'm always drunk. I've been drunk since I was fourteen. I used to drink a case of beer every day and a quart of whiskey every evening until I went to the hospital."

Burnett is right. How is an alcoholic witness going to play in court? "How drunk were you?"

"Well, I was walkin' home from Alma's, and I didn't have no problem gettin' here."

"Did you stay around after the accident?"

"Me and the cops don't mix. I walked by her. She didn't look like she was gonna die. . . . I don't know. I'm no doctor. She didn't die, did she?"

"Not yet." No Good Samaritan here. I stuff my notes in my briefcase and stand up. "Okay, Mr. Plumber, you've been helpful. You may be called as a witness."

"Me and the courts don't mix."

Obviously not a mixer. I put on my overcoat. "Thanks for your time." I smile again at Beeper's wife who appears as though she is on the verge of leaping off of her chair to bite me.

As I make a U-turn in the street to drive back to the office, I decide they're a lovely couple.

21

Burnett remains unconvinced. "John, the defense will tear Beeper apart in court, showcase him as the village drunk, and they'll have truth on their side."

First, I'm congratulated for finding an eyewitness to Ginger's accident. Next, I'm lectured for not obtaining a written statement from Beeper; what will he say the next time he is questioned? Then comes the praise for my efforts in the investigation. Now I'm in the position of defending Beeper's credibility. Burnett is bouncing me up and down like a yo-yo as we sit in his office.

"A less than sympathetic plaintiff backed up by the village drunk isn't an all star lineup." Burnett leans back in his office chair with his glasses off. "Also, we haven't seen the medical reports yet."

"Apparently her doctor is no longer sympathetic, so she thinks everyone sees her as a faker or a complainer."

Burnett taps his hand against the side of his head. "Were you planning to have the doctor bat third? Who's the cleanup hitter?"

I slump further into my chair by the fireplace. "I know what we've put together so far doesn't sound great, but I think we can do okay. We can . . ."

Burnett scowls. "Okay isn't good enough to win a jury case where you're facing insurance lawyers who handle PI defense full time. You have to do better than okay."

"I will. I misspoke. Although the defense lawyers may see Ginger as their dream witness, she could be a better witness than we thought. Maybe we initially misjudged her. Beeper may be another defense dream witness. He admittedly has a drinking problem. When I interviewed him, though, he was understandable and believable. The medicals . . . we haven't seen the reports." I pause to face Burnett. "Give me a chance."

Relaxing his facial muscles, Burnett looks at me and then toward the front windows. "I don't mean to be harsh with you, John. But there are too many 'could bes' and 'may bes' here."

"I know, but I've only been at this for ten days."

Burnett eyes me with a straight face. "I suppose this doesn't have to be decided today. Keep working on it." He puts his glasses on and sits up. "How about that strange man who came in yesterday, are you all right?"

"I'm all right. My imagination may have been working too hard."

"Not necessarily. There have been . . ."

"Go on."

"I don't mean to upset you, but attorneys have been killed by irate clients or irate spouses of clients. Ask Dick Minor. A distraught husband of a divorce client of Dick's popped into his office and pulled a gun on him. Fortunately, his secretary heard the shouting and called the police who arrested . . ." Burnett waves at a heavyset man wearing a denim jacket over bib overalls tromping into Margo's office. "Excuse me. We always need to greet our clients. He's picking up his tax return."

"I understand."

Burnett continues: "It's never happened to me, and it probably won't happen to you again. It's one of those things. I told you the first time we talked that you never know who is going to come through the front door." He purses his lips. "And this isn't Chicago. Some nut doesn't have to wade through a lobby, go up an elevator, get by a receptionist and find his way to the right office. . . . Be careful, John."

"I'll work out with Margo some kind of signal if I'm in trouble."

Burnett waves at the client again as he goes out the front door. I sniff. "What's that smell?"

"Probably manure. That was Marvin Krause, a dairy farmer over near Earl's place. Margo will have a fit. She says it a good thing we don't have many farmers for clients. Ah, most of them clean up before coming in." Burnett rises. "Let's get some coffee."

In the kitchen, I pour the coffee while Burnett selects a doughnut and sits at the table.

Margo strolls in and takes the coffee pot from me. "That Marvin Krause."

Burnett winks at me before turning to Margo. "Are you keeping up?"

"I'm keeping up."

"You're working a lot of overtime. It's only going to get busier."

I pull a chair for Margo to sit at the end of table; then sit next to her. "I have to do some abstracting at the courthouse this afternoon. Now . . ." I spread my hands in front of me, palms up. "This isn't because I don't like abstracting. If we hire a secretary who, in addition to helping Margo with typing and filing, can learn to abstract, it will free up more of your time, Bob, and my time as I get busier."

Burnett looks at Margo who appears pleased. I guess he's depending on Margo to do the mental math for the added cost. "If the secretary can also do abstracting, that will allow both of us to increase our billable hours."

Setting his half-eaten donut on a napkin, Burnett responds: "That might work if we can find someone capable of doing the work."

Margo speaks up: "There's a co-op program at the high school where business students work part-time in the afternoons their last semester, then go full-time in May after graduation."

Burnett nods. "I've heard of the program."

I push my proposal. "I could check with Ann's roommate, Shelly. She's the business teacher at the high school."

First observing Margo's affirmative nod, Burnett agrees. "Good idea, John." He finishes his donut and sips coffee. "Now that we've got that settled, let's go back to work and earn some money."

"I'm shocked, Bob." Margo beams as she speaks. "I've never heard you say that before."

I laugh as I slip into my office, hearing as I go Burnett's whisper to Margo: "He's just what we need." Margo's response is beyond my hearing range. Relief. At least for now, I'm no longer a yo-yo.

❧ ☙

"It's Benny," announces the caller.

"Benny?"

"You know, from Bear Path. The butcher sent me to another lawyer."

"Uh huh."

"The lawyer said he can get the ticket dismissed."

"How's he going to do that?"

"He said the judge throws 'em out if they're only two over."

I shake my head. "Benny, you were going seven over."

"You still don't get it, do you? The first five don't count."

"Sounds like you've got a good attorney, Benny. Good luck."

"I thought you should know for your clients."

"Thanks . . . and say hello to the butcher."

Margo buzzes me to pick up. "Carl Schultz here. Thanks for getting that check to me. I've got some more accounts I need to collect. Can I come in next week?"

"Sure, Carl." I check my calendar. "How about Tuesday morning about ten o'clock?"

"Good, I'll bring my file."

I write the appointment on my calendar and tell Margo on the intercom to put it on her calendar. She asks me to pick up again.

"This is Judge Tompkins."

I quickly sit up in my chair. "Yes, judge."

"Are you becoming acclimated to the area?"

"Everything is fine. As a matter of fact . . . "

"I'm appointing you as guardian ad litem in a divorce case with a custody battle."

"Thank you judge. I'll get right on it."

"The Clerk of Court will send you an order appointing you. I'll expect a written report."

"Certainly judge. By the way, I guess you know . . . "

"All right then. Goodbye."

How much has Ann told her father, I wonder as I hang up? The judge sounded more distant than he was on the day I met him. Is that his way with attorneys?

Depending on what calls I receive and who walks in the door, I determine to spend the morning completing the work on my desk—the tax returns, abstract examinations, the commercial lease I discussed with Burnett, and several real estate matters. I hear Burnett's admonition to me that if I put off too much, I'll soon be buried by the pileup. Burnett told me he revered his mentor, except for the fact Eggelston started every day by having his secretary bring in a huge stack of files. They went through the stack file by file. After he finished reviewing a file, invariably it went back into the pile and was returned the next day as part of a larger pile. Eggleston was, Burnett claimed, always slipping down the slope.

❧ ❧

When I finish abstracting at the Register of Deeds Office, I stop in the antique store on the side street across from the courthouse. The store is narrow but stretches back to an alley, with only the front portion heated. The shelves are crammed with glassware, milk and beer bottles, knickknacks, old skis and snowshoes, a few books, small furniture and tools from the logging industry. All junk, I decide, before acknowledging to myself I know nothing about antiques. I speak to a man sitting at a roll-top desk with his back to me:

"I'm surprised you're open in the winter."

The man swings around in a swivel chair. Heavyset and balding, he has a round face and wears large glasses that gives him an owl-like appearance "Mostly catching up on my book work. If someone comes in, so be it."

"I notice you have a few books and magazines."

"Not too much. I could probably sell more to the tourists in the summer. You can look at what I've got."

"I was wondering if you would be interested in purchasing some old magazines and newspapers, as well as some old farm implements and some antigue furniture."

"Might be." The man studies me. "Depends on what you've got and how much you want for it."

"I understand. My name is John Hall." I shake hands with the man who identifies himself as Mr. Denbrow. "I'm an attorney representing an elderly gentleman who has a farm with some items you might be interested in."

"I could take a look at them."

"Let me check with my client. I'll contact you again."

"We're going to be closed for two months. My wife and I usually travel around this time of year shopping for things for the store. Too busy in the summer when the tourists come through. You got a card?"

"I'm getting some printed. I'm in Winding River." I point at the desk. "Can I borrow your note pad?"

The man nods, and I write my name and telephone number on the pad. "Thanks, I'll be in touch."

"Okay, but I don't buy pornography."

"You don't have to worry. It'll be more like *Popular Mechanics.*"

❧ ☙

"I don't want to sell anything." Earl shakes his head as he sits at the checkerboard table while I stand next to the stove in his workshop.

"I thought we could raise some money to reduce your loan."

"How much time have we got?"

"Over a year. Smith hasn't filed an action yet. When he does, we can stall the process by getting the complaint dismissed. He gave you a thirty-day notice. The mortgage calls for a sixty-day notice before commencing foreclosure. He'll give the correct notice, though, and then re-file the action. Eventually, the bank will get a judgment of foreclosure against the farm. The redemption period in Wisconsin, that is, the time in which you can pay off the judgment before a sheriff's sale is held, will be a year, since your property is a farm."

"Auk," Earl throws out his hands. "I'm not worried that far down the line."

I warm my hands over the stove. "When Mr. Denbrow gets back to Lenora, why don't we have him appraise some of the property you no longer need? Maybe you have some things that are worth more than you think."

"I can't part with any of it." Earl fidgets in his chair. "You probably don't understand it because you didn't live through the Depression. You don't throw anything away."

"You won't be throwing your property away, Earl. You'll be paid for it."

"Ah," Earl waves his hands again. "Nobody's going pay anything for this stuff. It's only valuable to me."

I move to the door. "Think about it Earl. Mr. Denbrow won't be back for two months."

Earl keeps shaking his head negatively. I close the door on his world and trudge through the snow to *Rusty*. What is it I like about the old man? His genius in tinkering? His independent lifestyle? I have an overwhelming feeling I have to help him. If Earl refuses to sell some of his property, though, other than stalling the legal process what can I do to save the farm?

⁓ ⁓

Darkness has overtaken the village by the time I return to the office. Margo hands me several pink message slips when I walk in. I hold the slips as I sit in my desk chair and check my calendar for Monday. An appointment with an Ethel Franklin for a traffic citation is written in at nine o'clock. I flip back to Friday. Today is the end of my second week. Seemingly, months have passed since I drove up to Winding River in the snowstorm. So much has changed. Still holding the slips I slide my chair away from the desk and lean back.

Time. I recall sitting with a neighbor kid through a movie for the second time, and it seemed to spool by at twice the speed it did in the first run. If time is so important to existence, how is it humans developed without an internal biological clock that precisely measures the passing of seconds and minutes? I'm overwhelmed with the desire to protect every second of my time so I can get my work done, and yet, I so easily flit away hours drinking beer with Angie and Slider while what we discuss drifts away with the haze in the bar.

I slide my chair back over the plastic mat below it to pick up the ringing phone.

"John! It's Rick. How are you doing?"

"Rick. Nice to hear from you." I drop the message slips on my desk before again leaning back in the chair.

"I thought you could use a call after a couple of weeks in the boonies. You know, I haven't figured out why you didn't interview with our firm in Chicago."

"I've been trying to figure that out my . . ."

"You must be going nuts up there. What are you doing, examining abstracts and doing old ladies' tax returns? Jesus, John, you're living in a freezer. How far are you from the North Pole?"

"Funny, Rick. Actually, I'm . . ."

"You know, we're doing exciting stuff here. I'm sure you've heard of Xpecon. Well they've been sued by the feds, and we're defending them. Huge case, John. You probably read about it in the newspapers. If the government gets its way, the company could go under. We've got over thirty attorneys working the case. I'm on a research team. I mean we're working night and day, billing eighteen hours a day. This case . . ."

Burnett walks by the door, and I wave him in and put my hand over the mouthpiece of the phone. "Ever heard of Xpecon?"

Burnett shakes his head negatively and walks out.

"So, you see, John, this is really big stuff. This is the kind of case you think about when you're in law school. And I know they're watching all of us to see who handles the pressure and keeps up the billings. I did all right on my first year review, but you've got to keep it up if you want to become a partner. Real competitive, John. I mean this is big time stuff. The newspapers say there might be criminal charges filed. We're not commenting. You . . ."

"Rick."

" . . . could be a part of this. You could . . ."

"Rick."

" . . . be working with me. I probably could get . . ."

"Rick. Rick."

"Huh?"

"Rick. Do you see people? Do clients come into your office?"

"Of course we talk to clients, on the phone naturally."

"Do you sit in your cubicle or the library all day?"

"What? Jesus, John, it's getting to you, isn't it. Ah, you poor bastard. You should never have . . ."

"Rick . . ."

"As I told you, right now we're steaming full time on research. It's important. It's . . . ah John, give it up. Come on down here. You can do a lot better than, what's your place, Whipping River?"

"Winding River, Rick. How many attorneys do you have in the firm now, two hundred? Three hundred?"

"Oh, yeah. They're coming in so fast, I'm don't know half the new ones. We need them. We're doing some exciting things here. When it's over, I want to talk to you about this case. This is a biggie. This . . ."

"Rick. When's the last time a guy who shot a man in the back of the head until he ran out of bullets walked into your office?"

"It is getting to you, isn't it? That's scary, real scary. Oh, you poor bastard. Listen, I gotta go. We're working into the night. I mean this is big, John. Keep in touch, and if you want to come down here and interview, let me know."

"Thanks, Rick. And good luck with your case."

For several minutes I stare through the window into the dark, imagining myself being in Chicago with Rick. Then I wander to the table next to the couch in the hallway to check the morning newspaper. Finding it gone, I decide Burnett must have taken it home. I pick up the *Winding River Record* and skim through it while standing. A short front-page article catches my attention:

> Three cars were damaged on Main Street on Wednesday afternoon when a fourth vehicle went out of control.
>
> According to the Chief of Police, the driver Ethel Franklin, 78, was proceeding south on Main Street to her home when her vehicle allegedly sideswiped two cars parked in front of Jorgenson's Bakery, then veered across the street and hit a third parked car.
>
> She was taken to the hospital in Lenora and was released after treatment for minor injuries. The parked cars were unoccupied at the time.
>
> Franklin was issued a citation for operating a motor vehicle while under the influence of an intoxicant.

I fold up the newspaper and toss it on the table. Burnett and Margo have gone home. All the lights have been turned off other than those in the hallway and my office. The building is quiet except for the periodic running of the furnace fan. I try again to understand my role. Is it representing the Ethel Franklins in a village where they don't have any famous anything?

22

Four quick months pass. A lazy May air drifts through the village. The evening is the kind where everyone sits outside to seek compensation for the winter evenings spent behind closed doors. Ann and I sit on the front steps of the office, talking in the purposeful way she always structures our conversations; she resents idle talk. A sign of spring: she thinks again about opening an art gallery during the summer months. Lack of capital and an honest appraisal of the number of tourists passing through the village usually cut off her thought process during the winter months when she should be preparing for the tourist season. Then crisp May air arrives, and she's at it again, too late for the coming summer.

She purses her lips before she speaks. "Next summer, I'm definitely going to open a shop. I'm going to plan it this winter. I know several artists in the area who would bring their work to me. I have the summers off. I'm tired of being a camp counselor."

"Great. I'll help you set up the business. I wonder, though, how many tourists will stop. You know the locals and the Yoopers coming south from the U.P. won't buy much." Shoot. I need to be positive for her. Who am I to want to cut off someone's dream?

She goes on: "I'm getting tired of this annual business flu. The cure is the gallery. I've saved some money, and I'm willing to risk what I have on it."

"Hey, I'm the last guy to discourage you from trying something new. If I were, I wouldn't be here."

"That's true." She snuggles against me.

The sound of a siren screeches up the hill from the south end of the village, silencing the coyotes yipping in the far woods behind the office.

A few moments later a police car whizzes down Main Street past the intersection four blocks below us. We watch in silence. Then as I'm about to speak, the sound of a second siren pierces the air as an ambulance shoots by the intersection.

Ann looks at me. "What do you think?"

"I don't know, could be an accident, maybe another domestic dispute. I'm not an ambulance chaser." A recent conversation with a Chicago attorney comes to mind. "Is it really true," I had asked, "that when there's an accident on the EL you have to be careful not to get hit by all the flying business cards?"

Ann dislodges me from my reverie by poking me in the side. "Isn't that the telephone ringing?"

"You're right." I trot into the office and pick up the phone. The speaker is the Scandinavian looking officer I now know through Slider's as Sven, a sincere State Patrol wannabe without the qualifications for the job.

"You're client is asking for you."

"My client? You don't mean . . ."

"Who else? He's getting medical attention. An ambulance is on the way. If you want to talk to him, come over to Norma's house."

What now? I give Ann a hug and a kiss and jump into *Rusty* who had bedded down for the night but crankily turns over and starts up.

Norma's older, two-story house is near the village park stretching around the big bend in the river before the river flows south, parallel to the highway. When I pull up behind Sven's police car, I'm surprised by the number of people milling around the ambulance parked near the curb. A medic examines Suits, who has blood all over him, while Sven and another officer stand by. I push through several people to get to them.

Suits looks dazed and ready to collapse. He speaks listlessly: "She started it. It wouldn't have happened but for her. I was defendin' my rights. I'm still married to her. I'm . . ."

I throw up my hands. "Okay, okay. Be still."

"You should know . . ."

"Be quiet."

The medic and his partner put Suits on a stretcher and hoist him into the ambulance. He's still talking so I whisk my hand past my neck, but as the ambulance door closes, I can still hear him babbling.

I pull Sven aside from the crowd. "What is this? They had it out over the grill?"

He smirks. "See that elm tree next to the side of the house."

"Yeah."

"See how close that big branch is to the window."

"Yeah." For the first time, I notice most of the glass in the window is gone.

"Well, that's the branch your client leaped from when he crashed through the window."

"What? You've got to be kidding me. Why would he do that?"

"Because she was in bed with another man, and your peeping Tom couldn't stand it any longer." He smirks again. "Luckily he went in feet first."

"Unbelievable . . ." I glance around the crowd. "Where's Norma?"

"She's in the house, I think on the phone with her attorney."

"Oh, great. Who was the guy?"

"I don't know yet. She told me she would tell me after the medics got your client out of here." Sven looks at me before laughing. "Sorry, but I can't help it. Her lover apparently jumped out of bed naked when he saw your client crash through the window, and then ran out of the house. Your client chased him down to the river where the guy jumped in and swam away. We're looking for him on the other side. Guys like him always go to the far side of the river." He hesitates, as if reviewing his remarks. "Even if she doesn't tell us his name, his clothes are still in the house, probably with a wallet in them."

I shake my head. "You know my client wouldn't hurt Norma."

"Not physically."

"What's the charge going to be?"

"Oh, I don't know . . . breaking and entering, attempted battery, disorderly conduct . . . creating a public nuisance."

"Come on, this is a private matter, not a public nuisance. Anyway, it's not a public nuisance you could prosecute criminally."

"I don't know, counselor. I'm beginning to think your client *is* a public nuisance."

I walk away. I like Sven; he sticks to the truth, or least the truth as he sees it. He is also fair. Nevertheless, I sense he enjoys jabbing me, always referring to *your client.*

When I return from the hospital where Suits is being kept over night, Ann is parked on the couch in the hallway, reading the newspaper. She looks up as I enter. "Well?"

"You can read about it in the *Record*. Winding River burst wide open. My client and a man who lost his pants gave the village enough gossip to last through the summer."

❧ ❧

Monday morning. The main thing is I'm on the telephone; I don't have to see his face, or worse, have him see mine. Suits has dug a huge hole. Now I have to argue it is nothing more than a divot on a golf course.

"When you do sort it out," I plead to the Timber County D.A., "if you won't go for another ordinance violation or disorderly conduct, how about a misdemeanor disorderly conduct? That's still criminal. You know this guy would never hurt anyone. He's not a bad guy really." I'm choking. How do I argue what I no longer believe?

❧ ❧

After lunch, I drive past Norma's house to look at the crime scene in the daylight. Cardboard has been tacked over the inside of the window. Glass is visible on the ground below it. Otherwise, it appears as nothing more than a window shattered by a Packer fan heaving a chair through it after a close loss to the Bears.

Suits' legal matters spill out of the file cabinet of my mind as they always do whenever I think of him. I mentally review each one before I refile it. The matters all intertwine, though, through a thread of deviousness sometimes hard to spot even with a magnifying glass. Fear of allowing him to slip something by me forces me to continually review his files. I begin running through them as I drive:

Grocers Mutual. I settled Suits' claim for his fall in the parking lot. He seemed surprised the company doled out one thousand dollars, plus medical bills, which turned out to be the cost for one visit to Dr. Smeatshum. I credited the doctor with writing a good report, but there was nothing in the one page letter to indicate any injury other than a mild elbow sprain that would be cured, and was cured, with rest. When I briefly talked to the doctor about his report, the doctor laughed about the sling. Although the adjuster was suspicious it was a nuisance claim, fortunately, she had never handled a claim involving Suits. After I mentally close the first case, I think: what's the use? I gather up the rest of his files and jam them into what is now his own file drawer.

I drive slowly past the village park on the big bend in the river and then south along West River Road. With the melting of heavy, late winter snowfall, the banks of the river are swollen and water nearly laps the roadway. Activity is brisk at the West Shore Marina as houseboats are hoisted into the river and speedboats hauled to lakes to be navigated to their moorings. Most of the businesses in the village are preparing for the coming Memorial Day weekend kicking off the start of the tourist season. I wonder if I'll ever own a boat. First I need to work on my law school debts and trade in *Rusty*.

Passing a log home, I decide the home is the kind I'll build on the river. Thanks to my part-time jobs during law school, I should be able to clear up my debts in a couple of years and buy a better car. The log cabin will have to wait. If I had taken Rick's advice . . . I turn west onto Spruce Street to begin the ascent to Main Street, then on up to the office. I begin reeling out a daydream of myself holding a fishing rod while I recline in a chair on the pier extending from the front of my river cabin. Without warning, a new divorce client stands up in front of the screen complaining, and I shut off the projector. The daydreams are rapidly vanishing.

"Good afternoon," Suzy Steadmann chirps as I wave at her from the entryway.

I smile at the cheerful and energetic, young woman recommended by Shelly as I go down the hallway to my office and close the door. With two typewriters clacking and both secretaries often on the phones now that an additional line has been added, I seek shelter from the noise when I need to concentrate.

My calendar shows it's Monday afternoon, but the day of the week no longer has the significance for me it did in law school. Then I eagerly anticipated noon on Wednesday as being the fulcrum that tipped the weekly teeter-totter so I would gradually slide down to the end of classes on Friday afternoon. How dreadfully important it was then to get the present day behind so I could go on to the next day and the day after and the day after that to get to . . . what? Graduation? Then what? Now I have to make things happen today whatever day that may be with less of an eye on the future.

Suzy has made a difference in my practice. My work is typed sooner, and organization has set in. Of average height for an eighteen-year-old woman, with short, light colored hair, she has a pretty face with full lips and eyes that always appear wide open. Her smile makes her instantly likeable. A serious weight problem detracts from Suzy's appearance, having stifled high school dating. Margo's determined to get her on a diet. Now that Suzy is working full-time, having progressed from part-time when she was hired in March, Margo is subtlety addressing the problem. To make it successful, Margo claims Suzy must think the diet is her idea.

The young lady is mature for her age. An honor student, she scored well on a typing test Margo gave her. What surprises me are her organizational skills and motivation. In willingly accepting new tasks, she displays a calm and cautious approach, another brake on me. While pleased with her future replacement, Margo thinks Suzy is someone who should be in a law office as a lawyer, not as a secretary. Margo's displeased with Suzy's parents for having offered her a choice upon graduation from high school of a new car or money toward higher education.

Margo. I have let her adopt me. From overhearing a few lines of a phone conversation, I discovered Margo knew I was making inquiries about Jimmy. I have to come up with something to tell her, something that may ease the pain she so strongly suppresses. I also learned from an associate in the firm I worked for during law school that Margo checked on me before I came to Winding River. Maybe she doesn't know everything, but what she doesn't know, she works at learning, except for things she considers to be of no practical value to her, like the things The Dean knows.

Brenda Krueger smiles as she sits in a chair in front of my desk. "Good afternoon, Mister Hall." Her head is up, and her eyes meet mine and stay with them.

"Good afternoon, Brenda. You look great. I'm proud of you."

She blushes. "Thank you, Mister Hall."

As we talk, her transformation since the temporary hearing thrills me. Everything important about her has improved: her appearance, her attitude, her determination. Her struggles of the past four months behind her, she's excited about her home, refurbished through the help of her parents, friends and the Homemaker's Club. I attribute the change partly to the divorce and partly to Bill being in jail, his bail on the resisting arrest charge revoked after his arrest at the preliminary hearing.

Even though Bill is incarcerated, I worry about Brenda's safety. Bill has been granted work release privileges, and while he's restricted to going back and forth to his employment with a local construction company, I know he can easily deviate from his work route and find her. Except for the courthouse brawl, though, he has stayed away from her, perhaps on the advice of the attorney appointed by the court to represent him on the criminal charges. The attorney may have convinced him to stay away from Brenda so he would not violate provisions of the court order requiring him to have no contact with her.

I wish the final hearing in their divorce hadn't been rescheduled to December. The more I admire my client, the more I'm convinced Brenda has to sever her relationship with Bill. I worry that she may still change her mind.

"Have you seen or heard from Bill?"

"Nothing, and if I never hear from him again, I won't care. Oh, I understand I'll have to deal with him until the boys are adults." Tears form in her eyes. "I feel so much better not having to face him every day." She takes a tissue out of her purse and wipes her eyes. "I'm sorry. It's hard to describe how it was. People who haven't been through what I've been through the past nine years don't understand."

"You don't have to explain. I asked you to see me today so we could review the issues for your final hearing. The judge requires us to make an effort to reach a settlement with Bill so we don't have to try every issue before him."

"We won't get any cooperation from him."

"I'm sure you're right. But, we still have to do our part." I pick up a legal pad on which I have written the issues I want to discuss, with spaces between them for notes. I lean back in my chair as I remove a pen from my shirt pocket, noting with disgust ink has leaked out into the pocket. Why do I not take the time to affix the cap properly to the pen? "As to custody, there appears to be no contest. We'll have to come up with something on the visitation."

"Bill hasn't seen the boys since the day he was served with the papers."

"Maybe he doesn't want the boys to see him in jail."

"Maybe. His parents called me up a couple of times and said they wanted to see the kids. I wasn't sure what to say. I don't like them, and they don't like me. But, I know they're the boys' grandparents. What I worry about is the boys being taken to their place. They might not bring them back."

"Do you think that would really happen?"

"Oh, I do. The first time they called me after he was jailed I said they could visit the boys at my home. His dad swore at me, so I hung up. His mother called back, and we arranged for a visit at my place. She came alone and didn't stay long. The second time they called, they both yelled and swore at me and then hung up."

"Sound like nice people."

"They aren't, Mister Hall. I think that's the cause of most of Bill's problems. He has an older brother who lives at home. He's worse than Bill, been in jail several times. They live out near the village dump, north of the bridge on the west of the river. Their place looks like a junkyard. They're always bringing home stuff from the dump. You can hardly walk through their house with all the junk piled in it."

"Brenda, you know you can call me, John."

"Thank you, Mister Hall."

I suppress a smile. "I've been to the dump a few times. Other than the garbage, half the people were dropping off old furniture, appliances, car parts, toys, and the other half were picking them up."

"Bill's parents are the other half." A dark cloud covers her face. "The worst thing about their place is the dirt. Their place is always dirty—dirt on the floors, on the rugs, on the counters . . . even on the kitchen table. If you pick up anything, there's dirt on it somewhere. And in the summertime, the flies come from the dump in black swarms. I can't think of his parents without thinking of the dirt and the flies. I always took a shower after we left there." Her head drops.

I set my legal pad on the desk. "Look at me, Brenda. There's no reason you have to go to their place. Let me help you deal with them." I pause. "The problem we face is Bill being released from jail. He has no criminal convictions." Of course he would have if Brenda had followed through on the abuse complaints, but I can't tell her that now. "I'm sure his attorney will be able to plea bargain the rest of the charges against him, and Bill will get credit on his sentence for time spent in jail. Since he'll likely be out soon, we have to work out visitation. Unless something else happens, while the judge may place restrictions on Bill's visitation rights, I doubt he'll terminate them."

Brenda raises her head and nods slowly. "I know. I've been talking to a couple of women at work who are divorced, and I understand things better now." Brenda looks very serious. "I'm not bitter like they are, though. I just want to have a better life, like you said."

I wince. She believes in me and trusts me. She hangs on every word I speak. How can I always dispense the correct advice? It keeps coming to me there is this part of practicing law I did not learn in law school. On the other hand, how could it have been taught?

"Let's cover the items on my list as best we can."

✑ ✎

After Brenda leaves, I pick up Ginger Buckman's file. Depositions are set for the morning. I think of the insurance company attorney's snide remarks when I told him about the eyewitness; he had been forewarned of Beeper by the company's local counsel, my pal, Sanford Smith. When I received the medical reports on Ginger, I send a *demand letter* to the insurance company, outlining the accident, what I saw as the company's liability, her injuries and requesting a settlement. The insurance company expressed no interest in settlement other than as a nuisance claim, so I had to file suit after conferring with Burnett and Attorney Matt Willock in Ridgecrest. Well, barely after conferring with them, since I wanted to start the lawsuit as soon as I interviewed Beeper. Burnett held me back.

I study my calendar page for Tuesday:

  9:30 - *Deposition of Ginger Buckman*
  11:30 - *Deposition of Chief of Police*

12:00 - *Lunch*
1:00 - *Deposition of Eddie Plumber*
2:00 - *Deposition of Jeremy Wilson & Parents*
3:00 - *Deposition of Tommy Mathers*

The order of the witnesses is not what I planned. I wanted to wait on the depo of my client until I knew what the others would say. Working it out had been a matter of negotiation. Anyway, I expect no surprises from the testimony of the witnesses. We'll take depositions of Dr. Schloss, her family doctor, Dr. Andrews, her orthopedist, and the defense doctors later.

I begin leafing through her file. Having read my notes and the police and medical reports so many times, I have almost memorized them. Removing the metal fastener at the top of the file, I pull out the complaint and scan it, stopping at paragraphs 6 and 7:

6. That on or about October 16, 1975, at approximately 10:30 pm, in the Village of Winding River in Timber County, Wisconsin, the plaintiff was driving her motorcycle south on Main Street, and as she approached the intersection of Forest Street, an automobile operated by Jeremy Wilson with permission of the owners, the defendants, Ronald and Gloria Wilson, went through a stop sign on Forest Street without stopping, turned right onto Main Street, and swerved across the centerline of Main Street into the south bound lane, causing the plaintiff to swerve her motorcycle to her right to avoid colliding with said car, and causing the plaintiff to lose control of her motorcycle which ended up on the sidewalk in front of a commercial establishment known as Jorgenson's Bakery, with the plaintiff being thrown into Main Street.

7. That as a direct and proximate result of the negligence of said Jeremy Wilson and the ensuing accident, the plaintiff sustained severe injuries to her left elbow, left knee, left lower leg and left hip and other injuries, including permanent injuries, lost time from her employment, had extreme pain and suffering, and was otherwise damaged in the amount of two hundred and fifty thousand ($250,000.00) dollars.

I drop the complaint on the desk and swivel my chair around to face the side window. I stare at the pine trees in the lot between the office and the house down the street. What is her case really worth? The amount in the complaint is meaningless, a figure inserted out of the necessity to provide a figure high enough to cover her damages and high enough to make the insurance company pay attention. I still wonder if the case is worth anything; whether we can prove negligence to the satisfaction of a jury. What will turn up in the depositions? Presumably truth; however, I have already learned not to go to depositions without a rod and a reel and some good bait.

23

"Now," Burnett instructs Ginger, "Let's go over some matters pertaining to your deposition."

She sits next to me, across the library table from Burnett. The clock above the doorframe shows 8:35, and Ginger shows she is not an early riser. Burnett's eyes are fixed on her as he continues:

"Ethically, we cannot prepare your testimony, or coach you on it. We can, however, prepare you to be a witness. The purpose of these depositions is for the attorneys to discover as much as they can about your case, including you. The basic facts are known. The insurance company attorneys want to verify those facts. Mostly, they're looking for things they don't know, things they can use against you at trial, assuming your case proceeds to trial. And, we'll do the same with other witnesses. Facts will emerge that may have a large impact on your case." Burnett pauses to sip coffee and look at me.

"The insurance company will have two lawyers: Franklin Wells and Sanford Smith, their local counsel, whom you know. They'll delve into the details of the accident, your injuries and medical treatment, statements you made about the accident, except what you have told us. That's confidential.

"Now the lawyers can ask you questions that may be objectionable at trial. Since this is a deposition, you may have to answer them. Don't answer any question too quickly, though. That way the court reporter will be able to get everything on tape, and we'll have time to interpose an objection."

"They can ask me about anything?"

"They can ask; if the question is irrelevant, we'll object. If we don't tell you to answer a question after an objection, the other attorneys can ask the judge to rule on whether it should be answered. Do you understand?"

"Yes."

"The defense attorneys also want to gauge you as a witness. How do you answer questions? Are you straightforward or evasive? Is your story believable? Are you a complainer or a sympathetic individual? What's your appearance? Do you come across as being injured? How you appear and act can have a large impact on a jury. And, of course, they want to know whether you're telling the truth."

Ginger adjusts her position in the chair. "I'm nervous."

"That's all right. If you weren't, the other attorneys might wonder whether you're been through this before, or wonder about you as an individual. The important thing is that you tell the truth. Wells will do all of the questioning of the witnesses, as will John. Understand, Ginger, it's unlikely we will ask you any questions since we're not here to prove anything. If we want to ask you a question, we'll ask you off the record, in our presence only."

Burnett looks over his shoulder at the clock. "Now, Ginger, you should not guess at the answer to a question. Also, if you're sure you don't know the answer, then say so. If you're not sure, then say so. You may recall the correct answer later. If you're unsure about the answer today but give a positive answer anyway, and then later, for example in court, recall the correct answer and give it, then the other lawyers will ask you whether you were being truthful the first time or the second time. It's a bad trap to fall into. Do I make myself clear?"

"I think I understand."

I'm taking notes. I'm learning. I'm glad Burnett's in charge.

"Again, the most important thing, Ginger, is to tell the truth. Don't try to figure out whether it would be better to give an answer one way or another. They may ask a question several times, each time in a slightly different way. If you tell the truth, you'll always be consistent in you answers. If you try to manipulate the answers, you'll trip yourself up."

Ginger appears humbled. "I don't think I'm smart enough to figure out a certain way to answer a question."

"That's fine. Tell the truth, and we'll deal with whatever comes out. Be sure to listen carefully to the question. And, don't volunteer information. Answer only the question asked. Don't run on and on. You may wind up telling them something that will help them, something they had neglected to ask, or never thought to ask."

"What if I have to go to the bathroom or need to stand? My hip hurts more if I sit too long."

Burnett nods. "We'll take breaks between the witnesses and for lunch. If you need to stand at any time, do so. Be genuine in what you do, though. You're not here to give a performance. This isn't court. No judge or jury is going be here to watch you, and the other attorneys will see through any charades."

I speak up: "I told you it would be a long day. We want you to hear the other witnesses, though, and have them face you as they testify. You're a party and you're entitled to be here."

"Of course," Burnett continues, "If you're able to sit in that chair all day, especially without moving around, they'll wonder how you can do so if your injuries are as bad as you claim."

Ginger puckers her face. "I need to stand and to use the bathroom right now."

"Down the hall." Burnett points toward the door. After she leaves the room, he stands and puts his hands on the back of his chair. "I think she'll be okay."

I stand and stretch. "I told you that she wasn't as bad as we first thought."

"Let's wait until the depositions are over."

Margo carries in a coffee pot while Suzy sets a tray full of cups, cream and sugar in the middle of the table.

I thank them and turn to Burnett. "How am I going to sit across from Sanford Smith all day and behave myself?"

"Don't worry. I'll talk to him later and find out what grade he gave you."

❧ ☙

Suzy leads an amiable, older woman with dyed, curly red hair and unneeded weight under a loose dress into the conference room. Burnett introduces Maureen, a freelance court reporter. After brief chitchat, Maureen pulls a padded swivel chair away from the end of the table nearest the door and replaces it with a straight back chair from the corner. Then she arranges the chair away from the end of the table and facing, on an angle, the first chair on the opposite side of table. From a black case, she removes her stenographic machine and sets it up in front of her chair.

"Would you like some coffee?" Burnett asks.

Maureen declines as she feeds tape into her machine. "Do you have the caption of the case?"

I hand her a copy of the summons. She types in the information and hands it back.

Franklin Wells and Sanford Smith stroll into the room. I nod at Smith and nervously shake hands with Wells. According to Burnett, the difference between the two defense attorneys is that Wells, while also projecting a superior attitude, has the ability and experience to support the attitude. At fifty-one, the slender Wells, who has run in Boston Marathons, has the kind of graying at the temples and mustache that give him a distinguished look. His Milwaukee firm is well known for their insurance defense work. Initially worrying me that Smith had garnered help, I was relieved when Burnett pointed out the defense must have felt the case had merit or Wells would not be in it.

I sit to the left of Ginger, with Burnett to the left of me. Wells sits across the table from Ginger with Smith on his right. When the defense attorneys have arranged their files and documents in front of them and helped themselves to coffee, Maureen places Ginger under oath. Then Wells begins with explanations of procedure.

"So, Miss Buckman, if you don't understand any question, please let me know."

His smooth delivery in the preliminary remarks causes me to revisit the sick feeling I had in my stomach that long ago day in court on the Schultz collection. I doubt the feeling will disappear as it did in court; Wells is no Sanford Smith.

"You know, I had a motorcycle when I was your age," Wells tells Ginger. "How did you learn how to ride your bike?"

The question surprises me. I assumed Wells would go through her high school and other background information first. I wonder whether Ginger understands Wells is searching for a common ground, to get her to feel he is her friend, someone she can tell anything and everything to and hopefully will.

"My boyfriend taught me. Well, he was my boyfriend then. He isn't now. See, he got arres . . ."

I elbow her. Wells catches the movement and starts to comment, but proceeds to the next question. I berate myself for making the move. Why didn't Ginger listen to what Burnett told her? I miss the next two questions and answers while I try to relax.

As Wells purrs like a smooth running engine through Ginger's background, the answers to his questions are what Margo related to me, only in detail. It's not the kind of profile a plaintiff's attorney wants for his client. Fortunately, there's no mention of the janitor-closet affair. The time the janitor opened a door he had forgotten to lock and found Ginger and her boyfriend partially dressed. Or, the junior dance where Ginger, sporting green hair and dressed in jeans and a denim jacket, showed up intoxicated and barfed on the dance floor. The senior year incident where Ginger and five classmates destroyed the backyard of a history teacher they all hated, for a reason never determined, and all were suspended from school also escaped the transcript. Smith must know about her escapades. I guess they aren't relevant. Maybe he's saving them for later. Surely, Smith and Wells laughed about them.

As Ginger's deposition continues, at times repetitious and objectionable, it becomes clear to me the insurance company is still searching for ways to escape from the case based on the liability issues.

Wells asks, "Now to make the record clear, did your motorcycle *at any time* touch any other vehicle?"

"No it didn't."

"And again, so there is no mistake, Miss Buckman, there were no witnesses to the accident that you are aware of, other than Mr. Plumber?"

She pauses. "That's correct." Ginger's voice has begun to flatten out and fade along with her interest.

I look at her. "Do you need to stretch?"

"Yes, I do."

"Why don't we take a break?" Wells addresses the remark to Ginger in a manner suggesting it was his idea. "I need a stretch, too." He winks at me.

"What did the wink mean?" I ask Burnett after the defense attorneys leave the room and the court reporter goes down the hall to the bathroom.

"I didn't see it. Probably acknowledging you know what's going on."

"I wish that were true." Stretching and yawning, I pour more coffee for Burnett and myself. "A lot of this seems boring."

"That's because you know most of the facts, and you've been over them so many times. And, you should know them by now. You can't go into depositions without knowing your case. You wouldn't know what questions to ask. They're looking for what's in that second or third layer—some little fact, event, or character flaw that may help their case." Burnett pats me on the back. "Stay alert, John. Don't let anything slip by you."

"I'm listening to everything. I'm not sure, though, I understand the implications of every question. That bothers me."

Burnett lowers his voice. "I noticed upside down in front of Smith a copy of an investigative report on Ginger. I doubt, though, if there's anything they don't know about her that's relevant."

❦ ❧

When the depositions resume, I listen carefully as Wells explores Ginger's injuries—all of her complaints at the time of the accident, in the months that followed, and her present complaints. Wells questions why she's now unable to work as a waitress at The River's Edge. Hasn't it been over seven months since the accident? Aren't her elbow and knee and lower leg basically healed? Ginger brought her crutches, though she walks without them. I think she handles herself well in fielding his questions. Besides, shouldn't she still have problems? She was a waitress hustling around a supper club, carrying trays of food and dishes, a task that would now be hampered by the mended elbow and more so by her lower left leg. Wells dismisses her hip problem by asking few questions about it.

Wells then asks her what Burnett has described to me as a basic question in her type of case:

"Outside of your work, what is it that you can not do now that you could do before the accident?"

"Ride my motorcycle."

"Isn't that a dangerous pastime?"

Ginger curls her lip. "It's not a hobby. It's how I get around, how I get to work."

"You can drive a car with an automatic transmission, can't you? Then you don't need to use your left leg."

"Yes, but I don't own a car, and I can't afford to buy one because I can't work, and I can't work because I got hurt by the actions of your clients."

I pull the pen in my right hand back into a fist. *Good for you, Ginger.* Wells' smile, I decide, is his way of denying Ginger any satisfaction from her statement. The longer Wells questions her, the better I feel about her. Despite her high school record, she is smart, and despite her appearance and usually moody behavior, I'm forming the conclusion there is in the young woman the potential to be far more successful in life than she has allowed herself to be. I hope she will repeat her answers in court in the same words and tone of voice. Of course, then I will pose the questions. Wells won't give her the opportunity to provide such answers.

When Wells finishes questioning Ginger, I state I have no questions for the witness. I guess Wells is surprised by the *persona* she has adopted for her deposition. She might make a decent witness after all, I decide. Am I glimpsing the real Ginger?

Testimony from the overweight Chief of Police, fifty-seven and nearing retirement, is mechanistic, straight from his report, almost a recording of what he related to me. He had drawn a nice diagram of the accident on his report, with precise measurements, and had neatly filled in all of the blocks on the form; he had not done much of anything else. While he testifies, I ponder Wells' statement at the beginning of the deposition that while Wells subpoenaed the witness, the Chief is an independent witness. I know he works part-time for the Winding River Lumber Company, owned by Sanford Smith's family.

❧ ❧

On the drive back to the office from Wally and Laverne's with Burnett and Ginger, I recall Burnett's advice to eat a light lunch to stave off drowsiness. Hardly a problem for me; I'm keyed-up from coffee and anxiety over the depositions. Each time Wells pauses and refers to his notes, I slide to the edge of my chair as I wait for his next question.

Beeper provides most of the laughs for the day. Obviously, the defense attorneys sees Beeper as the kind of dumpy little man, wearing a three-piece suit and a bowler hat, with blood shot eyes and an engaging grin, that always appears in the saloon photographs from the early nineteen-hundreds. His testimony is essentially what he gave me at his home, except it's given without the presence of the huge woman glowering at me.

"So, Mr. Plumber," Wells asks, "that's all there is to your *story*? You haven't omitted anything?"

Beeper frowns and sits still. "Nothing else that matters, I guess. Well, when the boys went around the corner, a hubcap came off the rear tire and rolled across the street."

Wells appears perplexed. "A hubcap? It rolled across the street?"

"Yeah, it rolled to the gutter, in front of Jorgenson's Bakery or that gift shop next door."

"Did you look at this hubcap?"

"No."

"So, you can't describe it, other than it was a hubcap?"

"That's right. But, I know it came from the car them kids was drivin'."

"How do you know that?"

"Because, as I said, I saw it come off. I was there."

"Do you know what happened to this alleged hubcap, where it is now?"

"Nope. Never saw it again."

Wells hesitates. "So, you know nothing else about it?"

"That's right."

"Okay, Mister Plumber, thank you for your testimony." Wells looks at me. "I have no more questions for this witness."

I sit straight up in my chair while I try to comprehend the ramifications of the flying hubcap? I keep thinking about it as the other attorneys wait for me to question Beeper. I can't think of anything else I need to ask now. Beeper can corroborate Ginger's testimony. If the hubcap is found, I'll have corroboration of Beeper's testimony. I glance at Burnett whose cock of the head and pursed lips signal to me to let it go for now. "No questions."

My turn. It's my time to examine the two young men in the Chevrolet, Jeremy Wilson and Tommy Mathers. I soon realize from Wilson's testimony that the boys have, as have their stories, been scrubbed and tidied up. I stick to my script, the handwritten questions on my legal pad. Normally, Burnett told me, the lawyers make only an outline, or list of subjects and items they want to cover, framing the questions as they proceed. I want to get the questions answered without undue objections. Also, when I'm flustered, I can seek sanctuary in the typed questions before me; there's always a place to continue.

Their answers are what I expected: denials. Their facial expressions and shrugs signal me they can't be responsible for the imaginations of some crazy young woman. Missing from my list of questions is anything about a lost hubcap.

I put it to Jeremy: "On or about October sixteenth, nineteen-seventy five, did the Chevrolet automobile you were then driving, that was owned by your parents, lose a hubcap?"

"Objection." Wells shouts. "Begging the question, as they say. Mr. Wilson has denied driving the described vehicle on that day."

"Let me rephrase the question. To your knowledge, Mr. Mathers, did the Chevrolet automobile owned by your parents lose a hubcap on that date?"

"Not that I know of."

Not true. The answer comes too quickly and sounds practiced. Jeremy knew before the depositions the question might be asked.

"Did any car ever driven by you lose a hubcap while you were driving it?"

Jeremy hesitates. "No."

Wells looks worried for the first time. He must not have known about the hubcap. The coaching has not come from him. Sanford Smith? Probably the boys worked out the answers on their own. Ginger was right about them.

When I finish with Jeremy, who I decide tried to appear mystified by the missing car part, I depo his parents. The defense stipulated the Wilsons own the Chevrolet in question, having purchased it for Jeremy's use, and that he was the principal driver. The Wilsons claim no knowledge of the flying hubcap, and I believe them. One of them would have known if it was missing. I speculate the boys replaced it with a used one from one of the auto salvage yards in the area.

Almost as an afterthought, I ask Mr. Wilson, "Where is the Chevrolet now?"

"We traded it in to the dealer for a different car."

"The dealer being?"

"Pete's Used Cars in Winding River."

After I take Tommy Mathers' deposition, I'm convinced the boys are adhering to a carefully crafted plan that includes no one but them. Such a plan seemed implausible to me until I reflected on Margo and Suzy's comments about the two young men and their abilities, which include lying so skillfully that truth and prevarication blend seamlessly.

Then I announce I'm done. Wells advises he's also finished. We go over the exhibits marked by Maureen: the police report, diagrams, certified copy of the hospital report, doctors' reports, wage statements from the River's Edge.

After the reporter and the defense attorneys leave and Burnett goes downstairs to his office, I sit across from Ginger. "You handled yourself well today." She surprises me by blushing.

"I did the best I could."

"I know you did. Are you beginning to understand the legal process?"

"Sort of. This is a lot more complicated than I imagined it would be. You guys were right. Wells was sneaky at times. I did what Burnett told me to do. I answered his questions the way I remembered things."

"You did fine." I pick up the tablet I gave her before the depositions for taking notes. No notes, no handwriting. Did I expect there would be any? The top sheet is filled with drawings. "These are more than doodles; they approach art. I'm no artist, although I'm beginning to understand some things about art through a friend. You have talent."

Ginger blushes again. "I took all the art courses my school had. I like art."

"Why then don't you do art? Your lifestyle is none of my business, except as it pertains to your case. You're obviously a very independent person; you enjoy doing things that are different. In my life, I've done basically what I wanted to, sometimes for the best and sometimes, well . . . Have you considered doing things that are different but in a positive way? What about going to art school, or studying art in college? You could be creative, but still be different, the individual you want to be."

"I've thought about going to art school."

Tears are forming in her eyes. Am I stepping over that thin red line between my duties as her lawyer and my interest in her as a human being?

❧ ☙

Earl perches on a stool in front of one of his workbenches, assembling a small motor underneath the glow from a florescent light. His head doesn't turn when the door opens and closes. Suspecting his hearing aid is turned down, I shuffle loudly through the machinery and equipment on the floor.

Whenever Earl walks into his shop, the old man enters into his own universe—a place where grocery shopping, cooking and eating, washing clothes, and the other necessities for daily survival cease to exist. Earl controls his universe where the only rule he has imposed is to tinker with the ideas flowing through his mind. He controls everything about his universe except the ultimate fate of it. He can regulate the speed and direction of things like a marble in a rack, but not the destiny of the marble as it rolls toward the end of the last slide. Lately, he seems focused on that realization.

As I near the bench, Earl looks up, raises a finger and then adjusts his hearing aid.

I smile at him. "What are you doing?"

"Fixing the motor in the shop fan." He points at a window where the top half has been removed, leaving a flight path for flies and other flying insects who have suddenly adjusted their travel plans.

I pick up a small mechanical object. "What's this?"

"I don't know yet. I'm working on it."

"Where do you get the ideas for making these things?"

"I don't know. I start tinkering, and they come to me." Earl shrugs his shoulders. "Trouble with ideas, they aren't any good if you can't do something with them, make something out of them."

I lean against the workbench. "I wanted to remind you the judgment hearing on the foreclosure is on Friday afternoon."

"I know. It's on my calendar." Earl lays down a screwdriver and points to a dusty, farmer's co-op calendar hanging from a nail on the wall behind the bench.

"There are a few things we can persuade the court to allow that will help us to some extent, but the bank is going to get the judgment."

"You told me I'd have at least a year from the date of the judgment before the farm is sold."

"That's right."

"Well, I've been thinking about it. I'll just have to make other plans. I'm not worried, though. Something will come along. It always does."

"Spring is here. The tourists will be coming to the Northwoods. Think about selling some of your equipment, those old magazines and some of your furniture in the house. You have some antiques besides the furniture, like lamps and glassware. Maybe you should list some of the real estate for sale again. We'll raise some money."

"I'm not worried about it."

I'm sure he's not. Money and property and mortgage foreclosures do not exist inside his workshop. "I'll pick you up on Friday. We'll talk about the hearing further on the way to the courthouse." I place my hand on Earl's shoulder and then leave him to continue tinkering and to deal with the flies and bees arriving to tour the old man's universe, some of the insects already unpacking and settling in.

24

When I hear the familiar sounds of Margo dropping her purse on her desk and her brisk walk into the kitchen, I jump up from my chair and cross the hallway. "Tell me about the Jorgensons?"

Margo looks puzzled as she sets a bag of sweet rolls on the table. "Lloyd and Kathy. They own the bakery on Main Street where I pick up the pastry in the morning." She pours herself a cup of the coffee that I now brew each morning since I'm the first one in the kitchen.

"I'm sorry, this is about Ginger Buckman's case. They may know something that can help us." I explain Beeper's revelation.

"I see. Well, Lloyd goes in some time after midnight to do the baking, staying until late in the morning. Kathy comes in to open up and stays until closing to handle the sales. They should both be there until midmorning."

Abstract has checked out the rest of the office and strays into the kitchen, sitting next to me. I pet her as I speak: "Later in the morning, I'm going to walk downtown and talk to them. I'm also going to talk to Pete the used car dealer."

"I don't know anything about cars, but Red doesn't think much of him."

"I'm not buying, not yet anyway."

Suzy strolls into the kitchen. While she has adopted many of Margo's mannerisms and is an energetic young woman, she paces herself better than Margo who always appears to be in a rush. Suzy begins her morning conversation with Margo about the prior evening's events in Winding River. I smile as I return to my office. Burnett shrugs off their morning coffee klatches. He doesn't care what they talk about so long as none of it leaves the office.

In the middle of the night I woke thinking about the Buckman case. Stripping away the recitation of known facts, humor and gamesmanship, I summarized in my mind the day long depositions: the pitting of the heavyweight Wells against me is a mismatch, although with Burnett's help, maybe I can stay in the fight; Jeremy and Tommy are not going to deviate from their plan of prevarication, but if I can find the hubcap, perhaps I don't care about their testimony; and Ginger is a young woman who has the ability to drastically change her life. What obligation, what right, do I have to be the catalyst for her transformation?

❧ ☙

I push the files and papers strewn on my desk into piles. On my way to retrieve my sport coat hanging near the bookshelf I stretch out my arms. Standing over my desk, I rip two sheets of paper from a legal pad, fold them twice and stick them in an inside pocket of the sport coat. Burnett suggested to me that sometimes the best way to approach people to get information from them is to do so informally. If I walk in with a briefcase or a legal pad, he thinks they may be reluctant to discuss anything important. If, though, I do need to make notes so I won't forget something, I can use the sheets in my pocket. Conversely, Burnett pointed out that sometimes having the trappings of an attorney like a briefcase, legal pad or documents aids in convincing the witness to take you seriously. I recall the interview of Beeper at his home. Since I don't want to lug my briefcase around the village, I decide to use the pocket paper approach.

As I pass the bank on the way to Jorgenson's Bakery, I stop to talk to Mark Petersen who is walking up to the door. Petersen has kept his word by sending work to me. In return, I accepted his offer to sponsor me for membership in the Winding River Sportsman's Club. I have no aspirations to be a sportsman, other than doing a little fishing, but Petersen persuaded me that joining the club was another way to get involved in the community. Anyway, it pleases Margo who argues it's good for business.

Mrs. Jorgenson is waiting on a customer when I walk in. Mr. Jorgenson is in the back room, hunched over a table. Judging them to be their fifties, they are obviously victims of consumption of large amounts of their products. They're also both very jolly. They appear to enjoy being part of the whole bakery spectrum from the manufacturer to the distributor to the retailer to the consumer, especially the later.

"I found a hubcap next to the curb the morning after the accident," Mr. Jorgenson acknowledges. "I usually walk around in front and clean up every morning, including next door. The lady who runs the card and gift shop doesn't get around too well anymore, so I clean her sidewalk and curb, too. The hubcap was in front of her place."

"Was it from a Chevrolet?"

"It was. I remember it was smashed like someone had driven over it. Until you came in, I never connected it with the accident. Maybe one of the police cars or the ambulance drove over it."

"What did you do with it?"

Mr. Jorgenson considers the question. "I suppose I threw it out like I do all the trash I pick up."

"Would you be willing to testify to that in court?"

"Sure."

"You were closed at the time of the accident?"

"Right. We close at five o'clock in the afternoon."

"What time to do you usually take your cleanup walk?"

Jorgenson hesitates again before answering. "Around six o'clock, depending on the sunrise."

"I see. So, what time in October?"

"Probably about then, maybe a little later. It also depends on what I'm doing in the bakery."

"Thank you for your time." I shake hands with both of them.

"Are you eating your sweet rolls every morning?" Mrs. Jorgenson asks as I open the door to leave.

"They're terrific," I lie. I swore off of them after I gained ten pounds during my first month in the office, even with my gym workouts. Still, it's unfair to assess all the blame to their tasty products. I should attribute some of the new bulge in my waist to the beer at Slider's.

I walk the five blocks north to Pete's Used Cars, located on the corner of Main Street and Water, the cross street before the bridge over the highway. All along Main Street the sidewalks and street are free from trash. White, pink and purple petunias are planted in a thin space of dirt between the curbs and the sidewalks. Most of the older buildings are coated with fresh, bright colored paint and, in a few cases, the buildings have been restored. The effect is the appearance of a village with community pride. I wonder why other communities have the opposite appearance. Perhaps it takes a few concerned leaders in a town to turn the herd around.

Ahead I see strings of colorful pennants marking the perimeters of a used car lot. I lavished my praise too soon; Main Street would look better with the car lot on a side street. As I wend my way through the parked cars, Pete shoots out of a mobile home serving as an office. About forty, small and round with black hair and long sideburns, Pete rapidly covers the ground between us like a spider climbing down its web to see what it has caught.

"You've come to the right place." Pete extends his right hand. "This is one of the largest used car dealerships in the Northwoods. We've got a selection of cars you're going to love. Look at this beauty over here." He pats the fender of a Buick.

"Actually, I wanted to ask you a few questions." I introduce myself and then watch the smile evaporate from Pete's face as I shoot questions at him about the Wilsons' car.

"Yeah, I sold his parents the Chevy. Then I took it back as a trade-in on a Ford. That's what the kid is driving now."

"That's what I understand. So, you would have some paperwork on where the Chevy went from here?"

"That's true. I can show you the paperwork on it."

I'm excited. Wherever the Chevy has gone, I'm determined to track it down and check for the missing hubcap. Even if the boys replaced the hubcap, it may appear different from the others. Also, if . . .

"But, it won't do you any good. It went to the crusher."

I'm stunned again. "The crusher?"

"It was a beater. I couldn't get anything for it but junk price."

As I was rolling to the peak of the slide, I looked away in my enthusiasm and then rolled blindly over the top. I try to stop the descent, but, of course, I have no brakes. "Don't they strip the cars for parts first, or . . ."

Pete laughs. "Nobody would want anything from that car. Besides, who's going to take the time? They've got all the parts they can ever sell."

A dead end. Is that why Jeremy talked his parents into trading the car? "Well . . . thanks anyway. I might stop in again to discuss a trade-in on my car."

Pete flicks on the charm and enthusiasm. "Let me look at your car." His eyes scan the street.

"I walked down here. Maybe I'll be in toward the end of summer."

"It's never too soon to trade." Pete shoves a business card into my shirt pocket.

During the walk back to the office, the disappointment sets in. The Chevy is history. Still, I now have Jorgenson's statement. Forget the car, I have a witness to corroborate part of Beeper's testimony. What's the probability of a hubcap from a different Chevrolet winding up in the curb next to Jorgenson's Bakery between late evening and early morning on the next day? Especially in Winding River.

❦ ❧

The Parrington File. After lunch, I sit in Burnett's office while we discuss the significance of the morning interviews. Burnett yields some of his skepticism about the case. Deciding not to push it further, I bring up the new probate file.

"A middle aged couple came in last week. They're heirs in the estate of a guy named Parrington, a resident of Illinois who died in Illinois but owned a cottage on Thumb Lake. So there was an ancillary probate in Wisconsin. They hired an attorney named Herbert Krummel who has an office in . . ." I leaf through the papers in the file.

Burnett smiles. "Split Lake."

I close the file. "I assumed you knew him since Split Lake is in Timber County. So, Krummel handled the estate. The heirs are complaining about the amount of his bill, one hundred and seventy-four hours for handling something that appears to be uncomplicated."

Removing his glasses while he reclines in his chair, Burnett sucks in his lips and chooses his words. "Herb Krummel. It's too bad. He's a good man, but he should have retired. About eighty-five now, I think. He was a railroad attorney in Chicago until he retired twenty some years ago and opened an office in Split Lake. Never did much lawyering here, a little real estate and probate. He's a widower who spends most of his time hunting and fishing or reading on his boat while it drifts around the lake. The last few years it's been downhill. In spite of those who say attorneys never quit practicing, you have to know when to stop. Unfortunately, he's hung on so long he doesn't recognize the need to let go."

"I reviewed the probate file at the courthouse on Monday when I went down there for a traffic matter. There's no way he could have spent half that many hours on the estate."

Burnett sits up and puts his glasses back on, signaling the end of my consultation. "Go talk to him. Call him first, though. And . . . "

"I know you catch more flies with honey."

"Wait." Burnett pushes his open hands downward. "I was going to say, you won't forget your visit." He hands me a legal pad and a pen. "Here are the directions."

⁎⁎

From his manner of speaking, I have woken Krummel from a nap. He is friendly, though, and asks me to come to his home on the lake. Noting it's three-thirty and the sun is shining with a slight breeze, I easily convince myself a trip to his place will be a pleasant way to end the day. So, I agree to drive out to the lake.

When I drive past Pete's Used Cars, I slump down in the seat and look the other way. I imagine Pete is sitting by a window waiting for the next person to step foot on his web. I cross the bridge and head north on the highway to County Y where I turn west. At each road leading down to cottages along a lake, there is a stack of thin, white arrowed signs, each with the name of a cottage owner in black letters. The pinewoods come up to the ditches on the sides of the roads so I watch carefully for the turn back south on County PP. There must be a scheme to the numbering of the county roads, I reason. The way the roads wind around and cross each other, though, I cannot decipher it.

Several miles onto PP there appears an open, low bridge spanning an inlet connecting the two bodies of water composing Split Lake. Two boys, with their arms wrapped around their bare chests and their swimming trunks dripping water, are preparing to leap from the bridge. They plunge before I reach the far side. Not the smartest thing to do, I think; exactly what I would have done at their age.

I drive up to a crossroad with a gas station on the right and a tavern on the left. Across from the gas station is an old, three-story frame hotel and on the other corner a grocery store. Following Burnett's directions, I turn left, then pass the grocery, a barbershop and a block building with *United States Post Office, Split Lake* across the top, angle right and pull up in front of a log home on the shore of the lake. A birch-framed sign in front of the log house reads: *Herbert J. Krummel, Attorney At Law.*

Krummel stands in the doorway, clad in a short sleeve khaki shirt and trousers. Wiry, weathered and without hair, the tall, stooped man has the appearance of another outdoorsman. He beckons me in.

What was once the living room has been converted into an office. The appearance is startling. Mounted animals everywhere: a moose head, flanked by two antlered deer heads, hangs on the wall behind a desk; a couch and a stuffed chair are draped with fox and raccoon skins (what is that little animal?); assorted other creatures hang over the top of a bookcase stretching along the far wall. Is that a bobcat resting on the couch? A mounted coyote is curled up in one of two log chairs; the other is heaped with books and papers. A black bear stands in a corner, watching over everything.

Krummel shakes my hand before he shuffles over to the stuffed chair and sets books and papers onto the floor. "Sit down."

I sit carefully so as not to lean back against the animal hides draped over the chair. Krummel moves slowly behind his desk and sits in a leather swivel chair. I'm speechless. By my quick count, at least fifteen sets of eyes are watching me, not counting those of Krummel.

"This is some place."

"Got them all myself. Not all around here, though." Without turning, Krummel points over his shoulder. "The moose is from Minnesota."

We do the small talk for twenty minutes, Krummel seemingly interested in my background. During a lull in the conversation, I raise my briefcase to my lap and take out the Parrington file. "As I told you over the phone, I've been retained by two of the heirs in the Parrington estate about your bill." I remove the bill from the file. "They think, and, I have to agree, that one hundred and seventy-four hours is a lot of hours for handling this matter."

Krummel shrugs and speaks without sounding defensive. "I put in all of them. Did a lot of research. I'm sure the bill is right. I've never billed for work I didn't do."

"I know your hourly rate of seventeen-fifty is low, half of our rate. Still, your bill comes to over three thousand dollars. The bill for the whole estate in Illinois wasn't much more than that. This is one cottage."

Krummel stares over my head. "I know I put those hours in. It must be right."

I sigh. What is the common ground here? "If you would cut those hours to, say seventy, I think my clients will pay your bill right away."

"I can't do that. If I put those hours in, I have to bill for them. I'm entitled to payment."

Silent for a moment to phrase my remarks in a manner of respect, I continue: "I was hoping we could work out something. My clients like you and would hate to have to file a motion with the probate court. Burnett thinks a lot of you, too. He insists I try to settle the matter with you."

At the mention of Burnett's name, Krummel returns from a brief flight of mind. "Good man, Burnett. He's an honest attorney."

"Yes, he is. I'm proud to be associated with him."

"I'm sure I put in all those hours. I would not put them on the bill if I hadn't."

What you did, I say to myself, was to lose the decimal point in 17.4 hours.

We sit in silence. Finally, Krummel speaks, "My rate might be too high. I would take seven-fifty an hour. But, I won't cut the hours."

Unable to do the math in his head, I calculate the sum on the inside of the file. Circling the figure I rounded to thirteen hundred dollars, I ponder the result. The sum does include real estate work. Krummel's hourly rate is absurd, but so are his hours. The total amount is what matters. "I'll recommend it to our clients."

"All right then." Krummel looks relieved.

Checking the room again as we shake hands, I guess I won't see another law office like this one. Krummel has a tired, sad look, the look of a man near the end of a long journey, a man surrounded by mounted animals waiting for him to join them.

⁂

I pull into the gas station at the crossroads. An older woman with a wry smile, wearing a bandana and a long sleeve, denim shirt hanging over shorts, strolls out of the white painted building and ambles up to the car. I climb out and ask her to fill up the tank. After she sticks the nozzle in the gas tank, she moves to clean the windshield.

I lean against the driver's door. "Don't bother. It's okay."

"Suit yourself." She puts the windshield wiper fluid bottle and the brown paper towels she ripped out of a metal box on the top of the tank. Her eyes run up and down my shirt and tie. "You look familiar. You from around here?"

"I'm from Winding River." My answer sends a chill through me. Am I no longer from Milwaukee or any other place? Am I home?

"I think I seen you at the courthouse in Lenora."

"Could be. I go there almost every day. I'm an attorney." I reach inside my shirt pocket, take out a black cardholder, remove a card and hand it to her. At first I balked at passing out cards. A pretentious act? The act of someone like Pete the used car dealer? Margo persuaded me passing out cards is part of the business world; potential clients will want to know how to reach me.

The woman sticks the card in her shirt pocket. The smile is gone. "My grandson's in jail for hittin' a deputy after arrest for drunk driving. We have that Attorney Erickson from Lenora. Not much there."

"Not his kind of case, I guess." Easing back into my car, I wonder if the woman has saved any of her bitterness for her grandson for assaulting the law enforcement officer.

As I drive back over the bridge, I look for the boys, but they're gone. A speedboat with the outboard motor throttled down passes under the bridge. The driver waves at me, and I wave back. I know Krummel is nearing the end. Split Lake is the last slide and the perfect place for him.

⁂

Often when I sit in a barroom, even though I'm talking to the person seated next to me, in this case Angie, I enjoy watching the human comedy occurring within earshot. On this pleasant late afternoon in the spring, the lead actor is Slider.

As he pours me a beer, he says, "I'm tired, real tired." Then he shuffles away.

While surprised conversation fails to flow from him as usual, I see he *is* tired. After the boats went back on the lakes, his fishing guide business clicked into annual renewal. Angie told me Slider goes out early every morning when the conditions are right, naps in the late morning, helps out with the lunch at noon, sometimes napping in mid-afternoon, and is back behind the bar by late afternoon until closing. When he's gone, either his wife, who works the kitchen, or his nephew tends the bar. Usually he handles the routine well. Now he seems irritated at everything and nothing.

Angie explains: "He was up late last night and missed his mid-afternoon nap today to go to Lenora to purchase restaurant equipment."

The irritation is heightened by a heavy-set man, fifty something, with a barrel chest that enables him to bellow when he talks, wearing a T-shirt that accentuates his flabby stomach and a light blue cap embroidered with *Fishing Expert*. He delivers a lecture on fishing for the bass, walleyes and northern pike that populate the lakes of the Northwoods to everyone who comes into the bar, wherever they sit and whether or not they listen, causing some to leave early.

What apparently has elevated Slider's temperature, which he usually keeps at normal, is the fact the man has been in the bar for over two hours and is only halfway through his second glass of beer. Suddenly, Slider grabs the man's glass, fills it, and takes the price of a whole glass from money on the bar.

The man turns to Angie sitting a few stools away from him. "You'd think as long as I've been in here, the house would buy one."

Angie ignores him and gives me a wrinkled brow, squinty-eyed, puckered lips, look. He whispers to me to ignore the fishing expert, who is now relating a third version of a story, this time to a young couple on the other side of him.

Slider watches it all in silence. I begin describing the beauty of the Split Lake area to Angie.

Angie's face brightens. "Well, *Attorney* Hall, maybe some day you'll have a home on Split Lake."

The fishing expert has finished his story and downed the glass of beer. He rises to leave when he hears Angie's remark. "Who's an attorney here?" he shouts.

Angie points at me. "The finest young attorney in the Northwoods."

Walking over to us the man sneers. "I hate attorneys. You think you know everything." The sneer turns to a scowl as he faces me. "A lawyer like you ruined my daughter's life. Helped her husband divorce her. I hate attorneys. You're all one step down from used car salesmen and pawn brokers." He stomps to the door.

I look at Angie who shrugs.

Slider with a sunburned face and gritted teeth parallels the man's movements on the opposite side of the bar. Before they reach the front of the tavern, Slider explodes. "Sure you hate attorneys, until you need one. Then your attorney goes to the top of the heap, and you'll promote him as the best one around." Turning away, he quickly turns back. "And don't come in here again because I won't serve you. I hate *Fishing Experts.*"

The man slams the screen door. Slider glares at the door, then walks slowly back down the bar, his eyes fixed ahead.

Angie and I had rotated our barstools, as had the couple at the bar, and we are all staring at the door. One of the card players at a table strolls to the jukebox, inserts a few coins and pushes several buttons.

As the music plays, Angie speaks to me: "Tomorrow it'll be some other crazy thing. It's always some other crazy thing. Why get excited." He drains his stein.

I look down the bar at Slider and then back at Angie. "Have a good evening guys. I've got a date with the shrewdest fox in Timber County.

25

Hearing tapping on the wall above me, I assume Burnett is hammering something. I bound up the stairway to talk to him about Krummel. Burnett finishes hanging a picture on the wall to the right of the door to the library, a framed map of railroads in Wisconsin, circa 1898.

He stands back to admire the wall hanging. "I have a passion for maps, especially old maps or reproductions of old maps. This is an original. I've been meaning to hang it for years. Finally got it framed." He moves back to the map and with a finger traces on it. "See here is the rail line going north through Lenora and Winding River. It was built a few years before this map was made."

I move next to him. "Ann gave me some of the history of the railroad the first time I met her."

"There wouldn't have been a village here without it, certainly not then anyway."

"Where did you get it?"

"From heirs in an estate. They found the map, along with other documents, in the home of the decedent and weren't interested in it. After the estate was settled, they gave it to me. They wouldn't let me pay for it, so I deducted some time from my bill." He steps back again. "I don't know if it's worth much. But, it doesn't matter. I like maps. I like studying history."

Burnett continues as we go down to the kitchen. "Do you read much, John?"

"Not other than law books. I haven't had the time." I decide not to tell him the day before I was almost nabbed by The Dean. Maybe I should read something else. The dust jacket of something literary is all I would need. The Dean would fill in the rest.

"There's always time for the things you want to do. Reading outside of the law helps to keep your mind flexible. It also gives you new perspectives."

"Speaking of minds." As we sit and sip coffee, I relate my meeting with Krummel. "I talked to our clients this morning, and they're satisfied. Krummel is too. I have the feeling he didn't care about the money. He didn't want anyone to think he was padding hours."

"I'm sure that's true."

"What's going to happen to him? He can't go on like that."

"Tompkins is going to bring up his licensing with the Supreme Court. If pushed, I'm sure Krummel will surrender his license."

Burnett offers me a sweet roll. As I reach for it, I see Mrs. Jorgenson's smiling face and wave him off. "Too bad. I enjoyed dealing with him."

"He's drifting now, like he used to drift around the lake on his boat, lying on one of the seats reading."

"How did he keep from getting hit?"

"Oh, they all stay out of his way. He's dispensed a lot of free advice. And, most of the year round residents in the area are hunters and fishermen like him. I think there's an unwritten code in the area to look out for him."

"Well, his place is something else."

Burnett reflects: "I once went out there with two clients for a settlement conference on a contract matter, and Herb had fallen asleep in his boat. The boat had drifted into a cove on the far side of the lake, and I had to drive around the lake and walk down to the shore and yell at him. We anchored the boat to a tree, and I drove him back to the office." Burnett chuckles. "Our clients were very formal, and after they got inside Herb's office, they kept poking me to settle and get out of there. They couldn't stand all those eyes looking at them."

"It is distracting. The eyes are so real."

Burnett finishes his coffee and stands up. "Your clients come first in this matter, but when it's over, do what you can for Herb. If you have a few spare moments, drop in to see him or give him a call."

When I return to my office, I notice Suzy had straightened up my desk. She assumed the task from Margo, accepting without proof of it Margo's allegation that a neat desk and a neat mind go together and any attorney in general practice needs a neat mind. I refuse to accept the first part of the allegation, assuming Burnett's defense: my mind is organized, and I know where everything is located, even if a glance at my desk lends a different impression.

With tax season over, one stack of files has been eliminated from my desk. Now I have begun a system whereby each morning Suzy pulls all of the files on her calendar for that morning and puts them in my office. I work on some and pass on others. In either event, I mark a date on the top of each file when I want it returned, often the next morning. That way most of the files are always in the file cabinets or on Suzy's desk. Burnett has not caught on to my system, and has complimented me on my organization while fretting that we don't have enough work to keep the practice going.

I do not know where anything is located any better than before, but I have stemmed the complaints about files all over my desk. I smile when I see Margo chiding Suzy about all of the files on her desk. Instead of the constant pulling and filing, Suzy has piles in limbo.

After four months of constant switching from one legal matter to another, I understand the need for organization in the practice. Also, I am now more careful with details. My self-imposed rule: Stick to a regimen and be sure to dot all of the *i*'s and cross all of the *t*'s, especially in a matter such as a real estate transaction. I begin thinking of the closing scheduled for ten o'clock.

⚛ ⚛

Suzy has arranged the closing documents in three neat piles on the table in the library. A coffee pot and a tray with cups and saucers, a pitcher of cream, and a bowl of sugar, sit in the center of table. The blinds on the north window are opened wide. She has even straightened up the pictures always askew on the few wall spaces between bookshelves. The room has assumed as professional an appearance as can be expected in a Timber County law office. Only the cracks in the ceiling and the table desperately in need of being refinished are reminders the conference room won't be a threat to any of those south of the Pine Tree Line.

Six chairs around the table are enough, I decide, as I run through a mental checklist. In addition to me, there will be my clients who are the sellers and the couple purchasing the business. The buyers' attorney has reviewed all of the documents and is satisfied with them after negotiated corrections. She will, however, not be present, despite her advice to the buyers it is preferable to have an attorney present at the closing. No realtor is involved. The buyers are bringing a certified check for the purchase price. A check drawn on Burnett's trust account has been drafted to the sellers for the net sales proceeds. All I need to do is make sure the documents are reviewed and properly executed and keep the parties from volleying oral misrepresentations.

While pouring a cup of coffee, I assure myself there will be no wrinkles. I will follow my Closing Checklist and proceed in the manner Dick Minor used at the bank in January. Besides, I have been in many closings since then. The documents are there to cover the contingencies in the offer, for the transfer of the personal property of the Laundromat, and for the lease of the building on Juniper Street. Every day I'm beginning to feel more like a professional, a man with an assured competence in his field.

Suzy escorts the sellers into the room.

"Good morning." I say as I pump the hands of the older man and woman who respond with weak grasps and nods of their heads. I have them sit on either side of me while Suzy pours them coffee. The personalities of the sellers are the polar opposite of the Larsens. I feel like a dentist as I attempt to extract conversation from their mouths.

When the middle-aged buyers enter the room, nothing changes. They greet the sellers and then sit with them in silence. The four appear to have no personalities other than black names appearing on the white pages of the documents on the table.

"Well," I begin, paraphrasing a line from Mark Petersen, "I always start with the offer to purchase to insure that all of the contingencies have been met and everyone is satisfied." I smile, but no one utters a sound or looks up from their pile of documents. Suddenly, I am nervous. As I proceed through the documents and have them executed, I attempt a few jokes, and the silent four smile politely and nod. Maybe they don't like each other. It doesn't matter. I have to concentrate on the documents so I won't make a mistake, so I don't omit anything.

The parties keep their heads buried in the documents. When the last document is signed, I look at them and smile. "Well, that's it." I hand the keys to the Laundromat to the buyers. I'm pleased with myself; I *am* a professional man now. Not hard, really.

As I rise, they all stand. I give them the Henry Miller post closing congratulations, sans the ballpoint pens. They exchange polite remarks, shake hands, and the buyers walk out. "Perfect," I tell myself.

I face the sellers. "Thank you for allowing me to represent you. I'm glad everything went so well."

The smaller, older man nods as he folds the trust account check for the net proceeds from the sale and tucks it in his short-sleeve shirt pocket. "I followed everything you did. I was wondering one thing, though."

"Go ahead, I'll be happy to explain anything you don't understand."

He looks at his wife who is tugging on his arm. "Muriel says I shouldn't get into your business."

"Don't worry about that."

"Well then, where's the money from the buyers?"

"The money from the buyers?" Oh, my god. "Yes, of course. Excuse me."

I race down the hallway, down the stairs, through the front door and across the parking lot to the buyers' car, clutching the open window on the passenger side as they prepare to pull away. I bend over to speak through the window. "I'm sorry but you forgot to give me the certified check."

They both look surprised. The man leans across the front seat. "I don't think you asked for it." He glances at his wife. "You have the check?"

With an unsure look on her face, the woman reaches into an outside compartment of her purse, pulls out a certified check and passes it through the car window to me.

I force a laugh. "It's . . . it's one of those things. You know how hard it is to concentrate when there's so much talking going on."

Not a sound from them while they stare at me with frozen faces before driving away.

After I escort the sellers out of the office with thanks for allowing me to represent them, I watch their car drive off, too.

Another nice job. I use my hand to shield my eyes from the still rising morning sun as I view their car move slowly down the hill. "Can you imagine," I hear the woman say to her friend during their morning gossip call, "He even forgot to collect the money from the buyer." Then the reply: "I don't think they get the kind of training now that the older attorneys got. I never go to someone until they've had some experience." And the rejoinder: "Yes, well Attorney Burnett was busy, and you know we wanted to close as soon as possible. Anyway, we got *our* money. That would have been his problem, wouldn't it?"

❦ ❧

"Did you bring the letter from her doctor?" I ask Judy Larsen who sits across from my desk.

"Yes. She removes a letter from a folder on her lap and hands it to me.

"As I said, Judy, we'll need this for the hearing on the guardianship for Jerry's mother. Let me read it."

"Go ahead."

May 19, 1976

To Whom It May Concern:

I have been the doctor for Lucille Larsen, 37 West Superior Street, Winding River, Wisconsin for the past 16 years. I last examined her on May 17, 1976.

Mrs. Larsen is an 86-year-old widow, residing in a small home on property owned by her son and daughter-in-law. While it appears that she is presently able to handle simple daily functions of living, she has regular episodes of confusion where she is mixed up and disoriented. In addition, she has periods where she has paranoid ideas.

In my opinion, Mrs. Larsen cannot consistently handle her own affairs. I believe, therefore, that a guardian should be appointed for her and her estate.

Sincerely,
Herman F. Schloss, M.D.
138 North Juniper Street
Winding River, WI

"That's fine, Judy." I pick up a legal-sized form and hand it to her. "This is a Petition For Guardianship. Please review it to make sure I've got the correct information." I watch her as she reads through the document.

When she finishes, she looks up and hands it back to me. "It's correct." She frowns. "I do, though, hate that word *incompetent*. It has such a negative connotation. She was, well still is, a wonderful person. I hate to think we have to call her that."

"I understand; however, 'incompetent' fits her situation, the inability to handle her own affairs." I buzz Suzy to come in to notarize Judy's signing of the petition. Burnett and I are notaries; however, Burnett continues to preach to me to use a secretary, whenever possible. That way there is an additional witness who can later testify in court to the execution of the document.

Suzy leaves with her notary seal and the petition.

"We'll have to have a guardian ad litem appointed for your mother-in-law. That will be an attorney in the area appointed by the county judge in Lenora. The GAL's role is to protect the interests of the incompetent."

"Okay." She sits back in her chair. "Why is it that we have to go to court rather than have her sign a power of attorney?"

"Because, Judy, she can't legally execute a document if she's incompetent. It's too late to go that route."

"I see; that makes sense. You'll call me when a hearing date is set?"

"Yes." I toy with a paper clip. One of the reasons I like Judy is the way she peppers me with questions. The interrogation helps me; it makes me think carefully about what I'm doing. After this morning's fiasco in the real estate closing, I realize I have to keep working at my competency. If only Judy would talk more slowly.

Suzy returns with the petition and several copies, one of which I give to Judy.

"Okay, if that's it . . . " Judy puts the copy of the petition in her file and swaps the file for another file on the adjacent chair. "I have a few questions about corporate matters."

As she opens her file, I think the Larsens will have a successful business. They're great socializers, people I enjoy being around. Yet, when it came to the Winding River Manufacturing Co., Inc., they're extremely focused. They always know what they want and how to get it. Maybe, Judy dislikes the word incompetent because she is so competent. Judy Larsen and Mindy, the young woman who entered and departed my professional life during a single telephone conversation on my first day in the office, are going through life on different trains, one on a streamliner to a predetermined destination and the other on a slow moving freight to a nameless siding.

❧ ☙

Late on the Thursday afternoon I sit at the table in the library, facing the open window overlooking the vacant lot next door. The door is closed, trapping the incoming breeze that smells of the tall pines in the lot. I work on an opinion letter to the Bank of Winding River regarding a sticky check matter invoking a law in commercial paper transactions known as the "Holder in Due Course Rule."

When checks or other commercial documents come back to the bank dishonored, there's always a scramble among the parties involved as to who is going to get stuck with the worthless paper. As I see it, the HDC Rule is one of those laws of business transactions designed to determine the winners and losers. It's also one of those laws arguably stated as simply as possible yet interpreted variously and so often that in a particular situation, lining up the parties and assigning winner and losers badges is not simple. The law gives professors and law review members opportunities for scholarly articles and lawyers like me headaches. The *Bills and Notes* course in law school, which would have helped me in understanding the rule, was an elective subject I readily skipped out of fear and boredom and now wish I had not. Since this is the first piece of bank work referred to me by Mark Petersen, I must furnish the right advice.

How do I word the letter so it accurately conveys my opinion and, at the same time, protect myself, give myself room to squirm. Burnett, always honest, warned me that when something is not absolutely clear many lawyers prepare for the future dance on the opinion. Don't, though, he said succumb to waffling with weasel words: "perhaps, possibly, probably, usually," or the more subtle dance floor phrases: "it seems, it appears, it may be."

I debate discussing the matter with Burnett, working on it further, or setting it aside until after the long Memorial Day weekend. The smell of the pines ushers into my mind thoughts of the hike into the national forest Ann and I will be taking on Sunday. I eagerly await the trek.

I refresh myself by going to the kitchen and drinking a bottle of cola from the refrigerator before I resume the research on the bank matter. Unlike abstracting, this subject matter *is* why college students go to law school, to learn how to decipher the complexities of the law. Several months ago I would have sworn it was not why I decided to become a lawyer. I wanted no part of delving into the Uniform Commercial Code, or anything resembling it. Now, the reasons I attended law school seem as vague and contradictory to me as interpretations of the HDC Rule.

Back in my office, for a change of pace I pick up Earl Schmidt's file, placed by Suzy on the corner of my desk reserved for items demanding immediate attention. The foreclosure hearing is tomorrow. As always, I look forward to seeing Earl; I do not look forward to the hearing. I stalled the foreclosure process as long as I could. Now I have to find some other way for the old man to keep his farm. Earl has become more than a client. He is a friend, a friend who depends on me for help. The bank wants to take Earl's home away from him, and Earl doesn't blame the bank; neither do I. The money is owed. There must be a solution to saving the farm and enabling Earl to realize his dream of returning the land to nature. What is it?

26

Sybil Swain is the name she wants. I cannot decide whether the name tends to conjure an actress or a patron of the arts. Either image would fit her. She literally sweeps into my office as though she is acting the movement.

Undoubtedly older than the age of thirty-eight she gives me, no one would think so from looking at her. With a model's build—tall and slender, with light, long hair, high cheek bones and the first set of green eyes I have seen close up—thirty-eight would be a good guess. I determine she was married and upon divorce, took back her maiden name; remarried and divorced, again taking back her maiden name, Schlotzheimer, which she claims never to have liked; changed her name again to Christine Connelly and then to Frances Westfall, when she was trying to write a novel.

Distracted by her appearance and her penchant for names, all I can muster is: "You must be familiar with the procedure."

"Oh yes, I am."

Until she walked in the office, I never thought about a person adopting a new name. Actually, I had heard of it. But, five times? The hermit crab my mother gave me comes to mind. Part of her teaching me about life was the animal kingdom. I recall how the hermit crab moves into a shell it finds until it outgrows it and then moves to a new shell. My client apparently is the hermit crab of names, although an image of a seductive mermaid would be more appropriate.

While she watches me, I check the Wisconsin Statutes. Sure enough, there is a section permitting the change, so long as no sufficient cause is shown to the contrary that it should not be allowed. I look up at her.

"I'll prepare a petition for the name change. We'll have to publish a notice in the *Winding River Record.*"

"Oh, I know, dear." She speaks with an affectation that both disgusts me and suits her.

I search for the right way to put it. "As I understand it, you're in between jobs now, so you're not . . ." I run my finger over a line in the section of the statutes, "engaged in the practice of any profession for which a license is required by the state?"

"Oh, goodness no." She brushes back strands of hair with a hand displaying perfectly manicured nails.

"I had to ask that. Depending on the situation, we would have a hearing on . . ."

"Attorney Burnett explained that to me last time. Will we have the change finalized by the end of summer? I'm planning to go to the Caribbean in the fall."

Reading down the statute, I reply, "Assuming there's no objection that could hold us up in court, I would say yes."

"Wonderful." She pauses. "Hall. That's a plain, solid name. I like it. Hall. Have you always had it?"

Hunched over the statues, I lift my head. "Always."

"Hum. Well, I'll have to think about it."

"I can have the petition ready by Tuesday afternoon, if you'd like to come in then to sign it."

"Oh, that's terrific." She studies me for a moment. "I like your face. The brow shows strength; the nose, which appears to have been broken, toughness; and your mouth works with sensitivity. And the blue eyes, yes, I love blue eyes." She leans across my desk. "I don't mean to pry, but are you married?"

I freeze. The green eyes have magnetized me. She is so close to my face I can see her flawless skin and smell her perfume, and it smells good, and she is extremely attractive. "I . . . almost."

She sits back. "Really."

"Almost," I blubber again as I see in her mind the name Hall floating on a breeze into oblivion.

After she leaves, I enter Margo's office wiping my forehead with tissues. What a way to start Friday. Margo and Suzy smile at me as I speak: "That woman lives in Winding River?"

Margo laughs. "The last man she was married to was wealthy and had a large summer home on Loggers Lake. She got the home in the divorce."

"Does she really go to the Caribbean?"

"She goes where she wants to go," Margo sniffs. "She also got a lot of cash in the divorce. She knows her way around."

"How did I get the appointment? Isn't that Bob's client?"

"She was. She made Bob too nervous. He said he was too old."

Suzy giggles. "Margo calls her 'Mrs. All Names.'"

❧ ❦

Usually, Suits sits in my office on the edge of his chair, appearing as though he would leap and flee at the snap of the fingers of someone after him. This morning he looks subdued, a reason for me to worry. Whenever he's quiet, I'm suspicious he's calculating or plotting something I would rather not know. My comfort level is always higher when he fidgets and works over the room with his furtive eyes. He has bandages on his face. Are there cuts underneath the bandages, or has he slapped them on for effect? Does he still keep crutches, a cane and a neck brace behind the seat of his pickup?

I asked him to come in so we could review his divorce file, in particular the proposed property settlement, in preparation for the final hearing on Tuesday.

He addresses me without expression: "This is before the judge, right?"

"Right. You and I will be there along with Norma and her attorney, Dick Minor.

"I can have someone else there if I want."

What? Scary, how I'm beginning to understand the way he talks, how a flat statement can be a question. "Yes." I lean back in my chair. "Why are you asking? Do you plan to have someone else at the hearing?"

"Maybe." He looks at me. "You get a deal with the D.A.?"

"Too soon. I've got the criminal misdemeanor. Now I'm trying to wear him down to an ordinance misdemeanor. You've had your chance. I don't think he'll give you another one. Anyway, we need to discuss the situation for your divorce."

He wrinkles his forehead. "I told you I won't pay alimony."

Sometimes I wonder how much he listens to me. "I already informed you she doesn't want alimony. Besides, she makes more money then you do." I sigh. "Look we've been over and over this." I pick up a copy of the stipulation and hand it to him. "Take this home and look it over again. I want to be sure you're satisfied with the terms. I don't want any surprises in court."

Suits rolls up the papers. After he stands up, he shoves the roll into a pocket in the back of his blue jeans. "Three o'clock at the courthouse?"

"Three o'clock. And don't be late. The judge doesn't take kindly to persons who show up late for court."

"I know that."

"I guess you do. You and the judge are obviously well acquainted."

Suits steps through the door, then quickly backs up. "It's in there she doesn't get the grill, right?"

"Right."

I watch him disappear into the hallway. Grabbing my coffee cup from the desk on the way, I amble into the kitchen to get a refill. Then I climb the stairs to the library. Burnett sits at the table reading a Wisconsin case. He lowers the book to the table when I slide into a chair across from him.

"Suits came in. The final hearing in his divorce is next Tuesday." Burnett nods as I formulate how to ask him a question. "Tell me about him. No, tell me about those like him."

Burnett gazes at me. I hear the wall clock ticking as I wait for the reply. He starts in slowly as he always does; he enjoys being a mentor.

"There's one in every county, in every town, in every village. They're all looking for the colossal deal, colossal, that is, in terms of their small minds. Once they've received the benefits of the deal, then they begin searching for the frayed threads of the contract for their deal so they can escape the promises they've made. They're also searching for the insurance adjuster too busy to investigate all of the facts, the witness who looks the other way rather than become involved, the other party who would rather settle than fight. Are they dishonest or are they merely opportunists?

"They all know where the line of legality lies, and they all walk as closely to the line as possible. Once in a while, they stumble over the line or lose it in the dark and wind up on the other side. But, they'll never admit to crossing the line on purpose, or even that they have crossed it, unless they're caught in the act or found on the other side. In those cases, they will sort through their mental briefcases crammed with arguments, alibis and other vindications to create the illogical defenses that soothe their consciences while infuriating those of others. Eventually, some of them will face disgrace. The rest of them? Their obituaries will sanitize their lives except for those who remain that knew them, who watched them dance the line and will remember them for what they were."

His serious face dissolves into a wry smile. "Along the way they wind up in the office of the new attorney in town. They've been in my office in the past, in Sanford Smith's office, Dick Minor's office. Now they're crawling into your office." Before I can respond, he switches subjects:

"I see you met with . . . what does Margo call her?"

"Mrs. All Names." I breathe deeply and exhale. "Yes I did. She is *some* woman."

Burnett laughs. "Yes she is, and an interesting woman. She sheds names as she sheds husbands and the other failures of her life. I think her beauty has always been a curse for her." He smiles again. "Did you smell the perfume?"

"Yes, but it was the green eyes that did it to me."

❧ ☙

Earl Schmidt appears unperturbed by the foreclosure as I drive him from the farm to the courthouse for a four o'clock hearing. He wears bib overalls with a denim shirt and sports a seed company cap he has saved for the right occasion. When I remind him of the seriousness of the situation, Earl shrugs his shoulders. "What the hell. It won't be the end of me."

As we drive south to Lenora, Earl's complaints about his health concern me more than the judgment hearing. "So what do you think is the matter with you?"

"I don't know." Earl has his window rolled all the way down with his right forearm resting on the sill. As the air blows in, he has to adjust the new cap downward with his left hand to keep the cap from blowing away. "I just don't feel too good lately."

"Well, you had better go to the doctor," I shout at Earl over the wind and the sound of the tires slapping on the highway. "Who's your doctor?"

Earl laughs. "I don't have one."

"What do you mean you don't have one? What do you when you're sick?"

"I don't get sick." Earl reflects for a moment. "I went to the hospital and saw Dr. Schloss when I fell off the barn roof, but that was twelve, fifteen years ago. I got glasses and a hearing aid. That's all."

"You mean you haven't had a physical recently?"

Earl laughs again. "I've never had a physical. They're expensive."

"You must have gotten the good genes in your family."

"I suppose so since I'm the only one left."

"You know, Earl, I've collected a good deal of information on donating your property, and we still haven't worked out a will."

"I wouldn't worry about it none. Whatever happens, happens."

I slow down behind a car making a turn onto a road leading to a lake. "We need to worry about it. You should have a will."

"Why? The way I figure it the farm is going back to the bank. After that, what I'll have? All I'll have left is my health. I can't pass that on to somebody. If I lose my roof, I'll find another one. A will isn't going to help me now."

"What will you do for a workshop?"

Earl turns to me. "That's what's got me worried. I think that's why I'm not feeling too good lately."

We enter Lenora on the north end, the highway leading straight south through the city. As we approach the courthouse square, I mull Earl's situation while Earl stares out the window. I'm glad I've driven him. The drive would have been a struggle for him, and this way we can talk, even if the talk, as it always does, ends without resolving anything.

Earl still has a spry step, and bounds up the stairs to the courtroom. Whatever is bothering him must be psychological. Since there is a hearing going on, we sit on the benches in the back of the courtroom while we wait for his case to be called. I remind Earl to take off his cap. He sheepishly removes it, muttering, "Oops."

Sanford Smith and Mark Petersen sit across the aisle from us. I smile at Petersen who reciprocates with a weak smile. He has the appearance of a man who is in a place he does not want to be in. Angie looks up from his machine to find my eyes, showing no signs of impartiality other than not looking at anyone else.

When the parties and their attorneys from the case ahead of us have cleared their tables and we have settled in, the clerk gives a file to Tompkins who announces:

"All right, next case, *State Bank of Winding River versus Earl P. Schmidt*, Case Number 2908." When everyone is seated, the judge continues, "Please state your appearances."

Tompkins pays little attention to appearances when he knows everyone at the counsel tables. He looks at me in what is more than a casual glance. Ann talked her mother, Mildred, and the judge into inviting us for Sunday dinner a few times. The way we acted toward each other, Tompkins must know our relationship is a serious one. Maybe now he feels he needs to pay more attention to me. Ann told me her father liked the idea I served in the Army, as he had during World War II, a fact of which he is proud; that I present myself well, except for occasional rashness; and that I am an attorney. Ann said one of her sisters is married to a research chemist and the other one to a paper products salesman. Her father can't carry a conversation very far with either of them.

Lately, I sense Tompkins realizes he has been dismissive of me when I come to court. I wonder whether his past attitude resulted from a sense of showing impartiality or because he cannot let go of his remaining child. He now seems resolved to show me more respect. After all, I might some day become the father of some of his grandchildren. Still, I'm not counting on him making a huge turnaround toward me. I know I remain under his microscope, my arms pinned under the clips that hold the slides. He starts in:

"This a motion for Summary Judgment on a mortgage foreclosure brought by the bank. I dismissed this action in February based on the failure of the bank to give the defendant the notice required by the mortgage. It appears by the documents on file that the requisite notice was given and the action re-filed."

The judge continues looking through the file. "An answer was interposed by the defendant to the new complaint; however, it appears most of the allegations in the complaint are admitted." He peers over his bifocals. "Is that correct, Mr. Hall?"

"Yes, Your Honor. We admit the defendant is in default, the balance due, and the right of the bank to bring this foreclosure and be granted judgment. What we do object to is the allegation," I read from a paragraph in the complaint, "*that the property cannot be sold in part or parcel without material injury to the parties interested.* The property being foreclosed is a forty acre farm, and it's our contention that it can, and should, be sold in parcels."

The judge turns to Smith. I know Tompkins dislikes Smith intensely. Burnett told me Tompkins thinks the conceited lawyer is below par in his abilities and never hesitates to reflect that belief when asked by a lawyers' rating service. "Mr. Smith."

"Well, judge . . . " Smith looks out the window rather than at Tompkins and then glances at Petersen. "We've discussed this matter, and the bank would be agreeable to selling the property at sheriff's sale both in parcels and as a whole, whichever will bring the highest total bid."

"Mr. Hall."

"We agree to that, Your Honor." Why hadn't Smith agreed before? "The other objection is to the redemption period. Attorney Smith wants to begin advertisement of the property for sale six months after date of entry of judgment since the bank is waiving its right to a deficiency judgment against the defendant for any monies owed the bank after the bid price is deducted. The statutes on which the plaintiff is relying for argument are not applicable to this case. Since this is a farm, the statutes are clear that the property may not be advertised until after the expiration of one year from the date of entry of judgment."

"I believe that's correct." Tompkins picks up his copy of Volume 2 of the *Wisconsin Statutes* and begins leafing through the pages. "Mr. Smith."

"Well, Your Honor . . . " Smith begins to argue, but Tompkins has found the relevant section of the statutes and quickly cuts him off. "That's what the statutes say, Mr. Smith."

Smith looks at the window again as Petersen nods his head in approval and tugs at Smith's coat sleeve. He faces the judge. "We agree to commence advertising after the one year redemption period has expired."

Earl leans toward me and whispers, "Why'd they bother with that stuff?"

I whisper back, "Obviously the bankers want to get your place as soon as possible to cut their losses. They think they're not going to get their money out of it."

"Hell," Earl says a little too loudly. "I could've told them that. Why didn't they just ask me?"

Noticing Schmidt appears amused by the proceedings, Tompkins shoots a disgusted look at me. Does he think I haven't properly advised the old man of the consequences of the lawsuit? Tompkins struggles but is unable to restrain himself from stressing to Earl the seriousness of the judgment before he adjourns court.

In the corridor Earl, Petersen, Smith and I shake hands. When the allegations and counter-allegations have been pled, the arguments and the snide remarks said, the theatrics performed, the decision made, and the acrimonious air cleared, invariably parties and their attorneys shake hands. An oddity, I think. I surmise it's one of those moments when either the goodness of human nature overcomes the meanness and lack of civility created and nurtured by greed, hatred and revenge, or . . . everyone is simply glad the hearing is over.

"We'll come up with something," I promise Earl as we pull out of the parking lot to drive back to Winding River to pick up Ann. The three of us are going to dinner at the River's Edge, and it's obvious Earl is looking forward to it. The granting of a foreclosure judgment against a man's farm is not, I know, something to celebrate, unless you're a banker in a Jimmy Stewart movie. This case is merely an opportunity to treat Earl to a meal.

Passing the antique shop across from the courthouse, I brake *Rusty*, back up and park in front. I turn to Earl. "This will only take a few minutes. I want you to meet an owl that can get you some money."

27

We leave in the dark so we can reach the lake by sunrise. The public road into the forest ends in a turnaround, and from there we hike toward the lake. Even near the end of May, it is cold before dawn, so we wear jackets with our backpacks on top. A nearly full moon helps us follow a seldom used, winding path through maple and ash trees mixed in with the ever present tall pines, cedar and white birch.

"It doesn't look like many people use this trail." My soft voice carries easily through the still air.

Ann is leading the way and replies without turning around. "Not everyone wants to walk the mile and a half to the lake and then back."

When Ann proposed the hike, she assured me it would be easy and a lot of fun. She claimed to have hiked the trail many times. As a youngster, the hikes were with her girlfriends. In college, they were with roommates and friends she hosted on weekends or holidays. The treks had always been pleasant experiences for her, even when it rained. She now thinks of the lake as her own, her special place to take special friends.

I glance at the moon; then check the woods. "Which way are we going now?"

"Due east." Ann stops and turns around. "Do you want to rest? We've gone about a mile."

I pull up behind her her. "Hey, I'm the one that spent three years in the infantry. They didn't carry us."

"Didn't they teach you how to find your way in the dark?" She gives me a hug and leads on.

"What is that?" I speak quietly as I point forward.

"A red fox."

"I've never seen a fox before, at least in the wild."

"Maybe we'll get lucky and see a black bear."

I stop. "There are bears in here?"

"Could be." Ann halts up when she realizes I am no longer following her and turns around again. "What's the matter?"

"Isn't that dangerous?"

"The bears?"

"We don't have any weapons."

"We don't have any food either. That's why I told you not to bring anything except water. If we see any, they won't bother us."

"Are you sure?"

"Who's leading the way?"

I commence walking again. "Don't get so far in front of me."

Ann laughs. I know she thinks I'm a clown sometimes. The ski trip to the UP with Ann and the Larsens in February proved her right. My first few runs down the bunny hill and my leaping off the chairlift rather than waiting for it to nudge me forward as I got off provided the laughs for the day. I wasn't trying to be funny; I was apprehensive and too tense to do anything right. But, I caught on, and I think they were somewhat disappointed.

We reach the west shore of the lake as the sun creeps over the treetops on the east side, layering the sky in mauve, peach and powder blue. The woods surround the shores of the lake except for a few clearings. We stop at one of them to survey the lake.

I speak first: "This is beautiful. The lake must be a mile long by a half-mile wide. The water is so still and clear and clean. This looks like a painting."

"Actually, it's one of my paintings. I'll show it to you sometime."

Ann points out granite boulders she and her friends have used as chairs. We remove our backpacks and sit on the boulders and watch the sunrise. We are close enough for me to put an arm around her. She reciprocates. I wish someone with a camera would come along and take a picture of us.

As the sun moves higher, I take a bottle of water out of my backpack, offer it first to Ann, then drink from it. "I can't get over how quiet it is."

"If we're quiet, too, after awhile we'll start to see the fur and the feathers. We're being watched. So, don't move or make much noise, and they'll lose interest in us."

I lower my voice. "It's nice here. I like it."

"Are you coming to the conclusion that you're going to stay in Winding River?"

"I'm working on it. I still have a feeling I'm missing something by practicing here. How many people have ever heard of this place? I grew up in this state, and I had never heard of it. I mean, what's ever going to happen in Winding River?"

"Whatever happens anywhere? It's a matter of degree, isn't it? Don't you think what you've been doing to help Earl is important? He's part of a vanishing breed; it won't be too long before his kind will be gone from the countryside. And how about Brenda and Ginger?"

"I know what you mean. It's just . . . " A bird gliding into a treetop distracts me. "Did you see that? Must be a huge crow."

"A bald eagle."

"There's no white on its head."

"It's an immature eagle. They don't get the white right away."

I shake my head. "You always make me feel inadequate. Where was I when you were learning all this?"

"In the gym pounding on someone?"

I laugh. "You're probably right. On the other hand, learning a few moves helped me fend off Bill Krueger. I could be sitting here still mending a broken jaw."

"I wouldn't like that. You probably couldn't kiss me then."

"That *would* be bad." I edge closer to her.

☙ ☜

Sunday evenings in Winding River are dead, even in the spring. Except for Alma's, Squeaky's Southside Tap and two gas stations, every place in the village is closed. Most of the residents stay home on Sunday nights trying to rest from the weekends. Ann has gone home to prepare for Monday classes. I lay on my bed reading a paperback novel. Falling asleep on couches is becoming a less frequent event, though I did spend another night on the one at Ann's, again to Shelly's surprise. Burnett continues to urge me to read beyond the law; he has teamed up with The Dean to raise my literary awareness. A glance at the art on the cover of my paperback would tell them this is not a book from their list. Still, this is as close as I have ever come to making a dean's list of any kind.

Darkness has arrived, and I feel cool air flowing into the room through the front window. As I partially close the window, I stare at the lights in the houses below me, wondering as I always do what the people in them are doing, what stories are unfolding. Most of them are probably boring, but what about the house where Norma's lives, or the one where Brenda lives? I leisurely work my way to the kitchen to fetch a bottle of beer from the refrigerator. After I open it and take a few swigs, I cross the hall, switch on the light, and sit at my desk. I call Tim Waters.

"Were you able to find out anything about Lynch?"

"Sorry, John, I haven't. I'm working on it. Kind of interesting, though. I didn't realize the network of ex-marines out there. When I got out, I didn't want to think about it. If you remember, we were the bad guys then."

"I remember. I was a bad guy too, and I didn't go to Vietnam. I just wore the uniform."

"John, I'll keep working on Lynch."

I hang up and finish off the bottle of beer. Back in my bedroom, I lie on the bed and settle in with the paperback. It's mindless reading. Right now I don't need any more challenges. I almost finish another chapter before . . .

❧ ❦

Again the call comes after midnight, about two hours after I fell asleep. As I stand by the phone in the conference room, I hear nothing but sobbing. "Who is this?"

"I'm sorry, Mister Hall." Brenda's voice comes through the sobs. "He did it again. I can't believe it really happened."

"Bill?"

"It had to have been him." The sobbing continues, and she's unable to speak for some time. "The house. It's gone, burned, all of it, everything."

I have trouble comprehending her words. Were there sirens? "The house you just fixed up?"

"The police and the firemen think it was burned on purpose."

"Are you all right?" Of course she isn't. I cut off her answer. "Where are you?"

"At my parents. I . . ." The sobbing picks up again. "I give up."

"Don't do that, Brenda. You've come too far to give up now. As soon as I get dressed, I'll come over to your parents' place."

"Whatever you think." She cries as she hangs up.

Now that I have shaken off the sleep, I begin to get angry. As I dress, I resist the urge to find Bill and stop it. Then I remember Bill is in jail.

I drive to Brenda's house. Smoke from smoldering ashes rises toward stars twinkling as though, even at their distance, they are irritated by rising particles of soot. Several fire trucks along with a police car are parked in front of the now vacant lot. Firemen hose the ashes, while the captain and two other firemen sift through rubble. A few scantily clad neighbors stand on the sidewalk gawking. Sven sits in his car writing up a report. I park behind the police car, hurry over to the driver's side, and put my hands on the rolled down window. "Bill is in jail, isn't he?"

Sven nods. "And he's been there all day and night. In fact, he's been there all weekend since he only works on weekdays."

"Huh." Stumped again. "Brenda said you guys think it was arson."

"Absolutely. You can talk to the captain. It wasn't anything sophisticated. Looks as though someone forced open the back door, poured gasoline over the kitchen and living room floors, lit a match and poof. These old frame houses with no fire walls go quickly."

"No one was home?"

"Your client went somewhere for the day with her kids and her parents and decided to stay overnight at their house. Fortunately, our arsonist isn't a murderer."

I remove my hands from the window and step back. "Do any of these people know anything about the fire?"

Sven eases out of the car and stretches. "Not the people out here. We'll canvas the neighborhood in the morning."

"Someone needs to talk to Bill. He must be involved. I suppose, though, that may be a problem now that he has an attorney."

Sven smiles. "We'll work on it. We know where to find him."

"Thanks." I wave at the policeman and drive to the home of Brenda's parents. Sven has always been candid with me. I have developed a good relationship with the young officer, and, to the extent possible, treat our conversations as confidential. Perhaps Sven views my temporary appointments as District Attorney when the D.A. is out of town as signifying I'm one of the good guys.

⚮ ⚮

"What's the matter?" Ann speaks in a sleepy voice. "It's after two o'-clock."

"Someone burned Brenda's house . . . gone, completely gone."

"Oh, no. That's awful. Are she and the kids okay?"

"Depends on whether you mean by "okay" the fact they weren't in the home at the time. When I left her, Brenda was hysterical; her parents wouldn't talk to me. Even her boys gave me loathing looks. Now, thanks to Attorney John Hall, Brenda and her boys have no home, nothing except the clothes they're wearing. You think there's anything further I can do for them?"

"Here we go again. I suppose you've been lying in bed mentally listing all the things you've done wrong since you got here."

"Exactly. You want to hear my list? The first . . . "

"No, I don't. When are you going to accept the fact everything won't turn out the way you planned? Burnett is right, you can't blame yourself for everything that goes wrong, and you can't let yourself get so emotionally involved in your cases."

"Burnett told me on the first day I arrived here that I need to establish a good working relationship with my clients, make them feel I care about their problems."

"And that's what you're doing. The problem is you can't handle things when they suddenly turn sour, when your clients need you the most. Instead of wallowing in pity with them, you need to be formulating your advice as to what they should do next. Even if you gave bad advice, and I don't think recommending divorce to Brenda was bad, you have to move on. I'll bet every time you lost a boxing match you sulked awhile before you began preparing for the next match."

"That's true; I remember the defeats more than the wins. I recall every detail of a bout I should have won that kept me from going to the finals of a tournament."

"You're obviously competitive. That's a good attribute for an attorney." She pauses. "How many boxing matches did you have a year? What I'm wondering is how you're going to handle things when you start having legal bouts every day? How are you going to have time to wallow around in every defeat, in everything that goes wrong? Remember, you're not a psychologist or a psychiatrist or a social worker; your world is the world of law."

"My world is the world of people in which the law is only a part."

"Look, John, tomorrow . . . Hey, this is a new day. It's Monday, Memorial Day. Let's watch the parade in Lenora."

"They don't do fireworks, do they?"

"Go back to sleep, John. I love you."

"I love you, too. You know, I'm trying to do it right."

"I know."

28

Snatches of sleep last night. First it was Brenda, then Ginger, then Earl, then one client after another to the point I even thought about Billy. Should I have done something to try to help him? No one contacted me after I turned him in. Of course, he had to go back to the mental health center, and I did the right thing in turning him in; besides, how could I have know then he wasn't going to try to hurt me. What else could I have done for him? Further help for Billy requires skills beyond those of my profession. Yet, I'm obsessed with editing advice given to clients and mentally redrafting documents. I know I cannot change the past. Still, next time I'm in a similar situation . . . I continue to grapple with my lack of experience.

Foremost in my mind this morning is Brenda. What difference does it make to Brenda's divorce whether Bill himself burned down the house she lived in? I lean back in my office chair with my feet crossed and resting atop a bottom drawer of my desk I pulled out, a temporary footstool I discovered from watching Burnett. Sipping coffee while I wait for Margo and Suzy to arrive to begin their morning routines, I reflect on the events of yesterday as if I am still there.

I stand with Ann in the back of a crowd along the main street of Lenora. My eyes look at the parade but the messages relayed are mostly blocked as my mind sorts through possible suspects and their motives for the fire at Brenda's home. A police car and several fire engines with blaring sirens lead off the parade along the highway, followed by a convertible with a waving mayor and assorted other dignitaries. A Legion drill team comes into view. Floats. . . . *It could not have been Bill since he was in jail all weekend. No, it is possible. Someone could have let him out*

239

of the jail. Unlikely. Barricades block the cross streets. The sidewalks are lined with young men in T-shirts and shorts with children on their shoulders. Young women and other children stand in front of them and older people with caps and sun visors, holding small flags, sit in lawn chairs backed against the curbs.

Why should I be concerned about the cause of the fire? What difference does it make to Brenda's divorce whether Bill was involved in the burning of the home? . . . Kids streak back and forth into the street to grab candy thrown from the floats. The high school band marches in a formation I know would earn most of them extra KP duty in the Army. I cannot fault them, though, since I know many of them are marching to satisfy the requirements of others so they can then proceed with sunbathing on a pier or water skiing on the lakes, or slipping away with their boyfriends or girlfriends.

Ann scolds me. Somehow she knows the mechanism processing images my eyes are picking up is creating only flickering pictures. "You're supposed to be enjoying yourself."

"I know." I hate lying, so I cannot say I *am* enjoying myself.

Who is the arsonist? Now her home is gone, and she has no place to go but to her parents' home, pride or no pride. What should I do? What can I do? The clopping of horses at the end of the parade mixes with the clapping of the children and the clanking of the metal chairs being folded.

I empty my coffee cup, remove my feet from the drawer and close it. The answer is suddenly obvious. If Bill isn't involved, he may wind up with probation and can still be employed, thus, providing child support for his two sons. If he's convicted as being an accessory to the arson, in view of his other offenses, he will likely get prison time. That will sever his earnings and the child support. So, do I want him to be involved? If he is, the child support will be gone, but he'll get prison time. Brenda will be safe from him for a long time. Brenda worries about money; I worry about Bill. I think she can make it without his money.

Margo and Abstract arrive. I meet them in the hallway. Margo looks concerned, and I know it's genuine since she never portrays false emotions.

"I'm so sorry, John. I've heard about Brenda."

I try the philosophical approach. "It's one of those things." I avoid her eyes by leaning to pet Abstract, knowing she doesn't believe me.

I follow her into her office, where she drops her purse on her desk, with that resulting sound I hear every morning, and then into the kitchen where she pours a cup of coffee. Comfort has come to me from her routine, though I would not admit it. I sigh.

"Somehow we'll have to help her start over."

"That may be beyond us, John. Even if she can come up with more furniture and household items, she'll have to find another place to rent, and there isn't much in Winding River."

"Well, think about it. Talk to Suzy." What would Burnett say? No, what would he do? "You know Bob would go beyond his legal duty to help her."

"Yes, I know."

How do I interpret Margo's facial expression? Is it a sign of caring, or is it a look of resignation that she may have another poor businessman in her midst.

❧ ❧

As soon as I sit at my desk I call the police station. Sven is off, and the Chief is abrupt with me. Did he not like my questioning of him at the depositions on Ginger's case? Burnett warned me several times that being an attorney will not help me garner votes in a popularity contest. I learn Sven is on the second shift starting at three o'clock. I'll catch him later.

Suzy answers the phone now, diverting the calls around the office. When she buzzes me to pick up a line something prompts me to inquire as to the identity of the caller. "Do you know who it is?"

"A young woman. I believe she said her name is Mindy."

A voice from the past. I'm curious what has happened to her. I heard she commenced a legal action. I cannot, though, now yield to the curiosity even though I'm now in a position where I could probably struggle through her nightmare. I have to get to court. "Tell her . . . tell her anything except that I'm in."

"She said she just has a question."

"Don't listen to it. Make any excuse you can, but don't listen to the question."

"Okay. You're the boss."

I pick up my briefcase from under the back window and open it on my desk to toss in Suits file, a legal pad and two abstracts. Then I head to the courthouse for the final hearing on his divorce.

∻ ∻

During the drive to Lenora, I run through my mind the procedures for the final hearing. Through Dick Minor's assistance, the parties entered into a Final Stipulation settling property and other issues and avoiding a trial. I snicker thinking about the torture Suits endured throughout the negotiations, claiming he did not want the divorce and that Norma would come back to him, at the same time being eager to settle the money issues. For him: money before matrimony. Money. I played on Suits' life priority in persuading him to settle. In turn, Suits played on Norma's life priority, getting rid of him.

The terms of their written agreement: Division of Property. Norma is awarded the house along with the mortgage, leaving a small equity; her car and the loan on it, leaving no equity; and most of the household furniture, appliances and furnishings, the fire sale value of the items minor. Suits is awarded his pickup truck, with the loan on it; a boat with an outboard motor, two older snowmobiles, a rifle, a shotgun, and hunting and fishing gear, along with the loan on them from the finance company, and, the biggie, the grill. Why do some divorce settlements teeter on who gets the grill or the weed whacker?

The present dollar values are skewed in favor of Suits. Nevertheless, I reason, Norma has the house, and if she keeps up the mortgage, a large "if," she might have something of value in the future. Surely, Suits will run down most of the property he receives, and replacing it will depend upon the success of his latest scheme.

Strangely (what about Suits is not strange?), before the ink on the agreement was dry, he told me he got exactly what he wanted. With his penchant for dollars, I assumed he would fight for the house, recognizing the long-range investment, even though I knew for him, long-range is the limits of the scope on his rifle. Of course, he was way ahead of me. How could I have figured out he did not need the house because his indulgent mother, who apparently never understood what she had hatched, will let him live in her home, rent free, naturally.

Alimony: Each waives the right to receive alimony from the other. I understood Suits not wanting to pay alimony to Norma. At first, though, the fact Minor failed to insist on it for his client perplexed me. Thinking it over, Minor knows Norma earns as much as Suits does, more depending on who is asking, and chasing Suits for alimony payments or having him thrown in jail for not paying them would be lifetime pursuits. Since they have no children, there are no issues of custody or child support. I decide Norma wants a clean break from Suits, no continuing link like alimony.

Suits thinks reconciliation is still a possibility. If only he can talk to her, he claims, she will understand everything. The divorce is simply another deal, and he knows how to handle deals. Just watch him.

As I pull into the parking lot, I spot Suits' black pickup truck. Attached to the tailgate is a crudely painted sign reading *Norma's Man*. The lot is nearly filled with cars. Why? Although a Tuesday, due to the Monday holiday, it becomes the morning for traffic and criminal intake purposes. Yet, it's too early for those proceedings.

The hallway outside the courtroom is empty. I poke my head inside the door. A motley assortment of twenty plus adults, young to old, dressed in dated suits and dresses are packed on the benches nearest the door. Rising at the defendant's table in front of the crowd is Suits, dressed in the same out of style suit as the other men. Suits has the nervous, beady-eyed look he usually sports when he is guilty of something, like a child caught in a forbidden act. He meets me at the gate of the low wall separating the tables from the benches. I'm baffled.

"What is this?" I whisper to him.

"The Relatives. They wanted to come. You said it was okay."

Feelings of disgust, loathing. Why do I have to have Suits? Minor is the savior. I want his client instead. "This isn't a celebration."

"I wanted Norma to remember."

"Remember what?"

"Our wedding."

"Whaat? Never mind." I motion for Suits to sit back down at the table, glimpsing as I do so, Angie with his head down and a hand covering his laugh.

I try not to look at The Relatives as I move back into the hallway. Why is there always a surprise? Everything in their divorce is settled.

Why can't I have a simple hearing? Norma and Minor exit a conference room and stroll down the corridor toward me. I hear Minor ask Norma to sit on the bench outside the courtroom. When he walks up to me I ask:

"Do you know what's going on in there?"

"Norma said they're are all wearing the clothes they wore at their wedding eleven years ago." Minor chuckles. "She guessed Suits thought it would change her mind."

"Damn." Despite the disgust, the calm and levity in Minor's voice makes me smile. "Where did they get those clothes?"

"Out of their closets."

I burst out laughing and shake hands with Minor who also laughs.

"Every new lawyer in Timber County needs to get a proper initiation into his practice." Minor lowers his voice. "Besides, you'll have another story to remember."

❧ ☙

Grounds. Since the property and money issues have been settled, Minor doesn't want to put Norma through any more testimony than necessary to prove at least one ground. The infamous window leap, now famous throughout Timber County, would be a good start. Rumor has it kids have been seen jumping from a tree limb through a tractor inner tube hanging from another tree. Neither Suits nor Norma want to touch the highlight of the summer gossip. Suits is mum since his criminal case is pending, and Norma, Minor claims, is still embarrassed by the episode. Sven tells me the police filed no charges against her suitor but still hold his trousers as evidence. Of what?

Tompkins listens to Norma testify to what she and Minor are trying to convince him is cruel and inhuman treatment, the grounds for her divorce action. I suspect Tompkins thinks Suits' actions are neither cruel nor inhuman within the legal definition of the term. There is no evidence of physical or verbal abuse. Some muddled testimony surfaces about failure to support, a ground not pleaded nor pursued.

Mostly, I think, Suits' actions are devious, sneaky, perhaps illegal, but mostly plain stupid. Tompkins has presided over battles by Suits with the Department of Natural Resources, the Department of Revenue, Department of Transportation, and other state agencies coming into his sights, as well as Suits' ongoing traffic and ordinances violations. The judge no doubt sympathizes with Norma for being married to Suits, but the grounds have to be proven. He stares at Minor. Tompkins has established a practice with the attorneys in his court in a divorce action that when he is satisfied at least one legal ground has been proven he will say he has heard enough. In this case, he wants to hear more.

Tompkins establishes eye contact with Minor until he hears the attorney maneuver to a different line of questioning Norma. "Were you involved in any of the matters we've been discussing?"

"Well, I didn't want to be. He was always coming up with these weird ideas. Things I didn't approve of, things that were mean or hurtful to people . . . maybe even against the law. He always got me in the middle of it. And, we spent a lot of money for attorney fees." She looks at Minor as if expecting a signal. When there is none, she goes on: "My friends and the people I work with, even some I barely knew, assumed I was part of his schemes and approved of them. They started to shy away from me. They wouldn't come to the house if they thought he was there. One of my best friends from high school dropped me, and I know it was because of him."

I turn my head. Some of The Relatives are scowling and lip swearing. Tompkins scowls back at them until they stop. It appears to me the judge is beginning to be relieved, though, because Minor knows where to go with the testimony.

"Did all of this have a detrimental effect on your physical or mental health?"

"I started counseling with the pastor of our church, well my church. He wouldn't go. I also talked to County Social Services."

"How did your husband respond to the idea of counseling?"

"He became angry. He swore at me, called me names I didn't deserve."

Minor prodded her, "And how did that make you feel?"

Norma cries. "Worthless. The longer I stayed with him, the more worthless I felt. You can't imagine what it is to live with someone like him."

Suits starts to rise. I grab him by his suit coat and pull him back into his seat.

Catcalls issue from The Relatives. Tompkins bangs his gavel and watches their mouths open and then rapidly shut as the lips resume swearing. I wonder if Tompkins questions the veracity of her testimony. Norma's sobs sound forced to me, but her testimony is in the record, not the sobs.

The judge waves off Minor. "I've heard enough."

Minor shifts to the Final Stipulation. He carefully reviews the terms of it with Norma, asking her a few questions. "Do you want to take back your maiden name?"

"God, yes. I can't wait."

Boos from The Relatives clash with beats from the judge's gavel. Minor rests.

Tompkins gives me that *I have to ask you* look. "Do you have any questions for the witness?"

"No, Your Honor."

"All right, proceed with your case."

As Suits rises and walks to the witness box, The Relatives stand and clap and whistle. He stops, turns around and with a grin waves to them.

Tompkins face is flushed as he bangs his gavel several times. "Your behavior is not appropriate. If there are any more outbursts like this, I will have all of you removed from the courtroom."

The Relatives sit down in unison, and as I turn around to look at them, I see their lips curl and form more unkind expressions.

I lead Suits through the Final Stipulation as fast as I can. I also stay away from the grounds, a move I'm sure meets with Tompkins' approval.

At the end of his testimony, Suits pulls one more surprise. Without a question being asked, he stands in the witness box, faces Norma and lets it boom out through cupped hands: *Norma, come back to me! I love you! Norma, it's not too late! You can have the grill!* The Relatives jump to their feet and clap and cheer. The judge is livid. I'm red faced too, but for a different reason. I can't wait to exit the courtroom.

❧ ❧

I drop off in the secretaries' office the abstracts I brought up to date at the courthouse after Suits' divorce hearing. In my dazed state, I hope I didn't miss anything. The new photocopy machine has arrived. Margo and Suzy appear entranced with the demonstration of the machine by the salesman from the office supply firm in Lenora. I decide not to interrupt them. I know they've been looking forward to making decent copies of documents in a manner enabling them to avoid using carbon paper, the bane of all typists. They glance at me, and I give them a thumbs-up sign and head into my office.

Only because I cannot restrain myself from doing otherwise, I run through in my mind the divorce hearing: humorous, sad, a waste. Should the state adopt no fault divorce? Mental abuse was something I considered, but the kind used by Suits was different from that administered by Bill Krueger, without the violence, more insidious. How much of it was exaggerated, or even true? Norma is smart enough to know what she had to say in order to get the divorce. She wasn't going to leave the courtroom without it, and while I cannot condone perjury, I also cannot blame her for her testimony. Is that where no fault comes in? Now it's my turn to get rid of Suits.

Suzy brings the petition for Francis Westfall's change of name into my office and drops the papers on my desk. "She's coming in at two o'-clock to sign it."

I look at the petition without picking it up. "I suppose I should see her." I pause. "I probably don't need to see her. You can witness her signature." I pick up my calendar so Suzy is unable to see it. "I forgot to tell you I'm meeting with Earl and Mr. Denbrow from the antique shop in Lenora at Earl's at two o'clock."

"Chicken." Suzy picks up the petition and walks out.

When she is out of sight, I scribble the appointment on my calendar and call Earl and Mr. Denbrow to set up the meeting.

As I drive to the police station after leaving Earl's, I'm happy the old man has finally agreed to part with some of his property. We can raise money to pay off the bank after all. Perhaps. I know the emotional, as well as the practical toll, of failed optimism. On the other hand, doesn't optimism win more than pessimism?

Sven has come on duty and is in the process of sitting in a chair vacated by the Chief minutes before. I can tell Sven likes the fit, not just the chair, playing Chief. Maybe he would rather be a state patrol officer, but I respect him for recognizing his limitations.

"What do you know about the fire?"

"Not a lot. We're talking to Glenn."

"Whose Glenn?"

"Bill's older brother."

"You think he's involved?"

Sven rocks in the Chief's chair. "We're working on it. He's not too bright, and he's been in here a number of times." He switches subjects. "Say, whatever happened to that accident where Suits' car got rear ended?"

I frown. "I ran across an adjuster who knows Suits too well. He's dug in, convinced his company to fight it. Anyway, I've had enough of Suits for today. Thanks for the info."

Driving up the highway from the police station, I pass Beeper. He's wearing a dingy cap emblazoned with the name of the village fuel oil distributor on it and a T-shirt hung out over dark khaki pants. His gaze is fixed straight ahead, as if wearing horse blinders, and he's pulling the faded red coaster wagon with a case of beer in it. Apparently, his schedule for trips to Wills Grocery depends only on his thirst.

After I close the front door to the office, Suzy tells me I have a call.

"John. It's Rick. How're you doing?" He speaks slowly in a soft voice. If he hadn't told me his name, I wouldn't have recognized him as the caller.

"Good, Rick. How about you?"

"Tired. I'm not feeling too well lately. Stomach problems."

"You still working on Xpecon?"

"That's all I've been working on. The feds have been serving all kinds of Demands for Production of Documents, and Xpecon's shipping them by the carload. I mean they're sending so many documents, the government couldn't read all of them in a lifetime."

"Sounds like you need a rest, Rick. Why don't you come up here for a weekend? I'll get some of my buddies to take us fishing. There're some great spots around here. In the evenings I'll introduce you to Slider's Northwoods Tap, and if we drink enough, to Alma's and MM."

"MM?"

"You'll love her."

"Maybe I will. I don't know, though, if I'll be able to get away. This is a big case, John. I mean . . . "

"I know. You're steaming ahead on research and cranking out responses to the demand documents."

"That's it."

"Hey, we got what it'll take to set your stomach right. Come up to the Northwoods."

"You sound as though you found a new home."

"It's growing on me. It's not the North Pole, as you mocked, but I do a lot of abstracting and tax returns. There are those things you have to do if you want to be a small town lawyer."

"Sounds like you're having a good time, but I'd be bored."

"We do other work, Rick. As my girlfriend would say, "Work can be intense wherever you are and whatever you're doing. It's how you approach the work."

"You've got a girlfriend, huh? I don't have time for one. We're . . . "

"Rick, get up here this summer. You can forget Expecon for a weekend. We'll have a great time."

"I'll try, John. I'll see what I can do. You don't know what this is like." He pauses. "But what I'm doing is very important."

"I'm sure it is, Rick. I'm sure it is."

The Trial

29

Seven more months of 1976 have passed. Christmas is only two weeks away. End-of-the-year work in estate planning and for our business clients jams our calendars. Yet, none of that concerns us now.

We sit in Burnett's office, as we sometimes do in the early morning, with the fluorescent lights still off, sipping coffee. Logs in the fireplace have burst into flames, casting light onto Burnett's face. He looks wiser now than he did on that long ago day I met him in the law school. Monday morning. Ginger's trial begins a week from tomorrow, a date in the shadows of the future and at the same time within panic distance.

Burnett leans back in his chair. "Are you ready?"

"I'm not sure. I've never tried a case to a jury. How will I know until it's over?"

Burnett nods slowly. "That's a perceptive answer."

"I know the facts, and I think I know the law. And, I feel I know my witnesses well enough that I won't be surprised by their testimony. The depositions are complete except for their orthopod, which we're doing this afternoon in Lenora. I realize the defense witnesses may alter their testimony some. I doubt, though, there will be any revelations like the flying hubcap."

"I suspect that's true."

"I know I'm going to be nervous, probably very nervous."

Burnett nods again. "All lawyers become nervous before their first jury trial, and many of the best ones are edgy before any trial. Once you get into the case, your nervousness succumbs to your concentration. That's why knowing your case is so important; you have less things to worry about."

"I'm becoming nervous now just thinking about the case. I didn't realize how much more work a jury trial is than a trial to the court."

"That's one reason we don't have more jury trials than we do. Except in criminal and drunk driving cases where the defendants have little to lose, there's usually enough risk on each side to force a settlement. Unfortunately, there are also those cases that get settled because the attorney is over-scheduled, under-experienced, or lacks the drive to burst through the wall of preparation surrounding jury trials."

"Actually, although I'm nervous, I'm also anxious to get going."

Burnett sits up to look at his calendar. "You should be able to finish in three days, maybe two and a half. If the trial starts on Tuesday, you should have a verdict by Thursday afternoon.

"That's all the time Tompkins is willing to give us. If necessary, he said we can use Friday morning to finish up. But that's the day before Christmas, and we got the message he wants it done by Thursday evening. He plans to start early both days and finish late if necessary."

"He won't mess around with the jury selection and long-winded opening statements. You'll quickly be into the heart of the case."

"That's all right with me."

Burnett glances at his calendar again. "You've got the pretrial this Wednesday morning. You want me there?"

"Definitely. I know it's going to be hard on our schedules the next two weeks, but I need your advice and assistance."

"I'll be there, John. Any chance of a last minute settlement?"

"No. We're too far apart. Even though the hubcap threw them off course, the defense lawyers are still acting as though they're hung up on the liability. They've filed a *motion in limine*, to be heard at the pretrial hearing, to keep the hubcap out of the trial. I doubt, though, since Beeper surfaced they think they can escape liability."

"Posturing."

"Yeah, I think you're right. As far as Ginger's injuries, they don't believe they're as serious as she claims. The bottom line: they don't want to pay what we think the case is worth."

"What was your last demand?"

"Seventy-five thousand. That includes everything—medicals bills, lost wages, future meds, pain and suffering, permanency that applies to the knee and the lower leg. Admittedly, the percentages on permanent disability estimated by her doctors are low."

Burnett purses his lips while he contemplates my response. "I don't think we should go any lower, unless something new develops that could seriously affect our case. Still, John, you have to evaluate the risks: You never know what a jury will do. Timber County juries can be very conservative. And, you're facing a competent, experienced opponent in Franklin Wells. Stay flexible on settlement." Burnett looks hard at me. "At the same time, get ready. Do whatever you have to do to make sure that when you walk into the courtroom, you're in command of your case."

"I will." I'm the one who asked for the case, told him I could handle it. What was I thinking at the time? Burnett sits up and smiles at me. I know he sees the doubt in my face. He has become adept at reading the lines in my countenance.

"Actually, John, this is your second jury trial. Have you already forgotten the *Mueller* case in August?"

I laugh. "I've tried to. What I meant before was that I haven't tried a civil case to a jury. *Mueller* was a second offense drunk driving, as you know, criminal in Wisconsin. Anyway, I guess I should have told you what Tompkins laid on me after the trial. But, I was embarrassed at the time."

Burnett shakes his head. "You didn't have to; he told me. Forget it. Besides now that you hold the record in Timber County for the shortest time for a jury to return a guilty verdict, you have no where to go but up."

I laugh, then level my eyes to Burnett's eyes. "This is a test, isn't it? A test of me as an individual."

"Every conflict we face is a test, a test of how we respond to the challenge. There are those who relish grading lawyers on their performances in the courtroom. Those gratuitous grades are not final grades for the attorney. You'll receive your final grade when you're done practicing." Burnett straightens up a stack of papers on his desk before he continues:

"Anyway, this is a jury trial. Did I ever tell you about the criminal case lost by the district attorney here some years ago? No one thought it was an easy case for the prosecution. When jurors were interviewed afterward, though, it was revealed the verdict rested on the D.A.'s shoes. An old woman on the jury held out for an acquittal and eventually turned the other jurors around. Why did she hold out? She thought the D.A.'s shoes looked horrible. She claimed she couldn't believe anything a man with shoes like that said."

∾ ∾

As I step into the hallway, Suzy beckons me into her office to sign abstracts. I notice Henry Miller hidden behind the newspaper with Abstract curled up at his feet, no doubt to Margo's ire, digesting at least half a donut.

When I finish signing the abstracts Suzy hands me a citation. "Suits brought this in on Friday after you left the office."

I read through the form before I lower it to look at Suzy. "DNR. Shooting too close to the road during deer hunting season."

"I know. I read it. He said he entered a not guilty plea, and it's scheduled for trial in January." She giggles. "He says his shotgun went off accidentally while he was casing it."

I shake my head as I form a curse with my mouth. Suzy continues to giggle so I laugh and toss the citation back to her. "I'm going to think of something."

"He said The Relatives are still mad about the divorce. They didn't like the judge."

"Tompkins is probably in his last term. I doubt he'll care."

"And," Suzy extracts a postcard from the stack of mail picked up at the post office, "look what else you got?"

"Megans Bay, St. Thomas," I mumble as I view the beach scene. When I flip over the postcard I immediately recognize the handwriting. Is that perfume I smell?

> *Thank you again so much for*
> *helping me create my new identity!*
> *Looking forward to seeing you in*
> *the spring! You are a dear.*
>   *Sybil Swain*

❧ ❧

Music echoes off the smudged, cream color walls of the corridor leading to Dr. Brunholtz's office on the second floor of the old Lenora Professional Building. It sounds like some kind of Prussian march. I tail the sound to a dark wood door with opaque glass in the top partially covered by the doctor's name.

"Good morning," I offer to a stout woman with her gray hair in a bun and a cigarette dangling from her lips. "I'm Attorney John Hall. I'm here for the deposition."

"Umm." Looking up from a typewriter and eyeing me closely, she points to two chairs bracketing a low table covered with a lamp and scattered magazines. "*The Doctor* is with the other attorney." She returns to her typing.

As I remove my overcoat and hang it on a rack in a corner, I wonder why receptionists often refer to doctors by their title in voices that made the doctors sound like foreign objects. I set my briefcase on the floor next to a chair and plop down. The weight of Ginger's case is increasing each day.

The receptionist keeps typing. I assume she will not welcome the interruption of small talk so I focus my mind on Brunholtz. Burnett said he cannot be categorized as either a plaintiff's doctor, like Dr. Schloss, or a defense doctor, like those usually used by the insurance companies. Brunholtz works for whoever hires him. I recall Burnett's warning to be careful of the older doctor, that he knows his specialty, and can handle himself in court.

I greet Maureen, the free-lance court reporter, as she enters the room, removes her coat and sits in the other chair. While I chat with her, I'm curious what Wells is discussing with *The Doctor*. Probably what I discussed with Dr. Schloss before his deposition. Wells is getting an advance peek at the file to discover anything new since reports were last furnished to the attorneys. Surely they would not discuss anything that would lead *The Doctor* to be other than impartial in his opinions and testimony.

"Are you from this area?" I ask Maureen, with no purpose other than to keep myself from becoming further agitated over the case.

"From Algona, aren't you?" interjects the receptionist without looking up or missing a key on her typewriter.

"Yes, well I was born in the Twin Cities, but my family moved to Algona when I was in grade school."

"Your father worked in the office at the mill, didn't he?"

I'm impressed how skillfully the receptionist continues typing and engaging in gossip at the same time. Margo must know a lot more than I thought.

Wells enters the room, greets Maureen and me and leads us into Brunholtz's office. *The Doctor* is sitting behind his desk. Heavyset, he is mostly bald, with a large forehead and light skin. Glasses partially shield cold blue eyes. If I had to describe the appearance of the desk and the credenza behind it, I would say someone spread papers over them and then turned on a fan to make sure the papers were properly mixed.

Wells arranges Maureen to the far right of Brunholtz's desk, then has me sit next to himself so we face the desk. As he maneuvers us, it hits me like a smack in the forehead that Wells has taken over the case. From now on my real opponent will be the distinguished looking attorney who has tried countless PI cases; from now on it will be the two of us, each trying to win the same case by obtaining a different result. My anxiety level approaches the danger zone.

Maureen asks if the music can be turned down. Wells leaves the room.

This is my deposition. This is my chance before trial to go over Brunholtz's reports and to get a feel for him as a witness. His physical features, particularly the eyes, confirm Burnett's assessment Brunholtz will be a formidable adversary. I have a carefully prepared and typed list of questions for him. I am ready for battle. *The Doctor* surprises me, though, by smiling at me and chitchatting with us in an affable manner. Now, I have lost some of my edginess and realize the doctor is ahead of me.

The marching music is gone. As soon as Wells returns, I begin with a background question. "Doctor, do you have a curriculum vitae?"

Brunholtz hands me a three-page résumé. My eyes skim it. Burnett gave me an old one, and I now look for anything new. Some of it is puffing. I have a fleeting, bizarre mental picture of a fine restaurant waiter with a towel draped over his arm asking a customer, "Will you be having the curriculum vitae or the puffed résumé?"

"Are you presently doing a lot of independent examinations for insurance companies?"

Wells speaks up, "I'm going to object on the grounds of relevancy. I recognize this is a discovery deposition, but, as you know, it could under appropriate circumstances be used at trial without the doctor being present." Wells looks at Burnholtz. "Subject to my objection, you may answer the question."

"I don't know what you mean by a lot. I do some. I also do independent examinations for patients who are plaintiffs in lawsuits, like this one."

"You do a lot more examinations for insurance companies than for patients who are plaintiffs in lawsuits don't you?"

Wells: "Same objection."

"I do more. I don't know that I do a lot more."

"I understand doctor, that insurance companies are hiring you to do independent examinations for injured persons residing several counties away from here?"

"Same objection."

"Obviously my reputation." Brunholtz laughs it off with Wells joining him.

I remain straight-faced. "I take your response to mean yes?"

A slight color emerges in Brunholtz's pale complexion. "Yes."

Wells is right that the depo can be used in court under certain circumstances. I'm confident, though, they will produce the doctor in court. In either case, I need to test his temperament.

After questions on the details of Ginger's injuries, I begin comparing Brunholz's conclusions with those of Doctor Andrews, Ginger's orthopedist. "It appears to me, doctor, you're in basic agreement with Dr. Schloss and Dr. Andrews as to the nature of Ginger's injuries and the treatment she received. Is that correct?"

Brunholtz nods. "Basic agreement, yes."

"Is it further correct that one of the areas where you disagree is in the assessment of permanent disability as a result of her injuries?"

"Yes, that's true."

"For example, as a result of the continuing numbness in her left knee, you attribute only two per cent permanency as compared to Doctor Andrews's assessment of five to ten per cent?"

"I think he over-estimates her problems with the knee. I don't see it in the x-rays or other objective findings."

"What about her fractured tibia with the pin fixation?"

"Again, his estimate does not comport with my findings."

"How many times did you meet with Miss Buckman?"

Brunholtz looks at his medical records, starts to speak, but again reviews the records before answering. "Once."

"Once?" I smile at him. I'm beginning to understand how the medical expert game is played. If I hired an independent doctor as a rebuttal expert witness to Brunholtz, my doctor would probably not do anything differently. Still, *The Doctor's* cursory examination is something I can use later.

I pick away at Brunholtz's exterior, but it's all enamel, the way Burnett described it.

I pop into the Clerk of Court's Office to pick up a copy of the current jury list. Burnett, along with Margo and Suzy, will go over the names on the list, and I will call Dick Minor to review the list with him. After eighteen jurors are selected, each side will have three peremptory strikes, so I need any additional information about them that may not emerge during the *voir dire*. Burnett schooled me on companies offering investigative reports on the jurors, for a nice fee of course. But, this is Timber County he pointed out. Between the office staff and Minor and his staff they will know most of the names on the list and know things about the prospective jurors that may not be revealed by a report from a professional survey.

Through a door off of the Clerk's office I enter the law library. A slender, red headed man, in his mid-twenties, wearing a colored dress shirt and a tie, sits at one of the tables, taking notes from an open law book. As I approach him, he stands up.

I offer my hand. "I'm John Hall, one of the attorneys in Winding River. I assume you're the new lawyer in the area. Welcome to the Northwoods."

"Thanks. Dave Summers. The word travels quickly in a small village, doesn't it?"

"I'm sure you've been added to Mrs. Jensen's list."

"Huh?"

"Where is your office?"

"My main office is in Lenora, where I grew up, with a branch office in Winding River in that small, stone building around the corner from Swenson's hardware."

"I know the building you're talking about. How often do you plan to be there?"

"A couple of half days a week for now. I'll see how it goes. I've got a month-to-month lease on the place. It isn't much." Summers appears nervous. "I hope you don't resent my opening an office here. I thought there might an opportunity for some work where there are conflicts of interests."

I smile at him. "Not at all. In fact, I'm happy we'll have someone locally we can refer cases to since we don't have much of a relationship with the other attorney there."

"Yeah, I've heard about Smith. I thought about asking him to take me on as an associate, but then he spends half his time on family business. Also, I've heard the stories. Sometimes, I think I should have asked him. I'm finding it difficult to go it alone."

"I thought about going solo when I decided against the large firm. Not for long, though. I had the habit then of picking up people I needed. So, I latched onto the person who I thought could help me the most. It was later I realized I was the hitchhiker."

Summers stares at me as if I'm an enigma. I smile again. "Don't mind me; I have a tendency to slide off the track." I shake hands with him again. "Good luck, and if I can help you let me know."

"Thanks. I know what you mean. Sometimes, I think too much myself."

I walk down the corridor outside the Clerk's office. A dozen people, along with a man and a woman acting like attorneys, stand in two groups, separated by the distance of the carrying of their voices. As I pass the door to the courtroom, I hesitate and then duck in. The room is empty. The books and legal papers scattered over the counsel tables tell me there is a recess in some proceeding. At first I do not know why I'm in the room. Then I begin to experience an ancient criminal legal doctrine first hand: malice aforethought.

Glancing around, my eyes stop at Angie's work area and fix on a used stack of tape from his stenographic machine. The stack sits on a small table to the left of the machine, against the bottom of the witness bench and has a rubber band wrapped neatly around it. I look around the room again. I have more important things on my mind, but this is my chance to even things with Angie. Maybe if I pull off a good one, Angie will call a truce. I hurry over to the small table to pick up the tape.

I leave the courtroom with larceny in my actions, the stack of tape in my briefcase, and stupidity in my mind.

"Hey, John," Angie greets me as we pass in the hallway.

Before leaving Lenora I stop at the hospital on the northwest end of the city. If Earl is out of isolation, I hope to be able to visit him. It started with a lingering cold Earl brushed off and continued to brush off as it became worse. When I heard Earl was hit with severe chills, pain in his chest and a painful cough, I persuaded my friend to call an ambulance. The doctor who examined him diagnosed it as pneumonia.

"Are you a relative?" a gray-haired nurse with a kindly face, seated behind the counter, asks me.

"He doesn't have any relatives left. I'm his attorney."

"Oh, then you must be Mr. Hall."

"That's right."

"Mr. Schmidt has been asking about you."

"Can I see him?"

"No. I'm sorry. He's in isolation."

"What's his condition?"

"Not very good. He's not responding to penicillin. At his age, that's a real concern."

Until this moment I was concerned; now I'm deeply worried. "Is there anything I can do for him here?"

The nurse shakes her head. "Not that I can think of."

I reach into my shirt pocket. "Here's my card. If I can be of any help, please call me?" Then as an afterthought I add, "Do you know why he wanted to talk to me?"

"I'm sorry, I don't."

I walk slowly down the corridor, unsure if I should leave the hospital. Almost a year has passed since I joined Burnett, and I'm still riding the roller coaster. How far ahead is the next big drop and how soon will I reach it? Earl's marble is picking up speed as it moves toward the end of the last slide in the rack. I know there is no way to prevent the polished, rolling ball from eventually reaching its destination. Can I, or anyone else, though, slow it down?

30

The phone rings as I step out of the shower in the upstairs bathroom. Quickly toweling off, I ease up when I decide I can't get to the phone in the library before the caller hangs up. Since it keeps ringing, I trot to the phone, clumsily donning a bathrobe on the way. Who would call this early in the morning? It's Angie.

"John, you remember when we passed each other in the hallway yesterday afternoon?"

"Yes. There were a lot of people milling around and a couple of attorneys I didn't know."

"Look, John, please keep this to yourself. I've got a problem. I'm missing a tape. It was on that little table by the witness bench. You know where I mean?"

"I know."

"There was a motion hearing, and when it was over, the attorney on the losing side wanted a transcript. I said sure. After everyone was gone, I set some papers on the table and noticed the tape was gone. I've searched everywhere. I can't find it."

A smile creeps across my face. "Did you talk to Tompkins about it?"

"God, no. And, don't tell anyone. I've got to find it. I thought about it all night, and then I remembered seeing you in the hallway."

"I'd been in the Clerk's Office getting a copy of the current jury list."

"Yeah, that was when we had the break. I was on my way back from the bathroom. Did you see anyone go in or out of the courtroom when you passed?"

"No, I didn't." True. I couldn't see myself. Angie sounds despondent. I'm beginning to feel like a rat. What a way treat your buddy. Still, the buddy at times is a rat too. "Is there some way I can help?"

"Check around. See if anyone is talking about it. I can't figure out what happened to it. I was thinking maybe one of the attorneys took it. But, why?"

"I'll be around the courthouse this week. If I hear anything, I'll let you know."

"Thanks, John."

Why did I do it? I ask myself on the way back to the bathroom. And then, the short feature film emerges in my mind. It needs no editing. It's great!

❦ ❧

The caller introduces himself as the administrator of the hospital before continuing. "I understand you're the attorney for Earl Schmidt."

"That's right. I left my name in case there were any problems. He has no living relatives."

The administrator softens the tone of his voice. "I'm sorry, Mr. Hall, Mr. Schmidt passed away early this morning."

For a moment, it seems as though all of my bodily functions shut down. I knew Earl was very ill, but death? How could it have happened? I search the dictionary of my mind for words, but the pages are all blank. Finally I mumble, "From the pneumonia?"

"The official cause has not yet been determined. I'm calling you to find out what arrangements will be made for the deceased."

Death was not one of the options I envisioned for Earl's near future. Is there a funeral home in Winding River? I went to a funeral in Algona. Sure there is, on the southeast end of village, near the river. What's the name of it? What authority do I have to act for Earl now? "May I call you back?"

"Certainly. One of the nurses advised me that Mr. Schmidt told her before he died that if anything happened to him, there are instructions in an envelope on his dining room table."

"Thank you. I'll call back."

I shuffle through an air of disbelief into Burnett's office and slump in one of the chairs. "I need some advice."

⁂

We enter the house through the back door. The porch hasn't been shoveled for days. I kick snow and ice away from the door enough so we can squeeze through the narrow opening. When we're in the kitchen the feelings I experience are worse than I anticipated. Burnett's presence consoles me.

The newspapers and most of the magazines are gone. The sale of them to Mr. Denbrow, along with some china, old light fixtures and seven pieces of furniture, netted Earl nearly six hundred dollars. A start. Denbrow promised to return as soon as the snow melted to appraise the farm equipment and other items. Once Earl surrendered to my optimism that we could sell enough property to pay the bank, the old man had become excited about the idea. So had I. Now as I ease around the dining and living rooms, touching things as I go, I feel cheated. My film of Earl's future has not turned out the way I wrote the script, the way with the happy ending.

"This must be it." Burnett picks up an envelope from the dining room table and offers it to me.

"You read it, Bob." I begin pacing around the room for no reason other than to keep from stopping to accept the reality of the death.

Burnett opens the sealed envelope, takes out three sheets of lined tablet paper, and begins reading the first one. "Burial instructions." He keeps reading. "He wants his body to be cremated and his ashes spread over the farm, the same way he handled his wife's death."

"That's not surprising. He loved this place. He lived here away from the rest of the world. Why would he want his remains anywhere else?"

Shifting the first page to the bottom, Burnett begins reading the second page. "It's a will."

"A will?" I come to a halt. "He wrote a will himself?"

Burnett lowers the pages to look at me. "Yes, and in good form with his signature attested by two neighbors, as you know, the right number in Wisconsin." He raises the page and continues reading silently.

I smack the palm of my hand against the side of my head. "Now I know why he was asking so many questions I didn't think he needed to know. He wanted to make sure he got it right. No wonder he didn't want to discuss the will anymore." I commence pacing again, shaking my head from side to side as I move around the table.

As soon as he finishes reading the will, Burnett lowers it to his side. "Surprising. We now know why he didn't have you draft the will."

"What's surprising? What are you talking about?"

"He left everything he owned to you."

I stop pacing and rest my hands on the back of a dining table chair. The feelings I experience are strange and overpowering. I struggle to respond. "He left everything to me?"

"That's what the will says."

"Bob, I don't know what to say. Don't misunderstand me; that was a nice thing for Earl to do. Its . . . this isn't the way I thought it would end."

"In our business you have to get used to surprise endings and be able accept the finality of them."

"I'm beginning to understand that." Even if I can edit my dreams, there is no rewinding and editing of the reels of real life. "It's not the way I wanted it to turn out."

Burnett cocks his head. "Well, Earl was your client, and it was the way he wanted it to turn out."

While I continue to stand with my hands on the dining room chair, in deep thought, Burnett walks through the house. Then we leave in silence, and I wonder what he is thinking. Earl was one of his first clients when Burnett came to Winding River. I suspect he long ago crossed the professional line in his attachment to the old man. Why should I be surprised? At times, Burnett violates his own rules of conduct. He is, I've learned, very human.

❦ ❧

I clear my calendar for the morning. Suzy will do the abstracting at the courthouse and have Burnett check it over before she types it. A quick learner, she has already mastered the basics. Burnett will also handle my real estate appointment in the morning, and Suzy will refer an appointment on a traffic citation to Dick Minor. The afternoon had been kept clear, except for a sentencing hearing on a criminal matter, to prepare for the pretrial and motion hearing tomorrow morning on Ginger's case. I need time to think about Earl; at the same time, I need to fulfill my professional role in handling legal matters arising from a death. For the first time since my mother passed away, I am glad my brother delegated all her funeral arrangements to me. Experience is a massage for anxiety.

After I leave a message at the school for Ann to call me during her lunch period, I drive to the funeral home to make the arrangements. Until appointed as the executor of the will, I have no legal right to make the arrangements. A technical matter, according to Burnett, who assured me Tompkins will admit the will to probate. He also reminded me Earl has no heirs, and I am the sole named beneficiary of the will. Besides, I am following Earl's written burial instructions. By personally assuming responsibility for the funeral costs, I ease concerns of the directors of the funeral home. I doubt they would be as pleased if they knew I was a lawyer whose money is deposited in future billings rather than in the bank.

"There are a number of matters we need to go over," Suzy instructs me when I return to the office." She sits in one of the chairs in front of my desk, placing a stack of files on the other chair.

"Do we have to go through them now?" I wave off my question. She knows what I have to do next.

"Here's the Buckman file for the pretrial tomorrow. I made a sub file for the pretrial motion and another file for the proposed preliminary jury instructions and special verdict. You need to review them."

"All right." I take the file, set it on my desk and gaze blankly at her. The visitation at the funeral home will be on Friday afternoon. Who will come?

Suzy reaches over to the other chair for the next file, "Here's the Krueger divorce file. Everything should be set for the final hearing on Friday morning. You need to review her current financial statement form I typed."

I place the file on top of the Buckman file. "What about Bill? Did you check with the Sheriff's Department?"

"Yes. The deputy in charge of the jail told me they're going to bring him over to the courthouse for the hearing. Sounds like he doesn't want to be there, doesn't care about it. He told another deputy he wouldn't do anything for her any more no matter what the judge says." Suzy has a crooked smile. "At least this time *you* won't have to wrestle him."

"Hopefully. Who knows? There are surprises everyday now. They're coming in waves, one after another. When I first saw the river, the surface was frozen. I knew the water would begin flowing in the spring, but I thought it would be in ripples."

"Then . . . " She reaches for another file. When she began working for us, she looked bewildered on hearing my musings. Now she goes on without questions. Margo is her mentor.

I want to send her back to her office with the rest of the files. I want to hold up the two files I set aside and say, "I'll review these two. Right now I need to talk to Bob so I can take care of matters related to Earl." She will look frustrated and object, remind me that I have many clients to think about, and she will be right in everything she says. Margo again. We go through the rest of the files.

When we finish, I remind her, "Be sure to let me know if Ann calls."

I watch her walk out of the room. Then I scoot my chair over to the bookshelves, remove the marble rack, and examine it. The metal slides are so carefully formed and welded together and to the framework. Some child must have enjoyed the toy immensely. As a child I would have loved it; it would have been my favorite toy. I love it now.

I lean back with my hands on the marble rack resting on my lap as I recall my conversation with one of the nurses at the hospital. She assured me Earl's death during the night happened suddenly and quietly. That would, I reason, have allowed Earl to slip from existence without fuss, the way he would have wanted it.

What did it all mean? Earl got his wish for isolation from much of life, but wasn't that an illusion? What did it accomplish for himself or anyone else? Didn't the man waste his talents? If everyone maintained Earl's independence, how would civilization have advanced? Is not the principal purpose in life to move civilization forward?

Walking past the doorframe, Burnett glances at me, then stops. "It's all right to remember the man, but you're his attorney first. Let's get the legal work done."

I set the rack back on the shelf and swivel my chair to face Burnett. "I'm trying to sort out the man from his actions."

Burnett shakes his head. "You can't do that."

❧ ❧

I discuss the names on the jury list with Burnett. His experience and longevity in practice are again apparent. He knows something about most of the individuals on the list. If he doesn't know the person, he knows a relative or an employer or has heard or read about the person. The information adds to my profiles on the jury candidates.

Suzy buzzes me. Smith is on the line.

"Who is it?" Burnett asks.

"Smith."

"With the pretrial tomorrow, you'd better find out what he wants."

"You're right." I ask Suzy to put him on. I no longer bite my lips as soon as I hear his voice. Burnett has drummed patience into my mind.

"Have you reconsidered our settlement offer on the Buckman case? Given the many liability issues and her minor injuries, thirty-five thousand is a generous offer."

"That's not how we see it. We feel our offer of seventy-five thousand is more than fair. You know we've been over and over the details. So, I won't go through them again. We're still willing to negotiate, but you're going to have substantially increase your offer."

"Attorney Hall, you don't seem to be catching on. I've tried to be patient with you because of your obvious lack of experience and your naivety. At some point, you have to begin learning how to properly evaluate cases and situations and how to deal with them. You lack . . ."

Six months ago, I would have interrupted and said, "My problem is I can't deal with you." Patience. I keep listening.

"We're trying to be fair in this matter. I called so we can assure the judge tomorrow we've made a good faith effort to settle this matter."

"I've discussed the matter with Burnett and our client, and we can't accept your offer. As I said, we'll consider a higher . . ."

"Attorney Hall, have you witnessed Franklin Wells in the courtroom. I'm beginning to be embarrassed for you. He will shred you. He's as *smoooth* as a silk scarf."

I wouldn't know, I think. I've never owned a silk scarf. Some of us don't have that kind of money. But, I don't say anything.

"You need to properly evaluate your case, Attorney Hall. Think over what I've told you."

After the click, I turn to Burnett and stick out my hands.

Burnett smiles. "You've improved. I take it their settlement offer hasn't changed?"

"No. The call was for the record."

Burnett sits in silence for a moment. "Keep trying to settle. Keep trying to settle until you walk to the podium to make your opening statement. You always have to weigh the risks of a trial to unpredictable jurors against cash in hand. We'll see how the trial goes before deciding on settlement after the trial begins. At the same time, keep preparing, work as if there will be no settlement. I know how difficult it is to make a last minute settlement when you're prepared for trial, when the case from beginning to end is bottled up in you and you're desperate to spill it. But, that's what you have to do."

"I understand." My thoughts go back to Smith. "How does a guy get to be like Sanford?"

"I don't think he ever wanted to be an attorney. His father wanted him to be an attorney. Smith is going through the motions. His disdain for his fellow lawyers is some kind of subconscious disdain for a profession in which he was forced to practice. More lawyers than Smith have stumbled into the profession and don't know how to get out."

Suzy interrupts us again; Ann is on the phone. I tell her about Earl.

"That's terrible. I didn't realize he was so ill. Now I feel guilty for not visiting him at the hospital."

"You couldn't have seen him. He was in isolation." I discuss the funeral arrangements.

Ann speaks slowly. "Is there any point in having visitation at the funeral home? He's being cremated, and it's doubtful anyone will show up other than us."

"I've been thinking about that."

"Since his body is being cremated, why don't you arrange for a brief ceremony at the farm when you spread the ashes. Maybe we can get a few neighbors to attend and everyone from the office."

"I like your idea." I move on to the will.

There is a long pause before she speaks. "What are you going to do with a farm?"

"I don't know. I haven't considered it until now." I'm silent for a moment. "Do you want to live on a farm?"

"Sure . . . that is, if it's with you."

"It's something to think about."

"Can we have animals?"

"Animals? Like what? I don't know anything about animals."

"Oh, chickens, a couple of goats, some dogs and cats."

"We'll have to discuss that further. I've never had a goldfish. Listen, I have to go. I have other clients to consider right now. I'll talk to you later."

Burnett smiles. "She wants animals, huh?"

"Goats."

"Why not. You can milk them. Maybe find a market for the milk. Some people can only tolerate goat's milk."

"Milk a goat? I can't imagine myself doing that."

"Actually, I can't either." Burnett picks up the jury list. "Well, here's my opinion on the next name, Abner Dunkry. Good 'ol Abner. Let me tell you a story about Abner."

31

Ginger sits next to her father on a bench in the rotunda of the courthouse. Her parents have increased the support they've previously given
her for her injuries and her lawsuit. A rickety bridge now spans the
moat between Ginger and her family. I cannot, though, conjure an
image of them embracing in the middle of the bridge; rather, I see Ginger walking toward them and then stopping to look away, to look over
the railing, beckoned by the cool water below.

As Burnett and I approach them, Michael Buckman stands up. My
first meeting with him occurred after the Larsens hired him as their accountant. The resemblance between an undisguised Ginger and her father is evident. Tall and slender with narrow shoulders, he has a full
head of light hair, delicate facial features, and is clean-shaven and neat.
In his appearance and dress there are no loose ends. The way I would
want my accountant to be.

While we greet them I look across the rotunda. "Let's go up to the
courtroom."

Ginger starts toward the stairway, with her father at her side. I cut
them off. "Let's take the elevator."

Ginger has a determined look on her face. "I can make it up the
stairs."

"That's not the question. The question is who will be standing at
the top of the stairway watching you as you go up."

Michael Buckman nods as he steers Ginger to the elevator.

I feel a trifle smug about my awareness of the opposition's ever-
present eyes until I catch Burnett's eyes. He's the one who admonished
me to not let her struggle to do something she's really not capable of

272

doing, especially within the view of the insurance company lawyers who then have an argument for reducing their offer.

The courtroom is empty. I set my briefcase on the counsel table to the right as I face the bench. Though most of the attorneys adhere to the plaintiff using the table to the left, as Angie told me, I prefer the right one. My successes in court of late have improved and convinced me the table on the right possesses some magical quality lacking in its twin. I have Ginger and her father sit in the first row of benches, then take off my coat and toss it over the back of the bench.

Franklin Wells strolls into the courtroom, trailed a half step by Sanford Smith. He gives me just the right smile as he exercises a firm grip on my hand and stares into my eyes. Before I can recover to stare back, he turns to shake Burnett's hand and nod at the Buckmans. I'm immediately envious. It's all too easy for Wells. I watch him remove his overcoat and carefully fold it over the back of the first row bench across the aisle from me, then arrange his suit coat and tighten the knot in his tie. Wells does not have any loose ends either. Will I ever have that distinguished look? I begin fussing with my wrinkled sport coat.

Angie peers through the doorway of Tompkins' chambers into the courtroom. "The judge would like to see the four attorneys."

We move into the chambers and after greeting the judge, sit in the chairs in front of his desk. I immediately focus on Ann's pencil sketch, noticing as I do so Tompkins catch the look. He starts to turn around but halts the move and speaks:

"Gentlemen, is there any chance of a settlement in this matter?"

Wells quick response pre-empts my planned answer to the question. "I think Your Honor knows this is an unusual case. While the defense has not been successful in having the case dismissed, nevertheless, it is our position there is no merit to it. We . . ."

Tompkins cuts him off. "I understand your position, Mr. Wells. I don't want you to argue the case. What I want to know is whether there is a dollar figure that will settle this case. I assume that you two have been discussing settlement as instructed at the Scheduling Conference?"

I jump in. "I've tried."

Tompkins looks at me as though I'm a frog who's made a clumsy leap and missed the lily pad.

Ignoring me as if I were not present, Wells responds to Tompkins' question. "In view of questionable liability, the demands are excessive. We're very far apart, Your Honor."

Tompkins frowns. "If there is any chance of settlement, let's get it done today. I don't like last minute settlements. Once the prospective jurors are brought in, if you settle, you'll split the costs of the jury fees, unless you have a different agreement."

Wells nods. "Understood perfectly, Your Honor."

"I . . ."

"Well, then, let's get on with it." Tompkins sets aside the case file before him and picks through a stack on documents on his desk. "Let's review the jury instructions and proposed special verdict you each have furnished to me."

Tompkins uses his experience and forceful personality to quickly forge agreement on the jury instructions and the verdict. Burnett is right; he does know how to move things along. He proceeds with the next matter:

"Mr. Wells, you filed a *motion in limine* to exclude testimony from two witnesses . . ." Tompkins checks the motion. " . . . Mr. Jorgenson and Mr. Plumber, concerning an automobile hubcap. Do you wish to have the motion heard?"

"Yes, I do, Your Honor."

"All right then. Unless either of you have anything further, let's go into the courtroom."

I begin to speak, but Tompkins has already dismissed us and dials the Clerk of Court's Office to have a clerk sent over.

The attorneys settle in at their tables. Burnett and I flank Ginger who asks me what happened in the judge's chambers. Angie comes into the courtroom shortly after, a worried look on his face. I try to escape his attention by looking away from him.

Tompkins sits behind the bench, calls the case, notes the appearances, and asks Wells to proceed with the motion.

As Wells launches his argument, I sit on the edge of my chair. I can't afford to miss a word. If Wells can get the hubcap and Jorgenson's testimony regarding finding it excluded from the trial, there will be no corroboration of Beeper's testimony, and the whole case may collapse. At best for me, the jury will then have more doubt about the credibility of Beeper's testimony.

From the opening of Wells' argument, Tompkins appears antagonistic to the motion. Burnett is right again. The judge is no legal scholar and susceptible to plaintiff's testimony, but he is also a "quick study" on a case. He always grabs for the crucial artery and when he gets a hold of it, he is ruthless in his actions. He's known to be the kind of judge who can "slice bread." And after he has, he never throws crumbs to the other side.

"Excuse me, counselor." When piqued, Tompkins speaks slowly, carefully choosing his words. "If I understand this matter correctly, there is testimony by an eye witness that a hubcap flew off of the car as it rounded the corner in the late evening; the next morning a shop owner found a hubcap in the approximate spot it would land; and the hubcap is from the same make of car as that described by both the eye witness and the plaintiff."

Wells shoots back, "Your Honor, that hubcap could have come from any car of the same make. The plaintiff will not offer any evidence definitively linking *that* hubcap to the car allegedly driven by the defendants' son. We believe it will be highly prejudicial to our case to allow any reference to the hubcap found by Mr. Jorgenson. What he found was just a hubcap, any old hubcap."

"Well, Your Honor," I interrupt, jumping up, afraid the judge will leap to a decision unfavorable to my position. "It wasn't *any* hubcap. It was a hubcap from the same make of automobile. And, Mr. Jorgenson will testify that he picks up in front of his store and the one next door every morning, and the hubcap wasn't there on the previous morning. And . . ."

"All right, Mr. Hall, you'll get your chance to argue."

As I sit, Ginger tugs at my coat sleeve, whispering "Good job. I like this."

I glance at her. Not surprising. She likes controversy.

Wells continues: "Look, judge, as you know, this is a fantasy case to start with. It's sort of laughable. There will be no proof our insured's son was even at the scene. There will be . . . "

I still don't know much about the practice of law, but I do know when someone overreaches. Wells has gone too far, probably because he doesn't expect to succeed on his motion. Tompkins won't like the demeaning tone in which Wells refers to a "fantasy case" and "laughable." I know Tompkins dislikes the big city lawyers breezing into his court and intimating the local lawyers are all hicks in a hick town as the knowing, big city lawyers patiently educate him on the law. Wells crested the hill and is now slowly sliding down the wrong side. Keep it up Wells. I begin to feel my fingers forming fists.

As soon as Tompkins rules against the motion and leaves the bench, Wells, standing very erect and somehow taller than himself, shakes my hand again, this time with a less firm grip. He nods vaguely at Ginger and retreats from the courtroom, a half step ahead of Smith.

❧ ❧

Burnett and Margo agree with Ann's thoughts on the memorial service for Earl so I call the funeral home and cancel the Friday service. Everyone at the office assures me, the ceremony at the farm will be what Earl wanted, simple and away from the crowd.

Suzy buzzes me. "Can you talk to a man waiting in the hallway? He says it's real important."

I start to put her off, instead relenting and asking her to send him in. Thoughts of Earl still occupy my mind. When I see the prospective client, my mind becomes entirely focused on him.

The forty something, dark haired man is huge, not in height but in girth, and I'm concerned the man won't be able to get through the doorframe. The big man rotates his body sideways, sucks in his stomach, and barely eases through. He cannot fit in one of the armchairs, so I hurry into the kitchen to grab an open chair.

"Willard Hoff. They call me Half-Ton Willie." He has a high voice and is wheezing in between words and stretching the red skin around his mouth like a balloon ready to burst. "I ain't that heavy . . . not yet, anyway. You can call me Willie."

"Okay, Willie." I'm now concerned for the welfare of the kitchen chair, especially since it's the one I usually sit in. "How can I help you?"

"I bought this mattress in Lenora. Cost me thirty bucks."

I interrupt him. "A used mattress?"

"That's right, a used mattress, but the guy who sold it to me said it hadn't been used too much; he could tell. He said it was pretty firm, the mattress, I mean." Willie, still wheezing, cocks his head and screws up his face. "Well, I got it home and it sags in the middle. No matter how I turn, I wind up in the middle. That's no better than the mattress I had before." His excited voice jumps to a higher level. "That ain't right. But, he won't give me my money back."

Willie is no half-ton, I decide. A quarter ton? Probably close to it. "How about the springs on your bed. You think they need tightening?"

"They're the same as they were with the mattress I had before." Willie leans forward and stares into my eyes. "The reason I went for a new mattress was so I could get out of the middle. You know what I mean?"

"Yes."

"Hey, he knew I was a big guy."

Big guy? What kind of mattress is designed for this kind of person? "You said it was used?"

"For sure. The guy said it was in good shape. Shouldn't he have to take it back?"

"Did he give you any kind of warranty?"

"Nah."

"How about a bill of sale, a receipt?"

"This is that second hand store on Flintlock. He don't give you nothin.'"

I watch Willie sit back and breath deeply. "There is under the law a doctrine of implied warranty of fitness for purpose. There is . . . " I cut myself off. Where am I going with this thing? "You say you paid thirty dollars for the mattress?"

"That's right."

I suspect Willie will not like my advice. "Well, here's the problem you face if you want to hire us to work on this matter: We would charge you on our hourly rate which is thirty-five dollars an hour. Since you don't have a written contract for attorney fees to be paid to the success-ful party in a dispute, it's unlikely you'll recover any attorney fees in small claims court other than a minor amount. We can contact the store, write letters, start a lawsuit, but even if, and I say *if,* we get your money back, you'll wind up owing us a lot more money than thirty dollars."

To my amazement Willie looks relieved. "That's exactly what I told Myrna, my wife. I didn't want to go back to the store. I know that guy from way back. He's okay. That was Myrna's idea. Then she says, 'Go ask the lawyer.'"

As Willie struggles to his feet, I go on: "Of course, you could contact the consumer affairs department of the state. They might be able to help, and they don't charge. Maybe they could apply some pressure since he didn't give you a receipt and probably didn't charge sales tax and . . ."

Willie stops listening. He turns sideways and concentrates on sucking in his stomach to squeeze back through the doorframe. After he's in the hallway, he directs his stomach toward the front door. Without looking at me, he waddles forward. "I gotta go for a snack. This whole thing has made me hungry."

ℛ ℛ

Angie sounds frantic on the phone. "You hear anything?"

"I did, and I don't think you're going to like it. I don't know what else we can do, though."

"What? What do you mean?"

I hesitate. With Earl on my mind and Ginger's trial coming up, the prank seems trivial. I should fess up and forget it. On the other hand, Earl would have loved hearing about it. Ginger would want in on it. "I got a call this afternoon. Here's the deal: The caller will turn over the tape for one hundred dollars in cash. The demand is very specific. Bring two fifty-dollar bills. You're to meet with Santa Claus and Slider in the parking lot behind Slider's tomorrow night at nine o'clock and make the swap."

"Whaat? What kind of bullshit is this?"

I feign irritation. "Hey, you asked me to check around, and I did that. I let it be known that anyone wanting to talk to you about a confidential matter should call me. Someone did. Don't ask me who because the caller wouldn't furnish a name, and I didn't recognize the voice."

"Sure, Hall. I bet you'll be a skinny looking Santa Claus. And what's Slider got to do with this?"

"The caller doesn't want any trouble, just a simple exchange, and asked if I knew someone who could conduct the swap."

"I'll get you, you know."

"Get me? I'm beginning to get pissed off, Angie. You asked for a favor, and I did it." I hang up, and a few moments later hear the phone ringing in Margo's office.

"Okay. I'll be there. I'm looking forward to seeing you, *Santa*."

જી ભૂ

In the late afternoon, I phone Dick Minor to review the jury list with him. I read the questionnaires the prospective jurors filled out for the Clerk of Court, and I picked up additional information from the city directory for Lenora and from courthouse records. The data doesn't provide the sort kind of insight Minor, who knows many of them, can furnish to me. I'm struggling to keep up with my notes on his comments, when he comes to a new name and raises his voice.

"Now here's one I'd be wary of, Gertrude Goettelman. She's an older woman, a widow, very opinionated. You might call her the village busybody. She probably wouldn't like the idea of a young woman racing around the village on a motorcycle, holding onto the back of a convicted druggie."

"Good point. I'm taking notes. I really appreciate your help, Dick."

"Well, I suppose I owe you one."

"Owe me one for what?"

"Your referral to me yesterday of a traffic matter which turned out to be a drunk driving arrest. To think I could have missed the opportunity to defend a driver who when stopped by a policeman for a defective headlight and asked for his driver's license, handed the officer the floor mat."

I laugh as I hang up. As his remarks sink in, the scariness of the situation hits me. I have driven under circumstances where I should have tossed the keys into the bushes, but I never tried to drive when I was in that condition.

Rummaging through the files on my desk, I select the one on the probate of Uncle George's estate. Tomorrow is Thursday, and I will drive to the Milwaukee area in time for a late morning hearing on the decedent's will. I worry that *Rusty* may not be up to the trip. Still, I look forward to seeing Tim Waters. It's been almost eleven years since I last saw him.

32

Waters sits next to me in the first row of benches in a courtroom I've never been in before. We wait for a judge to preside over a hearing on admission to probate of the will of Tim's great uncle George. I feel uneasy as I always do in the midst of confusion. When I obtained the probate file from a clerk, her instructions were to "go across," which I assumed meant across the hall to the courtroom. The clerk's office in turn had been located with directions from an employee on a higher floor to "go down."

While we wait, I review the petition in the court file on Uncle George. Eighty-six and never married, he lived alone in a downstairs flat on the south side of the city. Tim described him as an odd duck, estranged from his relatives. Tim rarely saw him, yet Uncle George named him as the sole beneficiary of his will.

I turn to Tim, slightly taller than me and heavier, and still sporting a marine style haircut for his light colored hair and short sideburns. Out of nervousness, I ask a question I've asked Tim several times, "So, he had no assets other than the house and some furniture?"

"Not that I know of. I'm hoping the deed to the house is in the safety deposit box at the bank. If he had any insurance, which I doubt, the policy must also be in the box. I didn't find one in the house."

"No income other than social security?"

"I don't think so. Other than a few visits, I didn't know him that well."

"Maybe you were the only one who visited him."

An attorney and another woman enter the courtroom and sit at a counsel table. A court reporter strolls in through a side door and settles behind his machine as a judge ascends to the bench. The judge begins shuffling papers, pausing to skim through a file.

With a questioning face, the reporter looks at me. I hold up the probate file as I mouth "will." The reporter raises his right hand and circles it above his head. "What?" I mouth. Again the reporter raises his right hand and circles it above his head. Desperate for help I look at Waters who appears entranced by the hand waving.

When I turn back to the reporter, he says softly, "Go around."

I wrinkle my brow and extend my arms, palms upward.

Shaking his head, the court reporter pushes his chair back and walks over to me. He points to the door in the back of the courtroom. "Go out that door, turn to your left, go down the hall to a corridor, turn right and at the end of the hallway go into the Probate Commissioner's Office." He shakes his head again and goes back to his machine.

After we slip through the courtroom door into the hallway, looking like fleeced sheep, Waters laughs.

Then I begin laughing. "How was I supposed to know? Every courthouse and courtroom you go into there's something different. I'm always surprised."

Suddenly relaxed, I make what I consider a smooth presentation to the Probate Commissioner. The heavyset man smokes a huge cigar, while his smaller, female court reporter puffs on a cigarette. After the will is admitted to probate, through clouds of smoke, they probe me for a few minutes, no doubt intrigued by a Northwoods' specie of lawyer, and a novice one to boot.

As we leave the courthouse to go to the bank, I poke Tim. "Next time I come here, I'm bringing a gas mask and a list of courthouse hand signals and definitions of terms."

❧ ☙

The brick bank is located on a corner a few blocks from Uncle George's house in an area with blocks of weather-beaten, two-family homes, all with front porches on each floor. The elm trees that once graced the streets had, on their demise, been replaced, and the new trees are not large enough to hide the decay of the neighborhood. In the near background, smokestacks belch fumes, the odor sharply contrasting with the smell from the tall pines among which I now live.

Tim furnishes a copy of the order appointing him executor of the estate and a safety deposit box key to an officious bank employee. She uses the key, along with a bank key, to retrieve the box from a vault. She hands the large, gray metal container to Tim. Then leads us to a small room, barren except for a table and four chairs. "My desk is right down the hall, if you need me," is her prerecorded message as she exits the room.

Tim sets the box on the table. "Heck of a big box to keep a few documents in, isn't it?"

"That's what was I was thinking. Is it heavy?"

"Yeah. Strange, huh?"

"Well, open it."

As we lean over the box, Tim discovers a small padlock on the clasp in front. He turns to me. "Have you got a paperclip in your briefcase?"

I hand him one. While Tim straightens the clip and attempts to pick the lock, I reel off fuzzy film of going to a bank with my mother to open my first account.

Tim looks frustrated. "I can't get it to open. I'll be right back. I'm going to get a hacksaw from my truck."

During the wait I attempt to sharpen the images on the fuzzy film. They refuse to clear up, and the film goes blank. For some reason Rusty comes to mind as I sit at the table, tapping my fingers on the practical, hard plastic surface. I hated to ask Tim to drive to the bank. The way I saw it, though, I had no choice. *Rusty* has become an embarrassment. And then, there is always the reliability factor, even though I had bought new tires for the winter.

Tim saws off the lock and with the clasp freed, he prepares to lift the lid. He glances at me, then opens the box. "Damn. Look at that! There's nothing in it but money. It's packed with money."

I rifle through the bills, every denomination from hundreds to singles, some in packs with rubber bands, some loose with hasty folds. "You're right, no deed, no insurance policy, nothing but money."

"Why would he do that?" Tim pulls out a chair and sits down.

"Safety? He got the protection of the bank, but no interest."

"Man, I never expected that. What do we do now?"

I lean back in my chair. "We count it."

"Now? I was looking forward to lunch."

"Forget lunch. By the time we get done counting all these bills, we'll have cocktails and dinner."

❧ ❦

"Sixteen some thousand dollars ought to pay for the materials to fix up the house and pay the real estate taxes. And your guys can do the repairs." We talk as we eat a late lunch and drink glasses of beer in a booth in a neighborhood restaurant, alone except for the waiter and a bored cashier.

Tim halts his fork on the way to his mouth. "Sure surprised me. I can't imagine why he would do that. He was smart enough. All that lost interest."

"Burnett, my boss, says you can tell a lot about a person by their safety deposit box: what's in it and what's not, how the contents are arranged and identified, the monetary value as compared to the sentimental value of the items. Then there's the signature card for access to the box showing how often and when the box was entered and the haste or precision with which the signature was affixed."

"Sounds like clues for a detective."

"Well, lawyers often are detectives. They need to get the facts."

As soon as I speak, I realize I need to be more of a detective myself. Maybe I should have checked on the Wilson's car more after I visited Pete at his used car dealership. What else could I have checked on? Now, I'm almost to the trial date.

Tim goes on: "Still hard to understand why he kept all his money in a safety deposit box."

"Living through the Depression, Uncle George may have been afraid of losing the money if the bank failed and the cash was in an account. He may have figured the government couldn't take the money away from him if it was in the box." I sip from my glass of beer. "Also, who knows where the money came from? Those may be tax-free dollars."

Tim nods. "Both reasons are probably right."

"The government will get some of it now, through estate taxes."

Tim pushes his plate away from him. "Listen, John, I did get some information on Lynch. I wanted to wait until we got the other stuff out of the way to tell you."

Surprised, I sit back in the odors of garlic and other spices still wafting from the kitchen.

"Now I'm getting this second and third hand, but I think it's accurate. It makes sense anyway. Drinking water over there was always a problem. The streams and paddies were so polluted by cattle standing in them, human crap."

"I know. Didn't they give you those water purification tablets to put in your canteens?"

"Sure. And that was great if you had time to use them; sometimes you didn't. You were in a firefight, it was hot and humid as hell, you'd been running, you're canteen was empty. Sometimes you would take a chance on almost any water. Most guys, like me, never took that chance. If we weren't in a fight, when it rained, we took the liner out of our helmets and then held the helmets upside down on our heads to catch the rain water to fill our canteens."

"Makes sense."

"It does if you were in an absolutely safe area when you removed your helmet, but where was that? What you did was expose yourself to a headshot from a sniper or to a stray bullet. That's what got Lynch. I'm pretty sure of it. One of the sources said there was talk of it, and it had been mentioned the guy was from northern Wisconsin."

"He probably didn't suffer then."

"I'm sure he didn't."

I sit up. "Thanks, Tim. I know it probably seems strange that I'm looking into this after nine years. I did it because I think it will mean a lot to one of our secretaries and her husband who have been very kind to me."

"I understand. You know, in checking on this I learned several things I was curious about, including details of the death of a marine I knew. I tried to forget the war and maybe I shouldn't have. I'm glad you asked me to check on Lynch." Tim gazes over my head. "The questions about Vietnam continue to linger. It lasted so long; then ended so abruptly. But, I'll bet historians will be searching for answers forever."

☙ ❧

When I arrive back in Winding River it's close to eight-thirty. I call Margo from the office to ask if I can come to her house. I decided it would be best to talk to Red and to her together, at their home. Uneasy as to how I should approach them and unsure of the legitimacy of my prying into such a personal matter, I simply say I have something to tell them. On the return trip to the Northwoods, I rehearsed my presentation over and over. As I drive up to Margo's house, the prepared speech fades from my memory. I walk in and tell them exactly what Tim told me.

Margo has tears on her cheeks. "That would be Jimmy. He would worry about bad water. He would never take a chance on anything to eat or drink if he felt it wasn't safe."

"During deer season," Red added, "he was always concerned about the deer being properly gutted and kept cold enough before we delivered them to the meat processor. You know how when the weather is too warm during the hunt that after you gut them, you have to put ice in the chest cavity."

No, I don't know, and I find his remarks discomforting. I nod anyway. Now is their time to speak. Does it matter what they say?

Red continues: "When we took the kids out to eat, he always poked through his food before he ate it. Yeah, that would be him."

Margo wipes away the tears. "I suppose we should have looked into this more at the time. We were in shock. His body was never returned; we've reconciled ourselves to the fact it probably won't be. At least we can put one question behind us."

I continue to nod before offering: "I understand. I'm sure most people would have done what you two did."

As I stand to leave, Red rises and shakes my hand. "Thanks, John. We appreciate what you did for us."

Walking to my car, I feel they are satisfied, relieved that they will no longer have to dwell on the details of their son's death. I checked into the matter out of affection for Margo. My mother was a strong woman, too. Is that why I admire Margo?

☙ ❧

A long day. After ten o'clock. I want to collapse in my bed and drift into sleep, but I can't stop thinking about Earl. Whenever I exit the tunnel of my work, I lapse into reminiscences of Earl. Some force continues to impel me to sort out the man from his actions, regardless of what Burnett told me. Then I remember the sting. I grab a bottle of beer from the refrigerator and go into my office to call Slider.

"Is Angie there?"

"No. He's really pissed. An hour a ago he was still screaming out back."

I smile. "You have time to tell me about it?"

"Sure, it's a slow tonight. Here's how it went:

"I go out to the parking lot with Santa Claus, who's carrying a white bag over the shoulder, a little before nine o'clock, like you told me. Angie stands there trying to keep his hands and feet warm. When he sees us, he looks confused. You were right, he thought for sure you would be Santa. But Santa turns out to be short and sort of stocky.

"'Where's my tape?' he says.

"And I say, 'Where's the two fifty-dollar bills?'

"First he bites his lips and looks around. Then he takes two fifties out of his coat pocket.

"I give the okay sign, and Santa drops the white bag and takes out the tape.

"'No funny stuff now, Angie,' I say. 'I made a promise that this would be a fair swap.' Then I tell them to hand the tape and money to me. Angie looks Santa over pretty good but he can't figure it out.

"When I have the money, I give the tape to Angie and one of the fifties to Santa.

"'Why are you giving Santa fifty bucks?' he asks.

"Then Santa whips off the stocking cap, and her dark, long hair falls down, and Mary says, 'Because, you louse, each of us now has fifty bucks for drinks on the house.'

"Mary and I start laughing, and you can see the anger rising in Angie's face. 'Hall?' he asks.

"We don't answer him. But Mary says, 'And, I won't throw up any time for twenty bucks. Now it's at least fifty!'

"I walk away with Mary, and as we go in the back door of my place, we hear him let go: 'HALL! JOHN HALL! GOD DAMN YOU JOHN HALL!' He couldn't stop."

33

When she sees me amble into the kitchen to say good morning, Margo narrows her eyes, the sign I'm about to be chastised.

"Mrs. Jensen said she heard screaming coming from behind Slider's last night, and then she saw a red pickup truck roar out of the parking lot. She said the truck belongs to *that* court reporter. I suppose you don't know anything about it?"

"I wasn't there." The truth of the words cover the lie of the involvement so nicely I wonder if I have already represented too many criminal defendants. I cringe at my lack of honesty.

"He's kind of a wild one, isn't he?"

I turn away to hide a smile I struggle to suppress. "He has his moments."

Suzy greets us as she walks in, takes a quart of orange juice from the refrigerator and pours herself a glassful. "Suits has been calling and looking for you about that DNR citation."

"Tell him I'm working on it."

"He's been calling every day. He also wants to see you about some problem with the Department of Transportation."

"Tell him we'll get in touch with him next week."

"Next week? You know he'll be back tomorrow. He'll . . ."

I turn away.

Suzy looks to Margo for help, but Margo has returned to her office. With Suzy's back to me, I slip across the hall to my office.

The courtroom is empty. I direct Brenda to my pet counsel table. I arrange the pleadings and documents from her file and my notes in piles around a blank legal pad. Brenda appears to have recovered some of the confidence she lost after the fire. Still, she is so fidgety I try to get her to relax. Finally, after eleven months for me and an eternity for her, we have reached the final hearing on her divorce.

Angie enters the courtroom, moves to his area, and without looking at me begins to remove his machine. I walk over to him.

Holding his machine by the metal rod connected to the pedestal, Angie faces me. "Well, smart ass, it won't happen again."

"What do you mean?"

With his other hand Angie rolls his chair away from the table; underneath is a metal attaché case. From his pocket he extracts a key ring. "They're locked up now."

I force a laugh. "So, now someone will steal the case." I see the terror in Angie's eyes. Damn, I think, I came to apologize. "Look, why don't we agree to a truce. We don't need this." I stick out my hand. "Still friends?"

Hesitating as he eyes me, Angie suddenly shakes my hand. "Sure. But, I'm still pissed." He exchanges greetings with an older, woman court reporter, carrying her machine in a black case, who crosses the front of the courtroom to settle in his nest.

As I return to my chair, two heavy-set deputy sheriffs escort Bill Krueger into the courtroom. The deputy clerk of court trails them on the way to her desk. One of the deputies removes Bill's handcuffs and seats him at the other counsel table. I recognize the other deputy from the first time I visited the jail and ask him to step back from the table, out of earshot of Bill.

"How is he?" I whisper.

"Swore at us all of the way over here," the deputy replies in a loud and irritated voice.

Bill slumps way down in his seat, his head bowed.

The presiding judge enters the courtroom and sits behind the bench. A smaller and younger man than Tompkins, with a full head of dark, neatly combed hair. I recognize him as the county judge from Big Lakes County. I knew Bill had requested a different judge in the divorce, as he did in his criminal cases. What interested me was the form of the request. Bill did it himself on a written sheet of paper at the jail, yet in a form that he could have obtained only from an attorney. His public defender in the criminal cases apparently wasn't going to get involved in the divorce case *pro bono*, but bargained the disguised aid for begging off on the divorce.

The judge calls the case and notes the appearances. With a serious face he addresses Bill. "I understand Mr. Krueger that you are not represented by an attorney but are representing yourself. Is that correct?"

Bill sits mute, with downcast eyes.

"Have you sought assistance from Legal Aid? These are serious proceedings, Mr. Krueger."

Bill continues to sit quietly, without looking at the judge.

The judge turns toward his court reporter. "Let the record reflect that the defendant has been unresponsive to my questions, and I take his silence to indicate that he is representing himself and does not seek legal assistance. Mr. Krueger is not required to have an attorney, and he apparently does not want one. So we'll proceed."

Bill watches Brenda take the stand and be sworn by the deputy clerk. As I proceed through background questions, I feel my eyes occasionally drift toward Bill. I plod through the grounds since Bill has admitted nothing and refused to discuss settlement of the divorce issues. Brenda struggles to answer questions she has detailed for me many times during the divorce. Is it because of Bill's presence?

"Brenda, I know it is difficult for you to be here today and have to answer these questions, but the court must hear the grounds for your divorce. So, will you please answer my questions as best you can?"

"I'm sorry, Mister Hall."

The judge appears concerned as she relates details of the beating that led to her hospitalization. He interjects a few questions for clarification. As he does so, my eyes again drift sideways. What is relayed from Bill to the corner of my left eye is developed by my mind as the picture of a slow burning fuse.

"Were there occasions after that date in which you were physically attacked by the defendant?"

Before she can reply, Bill jerks his head up and yells at her: "You said you would never tell anyone what happened. You're nothing but a big liar. You . . ."

The judge cuts him off. "Mr. Krueger, you will have an opportunity to speak when Mrs. Krueger is through with all of her testimony. If you wish, at that time you may ask her questions, and after Attorney Hall concludes his case, you may offer testimony in this matter. In the meantime, please do not interrupt the witness unless you wish to make a proper objection to her testimony."

"Well, I object. I object to this trial. I object to what you're doing to me. I don't want a divorce and neither does she." He turns and points to me. "It's that goddamn attorney there. He's been brainwashing her. He's been telling her . . ."

Grim faced, the judge interrupts: "Mr. Krueger I again caution you on your remarks. I will not tolerate that kind of behavior in my courtroom. If you persist . . ."

Bill blows his lips at the judge "You think I give a shit. When all you assholes get done with me, none of this will make any difference."

As the judge again admonishes him, Bill leaps from his chair and starts toward Brenda, sitting on the far side of me. Catching the leap out of the corner of my eye, as Bill moves behind me, I stick out a foot and trip him. The two deputies pile on Bill as he sprawls on the tile floor. The deputy I talked to before the hearing gives Bill an unwarranted elbow in the back before they handcuff him.

I glance at Brenda. She stands in the witness box. Her face is blank as she watches the deputies drag Bill to the door. She catches my eyes before she slowly sinks into her chair.

Bill tries to turn around as the deputies drag him away. "You'll be sorry, Brenda. You'll regret this." The deputies push him through the door into the corridor.

The court reporter ceases taking notes and the room becomes eerily quiet. I interpret the passive acceptance on Brenda's face of Bill's outburst as evidence she no longer is surprised by anything Bill will do, that she no longer cares what he does because she senses the coming of the end of her anguish.

Shaking his head, the judge addresses us off the record. "I always find coming to Timber County an adventure. I think it's the anticipation of events beyond the powers of my imagination."

We proceed without Bill. The judge tells us he has heard enough testimony concerning the grounds. He awards full custody of the boys to Brenda but defers the issue of supervised visitation by Bill until conclusion of the criminal cases. The property and other issues are quickly disposed of, and the judge grants the divorce. Brenda looks washed out and limp as she leaves the witness box and returns to the counsel table.

The courtroom clears except for Brenda and me. We sit quietly for a few minutes facing each other. She wipes tears from her eyes. A struggle lasting for close to ten years of her short life has come to an end. The appropriate words for me to say hide when I call for them. I stick to what I know:

"Financially, it's going to be a struggle for you. The most important things, though, are that you've gotten yourself out of a bad situation, and you have your boys."

"I know that, Mister Hall, and I'm grateful to you for what you've done for me. But, if I'd known when I first came to you what I would have to go through, I'm sure I would not have started the divorce. It's good the bad things happened one at a time."

A wave of emotion sweeps over me like a surge of water when the ice breaks on the river. Brenda can find virtue in any situation. She's not a complainer; hardships are always minimized. I feel she has not told me the whole story. How much worse has it been than she related to me? Was she ashamed to tell me? Was she sparing me her grief? I realize I will never know. Then, do I need to know?

"Do you think I'll be safe from Bill now?"

"For some years. As you know, his brother confessed to the arson. You were right; he isn't the smartest guy around. He probably implicated Bill as putting him up to it because he was afraid to take the fall alone. They'll both do prison time . . . some years for you to get the boys on the right track." I shift the subject. "Are you going to continue living with your parents?"

"I think I have to. They fixed up one of the bedrooms for the boys. When I'm able to, I'd like to get my own home again."

"Would it help you to get a job in Winding River, so you won't have to commute to Lenora?"

"There aren't any jobs here I could do that would pay me what I make now."

"You can operate a machine, can't you?" I have trouble holding it back.

"That's what I do now at Northern Stamping. You know that."

"Do you know Jerry and Judy Larsen?"

Brenda shakes her head. "No."

"They own the Winding River Manufacturing Company."

"The one in the old warehouse by the train station?"

"That's it. They're expanding their operations, trying to gear up for a large contract. They need a couple of machine operators, and I told them I know a good one."

"Oh, Mister Hall."

"Call me, John. And, they'll give you a raise. I told them it would take an least another dollar an hour to get you away from your present job."

"Thank you, Mister Hall." She rises, kisses me on the cheek and hurries away.

I remain alone in the courtroom for several minutes while I assess Brenda's divorce. Suits' divorce was so much simpler. She wanted to get rid of Suits, and he wanted to get the grill. They each got what they really wanted.

❧ ❧

No new snow for ten days so the old snow piled along the streets has become the dirty white substance some call "snirt." I wish for more snow simply to return the pure white cover to the landscape. I cannot, though, attribute my somber mood solely to the snirt. I stop at the funeral home to pick up Earl's ashes and make arrangements to pay the bill. On the drive up to the office the little cardboard box rests on the passenger seat. I pretend it isn't there.

I set the box on the back of a shelf in my office, pondering why I elected to pick it up now rather than on Saturday which would have been in time for the memorial service at the farm on Sunday afternoon. I stack a couple of law books in front of the box and head into the kitchen.

Suzy pours a cup of coffee and hands it to me. "How did the final hearing turn out?"

"The only way it could have."

"I can't imagine it. Do you have time to go over some files?"

"Sure. Let me dictate the findings and the judgment for Brenda's divorce first. I need to get them behind me."

Suzy leaves and Abstract wanders in and sits before me, looking up with hopeful eyes. From the back of a lower cabinet I take a dog bone from a box. Glancing first at the door to Margo and Suzy's office, I give the bone to Abstract and whisper to her to go into my office. I follow her in and close the door. Abstract lies in the corner and cradles the bone between her paws and commits another violation of Margo's weight reducing program for her.

❧ ❧

After school Ann finds me in Earl's workshop sitting next to the cast iron stove radiating heat as it also heats the water in the pipes flowing through it. I had to build a fire in the stove to somehow bring the shop back to the way it had been. The small mechanical device I hold perplexes me.

She takes it from me, inspects it, and hands it back. "What is it?"

"I don't have a clue." I pull and poke at pieces of the gadget, finally setting it on the checkerboard table. I look at her.

Ann is moving around the cluttered room. "What are you going to do with this building?"

"What am I going to do with the house, the barn, the old smoke house with a tree growing through it?"

She sits. "We'll fix them up. We'll have fun. It will be something we can do together."

"A lot of work, that's what it'll be. A lot of work." I pick up a checker and begin tossing it in the air and catching it. "Will it be worth the effort?"

"Sure it will. We can make this into a great place, and Earl will be proud of you."

I smile. She knows how to set me up. How would I not want Earl to be proud of me? "I don't know."

"What do you mean?"

"Where are we going to get the money to do all this? There's barely enough in the estate to pay his current bills and funeral expenses. There will be inheritances tax. Then we'll have to pay last year's real estate taxes and pay off the bank. On top of those expenses, we'll have the re-modeling costs."

"I've saved some money. You said Mr. Denbrow would buy more items in the spring." She pauses to pad her argument. "We don't have to fix it up all at once."

"The first thing we have do is cut down the tree growing through the roofless stone building. That will improve the appearance of the place."

"Are you crazy? That's a beautiful maple."

"I love that smoke house. We can put a roof on it and turn it into a useable building."

"Well, we can also take the building apart and rebuild it somewhere else. We can't replant the maple, and you know we couldn't grow an-other one like it in our lifetimes."

I laugh.

"What are you laughing at?"

"You." I motion for her to sit on my lap. "Before we do anything else with the place, we'll have to honor Earl's intentions of returning the property to the forest by planting trees on all but a few acres. After that, I'll leave the remodeling program to you. You're the artist."

Ann sits on my lap and drapes her arms around my shoulders. "I ac-cept the job. What will we call the place?"

"I don't know." I pull her closer to me. "Can't we decide that later?"

34

Cold and darkness: two reasons not to rise early during the winter in the Northwoods. I cannot, though, wait for the sunrise; I need to get started early. This is my last day for preparation for Ginger's trial, and I've put off so many details I doubt I can get everything done.

After I quickly don sweat clothes, I bound down the stairs to the thermostat in the hallway and turn up the heat. A few minutes later, the coffee brewing in the pot is the only sound I hear as I pace the kitchen. Jaws of a gigantic vise grip me as the handle slowly tightens the vise. There are depositions, particularly those of the defendants' doctors, which I failed to review over the weekend. My questions for voir dire need to be critiqued. My opening statement contains the basic allegations of facts, yet lacks intensity. Questions for witnesses need to be reviewed. My cross-examination appears weak; I'll have to seek suggestions from Burnett. Corrections must be made to my charts. An exhibit list needs to be prepared. And, even now I need to sketch my closing argument. Then I need to arrange my case so that it will be a good story from beginning to end.

Holding a cup of fresh coffee in one hand, I use my other hand to switch on the lights in my office. I stand between the two client chairs facing my desk and set the cup on a spot of the desk not littered with files, open law books, depositions, documents and legal pads filled with notes. For a moment I stare at my calendar, upside down before me, showing a large red X that is not upside down, blocking out the day of Monday.

Since the service for Earl yesterday, I have been unable to think about anything other than the trial. I have to get the preparation done. I have to concentrate. If I work hard all day, will I get it all done? This is the final burst through the wall of resistance to trial preparation, the act Burnett described as being the worst part of the ordeal. Once I'm through the wall, I know I can handle the trial. First, though, I have to get through the wall. And, I will get through it because I no longer have any other choice. All of the stalling is over. All of the final exams for a first year lawyer have been rolled into one test to be given to me over the next three days. The pressure I feel is inversely proportional to the amount of time I spent on preparation; thus, the pressure is crushing me. I must stop the turning of the jaws of the vise.

I move rapidly to the windows and pull the shades to ward off the coming of the sunrise.

~ 35 ~

From my infamous jury trial in the drunk driving case, I discovered it's easy to tell when there is going to be a jury trial in Timber County. The parking lot and the streets around the courthouse square will be jammed with vehicles belonging to prospective jurors. Half of the vehicles will be pickup trucks. This time of year some of the pickups will have plows on the front; some chainsaws or hunting gear visible through the windows in the cabs. It's too early in the morning, though, for the individuals selected from the jury list. Instructed to be in the courtroom by eight-thirty, they will begin drifting in after eight o'clock.

Tompkins wants the lawyers in his chambers at eight o'clock. Allowing half an hour to arrange my file, exhibits and documents on the counsel table and take care of last minute matters, I arrive at the courthouse at seven-thirty, early enough to park a few spaces from the side door. I decide to leave my coat in the car. I rapidly walk through the frigid air to the door, toting a bulging briefcase in each hand.

For weeks, I have thought about the trial and planned for it. Some days it was work on the case—investigations like that of the flying hubcap, depositions, motion hearings, the pretrial, conferences with Ginger, the preparation over the weekend and on the prior day. Many days it was only thinking about the case. Something would pop into my head, and I would scribble a note before I forgot it, later researching the idea or discussing it with Burnett. Thoughts of the trial have so absorbed my mind I have almost convinced myself I've covered everything; in fact, Burnett has assured me I am well prepared. I want so desperately to believe his statement I conditionally accept it; the condition imposed by

298

the truth in my mind being that kindness does not always speak the truth.

The sound of my wet shoes squishing on the marble floor echoes through the corridor of the courthouse with each step I take toward the rotunda. In spite of all the preparation, the planning, the endless lists of "To Do Items For Trial," I missed one thing, one thing I did not plan on, one thing I failed to even think about, one thing now more important than anything else. I hurry into the men's room and throw up.

After I have cleaned up, I find the employees' break room on the first floor and purchase a roll of mints from one of the vending machines. This isn't the way I want to start the day. At least Burnett didn't accompany me, as I requested. He promised me he would be there by nine o'clock to offer assistance on the jury selection; otherwise, he would be in and out during the case. He made one thing clear to me: this is my case.

Until I raced into the bathroom, I had been willing, in fact had wanted, to accept sole responsibility for the case. Now, my lack of experience and feelings of inadequacy and doubt almost paralyze me. Trudging up the stairs to the second floor, I feel the height of the steps has grown. I want to be anywhere and doing anything other than walking toward a courtroom to try a personal injury case for a young woman who is depending upon me. I no longer want to be *The Great Attorney John Hall* in Rick's firm in Chicago. At the same time, I desperately want to try the case, to get it over, to get it out of my mind. I sense I'm not ready for the task before me; I sense failure. Then I think of the big kid in the ring with me as we shook hands before the bout. How had he made the same weight class as me? When the bell rang, his size was of no importance, and there was no time to fret over the outcome. I came out of the corner slugging.

Angie stands in the doorway of the judge's chambers, drinking coffee and chatting with the judge. He turns, waves at me, and turns back. I set my two briefcases on the floor next to my favorite table, on the right facing the judge. Unpacking the cases, I pause as it occurs to me Wells and Smith will be sitting next to the jury since the jury box is immediately to their left. They will be able see the jurors more clearly and can maintain better eye contact with them. All right, I decide. I don't want to be that close to the jurors. They can also see me more clearly, see me when I don't want to be seen by them.

I continue unpacking and arranging my law books with bookmarks for reference, pleadings, exhibits, sub-files for voir dire and opening statement, notes, witness questions and copies of depositions in piles around the table. In addition to the legal pad in front of me, I place another pad and a ballpoint pen in front of Ginger's chair.

The Clerk of Court enters the courtroom and begins arranging the court file at her station. I briskly carry my pile of exhibits, along with a copy of the exhibit list, over to her and ask her to mark the exhibits.

Angie backs out of the doorway of the judge's chambers, closes the door, and ambles over to me to shake my hand. "Good luck, buddy."

"Thanks. Please, though, no help this time. I'm nervous enough without any ringers from you."

Angie throws up his open hands in a defensive posture. "Don't worry about me." Then he smiles. "Not for now."

Walking back to my table, I feel underdressed in my dark blue sport coat and gray trousers. The last time I wore a suit was in Madison when I was admitted to practice before the Wisconsin Supreme Court, and that suit was borrowed from my brother. Margo and Suzy said I looked fine. Burnett told me to let Wells lead the fashion parade; let him show the jury the source of the money for the verdict. Besides, Burnett stressed, there is at least one study claiming jurors respond well to the color blue. Then, too, he had said, somewhere there is a survey showing whatever you want to be shown.

Wells enters the courtroom accompanied by Smith and Jeremy Wilson's father, who, as sponsor for Jeremy's driver's license, is also a defendant. Also with them is a scholarly appearing female legal assistant from Wells' office. They stop to greet me. Wells' assistant pulls a small handcart with two boxes of files on it. She places the boxes in front of the bench in the first row, directly behind where Wells and Smith sit. I assume she will sit behind the boxes and remove the papers and documents and hand them to Wells as he needs them. Then she wheels the handcart to the back corner of the room and becomes invisible.

Appearing more distinguished than usual, Wells sets a briefcase on the floor on the jury side of the table. He removes a black, three-ring notebook and places it alone on the polished, dark surface of the counsel table, where it stands aloof from the debris on my table.

I'm stunned. I've never seen a *trial book* before. Scanning my cluttered table, I feel like a junkyard operator in a swanky nightclub, a hick, a small town lawyer with no polish, no finesse, no legal cultivation, and no handcart.

I traipse into the hallway to look for my client. Accompanied by her father, she walks toward me. I lead them into the Clerk of Court's office and have them hang their coats on a rack there since the racks in the courtroom will be jammed with the coats of the prospective jurors. Then I escort them into the courtroom. Smith and Wells nod at them, Wells offering a polite "good morning." I arrange Ginger in the chair to the right of me at the counsel table, and then motion her father to sit near the end of the first row of benches where he'll have a good view of the proceedings and be close to Ginger.

Angie walks into the judge's chamber and returns almost instantly, moving to the counsel tables. "The judge wants to see the attorneys."

When we are settled in chairs, Tompkins addresses us in a voice and manner indicating he expects only one answer. "I assume, gentlemen there is no last minute settlement proposal."

"None, Your Honor," Wells speaks before I can open my mouth.

Wells is gradually taking control of everything, using his experience and reputation to dominate every scene. How do I stop it? I must not let myself be intimated by him. "No," I respond.

Tompkins shoots me a look of pity before turning to Wells. "I take it Mr. Smith will be assisting in this matter?"

"That's correct, your Honor. He will, though, unless you direct otherwise, not be present throughout the proceedings."

That's nice, I think; they're only going to double team me at the crucial times.

"How do you intend to present the case, Mr. Wells? Will you be handling all of the witnesses? I don't care if you divide up the witnesses." Tompkins leans forward for emphasis. "I will, however, allow only one of you to speak during any part of the proceedings. Am I clear on that?"

"Absolutely, Your Honor. I intend to handle all of the proceedings. Attorney Smith will be here from time-to-time to assist in certain matters but will not address the court."

I silently thank the judge, although I suspect his inquiry is standard procedure. While I know I'm no Franklin Wells, if I can get Burnett involved as much as Smith, the field will be somewhat more even. I hope.

"I do wish to the alert the court to one thing," Wells adds. "We're very concerned about the legal capacity to testify of one of the plaintiff's witnesses, Mr. Edward Plumber. He will probably show up in court intoxicated, and if so, we'll ask the court to bar his testimony."

I jump up, immediately realizing I need not have risen but am now stuck in my position. "That's a very prejudicial statement by Attorney Wells. Mr. Plumber may be a heavy drinker, but that doesn't mean he will be incompetent to testify. He . . . "

Tompkins motions for me to sit down. "I'll rule on any questions regarding competency to testify."

Wells has a smug look on his face. "Understood, your Honor. I merely wanted to bring this to your attention so that when the issue arises you won't think we are trying to delay the trial."

Now I'm irritated by the way Wells sneaked in the "when the issue arises." He knows Beeper will be a sober drunk. Where's the issue?

"All right." Tompkins continues, "I have rather extensive questions to ask on voir dire. You gentlemen may ask your questions afterward, but I want to select a jury as soon as possible. This is not a criminal case. As you know we're dealing with a five-sixths verdict, which in Wisconsin requires only ten jurors to agree, and the standard is 'preponderance of the evidence' not 'beyond a reasonable doubt.' I would like to have the jury selected, your opening statements and the first witness on the stand before noon. Any reason we can't meet that schedule?"

Hearing simultaneous "no's," Tompkins smiles and sits back in his padded, metal county chair. "That's all. We'll start the jury selection at eight-thirty."

The courtroom is now packed with the prospective jurors, most talking loudly among themselves, while a few sit silently, appearing embittered by their calls to duty. Several of the disgusted jurors glare at me. Are they holding me responsible for their being summoned to jury duty? Of course they are.

I glance at the clock behind the bench: twenty minutes after eight. I pause at the counsel table to tell Ginger I must leave the room for a moment. Another kind of duty calls; my stomach is turning over.

I rush to the men's room thinking I'm going to let go again. Somehow I stave off the upset. Standing before a sink I wet a paper towel and wipe my forehead. With my cupped hand I rinse out my mouth and drink water. How bad can it be? Then I recall the man who I thought was going to shoot me; that will always be for me the standard of what is really bad. I look at myself in the mirror above the sink. My face is pale and tired looking, hardly the face of *The Great Attorney John Hall.* I spent seven years in college and almost a year in practice to get here. I'm also a former boxer and survived three years in the Army infantry. Was my toughness itself a feint? I pop several mints into my mouth as I hurry back into the courtroom.

❧ ❧

While everyone waits for Tompkins to come on the bench, I chat with Ginger, vaguely hearing what she says. I try to remember pointers Burnett has given me, like staying alert for the objectionable question. He warned me how easy it is to let things slip by before you object. Once it's in the record, it's too late. He quoted Tompkins: "You can't unring the bell."

Burnett slips into the courtroom amid the chatter, the nervous laughter and the noise of the shuffling feet of the anxious prospective jurors. He eases into the chair on my left, directly across from Wells, exchanging smiles with our adversaries. Turning to me, he grabs my hand and shakes it vigorously.

He whispers to me: "This is something you can do, John. I wouldn't have turned this case over to you if I hadn't been confident you could try it."

"Thanks, Bob." I want to tell him how much I appreciate everything he has done for me, how grateful I am for the opportunity to handle Ginger's case. The congratulatory thoughts, however, are immediately cancelled by an overwhelming desire to be a bird so I can glide on the waves of the hot air flowing out of the window opened by the bailiff. I had wondered why the thermostat hadn't been turned down earlier to compensate for the body heat in the room.

Suddenly, the bailiff summons everyone to rise. Bailiffs, I learned are brought into the courtroom in Timber County only for jury trials. Jimmy Hacks, a retired deputy sheriff who is still husky but now bored, was dusted off for this one. Tompkins takes the bench; everyone else sits down; Tompkins tells the clerk to spin the tumbler containing the slips with the names on the jury list; and that's it. I no longer think of anything except the case. The bell has rung, and I'm on my feet, jabbing while shuffling my feet.

Near silence in the courtroom. An air of anticipation permeated only by the sound from the spinning drum. Tompkins leans toward the clerk but speaks loudly, "Due to the uncertainty of the winter weather over the few days, and the distance some of the jurors will have to travel to court, I've decided to have an alternate juror."

The clerk spins the drum until nineteen names are drawn and the twelve juror chairs plus an additional seven folding chairs, six for the preemptory or "free" strikes and one for the alternate juror, are filled. As each name is called, voices of relief outnumber the one from the selected juror trudging to a chair; then silence again as the whirling tumbler shuffles the remaining slips. Burnett fills in the name of each juror selected on a sheet with blank boxes furnished by the clerk while I refer to my notes on the jury list. Throughout the process we whisper back and forth.

After the jurors are all seated, Tompkins quickly explains the nature of the case and that it will probably last three days. He excuses several of the selected individuals who convince him that for health or other reasons they are not able to sit through a three-day trial and has the clerk draw names to replace them. Then he proceeds rapidly through his usual examination for cause. He has each of the attorneys and their clients stand as he introduces them and asks questions concerning them.

"Do any of you know Attorney Hall?"

A large man with dark hair reaching from his long sideburns into his mustache and beard, loudly proclaims, "Yeah, he's my attorney."

"Do you presently have any business with him?"

"Sort of. It's about . . . " His voice drops, "I'm going to make an appointment. . . ."

Tompkins obviously didn't hear the last part of the answer, since the judge speaks over the man's reply: "Would your association with Attorney Hall in any way prevent . . ."

I stare at the man, sure I've never seen him before, sure the man has never been in our office. I whisper to Burnett, "The guy is trying to get out of serving."

Burnett shrugs and whispers back. "If he is, you don't want him. Let the judge get rid of him."

"I'd go with whatever Attorney Hall thinks."

Tompkins glares at the man before excusing him, and then admonishes the remaining panelists to remember their civic responsibilities as electors of Timber County. The clerk spins the drum for a replacement.

When the questioning by the judge ends, I get my turn, followed by Wells. Tompkins dismisses a few more men and women called to the jury box. Clever arguments by the attorneys fail to persuade the judge to dismiss for cause any more of the panelists. Tompkins then allows each side to begin exercising their three peremptory challenges. The clerk passes the list back and forth between the counsel tables as names are stricken.

Burnett and I agree on the first two of our three strikes. The third is more difficult. I want to strike the older, stern looking woman Dick Minor warned me about, Mrs. Goettelman, convinced she will not identify with nor approve of Ginger. Burnett urges me to keep her and instead strike a middle-aged, smirking, over-weight man Burnett says is a known troublemaker, the kind who appears at village and school board meetings and creates havoc. There will, Burnett explains, be no way to predict how the man will view this case, and being a loud mouth could wind up as the foreman and herd the jurors down the wrong path.

Before he finishes, Burnett reins himself in. "It's your call, John."

"I don't know." I check Ginger out of the corner of my eye. I haven't paid much attention to her appearance. She's wearing a sweater over a blouse, slacks and low heels. Her hair is its natural blond color and neatly brushed, and she's smiling. What a change.

I check the jury list and note the older woman does reside in Algona and is retired. She probably has little connection with Winding River. I look up at the judge who is staring at me and tapping his fingers on the bench. The loud mouth is struck, and I sit back as the clerk removes the sheet from the table.

Burnett whispers, "You never know, though."

⁂

The deputy clerk comes up to me during the break before opening statements and hands me a slip with a message to call the office. I phone Suzy from the Clerk's of Court's office.

"I'm sorry," Suzy apologizes. "Suits has called several times this morning and driven by the office trying to spot your car. He wants to know when you're going to meet with him about some of his cases. He said The Relatives are now getting angry at you."

"For crying out loud. Have you got everything typed up?"

"As far as I know."

"Tell him to come in on Thursday afternoon. You know what to do." I hear a huge sigh.

"Okay. How's it going?"

"I'm still in the fight."

I hustle back into the courtroom and take my seat. I'm irked by the interruption until I realize it was a break for me, a distraction I needed. There is nothing I can do now with my opening statement.

Burnett gives me a pat on the back. Waiting for Tompkins to retake the bench, I begin to fret. I know the function of an opening statement is to briefly state the nature of the case, indicate the issues, and outline the evidence I intend to offer. The purpose is, according to an older Wisconsin case, "to advise the jury of the questions of fact involved so as to prepare their minds for the evidence." Remember, Burnett stressed, it's a statement not an argument. Nevertheless, Burnett pointed out, it's a crucial time to win the confidence of the jurors, and if done well, poison their minds against the other side. I recall reading a study claiming many jurors make up their minds about the case by the conclusion of the opening statements.

"Remember," Burnett whispers to me, "don't promise anything you can't deliver."

After the jurors are reseated, Tompkins looks at me. "Mr. Hall, you may proceed."

Carrying my notes and smiling at the jurors, I approach a podium moved into the area in between the counsel tables and the bench, facing the jury. My hands are sweaty as I place my outline on the podium and eye the panel of five men and seven women in ages ranging from twenty-two to seventy-four. There is no longer any other place to go. All remnants of *The Great Attorney John Hall* of my daydreams are gone. I am nothing other than John Hall, a first year attorney, apprehensive but not afraid. My eyes are fixed on the jurors. When the bell in my mind rings I begin.

In a way it's easy. I've gone over the facts so many times—with Ginger, the witnesses, in depositions, in the preparation for trial—the words roll out of my mouth. I assert that the witnesses will make clear what happened in the accident, how my client was injured through the actions of the other driver. I stress the seriousness of Ginger's injuries and play on the sympathy factor for a benign young woman.

A third of the way into the statement my words are rolling out too easily. I'm racing through the presentation, and some of the jurors appear inattentive. I'm using too many "ahs," and after I skip several lines in my outline, the statement is coming apart. The only thing capturing the jurors' attention is the flying hubcap. Out of the corner of my eye I catch the open window and wonder if I can still fly through it. Nothing flies, though, except the time. I sprinted through the statement in a matter of minutes yet half an hour has passed on the wall clock behind Tompkins. As I thank the jurors for their attention, I know my statement has been a disaster.

"Nice job," Burnett says to me in a voice to be heard by others as I return to my seat. I stare at him in disbelief.

When Wells walks to the podium, he carries nothing. Intrigued, I assume Wells is using some memory system to keep his outline at the ready in his mind. Wells leans an elbow on the edge of the podium and speaks as though he is at a fireside chat. His presentation is very natural and assuring, and the jurors sit like baby birds with their mouths agape waiting for their mother to feed them more. There are chuckles and grins and then laughter about the flying hubcap. Even Burnett is enjoying it. I want to crawl underneath the table. Instead, I lean back in my chair to see the jurors more closely.

Then it happens: the crash, the bang, the jurors and the judge all rising, Wells turning, and Burnett and Ginger peering down, to see me on my back in my chair on the floor behind the counsel table.

"Are you all right, John?" Burnett helps me up.

"I'm okay," I mumble. More loudly, I say it again to an astonished Tompkins and a shocked jury. I pick up the chair and sit down. Ginger tries not to look at me, no doubt to keep from laughing.

Tompkins frowns as he addresses Wells. "You may continue."

Wells hesitates. "Well, Your Honor, I can't top that, and I think the jurors have seen all they need to see. I'm finished." Wells turns and smiles broadly at the jurors, who smile back and nod.

I feel at though I've followed the Wilsons' old Chevrolet into the car crusher.

Burnett leans close to me to whisper in a consoling voice, "Tell me sometime whether you did that on purpose. It was a terrific way to cut him off."

36

A blowup of the Chief of Police's diagram of the accident scene rests on an easel near where the podium was located, within clear view of the jury, the judge and the witness. Before lunch, I had the Chief of Police identify the diagram. Missing from it is the Wilson's Chevrolet since the police discovered no physical evidence indicating it was ever a part of the accident. The Chief never believed Ginger, so he never treated the accident as a hit and run, or near hit and miss run. The choice between a rebellious young woman and two delinquent boys went to the boys. Regardless, I decided the diagram would aid the jury in visualizing the scene. Since the accident occurred near a principal intersection in the village, I surmise some of the jurors must have seen young drivers using a racecar approach to the stop sign on Forest.

The judge sits on the bench, and everyone waits for the bailiff to lead the jurors into the courtroom. Tompkins surely had Angie remove any clues that the jury's temporary home doubles as a practice putting green. I miss having Burnett at my side, at the same time understanding the office cannot shut down for the trial. Suffering a momentary delusion, I convince myself direct testimony is easier than cross-examination. Presenting the heart of the case through Ginger's testimony is simply a matter of adhering to my list of typed questions without overtly leading her.

"Are you okay?" I ask Ginger in a low voice.

"I'm pretty nervous. I wish we didn't have to do this."

I grab her left hand, lightly squeezing it. "You look great, and I'm sure you'll sound great. Just tell the jurors the way the accident happened. Don't be afraid to be emotional, but don't overdo it. They'll know when you're sincere and when you're not."

What about myself? I conclude the morning show was a disaster. If it had been a play, the audience would not have returned after the intermission. All I accomplished was to get through it. Anyway, it's over. I can do better; I will do better; I have to do better. I'm one of the lead actors in this drama. Still, Ginger is the star. I wonder if she can perform like a star.

As I watch the jurors file into their seats in the jury box, it occurs to me that presenting the heart of my case to a group that has only begun digesting a huge lunch is poor timing. I need to keep them awake. I look at Ginger again. What has precipitated her turnaround? The drug-pushing boyfriend has even disappeared from her life.

Tompkins peers at me over the top of his reading glasses, perched uneasily on the end of his large nose. "Call your next witness, Mr. Hall."

Walking slowly, Ginger approaches the bench. When she is sworn by the clerk and takes her seat in the witness box, she smiles at the jury. I notice several of the jurors smile back. That has to be a good sign. Ginger's courteous act is not the result of coaching by me, and it momentarily disrupts me as I study the jurors' faces.

"Whenever you're ready, Mr. Hall." Tompkins' fingers are again dancing on the surface of the dark oak bench.

I guide Ginger through my outline, retracing my steps several times after objections by Wells to leading questions. This is perhaps the most crucial part of the trial since the jurors must like Ginger and believe her testimony. From the standpoint of presentation, it's the easiest part. Presenting direct testimony, I reason, is like using scripted offensive plays in football. In both cases the defense can only guess what is coming. Of course, if the opposing attorney has the experience of Wells, the guesses will be good ones.

Ginger responds to my questions politely and thoughtfully, with no hint of the petulance present at our first meeting. If she's nervous, it's not evident in her calm voice. From hasty glances at the jurors, it appears to me they like her, though I'm so absorbed in presenting my case I'm unable to study their faces enough for a good read.

After I finish with her background, including employment history, I have her describe the accident in detail. I consider having her move to the Chief's blowup of his diagram, but decide her case will proceed more smoothly if she relates the facts and lets the jurors glance at the diagram as she testifies. I know most of them are familiar with the intersection. Her testimony is a polished version of what she furnished in her deposition. She must keep going over it in her mind.

Her injuries are presented as simply as possible; the doctors will hammer out the specifics. I want the jurors to be sure they understand and remember the basic injuries to her left side: the elbow, hip, knee, and especially the lower leg. My concentration is on the effects of the injuries—the pain and suffering, the permanent damage, the loss of ability to do things now that she could do before the accident.

One of the things she cannot do now is her job. "Do you plan to return to your job at the River's Edge?"

"No, I don't."

"And why is that?"

"I'm still having difficulty moving quickly. Being a waitress, especially when the supper club is busy, requires you to hustle. I can't move that fast."

"What about working there as a cashier where you can sit down most of the time?" I try to pre-empt some of Wells' cross-examination. Wells will go back to it, but if I explore it first, the jurors, having already heard her answers, might feel Wells is badgering her.

"There's no position there for me."

"Then what do you plan to do for employment?" Obviously, she's out of work, looking for a decent job, something hard to find in Winding River.

"I'm going to art school in Milwaukee at the end of January."

The quick answer paralyzes me. What? I glimpse Wells scribbling notes on his legal pad. When . . .

"I want to do something productive with my life. I want . . . Anyway, studying and being in class will give me more time to heal from my injuries."

I recover enough to check my outline and keep going through it. After I finish the long direct examination, Tompkins addresses the jury. "Let's take a fifteen minute break."

I congratulate Ginger on her testimony. I'm satisfied with it. Then I recall her revelation about future work. "Why didn't you tell me you had decided to go to art school?"

"I'm sorry. I forgot. I was very nervous this morning."

Ginger's mother rises from the first row of the spectator benches and moves over to us. There is nothing remarkable about her. A tall, trim woman, she is neatly dressed and wears thick glasses. With business like movements and a no nonsense voice, she fits my notion of a co-owner of an accounting business. Mrs. Buckman is the afternoon replacement for the comfort seat occupied by her husband in the morning.

First introducing her mother, Ginger then stretches. When she lowers her arms, her mother grabs a hand.

"How are you holding up?"

"I'm doing all right."

I guess the answer is partially true. Ginger was not overly concerned about the direct examination. She knew the questions I would ask her. Now I sense she's becoming anxious as she anticipates Wells' cross-examination.

"I'm sorry you have to go through with this."

"I don't think I had any other choice."

Ginger eyes her mother closely. I know they haven't been close since the beginning of high school. The way Ginger described it to me it was her fault they grew distant, yet she felt her mother's close grip and ever-present eye started the rift between them. I sense now Ginger was like a stretching balloon, needing space to expand, and her mother wouldn't give it to her.

I excuse myself to sit down so I can begin sorting through my notes of Ginger's direct examination. As I do so, I catch Mrs. Buckman easing Ginger away from me but not far enough away from my excellent hearing.

Mrs. Buckman whispers, "I wonder whether your attorney is capable of handling this case. He seems to know where everything is located, yet he doesn't seem as well organized as Mr. Wells. His delivery certainly isn't as smooth. Your father was embarrassed for you when Mr. Hall fell over backwards in his chair. You know, he . . . "

"He's doing a good job." Ginger twists her hand out of her mother's grip.

The ensuing dialogue sounds the way Ginger told me it always went with her mother: beginning with the foundation criticism. Her mother

and father are alike in that regard, Ginger claims; they always see everything as either black or red marks in a ledger, marks that must be neither smudged nor poorly printed. Ginger continues defending me:

"This may be his first civil jury trial, but he's tried cases before the
judge. And, Attorney Burnett is helping him. Burnett is your attorney,
isn't he?"

"Well, yes. You know, though . . . "

I turn to see a sneer on Ginger's mouth as she interrupts her
mother. "What I know is that he's doing a good job. I like him, and I
trust him. However the trial comes out, I won't be disappointed in him."

"This is about your future, you know?"

"Mother, who's the one suffering, the one feeling the aches and
pains. I'm old enough to do that on my own, aren't I?"

"Where did you come up with this idea about art school?"

"I've been thinking about it since last May."

Arching her brow, Mrs. Buckman moves closer to Ginger. "It would
have been nice for us to have heard that news from you rather than in a
courtroom."

"This is not what I need now, mother." Ginger steps backwards, out
of her mother's reach and looks for me, but I have turned back to my
notes.

I want to intervene, to reciprocate Ginger's defense of me, but let it
go and shuffle my notes as if my attention is elsewhere.

"You know, mother, you don't have to stay all afternoon. I'll do
fine."

"Well, there are many year-end things to do. Are you sure?"

"I'm sure."

"If it's all right, then I'll go back to the office. Your father can pick
you up." She nods at me as I turn around and watch her pick up her coat
from the bench and leave the courtroom.

I face Ginger as she sits next to me. "Nice woman, your mother."

"Yes, isn't she."

❧ ❧

Listening to Wells try to shred Ginger's testimony, I recall Burnett's comments about a well known lawyer whose book on cross-

examination was thought by many older attorneys to be the bible of cross-examination. A late nineteenth-century trial lawyer who established his reputation in the courtrooms of New York, the lawyer attributed any success he had not to skillful questioning, but to toiling preparation. It's obvious to me Wells has done his homework. He knows everything in the investigative report Burnett glimpsed at Ginger's deposition and everything that's not in it. He knows who she is and where she's been and what she's done, and he exploits it all. And, he does it without missing a beat. He *is* smooth as silk.

I know it all, too, and I watch the jurors carefully as they listen with rapt attention to Wells' questioning. Wells knows how to do it, and how to make sure the jurors know he knows how to do it. Burnett impressed on me that every lawyer knows you never asked a question on cross-examination that you do not know the answer to. The answers begin to come from Ginger's mouth as if she had been preprogrammed by Wells. And then in a blink, it all turns like a rotating stage set where the backside now comes into view.

Wells asks the question in a low, demeaning voice. "As I understand it, Miss Buckman, you were a waitress."

"Yes, I was." Ginger is sitting up very straight in her chair and looking at the jury. "I was going through a difficult time in my life then, and I needed some work, any kind of work, to keep me going, and help me pay for the support my parents were furnishing. I never expected them to have to continue to support me after I graduated from high school. I always knew it was my responsibility . . . "

I see the irritation in Wells' face as he is about to object to the answer, but instead interrupts her, "I think you've answered the question, Miss Buckman. If you would please just answer the question I ask you."

"Yes, I'm sorry."

But the jury has heard it, and I see in their faces they like her. They like the idea that she is trying to get through life like everyone else. That she is, after all, a young woman struggling to grow up in Timber County. That she has injuries from an accident somehow caused by persons Wells represents. The jurors are not drawn simply to the facts or the law. They're focused on the body in the jury box. They're drawn by what they see, what they like, what they want to believe.

I also witness Ginger's facial muscles and lips tighten up. I know she's holding in her anger over some of Wells' questions, as Burnett advised her to do: *Don't give Wells the opportunity to force you to say things you will regret, things that may cause the jury to see you in a different light.*

"You handled yourself very well," I assure Ginger when she returns to the counsel table.

She doesn't respond. She is visibly shaken and tired. She has been wronged and now she hurts. She told it exactly the way it happened, and now she doesn't care about it anymore. She wants to get on with her life so she doesn't care how the jury feels about her or about her accident. Wells at times made her look bad. I felt the stings along with her. She's not that bad. She is *somebody*, and someday can be more than *somebody*. She has the ability to achieve something significant. I know it, and now I think she does too.

The accident was not her fault. If she needs to be judged, perhaps the other things are her fault. I suspect she never wanted to ride a motorcycle; that, in fact she was scared when her boyfriend first suggested it. Then he signed the title over to her when he got in trouble and was afraid the cycle would be taken away from him. She found she liked riding the bike. She felt a sense of freedom when she rode it. She did it because it was a different thing to do in Winding River, and she wanted to be different. She did not want to be a perfect mark in a ledger.

Now, Wells attempted to make fun of her, ridicule her for roaring down Main Street at ten o'clock at night on her motorcycle. Her words and her face at times said she didn't care. Her doodles and her words to me said she did care; she cared very much. She cared about not doing something more with her life. It was not turning out the way she wanted it to. Perhaps I helped to push her into something she always wanted to do. She has changed. Still, I'm convinced she will always be different, will always want to stand outside the witness box. I hope, though, in future she will do it with a smile and with a thumbs-up sign.

She sits back as I prepare to question Beeper who is seated in the witness box. She didn't recall him being at the accident scene, yet she told me his description of the events in his deposition was the way she remembered them. She glances at the large clock on the wall behind the judge. I'm sure she now wants more than anything else to simply go home.

❧ ❧

"May we approach the bench?" Wells asks the judge.

Tompkins nods approval. I follow Wells to the bench where we huddle with the judge and speak in low voices. Wells sprinkles poison on Beeper:

"Your Honor, the defense is still very concerned about the competency to testify of the next witness. The jury should not hear testimony from an intoxicated witness." Wells leans closer to the judge. "I can smell alcohol on him from here."

"So can I," Tompkins whispers. "He always smells like alcohol." He rolls his chair closer to the witness box. The short, bald headed man is dressed in a sweater over a shirt and is staring at the floor. "Are you all right, Beeper? Ah, excuse me, Mr. Plumber."

Beeper looks up. "Same as I always am judge."

"You know why you're here today?"

"Yeah. I'm a witness in this case."

Tompkins rolls back to the center of the bench. "We'll proceed, Mr. Wells. He's as normal as he's going to get."

I haven't talked to Beeper since our meeting at his home. While the answers then were straight forward, I'm now apprehensive about the answer of each question I pose to him. I need not be as the responses are photocopies of the originals. It's going well, maybe too well, because I decide to try something I've thought about for some time. Can I get it in? Doesn't everyone know Beeper?

With my chair at an angle to the counsel table, I can see the witness, the jury and Wells all at the same time. "Mr. Plumber, you've been arrested in the past, haven't you?"

"Yes."

Out of the corner of my eye, I see Wells poised to make an objection, but does not.

"How many times?"

"Quite a few. Nothin' too bad."

"Well, you've been arrested for theft, haven't you?"

"Yes."

"And you were charged by the District Attorney with failure to provide support for your family?"

"Objection, Your Honor," Wells speaks with authority. "Counsel is leading the witness, the questions are immaterial, and, well, he's impeaching his own witness."

Tompkins had been leaning back in his chair, and he sits upright. "Yes, he appears to be. Why I don't know. I'll sustain the objection as to the questions being leading, and the jury shall ignore the answers."

I nod in agreement. "All right. Mr. Plumber, do you consider yourself an honest man?"

"I don't know about that. I stole some things, and I didn't support my family at times. I had my problems. I guess I was dishonest at times."

"Your, Honor," Wells is on his feet. "Where is counsel going with this?"

"I'm wondering that, too, Mr. Wells, but your question isn't an objection. And, please remain seated."

"Well, can a dishonest man tell the truth?"

"Objection!"

"Sustained. *Mister* Hall."

"That's okay, judge," Beeper interjects. "I get his point. I know I'm no good. I've never been any good, and never will be. I drink too much."

"Objection!"

Tompkins jumps in: "There's no question before you, Mr. Plumber. The . . . "

"But, I don't lie." Beeper turns to the jurors. "You can ask anyone, ask the Chief. He knows I don't lie. I saw everything I said I saw."

"Your honor, this line of questioning . . . "

"That's enough, Mr. Plumber." Tompkins has his hands up. "The jury will disregard those remarks by Mr. Plumber." He lowers his bifocals, and glares at me. "Please confine your questions to appropriate matters for direct examination."

"I'm done, Your Honor. All done."

Burnett had slipped into the courtroom and is sitting in a bench waiting to move up to the counsel table when I finish with the witness. As I square my chair to the table, I see a smiling Burnett creep into the chair next to me.

"I've got to take in more of this, John. This is better than I expected."

❧ ☙

"John, it's Margo."

A call in the evening? I lean back in my office chair and look at the clock over the door: 8:15. Always an interruption, yet I need a break.

"How's the trial going?"

"Okay, I guess. I don't honestly know. I'm working on the questions for my witnesses for tomorrow." I feel like that soldier (what's his name?) in Stendahl's war novel, the one where the soldier has no idea who is winning the war; he only knows what's happening around him. Maybe I should have read the book rather than skim through it as I did with most of the books on The Dean's list.

Margo continues: "I hate to call you in the midst of your trial. Lord knows you've got enough pressure on you already. I felt I had to tell you this before you heard it from someone tomorrow. It might throw you off your case."

"It's about the case?"

"No, the Swensons."

"Paul and Jean?"

"They decided to go to Florida for the holidays and take the kids since school's out."

"I know. I saw Paul on the street last week, and he mentioned they were going. Good for them."

"Apparently they couldn't afford to fly all of them down there, so they drove down. In Tennessee they ran into some fog." Margo's voice is strained. "A truck came across the centerline . . . and killed them."

"Killed Paul and Jean?"

No, well, yes . . . killed all of them."

It hits me worse than the news of Earl. At least I knew he was very ill. I can barely speak. "The kids, too?"

"Yes. I just heard about it. I hesitated calling you, but decided it would be better if you learned it now rather than during a break in the trial."

"You're right." I take a deep breath. As I exhale, I realize she must have heard it.

"All you did was draft some wills, John. You happened to hit on something that may never come up like this again. Don't blame yourself."

I nod several times before I'm aware she cannot see my head movements. "Thanks for calling me. I *would* rather have heard it from you."

After I hang up, I sit still for a long time. I feel bitter. Of course, who would not be bitter about the deaths of two lovely, young people with two nice kids? Images of the Sunstroms and their children flood my mind. The four Sunstroms leaving and the Larsens and their two young children arriving; population change in Winding River, zero. What does it mean?

The papers strewn across my desk come into focus. What else can I do about the trial until tomorrow? I push myself out of my chair, turn off the light and grab my coat in the hallway before heading out the door.

"What the hell," says Angie as he looks first at Slider and then me. "I never thought I'd see you in here during the trial."

"Two beers, that's all."

Slider moves down the bar to the taps.

Angie smiles. "Two beers? The courtroom standard: they always had two beers before they were stopped by the cops." He softens his tone as he eyes my face. "Hey, don't worry about it. You're doing a good job."

"Are you kidding me? What did you like best, my tumbling act or Wells pulverizing me during his opening statement?"

"Ah, every lawyer starts somewhere." He looks me over. "Something else eating you?"

Amazing how quickly you get to know your buddies, how soon you discern the pattern of emphasis on one problem as the cover-up for another problem. I watch Slider place a mug of beer before me. Then I relate Margo's conversation about the Sunstroms. After the remarks of regret, we sit silently, sipping beer.

Slider breaks the silence. "Say, we were talking about the past hunting season. Angie thinks that next year the three of us should go up to Hurley. I got a friend who owns a shack near there."

"Hunting? First of all, I don't know how to hunt, and secondly I don't have a gun."

Angie laughs. "You don't need to know how to hunt. And you certainty don't need a gun."

"That's right," Slider joins in. "If we're not playing cards and drinking beer in the shack, we'll be in the bars in Hurley."

"Have you ever been to Hurley?" Angie asks and goes on without my answer: "In the old mining days, Hurley was known as the hellhole of the whole iron ore range from Duluth to Detroit. The feds never could close it down during prohibition. Great place to go."

I frown at Angie. "You're a waste, Bellini."

"A waste. You hear that, Slider? Well, counselor, I happen to be the keeper of the words."

Slider laughs. "It's a good thing my house is behind this place. I can't tell you how many times I've had to drag this guy home. If he's the keeper of the words than I'm the keeper of the keeper of the words."

I shake my head. "You guys take it all for granted, don't you?"

"Ho, wait here," Angie barks. "We've got a philosopher tonight. You know what? When we go up to the cabin we'll stack our beer cans. By the time . . ."

"Nah," Slider interrupts, "we'll have to pile them outside, the ceiling . . ."

Angie shakes his head. "The wind will blow them over. You know what we could do, though . . ."

I pick up my money from the bar. "On second thought, one beer is enough. I came in here to escape. You guys have inspired me to go back to work on the trial."

Angie looks puzzled. "What's your problem? How would you stack the cans?"

37

Sleepy-eye time. Burnett sits in one of the chairs in front of my desk, trying not to spill the coffee from the full cup in his hand. I finish sipping my coffee, then open the early morning conversation: "I suppose Margo told you about the Sunstroms."

"Yes. Very unfortunate. I did some work for his parents many years ago. They have to be devastated. It's been said there's nothing worse than surviving a child when the death occurs at the hands of another." He pauses. "Looks like you handled the will situation correctly."

"I helped them do what they wanted to do."

"That's your job. Did they have much of an estate?"

"A house with a mortgage, some minor personal property. Mostly they had a lot of faith."

Burnett stares at me. His eyes tell me he's ready to discuss a subject that is a well of ironies and far too deep for me this morning. Copying his practice, I open the bottom right drawer of the desk, prop my right foot on it and lean back in my chair. "How do you think the first day went?"

He sets his coffee cup on my desk. "I think it's proceeding very well. Considering it was the end of a long day for the jurors yesterday, they appeared attentive throughout Jorgenson's testimony."

"Do you think Wells hurt us much on his cross-exam of Beeper?"

"No. Everyone around here knows Beeper, or knows who he is anyway. Wells tried to tear him down, which he did effectively. What did that accomplish? He presented him as he is. I think you did a good job of pre-empting the truth question."

"I've been thinking about that for some time. A dishonest man isn't necessarily dishonest about everything."

Burnett considers my statement. "I think you're right. I also think Wells' approach would have been more effective in a larger community where the jurors didn't know Beeper." He further reflects.

Rats. I closed a big door on him and immediately opened another one on honesty. I see it coming now, as it always comes when we start down these roads, and I will have difficulty sorting it out later. Usually, I want to hear it because I won't hear it anywhere else. This morning, though, as soon as I bring one question mark to the canvas, another question mark dances on its dot into the ring of my mind.

Burnett starts in: "I had the impression you were leading into the larger questions of truth. Be careful there. At this point in your life, perhaps at any point in your life, those issues are too heavy to carry. It has been said that truth is a liquid, not a solid. I believe truth can also exist as a gas, an odorless gas that defies all of our senses as it expands and contracts around us. Truth . . . " Burnett abruptly cuts himself off as he sees the look on my face. "So what's your schedule for today?"

Thank you. "Medical first. I'm going to begin with the technician who worked on her in the ambulance, then put on Schloss who saw her in the hospital, and then Andrews, her orthopod. If I can move it along, I can be through with the meds by noon, depending on their cross. Unfortunately, then I'll have to put our economist on after lunch."

"I wouldn't worry about that. Some of the jurors are going to lose their attention to his testimony on economic loss whenever you put him on. The main thing is to get the numbers in evidence so you can use them on final arguments."

"Then I'm done with our case."

Burnett gazes at the side window. "Do you think Wells will put the boys on the stand to deny they were there?"

"Interesting question. I didn't call them because I knew they would lie, which wouldn't help me. He doesn't have to call them either." I pause to collect my thoughts. "Wells must feel they're lying. In any event, I hope he doesn't use them. Let him argue later that they don't have to prove a negative. I've got Ginger's testimony, backed by Beeper's eyewitness testimony, which is supported by Jorgenson's testimony. Wells will certainly argue credibility of our witnesses. From what I could see of the jurors' faces, though, they believed all three of them."

"So you'll finish up on Thursday?"

"I think so. Other than the boys, if he uses them, Wells has his two doctors—a GP to offset Schloss and Brunholtz to cancel Andrews—and his expert on economic loss. He's planning to put the doctors on in the afternoon. So that leaves him using his economist on Thursday morning. Then he's done. Tompkins has some criminal matters he has to take care of on Thursday morning, so we'll start later. The judge also has an arraignment right after lunch. So, I think we'll be into final arguments in the afternoon."

Burnett empties his coffee cup and rises. "I'll try to stop in during the day. If you need me, call. And, good luck, John."

☙ ❧

The slight, dark haired, young medical technician is both nervous and imprecise as she relates what she discovered at the accident scene. Still, I reason, before her testimony the jurors had only a picture of the accident scene; now their minds hold the cries of agony of a young woman lying on blood spattered pavement and in the ambulance as she tries to out scream the siren. Ginger's version of pain and suffering was the black and white testimony of the self-serving. Now the colorized version comes from an independent party.

Dr. Schloss"s testimony of his initial visitation with Ginger at the hospital and his later care is what I expected from the plaintiff-oriented doctor. The thirty-six year old Dr. Andrews is better than I hoped for. A slightly built man with light colored hair and wearing glasses, he maintains a serious posture as he thoughtfully answers my questions. He gives the impression he is genuinely interested in the proceedings, that he wants very much to be here to explain exactly what happened to his young patient. The doctor is the right age, too; old enough to have the experience to support his opinions, yet young enough not to let serious thoughts of retirement impede his quest for medical truth.

Deftly using a shadow box resting on a table, something I previously viewed as an antiquated device, Andrews first illuminates Ginger's

X-rays. Then, with the aid of a pointer, he guides the jury through the fractures in portions of her skeleton.

"You can see here the pin fixation in her left tibia." He steps aside and glances back at the jury, and to be sure they did not miss it, points again to the bone in her lower leg.

While he speaks I observe the judge and the jury. They're hooked. How long that will last and what it will mean in the end, I don't know.

Ginger edges closer to me and whispers, "It's strange that a part of me is up there. It could be anyone."

I nod as I turn around and search the benches until I spot Brunholtz. He has a smirk on his face as he watches Andrews' performance. The more I see of *The Doctor*, the less I like him. Brunholtz is too sure of himself. I wonder, though, would I ever use him as my expert witness?

When Andrews finishes his tour and returns to the witness box, I address him. "Now, Dr. Andrews, do you have an opinion to a reasonable degree of medical certainty in your field as an orthopedist whether Miss Buckman has suffered any permanent injuries as a result of her accident?"

"Yes, I do."

"And what is that opinion?"

"She has suffered permanent injury to her left knee and her left lower leg."

"Doctor, would you please again use the shadow box to show the jurors those exact permanent injuries."

Dr. Andrews approaches the table with the shadow box on it and picks up the pointer. As he does so, the jury rotates their bodies to follow his movements. With an earnest face, Andrews looks at the jurors to make sure he has their attention, then turns and first points to the tibia. "Now here is the most serious injury."

Checking my list of questions for the doctor, I notice Ginger is adding the shadow box to the sketch of the courtroom she has worked on since opening statements. The sketch occupies the entire first page of the legal tablet I provided her. She has left the trial to me.

❦ ❧

The contest proceeds according to my outline. I put my economist on the stand after lunch, working through my questioning of him as rapidly as possible before the jurors' stomachs shut down their conscious functions. While the percentages of permanent disability are relatively small, regardless of which doctor the jurors determine to be more credible, I know that over a lifetime the amounts will be significant. Using life expectancy tables and his own dog and pony show, the economist confirms my opinions.

Wells' cross-examination seems to me to be perfunctory. A number of jabs, but not the systematic beating I anticipated. I surmise Wells will let his economist try for the knock down. That way, Wells will know the answers to his questions and not risk surprise.

When Wells finishes I sit back and speak in a voice I hope will assure the jurors everything has been presented to them that they need in order to return a favorable verdict for my client: "The plaintiff rests."

Tompkins peers at the jury over the top of his reading glasses. "We'll take a fifteen minute break. Mr. Wells you may then begin your case."

Ginger's father moves up to the counsel table as Ginger and I rise and stretch. He faces me and speaks through a smile, "That was certainly the most interesting part, wasn't it? His calculations were superb."

I smile in apparent acknowledgment of his remarks but actually as a result of witnessing the disgusted look on Ginger's face as she leaves the room.

"It was interesting." During Wells' cross, I noticed the mill worker in the second row of the jury box nod off and be joined by the hairstylist in the first row. The judge had whispered to the clerk to wake the bailiff to open a window.

☙ ❧

I was always a puncher, never a knockdown artist. Now, my punching consists of blows calculated well before the match. Despite the planned attack, most of the blows are missing my moving target. Brunholtz is the tough opponent Burnett described to me. I know I cannot sustain a beating, cannot move in for a knockdown. If I can land one solid blow, though, I will quickly move away. I hope the jury isn't looking for a knockout but is scoring the bout.

"Isn't it a fact, doctor, that Miss Buckman's sole visit to you lasted a total of forty minutes?"

Brunholtz checks the records resting his lap. "Yes."

"During that time, you had Miss Buckman describe to you the accident in which she was involved, correct?"

"That's correct."

"Also during that time, you asked Miss Buckman about her injuries, isn't that correct?"

"Yes."

"Now, doctor, isn't it true that of the forty minutes Miss Buckman spent with you, twenty minutes or more were spent in obtaining from her the accident history, her list of injuries, and general medical information regarding her?"

Brunholtz's eyes dart to Wells before he answers. "In that range."

"So, doctor, isn't it true then that less than twenty minutes were spent by you actually examining Miss Buckman?"

Sweat appears on Brunholtz's large brow over his cold blue eyes. "I wouldn't say *less than* twenty minutes."

"Doctor, please answer the question yes or no. Isn't it a fact you spent less than twenty minutes examining Miss Buckman?"

Brunholtz looks at his records again. "No. It had to have been half an hour or more."

"Well then, doctor, if that's correct, weren't you mistaken in your answer to my previous question of the time you spent interviewing her?"

Through his now damp brow I see the wheels of calculation gnashing their gears. "Well, doctor?"

"Apparently so."

I glance at the jury. Starting to pose a question, I change my mind. The jurors can do the arithmetic. I need to leave it alone. Besides, *The Doctor* has opened a new door.

"So you do make mistakes, doctor?"

"Everyone makes mistakes." Brunholtz smiles at the jury. "I don't make many."

"Could you also have been mistaken about your assessments of percentages on Miss Buckman's permanent disabilities?"

"No." His voice and manner are positive again. He has recovered and is ready for the next rush over the top. "Based upon my examination of her and the medical records, my assessments are correct."

"Based upon your examination of her one time for less than twenty minutes as against Doctor Andrews' exhaustive examinations of her over the past fourteen months?"

"Objection. It's argumentative. It's . . ."

"Sustained. The jury will disregard the last question. Mr. Hall, need I again remind you . . ."

"I'm sorry, Your Honor. I have no more questions for the witness."

I glimpse an affirmative nod by the small, middle-aged retired man in the last chair in the second row. Did I land a solid punch?

☙ ❧

After five-thirty and dark outside. I unlock the office door and turn on the hall light. First dropping the two bulging briefcases in the hallway, I go right to the kitchen to grab a bottle of beer from the refrigerator. While I take a long swig on the beer bottle, I stroll back into the hallway and plop down on the couch. Weariness immediately seizes control of my unguarded body. Was I ever this tired? I recall the crazy fifteen round sparing match when I was sixteen and my first long march in basic training with a full field pack on my back. This is a different kind of fatigue, but it affects me just as much.

I reach over and paw through the newspapers on the table next to the couch. Setting aside the crossword puzzle worked by Henry Miller, I locate the front page of the Milwaukee paper. I scan the news as I do each day. Suddenly, I sit straight up.

> Chicago—Jonathon Stone, CEO of Xpecon, and several other high ranking officers of the Chicago based conglomerate, have been indicted by a federal grand jury. The indictments, handed down yesterday, resulted from a lengthy investigation of the company by the United States government.

"Where's Rick?" I mumble as I hurry into my office and dial my friend's home telephone number in Chicago. Unlike on Monday afternoon when I called and the home phone rang without being answered, a mechanical voice answers, "This number is no longer in service."

I hang up the receiver and finish the bottle of beer. What happened to him? My prior search runs through my mind. When I called his office on Monday, the receptionist said Rick was on sick leave; that was all she would say. He wasn't at his apartment. Where is he? He hadn't come up to the Northwoods during the summer, and now that I think about it, he didn't sound well the last time he called. If I could remember the name of Rick's stepfather, I would call Rick's parents in Milwaukee. The name refuses to step forward. Maybe Rick will call me.

I carry the two briefcases into my office and sit way back in my swivel chair. Then, remembering the fall in court, I ease forward. One day of trial is left, the day that can be the best or the worst. The trial has proceeded so swiftly two-thirds of it is completed. Yet, every minute of the trial has seemed to me like an hour. I've concentrated so hard, now I can barely think. I have to keep my focus on the case, though; I have to prepare for tomorrow.

I remember Margo baked me a casserole I can warm for dinner. After dinner, I will rework my closing arguments. No significant surprises, other than Ginger's plan to attend art school, surfaced during the trial. Burnett assured me there wouldn't be if I adequately prepared for the battle, and he was right again. One more day, I . . . I answer the ringing phone. Brenda Krueger.

"Mister Hall, I wanted to tell you I got job with the Larsens' company. Thank you very much."

"No thanks needed, Brenda."

"I'm going to do okay, Mister Hall."

"I'm sure you will." As I hang up the receiver, I reflect on her divorce, then drift back to Ginger's case. What is her trial really about?

38

A bulky deputy sheriff leads a handcuffed, unshaven young man, with long hair hanging over the top of his jail suit, into the courtroom. Trailing them are Attorney Lester Erickson and the older woman I met at the gas station in Split Lake. Ginger and I sit on the bench outside the courtroom door, waiting for Tompkins to handle arraignment of the young man on criminal charges. As I return the woman's nod, I wonder what caused her and her grandson to stick with Erickson after her complaints about him.

Ginger elbows me. "I know that guy. He's a friend of my ex-boyfriend." She shakes her head. "I don't know how I ever got in with those guys. Well, maybe I do. They're different."

"I guess it depends on how you want to be different."

"I'm beginning to understand that."

"Are you serious about art school?"

Ginger turns her head to me. "Yes, I am, however this turns out. I've got some money saved, and I can get a part-time job. I know a girl living in Milwaukee who will let me share an apartment with her."

Mrs. Buckman walks precisely within the patterns of the marble floor as she takes measured steps down the corridor toward us. I notice the wince in Ginger's eyes. "I think it's a good idea, Ginger."

Several juror heads bob and fall during the testimony of Wells' economist. I'm beginning to understand that presenting testimony of expert witnesses, unless handled timely and skillfully, is akin to serving the jurors drinks laced with knockout drops. I proceed quickly through my cross-examination of the witness, trying not to awaken any of the dozing jurors. How do I attack something they haven't heard? Anyway, if the jurors are no longer going to pay attention, why should I risk letting the witness open Pandora's box.

When Wells utters, "The defense rests," the testimony phase ends.

Tompkins calls a fifteen-minute recess before closing arguments. I rise and stretch while Ginger and her mother leave for the bathroom. Wells is conferring with Smith. I look toward the door to the hallway. Where is Burnett? I sit down and begin scribbling notes to my closing arguments. I will go first since I have the burden of proof. The anxiety is returning, yet I'm buoyed by the thought my closing argument cannot be worse than my opening statement. Burnett enters the courtroom and slips in next to me. His presence gives me immense relief as I prepare to plunge into my argument.

After the jurors are led back to their chairs by the bailiff, Tompkins peers at me. "You may proceed, Attorney Hall."

This time I approach the podium with the confident steps of my mentor. I place my notes on top of the lectern. During the break, I placed an easel with the blowup of the accident scene on it slightly behind me, to my left. The shadow box with the x-ray of Ginger's tibia with the pins in it is on a table to my right. I switched on the light so their eyes can flit back and forth from me to the box as I speak.

Turning to the easel, with a rubber-tip pointer I slap the accident intersection. "This is what the accident is all about: a healthy young woman riding her motorcycle down Main Street toward the south end of the village, on her way home from a visit to a friend, when an irresponsible teenager runs the stop sign at Forest Avenue, swerves into her lane, causing her to swerve to her right to avoid a collision, resulting in her losing control of the bike and suffering painful and permanent injuries that should never have been incurred."

I face the jury. "Despite Ginger Buckman's explicit testimony, the believable testimony of an eye-witness and the testimony of another witness who found the hubcap that flew off the driver's car as the teenager rounded the corner, the defense would like you to believe, and therefore find, the defendants blameless. Yet, the defense offered no testimony to rebut that of the plaintiff's witnesses. The defense offered no plausible explanation how she could have taken her spill. Sure, there was some idle speculation about the plaintiff being tired and dozing off and about her being a diabetic. I know that you know how the accident happened, and it was exactly the way Miss Buckman described it to you."

As I continue, I find myself picking up speed. This time I feel it's right. I want to build to the climax.

"The defense managed to portray Mr. Edward Plumber, the eyewitness to the accident, as an unsavory individual. Why, I don't know. Mr. Plumber already told you he was, to use his own words, 'no good, that he had never been any good.' We're all in agreement he's a tragic figure, tragic not because he's an alcoholic nor because he has trouble holding jobs nor because he has been abusive and unsupportive of his family, tragic because his life is empty of purpose. That does not mean, though, that he is incapable of telling, or has not told, the truth in this matter.

"The defense implies he is a dishonest man because he has stolen and that a dishonest man cannot be trusted to tell the truth. Who can define the meaning of that abstract word 'honesty'? If committing an offense against the law makes a person dishonest, are those people who exceed the speed limit while driving their automobiles dishonest? Does the fact some people take deductions on their income tax returns they know they shouldn't have taken render them dishonest, and thus, unable to tell the truth about something else? How about the remodeling or addition to their homes some people make without first obtaining a permit, as required by law? Does that act alone permanently remove them from the ranks of the honest?"

Out of the corner of my eye, I see Wells about to make an objection, instead scribbling furiously on his legal pad. I also note two of the jurors nodding. I keep punching. I'm beating out a rhythm. I'm in the ring with my hands up, and I'm light on my feet as I shuffle and pivot while keeping my head moving and my eyes always on my opponent. I do not want to lose.

Still holding my pointer, I move to the shadow box and begin hammering on Ginger's injuries, exchanging x-rays as soon as I am confident the image of the previous one has been etched on the minds of the jurors. I replace the blowup of the accident scene with a chart showing the dates of all of Ginger's visits to Dr. Schloss and Dr. Andrews. Then I hammer on the number of visits as I mock the time spent by Brunholtz with Ginger. The economic loss is next. I substitute a chart prepared by my economist for the medical visitation chart and then pound on those numbers. Finally, I step aside from the lectern and lower my voice.

"Those are the cold facts, the stone facts. If those facts were all there were to this case, you would have witnessed a silent movie in black and white, like the illuminated x-rays in the shadow box." I gesture to my right. "But, that isn't the movie you saw, was it? As the witnesses testi-fied, you ran through your minds a movie with color and sound. You saw the gray of the asphalt, the red of the blood, the white of the ambu-lance, the ashen face of the plaintiff. And as you saw it, you heard the moaning of a victim and the wailing of a siren as the ambulance sped through the black of the night."

I pause to let the words sink in as I replace the last chart on the easel with one listing by categories the dollar figures I want the jury to use in answering the special verdict form. My voice climbs as I run the pointer down the items of damages and recite them to the jury: past medical bills, future medical bills, pain and suffering, temporary disability, per-manent disability.

"This lawsuit is about Ginger Buckman being fairly compensated for the severe injuries unfairly inflicted upon her by the defendants. What sums of money will do that?" I slap the pointer on the easel as hard as I can. "The figures on this chart. I know these amounts may appear to you like huge amounts of money, and they are. BUT, and I speak that word in capital letters, I ask you to remember as you deliberate the movie you witnessed." Several heads in the jury box turn to look at Ginger.

Suddenly, the sounds of the hammering are gone. I'm through throwing punches. I think my opponent is on the canvas, although I can't be sure. There are twelve referees, and they're all watching in wonder. I drop my hands and return to my corner. There is no crowd noise, only the silence of my mind. Are the twelve referees counting down?

Almost oblivious to my surroundings, I sit at the counsel table shaking hands with Burnett underneath the table and feeling Ginger's hand on my right arm. My body is quivering, and at the same time I'm relieved everything has poured out of me. The words are all gone, drifting into the depths of the universe. I am now a crumpled sheet of paper on which the printed words have somehow disappeared.

In what seems like slow motion, I watch Wells rise and move to the table with the shadow box to turn off the light. Then he places his first chart on the easel. Wells' face has the confident smile and the superior look of a professional man at his peak. I smell the lemon-flavored words dripping off his tongue as he begins:

"We all suffer at times from unfortunate situations. And we are indeed sorry for those who suffer what we do not. You should not, however, permit your sympathy to interfere with your determination of facts, the purpose for which you are here assembled."

All theatre. It's probably Wells' hundredth performance. I didn't intend nor try to be theatrical, well, maybe a little. I argued the case the way I believed in it. At the same time, I suspect I'm learning to be an actor; that is part of it. I borrowed from those lawyers I watched in the Milwaukee County Courthouse and in the Timber County Courthouse, from Burnett, from trial books I read. Will any performance, no matter how good, really sway a jury, or is that a false idea spread by the egos of those trial lawyers who have risen to the top? All I care about now is whether the jurors have listened and believe Ginger and understand her suffering. I sit back carefully and study the faces of the twelve persons in the box as I listen to Wells' argument.

He finishes with a flourish. Tompkins looks at me. "Mr. Hall, any rebuttal?"

Burnett whispers to me, "The jurors appear tired and ready to deliberate. What else can you say?"

I ponder the advice while glimpsing Tompkins' fingers begin another dance on the bench. I fire back the remarks Wells shot at the jury after my chair tipped over. "None, Your Honor. I think the jury has heard and seen all they need to." As the sentence leaps from my tongue, looks of relief appear on the faces of the jurors and a pleased Tompkins.

Just like the start, the trial ends abruptly. There is nothing left except the judge's instructions to the jury and then their deliberations and return of the verdict. I feel as though I have lost a piece of myself that will never be exactly replaced. I'm emotionally drained, yet energized by anticipation of the verdict.

⤫

Burnett smiles while he eyes me. We sit across from each other at the oval table in the conference room where I wrestled Bill Krueger. The door closes as Ginger goes down the corridor to a water fountain. Her mother had gone home after leaving detailed instructions with Ginger to call when the verdict was in.

"I'm impressed, John. That was some oratory for a first jury trial."

I laugh. "First jury trial? Remember *Mueller*? Now I hope I break my record."

Burnett laughs. "I'm sure you'll break it on this one."

"I did get carried away with it, didn't I? The Dean finally caught me a few months ago and gave me a reading list. I got some ideas from a couple of the books. He wants me to join you two at his January picnic."

"You're welcome to come, John."

"Actually, I ad-libbed quite a bit; I lost my place in the script. I'm surprised Wells didn't object to some of my statements."

"There's an unwritten rule that you don't object during closing arguments unless something said is totally impermissible. Besides, he probably thought you would hang yourself with a necktie of amateurism. I was beginning to wonder myself."

I laugh loudly. Burnett joins me. Maybe it's relief from the testimony being completed; whatever the reason, we continue to laugh. Finally, I interlace my fingers and put them behind my head so I can stretch my shoulders. "How long do think the jury will be out?"

"There's no way to tell. It's unlikely they'll return in less than an hour since they have to pick a foreman and discuss the case. On the other hand, it's almost four o'clock. My guess is they'll want to get home for supper. Maybe an hour and a half to two hours."

"You don't think they'll be out longer than that?"

"As Tompkins pointed out, this is a civil case with the lower burden of preponderance of the evidence, not beyond a reasonable doubt as in a criminal case. And, in Wisconsin, with its five-sixths verdict rule, they only need to get ten of the twelve jurors to agree on each question. One holdout can't upset the verdict as it can in a criminal case."

I rise with a can of soda in my hand and begin pacing around the table. "This is tough. I'm tired but I can't wait for them to come back." I stop to drink from the can and then continue pacing. "What's your opinion on how we did?"

"I already told you that you did a fine job. I also told you the first time we discussed juries that they're a crapshoot. With most juries, a likeable and believable plaintiff with serious injuries versus an insurance company with large reserves favors the plaintiff. This is somewhat of an odd case from the liability standpoint. I still don't understand why the insurance company failed to up the ante considerably after the hubcap flew into the facts. They probably felt that an upstate, small county jury would be conservative. They may also have counted on you caving in before the trial began."

I cease pacing and lean my back against a wall so I face Burnett. "You know I wouldn't have done that. This case is important to me."

"I know that. So do Margo and Suzy. And, so does Ginger. I hope, though, if the jury comes back with a small sum, or, unlikely but possible, you lose on liability, you'll be able to handle it."

"Do you really think I could lose on liability? I mean, that's worried me from the start."

"I understand. No, I don't, since we have comparative negligence in Wisconsin. Even if they find say ten per cent negligence on Ginger's part for, say failure of lookout, that won't bar her recovery as it would in some states. It will merely reduce her damages by ten per cent." Burnett sits back in his chair. "Look, John, don't rehash for the next hour or two everything you've done. Do that some time later when you have some distance from the case. When Ginger comes back, take her mind off of the case, too. Talk about anything else."

"I'll try." I sit down again across from Burnett and finish the can of soda. "You know, Bob, when you told me I could try this case, all I thought about was winning. I wanted the jury to return a verdict larger than the best offer the insurance company made, which was thirty-five thousand dollars, with a maybe on forty-thousand. I felt I owed it to you for your confidence in me. And, honestly, I wanted to win my first jury trial. I still don't like to lose."

Burnett cocks his head. "I don't know any trial lawyer who does."

"Except, Bob, its not about any of that anymore. I want the jury to return a good verdict for Ginger, not for me, or you." I stare at Burnett. "I really mean it. I'm beginning to view some things differently."

Burnett nods. "I always knew you would. That's why I hired you."

❧ ❧

At five forty-eight, the deputy clerk knocks on the door to the conference room and opens it enough to stick her head through the doorframe. "The jury has reached a verdict."

I jump up and head out the door before Burnett and Ginger can stand. Halfway down the corridor, I halt and wait for them to catch up to me. "I'm sorry. I'm nervous."

We sit together at the counsel table for the final time in the trial. Burnett and Ginger form a sandwich around me. Wells, Smith, and Mr. Wilson are seated at the other table. The bailiff knocks on the judge's door and sticks his head in. Moments later, Tompkins takes the bench. After surveying the room, Tompkins turns to the bailiff and asks him to bring in the jury.

There is complete silence in the large room. The attorneys stand as the jurors file into their seats. The sounds, the smells, the shuffling of bodies and the smothering heat of the room I experienced during the trial have all vanished. I try in vain to read in the faces of the jurors their verdict. Some are smiling, but at no one. Most of the faces are blank, with their eyes fixed straight ahead of them. My stomach has turned on me again, and for the first time during the trial my hands begin to tremble.

As soon as the jurors are seated, Tompkins addresses them. "Ladies and gentlemen of the jury, have you reached a verdict?"

"Yes we have, Your Honor," voices a slight, older man wearing glasses, rising from his seat in the third row."

Shocked. I paid little attention to the quiet man who seemed unlikely to be a leader. Now I understand why the man had not exercised his statutory right in Wisconsin to be excused from the jury because he was over sixty-five; the man wanted to be on the jury, to be part of what transpired. Now I think he may have been the only juror to sit in the box for three days with his eyes always wide open.

The bailiff collects the verdict form from the foreman and hands it to Tompkins; he reviews it and hands it back to the bailiff to give to the foreman to read.

My right hand is shaking as I hold a pen over my copy of the verdict form. I drop the pen, flex my hand and grasp the pen again as the foreman begins reading the verdict:

"On the first question, we find the defendants one hundred per cent negligent."

I sigh. The worst part is over. Then panic attacks. What if the negligence was not causal of her injuries?

"On the second question, we find that the negligence of the defendants *was...*"

"That's good, isn't it?" I hear Ginger say softly.

"Yes." Again the relief. At least we have proven her case. Well, except for the damages. Now the question is how much?

"On the third question as to what sum of money will fairly and reasonably compensate the plaintiff Ginger Buckman with respect to past pain, suffering & disability, we find the sum of . . . "

I try to pen in the figures as the foreman reads them off. They seem higher than I hoped for. " . . . loss of earnings, the sum . . . " My eyes are fixed on the form. " . . . future medical expense . . . "

When the foreman finishes, I slide the form over to Burnett. "Add it up. I'm too nervous." I sit still as I hear Tompkins confirm the verdict.

Burnett slides the form back to me with the total circled. I want to look at it, but somehow cannot. Finally, I eyeball the circled total: $100,000.

Ginger peeks over my shoulder. "Wow!" she utters at the jury. Several of the jurors smile at her.

Burnett grabs my unsteady hand. "Congratulations, John. Great job."

Vaguely hearing the judge dismiss the jury, I mumble, "Amazing. One hundred thousand even. I never would have guessed that."

As the jurors file out of the room, several glance at Ginger and me and smile.

"Is there anything further, gentlemen?" Tompkins asks the attorneys.

"No, Your Honor," Wells speaks with irritation in his voice.

"Mr. Hall?"

Unbelievable, I think, unbelievable. The damage amount sinks in. Burnett was right; there are always the surprises. This time it has been a pleasant surprise. I feel elated.

"Mr. Hall?"

Burnett nudges me.

Seventy-five would have been a good verdict, even fifty, especially for me. One Hundred thousand is beyond my wildest predictions. Was it Ginger? Did I do a good job? Wells was good; he was very good. Maybe . . ."

Burnett speaks: "Nothing further, Your Honor."

I look up at Burnett and then at the judge who smiles at me for the first time ever.

Tompkins slams down his gavel. "Court is adjourned."

39

"Were you nervous when the verdict came down?" Slider asks as he pours me another glass of beer.

"Not a bit. I've been through tougher things before."

Angie draws his head back, smirking, "Bullshit. From where I sat I could see your hands shaking."

"Have you ever been in a ring, Bellini? That's tough."

"No, but I've never seen a boxer shaking in a ring. That had to be the biggest money bout you ever fought."

"One dollar would have beaten my record."

Angie smiles. "Tompkins said afterward he was surprised you didn't get killed in the courtroom."

I laugh. "Well, at least now he's giving me backhanded compliments." Clutching the glass of beer, I move to the center of the room where Ann stands with Burnett and his wife, along with Margo and Red, all toasting each other to something. Couldn't be me. After we all dined at the Rivers Edge, Ginger went home with her parents, and Suzy left to visit a friend.

Burnett clanks his glass against mine. "I guess I no longer have to worry about trial work."

Smiling, I wish the compliment contained even an iota of truth. Still, in a world where many of the inhabitants are bent on peering into themselves, I have come to understand why one accepts the praise of others without inspection of it for truth.

I turn to Burnett. "Bob, I still can't fathom it. The old woman from Algona, the one with the gray bun, I figured she would be the clinker. But there were no dissenters on any of the questions. Amazing. You remember how I wanted to strike her, and you said to get rid of the loud mouth."

"That was a guess."

Margo appears perplexed. "Who was the woman?"

"Ah . . ." I stall to fire a search request to the keeper of names in my head who has been battered and bruised, but not beaten, by the ordeal of the trial. " . . . Mrs. Goettelman . . . from Algona."

"Mrs. Goettelman? Mrs. Goettlemen." Margo frowns. "Oh, gosh, I forgot that was her married name when I reviewed the jury list." She faces Burnett. "Bob, you know her."

"I don't think so."

"Sure you do. She's Mrs. Jensen's sister. Boy, I'll bet she's gotten an earful over the years from Mrs. Jensen about *those young people*, as she calls them, going through the stop sign on Forest and speeding on Main Street."

Burnett looks at me as we burst out laughing. I make a wide sweep for his hand.

Margo smiles. "What did I say?"

"Nothing, nothing at all." Burnett continues to laugh. "It's just Timber County."

Sure, I think out loud, "The shadowy Mrs. Jensen."

Recovering, Burnett nods. "Conscience is a shadowy thing. It always lurks behind the window curtains."

Ann puts her arm around me. "Does this mean you're going to stay in Winding River?"

"I guess I have to. I have to take care of my country estate." I think of the maple proudly protruding through the roofless old smokehouse.

Excusing myself first, I walk over to the bar stool next to Angie and ask Slider to give me a table knife resting on the back bar. I bang it against the side of my glass. "Listen up, folks. I've got an announcement to make." I wait for them to quiet down. "Get this: Ann and I are engaged."

The sound of clapping fills the air as Ann hurries over to me and whispers in my ear. "But you haven't asked me yet."

"Sure I did. Didn't you tell me you wanted to live on the farm?"

"That was it? That was a proposal?"

"You didn't think I'd ask you to live with me if I wasn't going to marry you, did you?"

"Well, you . . ."

Angie climbs off his barstool. "Apparently, we have a questionable contract here, whether there has in fact been an offer and an acceptance."

Laughter rings out. Burnett turns to Margo. "That's John."

I wave my hands at Ann. "What do I need to do?"

"Ask me. You know, ask me."

Reaching my arms behind my back, then grasping my left wrist with my right hand and forcing the left arm upward, I bend down on one knee and ask her amid further laughter.

Ann laughs with them. "I accept."

As I stand up, Angie picks up the knife and bangs it repeatedly on his beer mug. I embrace Ann.

She whispers in my ear again. "Didn't you violate a cardinal rule of trial lawyers about not asking a question unless you know the answer?"

I shake my head. "No, I don't think so. I knew the answer. I just forgot to ask the question."

🙈 🙊

I wrap my arm around Ann as we walk out of Slider's into the parking lot in back. Despite the winter evening, I feel very warm and in no hurry to crank up *Rusty*.

I hug Ann. "Angie will be the last one to leave. You're right about him. He's stuck at noon on Wednesday."

Ann presses her back against my arm. "That's why I've got you. You have the best story."

I laugh. Then looking around the lot, I drop my arm. "My car's gone."

"You're right. That's strange."

I glance around the lot again. "Maybe someone stole it."

"In Winding River? It's no fun to steal cars in Winding River. They're always unlocked with the keys in them."

"Angie." I put my arm around Ann again and lead her into the back entranceway of Slider's. I stomp down the bar to Angie. "Where's my car?"

Slider walks away as Angie turns around. "What are you talking about?"

"Okay, where's my car? I have to take Ann home."

"Beats me. If you need a ride, take my truck." He reaches into a pocket in his trousers and tosses me a key ring. "Take it easy pulling out onto Main Street. You don't want to upset Mrs. Jensen."

"You're going to start it all over again, huh?"

After we climb into the pickup truck, I glance at Ann. "I'm sorry about tonight. How about Saturday night I take you to that new restaurant in Lenora that we've been talking about since summer?"

"Great."

As I turn onto Main Street, I dip my head to spot Mrs. Jensen. Was that her? The movement was too quick for me to make a positive identification. On the other hand, who else could it be? Is there any substitute for conscience?

"Now, as to the wedding," Ann intones matter-of-factly, "how about in the early summer at *My Lake* in the national forest?"

"I don't know, we would need to consider a number of things: Are weddings allowed in a national forest, at least that forest? How many of the guests will be able walk to the lake and back? What if it rains? What if . . ."

"You lawyers, you always spoil the hopes and the illusions."

"Besides, what year were you thinking of?"

Ann pokes me. "Do you really want to stay in Winding River?"

"I always have to be careful how I answer your questions. If I say no I don't want to be here, then you will be unhappy about the thought of leaving here, which in turn will make me unhappy and then you unhappier. But, this question is easy. I like it here."

"That's good." Ann snuggles up to me.

I turn onto Spruce Street and drive up the hill to the office.

"Where are you going?"

"A hunch." I pull into the lot and park next to *Rusty*. "I thought so. How about helping me?"

"Sure."

Some time later (If it's love and not something else, time is irrelevant, isn't it?), I drive home. As I reflect on the aftermath of engagement, I pull up in front of the office. The lot is empty. I lock the truck and go inside. The phone is ringing. "Burnett Law Office."

"This is Angie. Where in the hell have you been? I've been calling all over for you?"

Why should I tell him I took the phone off of the hook at Ann's house since I knew he would be looking for me? "Yeah, what do you want?"

"My truck. I want to go home. Slider has already shut off the outside lights and locked the doors. He wants to go to bed."

I feel no sympathy. "I don't know if I want to give up the truck. It's in a lot better shape than *Rusty*, especially the brakes. Anyway, *Rusty* is outside of Slider's with the keys in it. If you had bothered to get off your barstool, which I knew you wouldn't, you would be home now. See you tomorrow. By the way, that's Friday for the rest of us."

✧ 40 ✧

Sunlight streams through my bedroom window overlooking the village. Without checking the clock, I know it's midmorning. I've been lying in a stupor for some time. The exhaustion from the trial and the exuberance from the verdict have cancelled each other resulting in a neutral feeling that renders me powerless to move.

I did it; I got through the trial. I managed to burst through the wall of resistance and out run the defenders, but I collapsed as I stumbled into the end zone with a hand grabbing me from behind. Now it's over, and I should be celebrating something. Yet, I have things to say to the judge and to the jury that I forgot in my haste to the goal line: small facts, minor points of law and clever arguments. They're all important; they must be. They're all bottled up in me, and if I don't release them now they'll be lost forever. Next time I must follow my script more carefully. Next time I may not have a sympathetic jury.

Always the questions: What was it all about? What is winning? What is losing? If the jury had rendered a verdict awarding Ginger a third of the amount it awarded, roughly what the insurance company offered, would I then have done a poor job? Would the insurance company have won? What about their costs of trial? Isn't Ginger still a loser? Unless desperate for survival, who would trade her permanent injuries and past pain and suffering for dollars?

Ginger. She never cared about the money. She wanted to prove she *was* somebody.

And then more questions: Wells and Smith sloughed off the verdict as an anomaly rather than a victory. What would I have done if I had been in their position? Would I have settled the case? For how much?

How can I ever be sure what a jury will do? If it is a crapshoot, how far should I go with someone else's money before I stop rolling the dice?

In a mid-wake state of nonsense I want to go back to the court-house and continue trying the case; at the same time, I want to sleep all day. I can do neither. Unsteadily, I bring myself to my feet and head to the shower.

❧ ❧

Burnett sits down in my office. "Congratulations again, John. You did a fine job."

"I had a good jury. I wonder what the results would have been with a different jury. When everything else is stripped away, does it come down to luck?"

"I suppose there are those who would support that thesis. If you tried the case to ten different juries, you would get ten different verdicts." Burnett leans back in the chair and props one leg on the other. "I'm not sure what luck is. Who was it that said something to the effect luck is where preparation and opportunity meet? You were prepared and seized the opportunity. To a large extent, John, I think you make your own luck. I think you made some luck this week, and I think you'll make it again."

"I don't know about that. What I learned in this trial is how much I don't know about trial work."

Burnett laughs. "You haven't tried enough cases to know how much you don't know about trial work."

I answer the phone. The voice: "This is Attorney Smith." I shake my head. Smith is the only attorney I know who prefaces his name with his occupation even when talking to an attorney he deals with on a daily basis. Somehow, I don't care much about Smith right now, and I let him drone on.

"I've been conferring with Attorney Wells, and we wish to advise you we won't appeal the verdict if you drop all court costs assessable against the defendants. At this point, Attorney Hall, I'm sure you'll agree we should all get this behind us."

Screwing up my face at Smith's proposition, I wonder why *we*, who-ever that is, should want to get the trial behind us? I'm still possessed by this neutral feeling so the teeth gritting and sarcasm rest in the limbo of my emotions. Besides, I'm mostly over that now. "I'll have to talk to our client. Personally, I wouldn't forgive anything. You could have settled this case for less money."

"My, my, Attorney Hall, you have still that ungracious manner about you. Call me back."

As I hang up, I look at Burnett. "That was Smith. He found a new word."

Burnett sighs. "Has it occurred to you that Smith has you right where he wants you?"

"What do you mean? I beat him in the trial, didn't I?"

"No you beat Wells, which is an achievement. Beating Smith would not have been. You've already beaten him. Anyway, the practice of law isn't about beating other attorneys. Before a judge, you win by hammering the merits of the case; in a jury trial you win by skillfully picking a jury and skillfully presenting a winning case, regardless of what the other side does."

"I'm beginning to understand that."

"Anyway, what I meant about Smith is he gets you riled up without lifting a finger, without using a harsh word. You're the best bait he's found. He can slip you onto the end of a fishing hook and dangle you in the river at will. Quit giving him the opportunity to degrade our profession."

"I'm handling him better now. I've learned . . . " A number of retorts come to mind, but I'm no match for Burnett, especially this morning.

Burnett relents: "So what did Smith want?"

"They won't appeal if we agree to drop court costs."

"What's the total of our expenses we can collect as court costs?"

"Maybe fifteen hundred dollars, mostly the deposition costs and statutory expert witness fees. I did make an Offer of Settlement for seventy-five thousand. Since the verdict was more, as you know, under Wisconsin law we're entitled to double the costs."

Burnett meditates. "What have they got to appeal?"

"An adverse ruling on the admission of the hubcap and the testimony on it. A few objections they made that were denied. As you know, some of what I said in closing was probably impermissible argument. They agreed on the form of the special verdict and the jury instructions."

"They're not going anywhere with those matters. Besides, with the verdict drawing interest at twelve percent in our state, how long do they want a judgment out there? They want to cut their loses." Burnett pauses again. "On the other hand, you had a good jury. What would you get on a retrial? Also, if Ginger is going to start art school in January, she's going to need some money right now. There's a slim risk they might appeal, or at least delay issuing a check to her. I'd tell Smith we'll waive doubling the costs if they don't appeal, but we still want costs, and . . . and provided they issue a check within a week. Be firm on that. They can do it if they want to."

"All right." I pick up the phone. While I obtain Ginger's approval and talk to Smith, Burnett grabs a cup of coffee from the kitchen and returns. I relate the call to Burnett. "I've never heard Smith so humble. He said okay, and that was it. I still don't like him."

"Smith will never admit it, but you've gotten his attention. Now, you have to figure out how you're going to get along with him."

"I know. I'm doing better. He has to stop patronizing me."

Burnett cocks his head. "Anyway, the case is settled. "Now John, we need to discuss how we're going to split our fee?"

I wrinkle my brow. "What split? I work for you."

"I know you do. I also know I would not have kept that case if it were not for you. I've been thinking about a fifty-fifty split."

"Bob, I wouldn't consider that. This is your practice, and I wouldn't be here if it weren't for you. You supported me until we got receipts from my billings. Besides, even if we had referred the case, you would have gotten part of the fee for acting as local counsel."

"I would have gotten a lot less than I'm getting now. Besides, I've been making more money since you came here." He laughs. "Making money is something new for me. You'll have to help me figure out what to do with it."

I begin scratching on a legal pad. "I could use some money to pay off my law school debt and buy a reliable car. Still, I feel I should give the money to Ginger. . . . On the other hand, I suppose if I hadn't gone to law school I wouldn't have been able to do what I did."

"That's true. How about the farm? How are you going to pay off the bank? Pay the estate taxes and the real estate taxes?"

"I'll work it out. There are still items on the farm I can sell. How has Ann figured it out? I should have paid more attention. I'll still be earning money here, won't I?"

"Absolutely. And, I'll have to give you a raise after one year." Burnett rises.

I stand and reach across the desk to shake Burnett's hand. "I appreciate all you've done for me, Bob. I'm very happy here."

Burnett lets go of my hand. "Is the arrangement fair, then?"

"More than fair. I'd be happy with half that amount. You're going to need that money for your retirement."

"I'm not done yet. Cases like Ginger's don't come along very often. With you around here, though, I sense there'll be more."

I listen to his steps down the hallway. He knows where he's going. For a few moments I lean back in my chair, now a measured amount. Coffee has shifted my state of awareness into positive gear. I follow his steps to the front door.

As I put on my coat, I duck into the doorway of the secretaries' office. "Suzy, I'm going over to Weber's Garage to drop off my car."

"Do you want me to follow you over there and drive you back. That's a long walk, and the sky is becoming overcast. The forecast is for more snow today."

"No, thanks. I need to walk off the trial." The verdict is sinking in. Am I really *The Great Attorney John Hall* after all?

"Well, when you get back to the office, you need to call a man from Bear Path. Benny? Sounds a little strange. And, I've got a pile of abstracts for you to examine."

❧ ❦

I drive to the repair shop on Hickory Street, around the corner and across the street from Swenson's Hardware, and drop off *Rusty*. Ann has Christmas break, and we can share her car. With the brakes nearly gone, Angie must have been irked driving the car up to the office. I know I was lucky about one thing; if it hadn't been winter, Angie would have abandoned *Rusty* somewhere in the village where it would have taken me a lot longer to find her.

I cross the street from Weber's garage to the old stone building behind the hardware store. As I approach the door, through the bay window in front I see Dave Summers sitting behind a desk talking on the telephone. Inside, I hover in the hallway as I wait for the new lawyer.

A few minutes later, the lean, red-haired young man with a freckled face appears in the doorframe. "Come in John." He appears embarrassed. "Not too much here as you can see."

Two wood chairs in front of a third-hand desk hide part of the threadbare carpet. Over a table pushed against a wall hangs a framed picture of a hunter standing under a tree, smiling as he holds his gun with the barrel pointed down at the dead rabbits piled near his feet. A picture from a yard sale? Photographs Rick sent me of his firm's offices in Chicago flash through my mind as I sit in one of the chairs.

"I'm going to see how things go before I put too much into this office."

"This looks fine for your purposes. What days are you here, Tuesday afternoons and Friday mornings?"

Summers checks his calendar before answering. "Yes. I'm not sure those are the best times. Right now they work out with the schedule at my office in Lenora."

"Well, it'll take awhile for the business to come your way, especially this time of year. Most of the people in the village have better uses for their money at Christmas than shopping for a lawyer."

"That's crossed my mind." Summers shows a serious face. "John, you've been here for a year now. I know that's not a long time, but it's longer than I've been in practice. I have a question for you. It may seem somewhat strange, and I hope you don't mind my asking. It's one of those things you think about when you have too much time to think. As small town lawyers, what do you feel is our role?"

I sit back. His boat trails my mine as we work our way up the river. "You're asking the wrong person. I'd have to try to quote Burnett." I stare past Summers. My reply comes slowly, spoken with words borrowed from one who has cruised the waters of the law for forty years, words I have repeated to myself a number of times:

"Burnett says the law is something that's never-ending. It's a network of endless rivers winding through humanity. As lawyers, we're the boatmen on the rivers, and as small town lawyers, we're the boatmen on the rivers known mainly to those who inhabit their banks. We learn to navigate the waterways and transport those who need assistance. We advise on points of early departure and eventual destinations. Unlike our brethren who are pilots on the big rivers, we rarely make waves. Sometimes, though, even the smaller waters are tricky. And Burnett says, if we're not careful, we can be swept away by the current."

Summers starts to speak, ceasing before a word is uttered.

I quickly change the atmosphere. "Dave, I'd like to help you get started. That's a Timber County tradition. I've referred a client to you. He should keep you busy. He'll be bringing in his files with Consent to Transfer forms for you to sign."

"That's very nice of you."

"You don't need to thank me."

"What's his name?"

"Wolner. His full name is James Bernard Wolner. Some call him Jim and some call him Jimmy. Around here all the attorneys know him as Suits."

I shake hands with Summers. "Good luck on your practice here." I start toward the door to the hallway.

"Tell me, John, why are you referring him to me, because of a conflict?"

I turn back. "You might say that. I didn't get along well with The Relatives."

❧ ❧

The sun hides behind gray clouds; the temperature has dropped. I turn the corner and head down Main Street for the six-block hike to Spruce. Snow begins to fall in large flakes that collect on the tops of the cars parked at the curbs and on the tops of the plastic decorations affixed to the utility poles: wreaths with red bows, candy canes, golden horns and miniature Santa sleighs. I pull up the collar of my overcoat.

Carols are drifting from an outside speaker at Records, News & Books. Through the large front window I see The Dean leaning against a bookshelf, absorbed in the book in his hands. As I near Wally & La-Verne's, I look up and spot Mrs. Jensen shrink back from her window. Before I reach the window of the restaurant, I notice a door. I try the handle, and the door opens into a small hallway with a single mailbox before a long staircase to the second floor. From an inside coat pocket, I remove a twice-folded sheet of legal paper, rip off a piece and pen a quick note: *Thank you, Mrs. Jensen. Merry Christmas. Santa.* Smiling, I stuff the note through a slit in the mailbox, then step back into the falling snow.

Up the opposite side of the street, wearing his cap with dangling earflaps, Beeper pulls his faded red coaster wagon with a case of beer in it. I keep walking. Mr. Jorgenson waves at me as he leaves his bakery for the day. Crossing Main Street at Spruce, I wait for a car to pass me. The driver is Judy Larsen who honks. Waving, I finish crossing the street and head up the slope.

The sidewalk past the bank is covered with snow from the day before. An old woman, bundled in a heavy coat and bent almost into an inverted U, plods ahead of me. Before each step forward, she plants in the snow a ski pole held in her hand. I stop alongside her.

"I like your cane."

She looks up, smiling. "Oh, it's wonderful. And, if I break it or lose it, I've got another one just like it at home."

I return the smile and continue walking. Ahead, the red brick building comes to me. I think of Burnett, Margo, Ann, my clients and friends, and then Rick. Rick. He was on his way; he was getting close; he was going to be the attorney I once wanted to be. Although I know he cannot hear me, I voice out loud to my ailing friend the sole thought in my mind:

"Ah, Rick, you poor bastard."

Afterword

An evening
in June 1977

I glance at the dozen lawyers from Timber County seated around a table in a side room of the River's Edge Supper Club. They have wolfed down the Northwoods' version of deep fried chicken and barbecued ribs served home style with lots of mashed potatoes, dressing, corn and coleslaw, and then washed it over with refills of drinks from the bar. Now they await dessert: my speech. As I stand and place my hands on the back of my chair, I possess the anxiety one always has when addressing a peer group. I speak, though, without notes since the words come from my heart.

"As you know, this past month Herb Krummel, at age eighty-six, passed away. Although I have known him for barely a year, we talked often, and he selected me to probate his estate. . . . I think he figured I needed the work."

I pause for the laughter to subside.

"His handwritten, lengthy will is both a legal document and an expression of optimism. It contains a stipend for the lawyers of Timber County and a stipulation for his heirs. The sum of five thousand dollars is to be placed in an income earning investment, and each year the income is to be used by us to purchase food and beverages, of any kind, for a day at his home on Split Lake. It is stipulated in the bequest of the home to his children that one Saturday in August of each year the home be reserved for us, as well as our spouses and children, and that we may also have the use of his boat so we can enjoy the lake. Should the home be sold, which he anticipated would not be in the near future, the trust funds shall remain for us so long as we wish to use them. In the event we do not, they shall pass to enumerated charities.

"It was Herb's expressed desire that we continue to engage in the comradeship that has bound our predecessors and us together for so many years. He noted that while he was counsel for a railroad in Chicago, living and practicing in a world seemingly different from ours, both worlds contain practitioners sworn to uphold the same fundamental laws and practices. We are, after all, he said, all lawyers. Besides, in his second career as a lawyer, he became one of us.

"He hoped that during the Saturday outing we would continue to share our knowledge, our experience and our wisdom. Herb also hoped we would continue, in an appropriate fashion, to share our stories. He admitted he too liked stories. During our brief friendship, he related to me many stories, including the following one:

"He described walking out of the courthouse in Lenora several years after he moved to the county. A pleasant appearing, middle-aged man stopped him and shook his hand. 'I never got the chance to thank you for all your help,' said the man. 'I'm sorry, but at the time I didn't have the interest I have now.' Herb was obviously pleased by the flattery; he thought it was nice to be remembered for his professional work. Though he could not place the man, he told him it was good to see him again. 'It's good to see you, too, Mr. Pratt,' the man replied. 'I assume you're retired now?' Herb's expression of pleasure faded to puzzlement. 'But,' he explained, 'My name is not Pratt.' The stunned man stammered, 'You, you were my high school English teacher weren't you?'

"It was not only the humorous incidents he remembered. Herb referenced in his will a conversation he had with Burnett wherein they agreed there is more to the practice of law than drafting documents and performing in a courtroom. So much of our practice, he wrote, is about people, understanding them and their relationships to each other and to society as a whole. Sharing that understanding, he felt, would only lead to better lawyers.

"When Herb moved to Timber County from Chicago, he soon realized he was not prepared for the life here. To use his own erudite words, 'Initially, he felt the pulse of the pace of life drop to a precarious level.' He fretted 'that he had given up on life too soon, that he had put himself out to shuffle along with the sleepy inhabitants of the river, people with strange nicknames designed to distinguish one from another.' Then in his practice, he discovered in first person the reality of their sicknesses, heartaches, loves, shocks of loss of others, and the collapse of their virtues and dreams.

"Herb intended the wisdom we lawyers of Timber County will share, will be the lessons we have learned from the happy and sad stories of the Northwoods people: a woman who cannot bear her name, a retired professor who picnics in the winter, a young woman whose automobile accident rerouted her life, an elderly tinker whose waning years were spent in another universe, and an abused woman who finds goodness in life; the stories of small town lawyers and their clients in a county tucked away in a part of the United States of America that with a change of scenery and dialect could be anywhere."